THE PIECES WE KEEP

THE PIECES WE KEEP

KRISTINA MCMORRIS

THORNDIKE PRESS
A part of Gale, a Cengage Company

LIBRARY OF CONGRESS CIP DATA ON FILE.
CATALOGUING IN PUBLICATION FOR THIS BOOK
IS AVAILABLE FROM THE LIBRARY OF CONGRESS

ISBN-13: 978-1-4328-7333-2 (softcover alk. paper)

Published in 2020 by arrangement with Kensington Books, an imprint
of Kensington Publishing Corp.

Printed in Mexico
Print Number: 01   Print Year: 2020

To Danny, for your unwavering faith in me,
our family, and our journey

Thank you for believing.

ACKNOWLEDGMENTS

Once more, I owe the inspiration of my latest novel to true accounts. Although the characters within these pages are fictitious, the astounding case of German saboteurs in America during WWII is not. I am indebted to Melissa Marsh for bringing this slice of history to my attention, without which this book would not exist.

Likewise, the tale of a young boy inflicted by night terrors and memories beyond logical explanation is also based on a true story (more details in the Author's Note). For guiding me to this documented instance, as well as suggesting the two storylines were in fact the makings of a single book, I am enormously grateful to my dear friend and devoted champion Jennifer Schober.

Research for the writing of this novel would have proven overwhelming if not for the generosity of many diverse experts. For enduring countless questions and even reading sections of the book for accuracy, I owe my deep appreciation to Detective Mike Hall, veterinarian Tammy Tomschin, child psychologist Kevin Wright, hypnotherapist Jennifer Boose, and Afghanistan combat veteran Bryan Wood. I am truly in awe of the selfless service you all provide to others. Thank you for allowing me a glimpse into your inspiring worlds.

An equal amount of gratitude goes out to the following people for their insight regarding the very difficult topic of child abuse: Meta Carroll, Judith Ashley, Terrel Hoffman, Erica Strauss, and Anna Stiefvater. I also thank Sheri de Grom for invaluable information on traumatic brain injuries, John Meehan and David Davis for educating me on airline emergency protocols, David Noble for confirming details on River View Cemetery, and Steven Burke for tirelessly addressing questions on court procedures and legalities. The compilation of answers you all provided could easily amount to an entire book.

I am immensely grateful to Ursula and Les Stomsvik, who spent half a day at my kitchen table sharing stories about growing up in Germany and the tragic hardships of those caught in-between. You have not only broadened my mind but also embedded yourselves in my heart.

Additionally, I relied upon the historical expertise of archivists from the Women's Army Museum, Francoise Bonnell and

Amanda Strickland, as well as Carol Fletcher from the Telephone Museum Foundation of Gridley, who treated me to tales of working as an operator since childhood when she had to sit on books in order to reach the switchboard.

Forever I will be grateful to: Al and Karen Cagle for their unrelenting support and help in all areas of WWII that otherwise would have eluded me; WWII airman Kenneth Tucker for his information about cargo transports; Richard Cox for his hard-found historical facts regarding Fort Hamilton; and, of course, to the Multnomah County Research Librarians for once more assisting my hunts for obscure details.

I owe another serving of thanks to Brian and Janet Taylor and Helen Scott Taylor, who were all kind enough to read excerpts featuring 1940s London in an effort to ensure authenticity; to Joan Swan, my wonderful medical go-to person; and to Lynne Krywult for enlightening me on the ins and outs of farm life. The hayloft scene is for you!

Thank you to Heidi McDonough and Lisa Osnes for helping me find the perfect title (and not letting me settle on a simple *THE*). For trudging through the lengthy outline and assuring me I was on the right track, despite my propensity for fading to black, I thank Rachel Grant, Elisabeth Naughton, and Darcy Burke. My early readers of the manuscript are all super-bionic women whose encouragement and/or suggestions were invaluable: my beloved Sue McMorris, Kathy Huston, Molly Galassi, Sharon Shuman, and literary soul sisters Erika Robuck and Therese Walsh.

Of all the stories I have written thus far, this one undoubtedly presented the greatest challenges. My saving grace was the team of cheerleaders who kept me going, page after page, month after month. Everyone should be so blessed as to have Tracy Callan, Sunny Klever, Stephanie Stricklen, Jenna Blum, and my "twinsie," Alyson Richman, waiting at the finish line with pompoms and Gatorade cocktails in hand. I love and admire you all to no end.

Thanks, as always, to the amazing Kensington team for managing to bring stories from my imagination to pages in readers' hands. I am especially indebted to my editor John Scognamiglio, who believed in my work from the beginning; Vida Engstrand, whose energy and efforts are utterly infectious; and Kristine Mills-Noble, who continues to gift me with covers which are truly works of art. I also extend my sincere thanks to all of the readers, book clubs, and reviewers who have enjoyed my novels and generously helped spread the word. For a writer, there is no greater compliment.

Finally, above all, I'm grateful to my husband, Danny, and our sons, Tristan and Kiernan. From marriage to motherhood, the lessons and memories I treasure more than any others have all come from you. You are the "pieces" that eternally fill my heart. Thank you for blessing my life in ways beyond measure. My love for you overflows.

■ ■ ■ ■

PART ONE

■ ■ ■ ■

Back on its golden hinges
The gate of Memory swings,
And my heart goes into the garden
And walks with the olden things.
                — from "Memory's Garden"
                   by Ella Wheeler Wilcox

1

Mid-May 2012
Portland, OR

The sound of her name, in that deep familiar timbre, swept through Audra like a winter gale. Her lungs pulled a sharp breath. Her forearms prickled. In line at the airport gate, she clutched the shoulder strap of her carry-on, a makeshift lifeline, and turned toward the voice.

"Babe, you want anything else?" the man in a floral-print shirt hollered from the coffee stand. "Andrea?"

Andrea. Not Audra.

And the man wasn't Devon.

"Just the vanilla latte," a woman replied from a nearby table, then resumed chatting on her phone.

For an eternal moment Audra Hughes remained frozen. She braced against the aftershock of hope, like the rush of a near car collision, when blood rages in your ears and every pore yawns open. Even now, two years after her husband's death, she hadn't conquered the reflex, nor the guilt. But in time she would, and today's trip would serve as a major step, regardless of others' opinions.

"Ma'am?" The male attendant stood at the door of the Jetway. "Are the two of you boarding?"

Audra and her son were suddenly the only passengers at the gate. She would usually make a quip, about the plane not coming to them, but her senses were still recovering. "Sorry," she said, striding forward. "Not enough coffee."

Truthfully, she didn't drink the stuff; too hard on the teeth and heart. But the excuse flowed out, plausible for any Northwest native, the caffeine kings of the world. A person couldn't walk the length of five gates at Portland Airport without hearing the turbo blast of an espresso machine.

The man scanned her boarding passes. *Beep. Beep.*

"Enjoy the flight."

Audra was about to continue through the doorway when she noticed Jack hadn't followed. The seven-year-old stood several yards away, the rolled cuffs of his jeans hanging uneven from dressing himself. Beneath his Captain America backpack and favorite gray hoodie, his hunched shoulders downplayed his sturdy form. His attention remained on a window dotted by Thursday-morning rain. The sight of their idle plane widened his slate-blue eyes, same shade and shape as Devon's. Their hair, too, had been a perfect match, the color of sweet molasses.

If it weren't for that rounded nose and chin, Devon's father used to jest, *you'd never know who his mom was.* It was actually a fitting claim in more ways than one. And every day Jack looked more and more like Devon. Or less and less like Audra, depending on the choice of view.

"Buddy, time to scoot," she told him.

Still entranced, he stroked his little toy plane, its silver paint worn thin from the habit. He'd been awed by aircrafts since the age of three, when Devon gave him a 747, stuffed and plush with cockpit eyes and a propeller nose.

"Jack!"

He snapped his head toward her.

"Let's get onboard."

She expected dazed excitement to fill his eyes; what she caught was a flash of dread. Not the common kind among kids at the dentist's or on the day of a quiz, but the type she'd witnessed a hundred times over, from animals being led into surgery or about to be put down. A look saying they knew what was coming.

Could it be Jack sensed something wrong with the flight?

"Mom," he said in a hush. It was the way he often spoke these days. But this time, the plea in the word leapt out and cinched Audra's chest.

17

"Ma'am," the attendant repeated, "we have to close the doors."

If Audra missed this flight, there would be no final job interview. She was currently the top pick according to her contact, who encouraged her to bring Jack along. A smart idea. The transition would be easier if he was involved in the process. Together they'd scout out houses with plenty of acreage and top-rated schools near the brand-new animal hospital. At the facility just outside Philadelphia, everything would be shiny and flawless and unused. An empty slate.

She assessed the plane, a strong and trusted transport. Flying ranked safer than driving according to statistics.

This had become her method of reasoning: the tangible, the provable; X-rays and blood tests. Any faith in the spiritual realm — airplane premonitions included — had been buried along with Devon.

"Jack, let's go," she told him. "Now."

The command prodded him forward, though only increased the pursing of his lips. She clasped his hand to hurry him onto the jet bridge. The gate door sealed, dimming the snaking tunnel. Jack tightened his hold, so snug she could feel waves of apprehension pulsing through his body.

Instinct implored her to pick him up, yet her own lecture slammed back. *Let them walk on their own.* It was the instruction she gave any clients whose coddling, albeit well intentioned, stunted the confidence of their Chihuahuas, Yorkies, any number of small breeds. *Treat them like big dogs and they'll believe they are.*

Whenever applied, the lesson proved reliable, swelling Audra with pride. A stark contrast to this moment.

If Devon were here, what would he say? What magical phrase would rid the stiffness from Jack's steps? There was a huge difference between nurturing animals and children. It was her husband who excelled at the latter.

Audra rubbed the crown of Jack's head, the airplane now in sight. His hair smelled of green apple, from a shampoo that claimed to prevent tears. "Nothing to worry about, buddy. I told you, this is going to be fun."

"Good morning," a uniformed woman said from the plane's entryway. An ash-blond updo topped her petite form.

Audra was about to return the greeting when something yanked her arm. Jack had concreted himself a few inches from the door. His eyes went wide, not blinking.

The flight attendant leaned down to his level. "Is this your first plane ride, cutie?"

Jack didn't answer.

Audra explained, "He flew a few times when he was a baby. But this is the first time he'd be old enough to remember."

"Well, in that case," she told Jack, "I'll have to make this flight extra special. How about you take your seat, and I'll see if I can scrounge up some pilot wings. What do you say?"

Jack perked ever so slightly. After a moment, he gave a nod and inched onto the plane. The red lights on his sneakers flashed like a warning.

Thank you, Audra mouthed.

She followed Jack's shuffling into First Class, through wafts of a Bloody Mary and champagne from mimosas. Business travelers flanked them in suits and polished shoes and perfect layers of makeup. Audra, with her cushioned sandals and faded khakis, winced from the heat of her neon sign: *Coach Class Passenger.*

She tucked away stragglers of her bound black hair, a looped ponytail parading as a bun. For a moment she had the urge to overhaul her trademark look. But as she continued down the aisle, a smattering of baseball caps and windbreakers reinforced her practical nature.

Their assigned row waited empty near the rear. It was the usual quarantined section for those with children, of which today there were few. She encouraged Jack to take the window, a coveted seat for any kid.

He craned his neck to peer under the half-raised shade. Seeing where they were going would alleviate his worry.

But Jack shook his head.

The blond flight attendant announced over the intercom, "We'll need all passengers to take their seats at this time." By *all passengers,* she

20

meant Audra and Jack. Pressure mounted around them from people anxious for departure.

"All right, you take the middle," Audra sighed. She slid into the row, stowed their carry-ons, and buckled their seat belts. Surely, before their layover in Chicago, Jack's nerves would morph into a thrill over their adventure. And maybe, just maybe, the excitement would resuscitate even half the innocence he'd lost.

Soon they were pulling away from the gate. Lights dinged, engines groaned, overhead compartments were clicked closed. A dark-haired flight attendant demonstrated the use of life vests and oxygen masks, the audience more interested in their conversations and magazines. Not long ago Audra, too, would have paid little mind. Now, solely responsible for the human beside her, she hung on every word, fending off doubts about a thin, aged seat cushion as a reliable floatation device.

When the emergency charades ended, she realized she wasn't the only one absorbing the worst-case scenarios. Jack had latched onto the armrests. His knuckles were white, the toy plane glued to his palm.

"Everything's going to be fine," she said, trying simultaneously to convince herself.

His face had gone pale.

"Jack, really, it's okay." She layered her hand on his. And then it hit her.

This was how Devon had held Audra's hand the day they met. They were strangers seated

21

on a flight together, bound for various conferences, when a winter storm lashed out at their plane. Once back on the ground, passengers burst into prayers and applause, not a single complaint of connections being canceled. Supplied with vouchers for a meal and hotel, Audra and Devon shared a booth at a local diner, chatting nonstop until closing. She'd never been one to trust easily, but there was a kindness in his eyes, sincerity in his smile. Somehow everything about him made her feel safe. She had realized this in the hotel hallway as they lingered in a handshake before going their separate ways. Then a week later Devon tracked her down, and by the end of their date they joined in a kiss that ultimately led to an aisle lined with pews and candles and promises.

This had been their story. A suburbanite fairy tale. Eight years ago, during a toast beside their wedding cake, Devon had regaled their guests with the turbulence, the fates, that had brought them together. Later he would repeat this to their son, soothing him at bedtime with a happily ever after — not foreseeing how quickly Jack would learn such an ending didn't exist.

No wonder the kid was frightened. The guarantee of safe flights would be lumped into a pile of Easter bunnies and Christmas elves. Deceptions, like kindling, worthy of a match.

She squeezed his small hand, scouring her mind for a solution. A distraction. "Do you want me to get a notepad out? We could play Tic-

Tac-Toe."

He shook his head stiffly.

Strike one.

"It's kinda fun, missing school today, isn't it? I bet all your friends are jealous." The words, once out, cracked and withered. He rarely socialized with classmates anymore.

A second strike.

"Hey, how about some food? Are you hungry?"

She reached into her bag. Amid her just-in-case travel supplies — Tylenol, Tums, and Pepto, all for Jack — she found a granola bar. She offered the snack, to no response, so put it away as the plane launched down the tarmac.

The wheels bumped and rumbled as they picked up speed. Jack's breaths shortened to choppy bursts, reflected in the pumping of his chest. Crinkles deepened on his brow. Tension condensed in their arched confinement.

At the sensation of going airborne, a smooth release from the weathered runway, Audra glanced out the window. In the sky, on the ground, tragedies happened every minute of every day with no rhyme or reason. The thought closed in around her.

She used both hands to lift the stubborn shade that ultimately yielded. They were at treetop level and climbing. Before long, the cars and buildings would all shrink to a size fit for an ant. This was something she could point out, to calm Jack down. Everything seemed safer, less real, when viewed from a distance.

"Jack, look. It's like they're all toys down there." She gestured to the window and turned for his reaction.

Aside from his little gray plane, the seat was empty.

"Jack?" A blade of panic whisked through her.

Across the aisle, a plump woman gawked toward the front, where a din of yells erupted.

"Let me outta here!" a voice screamed. "We're gonna crash! *We're gonna crash!*"

Audra fumbled to release her buckle. She dashed down the aisle that stretched out for miles and struggled to comprehend the scene. The flight attendants were both on their feet, attempting to restrain Jack. He flung his arms fiercely, a wild beast battling captors.

"We're all gonna die!" He lunged for the handle of the cabin door. "We have to get out!"

Almost there, Audra tripped on the strap of a purse. Her knees hammered the ground and her forehead rammed an armrest. Dazed, she grabbed the back of a chair to rise, just as three passengers sprang to help the crew. Their bodies created obstacles denying her passage.

"I'm his mother. Let me through!" In spite of her trim build, she was no longer the athlete she once was, and she suddenly regretted this.

"Nooo," Jack shrieked in a muffled tone. A husky man had wrapped Jack's mouth and chest from behind and wrenched him away from the door.

"Stop it," Audra roared. "You're hurting him."

24

Logic told her they were doing the right thing for all aboard, including Jack, but primal instinct dictated she claw at this person who could be strangling her child.

By the time she'd wrestled her way to the front, two male passengers had secured Jack to the floor, facedown, by his wrists and ankles.

She folded onto her throbbing knees. Through the tangle of limbs, she placed a shaking hand on his back. "It's okay, Jack. Everything's okay."

His gaze met hers, and his squirming body went limp. Confusion swirled in his features. "Mama?"

The endearing address, for the keeper of wisdom, the provider of all answers, delivered a punch to her gut. She replied with the single truth in her grasp. "I'm here now, baby. I'm right here."

The captain made an announcement that Audra barely registered.

When they guided Jack to stand, he flew into her arms. He clung to her shirt, convulsing with sobs. She swooped him up, her adrenaline rendering him weightless.

They were led down the aisle like prisoners to a cell. The silence was deafening, the stares nearly blinding. She wished her arms were wide as sails to fully blanket her son.

The plane tilted and lowered in a U-turn for the airport.

At the very last row Jack was directed to the window seat. This time he didn't resist. Audra assumed the middle, the cushion warm from a shuffled passenger. She cradled Jack's head to her chest, his trembling lessening with their steady descent.

A flight attendant took up post nearby. Spectators stole glances through gaps between seats. What a story they would tell. The online posts, the e-mails and texts.

Once parked at the gate, Audra waited for officials to help gather her and Jack's belongings and escort them off.

"Look outside," she told Jack. "See that? We're safe now. We're safe." She offered the assurance twice, hoping through repetition to believe her own lie.

2

Light flickered over his face, a mask of shadows in the darkened room. Vivian James edged closer in the velvety seat beside him. Once more she exaggerated a sigh.

Alas, Isaak's gaze remained glued to the screen. In black-and-white glory, a squadron of Spitfires roared off the runway. British military had become a standard of these newsreels, a flexing of royal muscle, a pep talk for patriots. From Isaak's rapt interest few would guess he was actually an American, the same as Vivian. Before each picture show the RAF propellers would appear, and on cue his spine would straighten, eyes wider than a full moon over the Thames.

So easily she could see him as a child, even without the projector's softening beam. Youthful curls defied hair tonic in his thick golden hair, and a light dimple marked his chin. His entire face had a striking boyish-

27

ness, save for his gray-blue eyes that reminded Vivian of the locked file cabinet in her father's den: prohibitive and full of mystery. A good reason, in fact, to have kept her distance from the start. After only three months of their clandestine courtship, her yearning to be with him, her fear of losing him, had grown to a point she despised.

Was Isaak aware of the power he held? She wondered this now, studying the profile of his handsome lips. His unbuttoned collar pulled her focus to his medium-framed chest and down the series of buttons. She forbade her gaze from wandering on.

Determined to balance the scales, she brushed aside finger waves of her long brown hair. The motion freed a waft of the perfume he had given her, Evening in Paris. Raising her chin, she exposed her neck, the slender, bare area he had declared irresistible.

A claim now proven false.

She recalled Jean Harlow, the elegance of her feline moves. Brazenly, Vivian arched her back as if stretching for comfort. Against constraints of a girdle, she showcased the curves of her trim, belted dress. She parted her full lips, painted deep cherry red, to complete the sensuous pose.

Still, Isaak stared forward, where Nazi soldiers paraded in goosestep. They steeled their arms in angled salute. A narrator recycled the usual reports: Germany's pact for alignment with Italy, an increase of rumored threats to Poland, the troubling ambitions of Adolf Hitler. It was hard to fathom how a pint-sized man with the looks of Charlie Chaplin could cause such a stir. Back in Washington, DC, her family's home until two years ago, he was surely fodder for the Sunday funnies.

"Isaak," she whispered.

He nodded absently, not turning.

She said his name louder, with no distinct plans of conversation. A flash of his slanted smile would simply confirm knowledge of her presence.

But her efforts produced a mere *shush* in the row behind them.

On their last two dates he had been no less distracted. "Just have a lot on my mind, darling," he'd explained, "with research for Professor Klein, and all the rumblings in Europe."

Politics. The ubiquitous topic.

Her father, a veteran of the Great War, rarely detailed his work at the embassy. But that didn't stop *politics* from maintaining a strangling grip on their home. That was not to say Vivian was uncaring, for Isaak's family in particular. He had been born to Swiss emigrants in upstate New York, he'd explained, and was only fifteen when a factory accident ended his father's life. Then Isaak and his mother had moved to Lucerne, where

29

she now remained with family. Although Switzerland was famed for its armed neutrality, the expansion of Nazi power gave just cause for apprehension.

Vivian just wished, for a slice of a moment, that global bulletins would take a backseat. Did this stance make her selfish? She pushed down the notion. There were times when a woman ought to put herself first.

At a second *shush* from behind, Vivian became aware of her bouncing heel. She tended to fidget whenever her mind wandered. As she crossed her legs, a bold idea formed. Subtle options had failed. She inched her dangling foot over the border of Isaak's space. With the toe of her slingback, she brushed against the calf area of his trousers.

Oblivious, or so it seemed, he moved his knee away.

Vivian retreated to her side.

His summer holiday, free from his classes at the University of London, was supposed to afford them quality time. But demands of his campus job had kept them apart this entire week. The separation should have caused his affections to spill over — as exhibited by the couples sprinkled about, already necking, embracing, hands roaming. Was this not the reason he had chosen a matinee? For its offering of relative privacy, an element he favored?

It had been Isaak's suggestion, after all, to

keep the relationship under their hats. His benefactor would be far from pleased, he had said, in light of Isaak's studies; a romance was not to detract from his final academic year. Vivian had accepted this reasoning, admittedly enticed by the thrill of their secrecy.

But that thrill had run dry, and suspicions were trickling in.

While Isaak had asked plenty of questions about her life, her family — less a mark of interest, perhaps, than the habit of an aspiring journalist — he shared so little about his own. Did he view her as a passing fancy, a fling not worthy of investment? Maybe he was divulging a great deal, but to another girl.

"Isaak."

He raised his pointer finger, a sharp signal to wait.

Vivian clutched her pocketbook. She would be a fool not to see where she stood. "A grand idea. Why don't I wait outside?"

She rose and strode up the aisle.

"Vivian?"

In the span of her twenty years, she had rebuffed an abundance of other fellows. More than a few had likened her fair skin and fine features to a porcelain figurine, her copper eyes to a field of autumn leaves. Yet here she was, ashamedly willing and questioning her very worth.

No more. She was reclaiming her indepen-

31

dence, a possession she swore she would never concede.

Sunrays blinded her as she burst from the theater and onto the sidewalk. The pain behind her eyes rivaled the squeeze on her heart.

"Vivian . . ." Isaak's raw, natural rasp tempted her to turn, but she resisted.

"How lovely. I have your attention."

Dots of light faded from her vision, clarifying a view of honking Hilmans and double-decker buses. Hats of every sort floated through the West End: fedoras, flat caps, bowlers, and wide brims. Off in the distance the bells of Westminster chimed.

She raised her palm for a cab.

"For Mercy's sake, where are you going?" He sounded bewildered yet almost amused, fueling her frustration. If she was acting dramatic, he alone was the cause.

He touched her elbow. "Darling."

Shrugging him off, she lifted her hand higher. How could a single taxi not be empty?

"Miss, are you a'right?" a man asked. He paused from pushing a cart of flowers for sale. "Is the gent 'ere bothering you?"

"Yes, he is," she replied pointedly. "But I'm fine. Thank you."

Though reluctant, the man nodded. He disappeared behind a cluster of ladies, thick with pretension and talcum powder. Bags and boxes in their gloved hands denoted an afternoon spree at Marshall & Snelgrove.

"I don't understand." Isaak suddenly grew serious, his brow in a knot. "Tell me what I've done."

For as long as she could recall, she had envisioned a future that broke the mold of convention. Yet because of Isaak, she had been tethered by emotion, her goal kept out of reach. She simply hadn't realized it until now.

"I've meant to tell you," she said, not quite meeting his eyes. "I think we need a break."

"A break?"

"Really, at our age, there's no reason to be tied down to one person."

A shocked, humorless laugh shot from his lips. "Whatever are you talking about?"

She gripped her purse with both hands, firming her will. "It's over, Isaak. Please let me be."

To hear an objection would be as damaging as his agreement. Not waiting for either, she bit out "good-bye" and headed for the Underground, longing to escape into the deepest levels of earth.

3

It was a striking visual of the entrapment Audra felt, yet a disconnect from her old self. In the gilded oval mirror, her reflection gazed back like a stranger stuck behind the glass. She leaned closer, hands gripping the pedestal sink. Could this person really be her? Maybe it was just the lighting, here in the home of Devon's parents. But, more likely, the harshness of reality.

Though just over thirty-five, she could easily pass for forty. Gone was her youthful glow born of skiing and hiking trips, now faded by duties and worries. Circles under her hazel eyes, like stains of grief, had darkened even more from the past four days. The airport interrogation, the media evasions, the lack of sleep. Every night since the in-flight disaster, Jack had wakened her with his chilling screams.

Audra had never seen nightmares like these. Eyes wide open, he would flail around as if fighting for his life. *Get out! Get out! We're gonna crash!* Over and over he would yell in desperation until exhaustion seized him fully.

You're not supposed to wake them. That's what her husband had warned on the few occasions when Jack had sleepwalked. Devon even caught one on video. He thought it was adorable that their son, while asleep, tried to brush his teeth at midnight.

But this wasn't adorable. It was terrifying — for Jack and Audra both. These went far beyond his bad dreams at age five, when comprehending that Daddy was never coming home. Audra had been grateful, so grateful, those teary nights had waned. The stab of self-blame had been painful enough without a child's cries twisting the blade.

She tossed cold water at her face. It splashed the thought away, yet failed to make her more alert. Fortunately, the drive would be only fifteen minutes from here in Wilsonville to her job in Sherwood. Ten minutes shorter than her commute from home.

She had no obligation to work today — after all, she had taken vacation time for the trip — but the clinic remained her sanctuary. There was no better place to regain confidence from something at which she excelled. Of all days, Mondays offered ample opportunity, packed with pet mishaps from the weekend. Meanwhile for Jack, with no classes on a teacher in-service day, an afternoon with the grandparents would be a nice treat.

Patting her face with a hand towel, Audra

winced at the tenderness of her forehead. A knot left from the plane. She smoothed her hair to cover the bruise, hoping to hide her emotions as easily, and headed for the backyard. On the way, she averted her eyes from the photos of Devon. They dappled the bookcases and end tables and walls, artifacts in a museum of memories.

She focused instead on her path through the house. Design wise, the English colonial was the perfect balance of luxury and practicality, as would be expected from the owner of a construction company. Robert had built the place for his wife, Meredith, soon after Devon was born. *A good cure for the baby blues,* Robert would say, explaining his motive behind the elaborate kitchen and elegant bathrooms. The walk-in closet off the master bedroom was half the size of Audra's apartment.

Years ago, during a late night of holiday baking, after their spiked eggnog and laughter had dwindled, only then did Meredith tell Audra about her bout with depression. Though the comments were brief and slightly slurred, Audra gathered it was a much darker period than the family let on. She always wanted to find out more but chose not to pry. And now, with the widening gap in their relationship, she would probably never know.

"Well, I'd better get going," she announced on the back deck, where a hammering noise drowned her out. Robert was on his knees, repairing a wobbly rail. She spoke louder: "I thought you were close to retirement. Don't you have people to do that for you?"

He smiled, his silver-gray mustache trimmed as neatly as his hair. "Yeah, but then I'd have to pay them. And I'm way too cheap for that."

"Ah, yes. I forgot that part."

Robert rose in his carpenter pants and boots. Aside from a solid build, his rounded face and widened middle resembled a teddy bear from the county fair. "I imagine you're looking for those two culprits." He used his hammer to indicate the far corner of the yard.

Audra should have guessed where Meredith would take Jack on a sunny day. Already, just minutes after his arrival, his grandmother had him crouched down for a chat in her enormous garden. Lessons about nature — from roots and leaves to caterpillars and bees — were always appreciated. But inevitably she would move on to all the varieties of lilies Devon had given her, and the memories attached to each Mother's Day on which he had planted them.

While the sentiment was a sweet one, Audra wished the woman would center on the future, rather than the past. At least where Jack was concerned.

"Hey, buddy!" Audra intervened. "Come on over and tell me good-bye."

Jack came to his feet. He treaded over with his shoulders up and the bill of his baseball cap lowered. Raising his eyes, he said in a tight voice, "When'll you be back?"

She recognized the true question, one she hadn't detected in over a year: Would she *ever* be coming back?

The crushing doubts in his face tempted her to stay. Yet she heard the echo of a teacher's voice, back when Jack started to cry during his first preschool drop-off: *By proving that when you leave it's not forever, you'll build your child's trust.*

Audra knelt on the deck and cupped his baby-soft cheek. "I'll just be gone for a few hours, then we'll go get pizza together. Sound good?"

After a beat, he nodded sharply in a show of bravery. But when she leaned in for a hug, his tentative hold confirmed that the boy she missed — the ever-beaming Jack who found wonderment in a potato bug and made drum sets out of Cool Whip tubs — was a thousand miles away.

She smiled at him. "You're going to have so much fun today. I want to hear all about it when I pick you up."

He didn't respond, and it was plain to see that his summary of the day would be no different, regardless of her efforts.

"You know what, Beanstalk?" Robert said. It was a nickname from Jack's first growth spurt. "Just remembered, I got a surprise for ya. Picked up a full-bird colonel for your collection."

"Wow," Audra said, "that's amazing." Then she whispered to Jack, "I have no clue what a full-bird colonel is, but it sounds very cool. And twice as good as a half bird, for sure."

Jack's mouth lifted, a shadow of a smile.

Meredith removed her garden gloves while joining them. "Dear," she said to Robert, "why don't you take Jack inside to play, and I'll throw some snacks together?"

"As you wish, milady." He winked at Audra and ushered Jack in the direction of the "music room," a space that produced no music. The piano there, passed down through generations, apparently hadn't been played since Meredith's years as a music teacher. Now it sat in a tomb of canvas, retired — like Meredith — and being edged out by a battlefield. Spanning the room, more than a hundred tiny army men held positions behind Tupperware bunkers and bushes of packaged moss, soon to be joined by a full-bird colonel.

"Thanks again for watching him," Audra told her by way of parting.

But Meredith cleared her throat, expression pulled taut over high cheekbones. Her hair was sleek and short in the fashion of an eagle, with eyes just as penetrating. "Audra, before you go . . ."

"Yes?"

"I was hoping we could talk for a minute."

The intensity of her tone told Audra to sprint for the car. What usually followed were strong "suggestions" of putting Jack in a contact sport, or signing him up for an outdoors camp, or sending him to the Sunday school where Meredith volunteered. However well-intentioned, none of those ideas would keep Jack safe in a world that refused to be controlled.

"I really do need to head out," Audra said, but Meredith persisted.

"How's Jack been doing in school lately?"

The detour was surprising.

Then again, Meredith and her husband would soon be watching Jack on Audra's workdays, same as they did last summer. The status of his academics would be helpful to his progress.

"He's good overall. His reading's still amazing, but he could use more practice in math. When school ends in a few weeks, I'll drop him off with workbooks, so you can quiz him if you don't mind."

"That's all fine. But how's he doing with everything else? With other kids, I mean?"

"He's great," Audra lied. "Everything's great."

"The reason I ask is — well, I couldn't help but wonder. Have kids at school been playing rough with him?"

Audra blinked. He had never mentioned it to her.

Not that he necessarily would these days.

"Why? Did he say something?"

"He didn't. I just noticed, over in the garden . . . I know he tends to bruise easily. But there are quite a few marks on his arms."

The bruises. From the plane.

Audra had informed Meredith of the basics —

that Jack's "disruption" from anxiety had caused the pilots to turn back; that in the wake of 9-11, it didn't take much to shake up the crew. Had it been up to Audra, she wouldn't have shared even that much with her in-laws. But a Port of Portland authority had warned her that if the media pounced, local relatives were rarely spared.

She had little choice now but to elaborate.

"The plane ride might have been more . . . involved than I mentioned. When Jack panicked, he actually tried to get off the plane, and some passengers had to hold him down."

A crease divided Meredith's brow. "But — that doesn't fit him. He's always been so agreeable." Audra couldn't argue with this. "Did you explain to him what to expect? About traveling on airplanes? Maybe that would've helped."

With Meredith, every moment offered a teaching opportunity.

"He never seemed worried," Audra said, "until it came time to board. You know how fascinated he's always been with those model planes Robert gives him. I thought he'd love it."

"Mmm," Meredith said simply.

The woman was problem solving, but her remarks only magnified Audra's insecurities of parenting without Devon. She felt her defenses rise.

"Doesn't matter now anyway. They're not going to let him fly for a long time."

"Ooh. I suppose they wouldn't." Meredith tilted

41

her head, thin eyebrow lifted. "So, does this mean you won't be moving to Philadelphia? Since you missed your interview?" She didn't do much to hide her enthusiasm.

"I'm still in the running," Audra contended. "The owner was willing to set up a videoconference with me later this week."

There were three other candidates being considered. Audra didn't have to be told she'd lost her top rank, viewed now as a single mother whose "family emergencies" already interfered with her work. But she wasn't up for dwelling on that.

"You know, Audra . . ." Meredith blindly scraped dirt from the tips of her gloves. "I could be wrong, but maybe it wasn't the flying part that Jack was anxious about."

"What do you mean?"

"I'm just saying. Moving him cross-country could actually be the core of the problem. A new school, a new city with nobody he knows. He's already changed homes once this year."

Yes, and Meredith had made it abundantly clear how she felt about that too.

"After everything he's been through," she went on, "I would think some consistency would be good for him. Maybe he'd prefer to stay where he's grown up, close to where his dad is."

"His dad?" Audra was astonished by the tactic. She understood why Meredith would want her grandchild nearby, but that didn't

42

justify using Devon as an excuse. And what about Audra's needs? Every restaurant, every street here contained a memory dense enough to smother her. How could she possibly be a good mother until she could breathe?

Meredith clarified, "Oh, of course, wherever Jack is, I know Devon's there, watching over him. I just meant it might be important for Jack, especially as he gets older, to visit Devon's grave, to feel closer —"

Audra couldn't take anymore.

"Devon is gone. In every way. *Gone.*" Her voice trembled, gaining momentum. "He's not hiding behind a headstone. Not floating around like fairy dust. And he sure isn't sitting on a cloud somewhere with harps and wings."

When Audra stopped, silence burned the air. The heat of it crawled up her arms, her neck. In contrast, utter shock blanched Meredith's face, triggering Audra's mind to replay her own words.

Though formed in truth, the outburst wasn't meant for Meredith. It was for the doctor who had given Devon a clean bill of health. It was for herself, for chalking up Devon's headaches to caffeine withdrawal and his increased forget-fulness to being "a typical guy." It was for every condolence card that insisted she cling to her faith, because goodness knows that her hus-band — at barely thirty-four, with a family he loved and a great consultant job from home — wouldn't die in a blink without reason. It had to be part of a "bigger plan."

43

A plan that didn't exist.

Vision clouded by tears, Audra swiped at her eyes. Meredith's gaze had fallen to the garden. From the pain in her features, an inescapable truth struck back.

Sure, Audra had lost her husband and Jack had lost his father; but Meredith and Robert had lost their only child. For any parent, was anything more devastating?

"I'm so sorry, Meredith. I shouldn't have said that. I didn't mean to hurt you . . . ."

Slowly Meredith looked at her. From the start, she and Robert had welcomed Audra without question or condition. They were the picture-perfect Christmas cards, the movie nights and cribbage games. They were everything her own parents weren't.

I've missed you. The declaration gathered on Audra's tongue. But before it could find a voice, Meredith turned and left.

4

All thoughts of Isaak should have been left at that theater, cast off like an old ticket stub. Yet in the full day since their parting, Vivian could think of nothing else.

"No, no, Miss James," Mr. Harrington said in his proper English. "I requested the brown peep toes, not the black." Low on his stool, he handed the pair back, and she confirmed yet another error.

"Good grief, I apologize."

The owner of the shoe store was typically as gentle as his dove-gray beard, yet his impatience began to show. "Please do hurry."

"Right away." She proffered a smile for the seated customer.

The robust woman looked on in disapproval, flushed from straining, by choice, to sample shoes too small. Her sons, young twins in matching jumpers, sparred in the corner with metal shoehorns.

Vivian was halfway to the back room when she heard the woman cluck, "American girls.

They are simply not raised to listen." Then tersely, "Matty. Natty. Stop that horseplay at once."

During moments like this, protests from Vivian's mother rushed to mind. *The daughter of a U.S. diplomat has no business working at all, let alone to service the feet of strangers.*

The implication of being paid to tickle and massage British toes would verge on amusing if not for the added point: *How do you expect to find a good husband this way? I did not raise my only child to become a spinster.* Her inflection conveyed a fatal disease, as though her own marriage encapsulated sheer bliss.

Vivian knew better.

She had also known, when offered the job at the store, to bypass her mother in favor of her father. Perpetually distracted, he had mumbled his consent. In doing so, he had spared her from torturous hours of knitting and playing bridge with her mother's gossipy socialites. And most important, Vivian's personal savings had continued to flourish. Stashed in an old coffee tin since early girlhood, each dollar and pound was a step toward her dream. Traveling. Self-reliance. Freedom.

That wasn't to say she opposed marriage entirely — only the dreary, passionless type. She refused to be a caged and clipped housewife, with love deemed an afterthought. She would rather be alone forever than deprived of her independence.

Focusing on that divine word, she approached the storeroom's mustard-colored curtains. Split down the middle, they draped to the ancient wooden floor. The scents of leather and black polish welcomed her entry. A single bulb threw dim light over the ceiling-high shelves.

She set aside the mistaken pair and scanned the array of choices, grouped by color and size. What a poor habit she had made today of placing shoes in the wrong slots. All because of foolishness over a boy.

At last, she spotted the chocolate-brown peep toes. They were up on a high shelf, but retrievable without the rickety stepstool. She rose onto the balls of her feet, stretching her arm. In her haste, her fingertips pushed the shoes away. She needed to concentrate, to be patient, if she wanted her life to improve, much less her workday.

"I can get those for you," came the voice.

Her muscles petrified, rigid as stone.

Isaak.

For a second that seemed an hour, he reached over her from behind. Her head grew faint from the faded aroma of cigar on his clothes. His chest pressed against her shoulder blades. The warmth of his skin seeped through her flimsy cotton blouse, the drape of her skirt.

47

"There you go," he said. That maddening rasp.

She fended off a shudder, and realized her eyes had closed. Opening them, she swung around and backed away, imprisoned by stacks of shelves. He peered at her from beneath the plaid bill of his flat cap. His black jacket hung unzipped.

How had he managed to sneak in here?

Before she could ask, he motioned toward the curtain. "Door was open from the alley."

The side door was used for supply deliveries. And apparently, stray tomcats. "How fitting."

"Vivian?" Mr. Harrington called out.

The customer.

The shoes.

She swiped them from Isaak. They were larger than requested, but she would present them regardless. It was silly, she had learned, to pretend something fit when it didn't.

"One minute, sir," she replied, then cut to Isaak in a hush. "You have to go."

She attempted to stride past him, but his arm shot to the side. "You owe me an explanation."

"I don't owe you a thing. Now, let me pass, or — or I'll have Mr. Harrington escort you out."

Isaak drew his head back, emitting the same edge of mischief that had first lured her in. "Even though you'd left the back door un-

48

locked for me? So we could mingle here in the closet?"

"I did no such —" She caught her raised volume. Was he trying to get her fired? "He'll never believe you."

Isaak folded his arms and leaned against the doorway, a bald dare.

At his outright arrogance, blood sped through her veins, spiking her temperature. "I can't do this now."

"And why is that?"

Didn't he see she was at work? Or was it that he viewed a woman's occupation as a piddly hobby?

"If you must know, I have inventory to take, supplies to stock, and a customer who, despite her toes being overstuffed sausages, is convinced she wears the same size as the Queen. Therefore, as I said, now is not a good time." She pinned him with a glare, pressing him to relent.

Neither of them budged.

Finally he said, "A simple explanation. Please, Vivian. Give me that and I'll leave you alone." His tone suddenly shifted, tender as the memory of his hand on her skin, of his lips trailing the side of her neck.

She swatted away the thought, battled back with the truth — at least in basic form.

"Fine, I'll tell you," she said, at which he nodded. "I'm tired of being hidden away like something to be ashamed of. If Mr. Mueller is such a kind benefactor, he shouldn't take issue with our relationship. Either way, I don't see the point of sneaking around anymore." She tried to leave it at that but added, "Unless you're afraid a woman who you're truly smitten with might spot us together."

His eyes narrowed. "Is that what you think?"

Honestly, she didn't know what to believe or how to feel. But then, how could she possibly with his dwindling show of interest?

"Whenever we're together anymore, your mind is elsewhere. And frankly, I've endured enough of that with my father. So unless you can argue otherwise, it appears our relationship has run its course."

Through her matter-of-fact delivery, she had taken control of the situation, even mercifully provided him an easy out. The air should have lessened in weight, not turned to lead.

Whoops and hollers burst from the front room. No doubt, the twins were escalating their antics out of boredom.

"Vivian!" Mr. Harrington yelled. His urgency for a sale had been buoyed by the need to salvage his store.

"Coming, sir!"

Isaak's jaw twitched and his Adam's apple bobbed, as if a reply were clinging to his throat. In the silence, an infinite wavering stretch, his eyes glinted with . . . something.

But as swiftly as it appeared, the spark vanished.

"Princess Beatrice," he said.

She blinked at him.

"Princess Beatrice has large feet." He moved from the threshold to permit her through. "It ought to help with your customer."

A fact about royal feet. That's all he was willing to share.

Vivian treated the appeasement with the respect it deserved, by not responding. She charged through the curtains and out to the front. She steadied her emotions as best she could.

"Sorry for the delay. These were tucked away on an upper shelf."

Mr. Harrington accepted the shoes without thanks. "Here we are, madame," he said, sliding the woman's feet into the pair. "They are utterly lovely. Don't you agree?"

The heels wobbled as she stood, like thumbtacks propping a sack of flour. "Yes, yes, these are splendid indeed." She admired them at various angles while her sons spun in place, using arms as propellers, to the point of falling down. "I do say, they are exceptionally comfortable. Are you certain these are my usual size?"

As the woman reached down to check, an answer flew from Vivian's mouth: "Princess Beatrice."

Mr. Harrington and the customer turned to her, staring.

"Wears . . . the same size," Vivian finished. She resented using Isaak's help — who knew if the claim was even true? — but it was too late to retract. "A smidge wider, I believe, but just as stunning."

"Oh?" the woman said, a tad dubious. "Is that so?"

Mr. Harrington's beard twitched as he cleared his throat. "Rightly so, madame. Precisely the same. Shall I wrap them up for you?"

After minimal contemplation, the woman agreed and followed him to the counter.

A click traveled from the hall, a sound only Vivian noticed. The closing of a door. In its wake flowed a sense of finality. She bristled at an absurd tide of angst, and her thoughts returned to Isaak's eyes. A secret had risen from the depths, peeked into the open, and scuttled back inside. What admission had he almost made? What was so terrible that he could not say?

Then came a creak, like that of the step-stool.

Her imagination surely.

Or perhaps his return.

"I'll be organizing the storeroom," she told Mr. Harrington, who waved her off.

Down the hall she held her breath. At the curtain she let it out. She envisioned Isaak inside, hat in his hands, his defenses finally lowered. She flung open the drape.

Only to find the room empty.

5

Audra was the only person there, waiting at the counter. Anxious to check in — a packed day awaited at the clinic — she attempted eye contact with the school receptionist. But the woman didn't engage. She continued on the phone, her pace impossibly slow, addressing a student's absence. She had a thick helmet of hair that smelled of Aqua Net.

Past the interior window a line of kids slogged toward the gym. A backdrop of handmade posters featured glittery medals and lopsided trophies. *Reading is for Winners,* they declared.

Reading . . . Friday.

Was this Jack's library day? Had he packed the Magic Tree House book to return? Or did they have PE class instead? She couldn't keep track of his ever-rotating schedule, even before sleep deprivation hit its current high. Other distractions weren't helping her focus — namely, that the job in Philly had been taken.

"Mrs. Hughes?"

Audra turned.

The principal, Miss Lewis, strode from her office in a beige pantsuit. She boasted the energy and build of a devoted runner. "Thanks for coming in."

Audra greeted her with a handshake. "Sorry I'm a little late. I was about to leave when our fridge decided to create a man-made lake." As proof, she motioned to the damp spots on her light-blue scrubs.

"Not to worry. It actually gave Dr. Shaw and me more time to discuss the . . . *situation.*"

Emphasis on the last word struck all too familiar. It was the padded introduction Audra often used when delivering fatal news about a family's beloved pet.

"Dr. Shaw's joining us?"

"He is. Did I forget to mention that?" The oversight sounded genuine, her deportment casual, as she led the way to her office. Still, Audra had learned to be wary of surprises. She had come here expecting a routine update.

Ever since Devon's death, Miss Lewis had been kind enough to keep tabs on Jack's change of demeanor. She was one of the few reasons Audra had remained in the same district when switching from a house to an apartment last year.

They entered the room to find Dr. Shaw parked in one of the two visitors' chairs. The school counselor wore thick black glasses, commonly known as geek-chic, and a skinny plaid tie that completed his look of a yearbook shot from the seventies. "Good morning," he said with a smile crafted for disarming, resulting in the opposite effect.

"Is there a problem with Jack?" Audra asked.

Miss Lewis closed the door — a private conference. "We'd just like to talk to you about some concerns we have. Please, make yourself comfortable."

Ruling that impossible, Audra settled for taking a seat. She gripped her purse as the principal reclaimed her rolling chair. On the corner of the desk sat a cup of pencils with troll-like hair and wiggly eyes that stared back.

"I'm afraid we did have an incident this morning. Everyone is fine now" — Miss Lewis raised a reassuring palm — "but whenever a conflict becomes physical between students, it's standard for us to alert the parents."

Physical? Audra tamped the urge to demand who specifically had tried to hurt her son, already wanting to have a word with the child's parents. "What happened?"

"In the middle of morning announcements, a couple of military jets roared past the area. There was a lot of noise and some shaking of the walls. Apparently Jack crawled under his desk. A girl tried to coax him out by pulling his arm, and that's when Jack hit her in the face."

Audra went speechless. She felt as if she, too, had been struck.

"The teacher agreed it was a result of circumstance, and not malicious in any way. Really, if it weren't for other factors, I would've just told you this over the phone."

Miss Lewis then gave the counselor a nod. The handoff of a baton. A cue in a vaudeville act before the damsel was sawed in half.

"Mrs. Hughes," he said, "we'd like you to take a look at something." He opened a red file folder, and more than its color reminded Audra of the lights on Jack's shoes. "They're from assignments in your son's class. All of these are drawings he created just this week."

Audra cringed inside while accepting the stack, though the subject matter came of no surprise. The picture on top featured an airplane in gray marker, diving toward the ocean. Orange flames sprayed from the wings. Smoke curled from the tail. A star adorned the side, like his model planes at home. It was no doubt the looping scene that haunted her son every night.

She flipped to the next sheet, and the next. Each depicted a similar crash, but with passengers in a plummet. A girl and a boy stick figure held hands in midair.

The illustrations grew more frenetic. Thicker lines. Jagged faces. Fiercer flames. It was the product of an angry artist, emotionally unstable.

She had to remind herself the artist was Jack, and with the thought came reason.

Their plane ride had been a traumatic one. His nightmares reflected this. Each episode required more time and effort to soothe him. He claimed to not remember a single thing the following mornings. Subconsciously, though, he had to be affected. This, too, would explain his cowering under a desk and the instinct to fight for that haven.

Audra confessed: "We experienced a bit of a problem with an airline trip last week."

"Yes, of course." Dr. Shaw was clearly aware. "We both agreed that's where a lot of this was coming from."

The media had withheld Jack's name, being that he was a minor, but not Audra's. Until now she had hoped the news had bypassed her local community.

"I'll definitely talk to him when he gets home," Audra said in conclusion. Contrary to ten minutes ago, she was now anxious to check *out* of the building. But Dr. Shaw wasn't finished.

"I think you'll want to take a look at the next picture first."

Audra felt her reaction being monitored, analyzed. She aimed for a neutral expression as she revealed the image.

No plane this time — gratefully. Rather, a wild-eyed figure sat in a chair, a domed helmet on his head and bands on his wrists. A wiggly *X* covered his chest like a shield. A Viking warrior, or a king on a throne.

"He did this one yesterday," Dr. Shaw said, "for a cause-and-effect assignment. Other kids drew things like sunlight that turned a seed into a flower. Or a rainbow that appeared after a storm."

If a warrior won a battle, Audra supposed, the *effect* would be his ruling from a castle. It wasn't a rainbow or a flower, but still harmless enough — unless you were seeking out an issue. "I really don't see the problem," she said with a touch of relief.

Miss Lewis chimed in. "When asked about the man, Jack said the chair had killed him."

Audra more closely inspected the drawing. The wavy lines, common indications of movement, were jagged enough to suggest . . . electricity. The man was being electrocuted.

"My God," Audra said. Where had Jack seen such a thing?

"Naturally," Miss Lewis added, "the teacher asked him questions, to get an idea of what prompted the idea. But the only thing she could get out of Jack was the reason behind the man's death."

Audra swallowed, tightening her hold on the folder. "And? What did he say?"

"That the man was a Nazi spy."

Then it became clear: The spidery design wasn't a shield, but a swastika.

Miss Lewis attempted an encouraging look. "When asked by his teacher, Jack did agree to draw . . . happier things. Even so, we felt the need to bring this to your attention. Especially since one of the class volunteers is an elderly Jewish woman. You can imagine why she was pretty shaken up."

Dr. Shaw leaned closer, elbow on his wooden armrest. "Do you know if Jack is watching any movies that might be giving him these ideas? Kids often absorb images, or song lyrics from the radio, and actually don't understanding their meaning."

Audra grappled for the source, hindered by an overload of thoughts. "We don't watch TV at home. Rarely anyway. When he does, it's only cartoons. Disney. Pixar."

"Maybe when you're not around, then?"

"I'm always around. I mean, I wasn't in the beginning, but — that was before."

He was only three months old when she entered her final year of veterinary courses at Pacific University. Yet it was never a challenging juggle, with Devon's dedication as a father.

"Jack does stay for after-school care now," she admitted, "but just for a few hours. I get there as soon as I can. Being the only parent, and working full-time —"

"It's okay." Miss Lewis reached forward and gave the desk a light pat, as if meant for Audra's arm. "Nobody's criticizing you as a mother. We're just trying to solve this, to create the best possible environment for Jack. And for the other children."

So that was the point of this meeting: to keep the class safe from Jack.

"My son wouldn't hurt anyone," she told them. Then had to add, "Not on purpose anyway. It

60

was obviously an accident."

"I'm sure it was."

"As for these drawings," Audra said, "he could've learned about all of this from another kid. Maybe from a video game. Somebody might've snuck one into class. Just think about how violent those things have become."

Whatever the case, Jack had every right to be fascinated by death. He was still comprehending the passing of his father. At the clinic, plenty of children processed loss in their own ways, at their own speed.

"You're absolutely right," Miss Lewis said. "That might be all it is. However, coupled with his behavior this week — more distressed and isolated than usual — it might help Jack to see someone. A person he can talk to."

Distressed. It seemed a lightly veiled word for *disturbed,* a description that didn't pertain to Jack. The label applied to other kids, violent ones. The vicious shooters at schools and malls and movie theaters who took their own lives when cornered by a SWAT team.

Miss Lewis produced a business card from her top drawer. "With summer around the corner, I thought you might consider setting up a private session with Dr. Shaw."

"Or if you'd be more comfortable," the man assured Audra, "I also know several other therapists in town who are excellent. I'd be happy to refer you."

Audra studied the card without taking it. All

points and edges like a perfect paper shard. She looked up at Miss Lewis before making her own cause-and-effect inquiry. "And, if his behavior continues as it is . . . ?"

The woman glanced at Dr. Shaw, a message traded between them. "Why don't we cross that bridge when we get there."

6

The air was moist from the river below, crisp with summer's decline. On the block of concrete stood a lone iron lamppost. Beside it, Vivian pulled her cardigan closed and hugged her elbows atop the rail.

She stole a glance at a passing couple, then a second pair and a third, half expecting to spy Isaak's face. As if catching him with a lover would put her feelings to rest.

It had been several hours since they'd parted in the storeroom; still, the ache refused to dull. She trained her attention on the landscape. The setting sun cast London's skyline in silhouette. Orange rays poured liquid ribbons over the Thames, guiding a flock of boats downstream.

Following long workdays, this spot was her cherished retreat.

Faced by such surroundings — the vast winding river, the grand Houses of Parliament — many would be discomfited by a feeling of insignificance, reduced to but a speck in the universe. To Vivian, the scene gave proof of purpose. For why else would humans exist? Each played a small but integral part of a massive design, so intricately crafted that only upon its completion could one grasp the perfectly logical beauty.

The theory required faith, of course — an asset of hers now put to the test. She leaned her head against the cool metal post and listened to the rush of the current. A force even stronger had swept her away the day she first met Isaak.

She was buying fruit at the outdoor market when an air-raid siren wailed. Another tiresome practice drill. Startled from her thoughts, she knocked a large tomato onto the cobblestone road. Its juices sprayed an arc over a pair of wingtips. When she looked up to apologize, expecting a stuffy man to fill the suit — after all, what in England wasn't stuffy? — she instead met eyes that drained her of words.

The craggy vendor interrupted, demanding due pence for her loss. Fear of poverty trumped that of a German attack. Vivian hastened through her coin purse while the siren blared and people all around bustled toward shelters.

"This should cover it, ma'am," the suited man said, paying the vendor double. Before Vivian could object he wrapped her hand with his. Words again eluded her. "Come with me," he said, not a question, and she wasn't sure which surprised her more: his American accent or her willingness to follow. Not that her assent was fully voluntary. A magnetic pull radiated from his touch, making every layer of her skin hum.

He guided her into a public air-raid shelter. It was there she detected a trace of his German vowels — residual of his time spent in Switzerland, he explained, after moving from the States. Only a year her senior, he spoke of the American delights he missed, the drugstore confections and radio shows of his youth. She nodded along, prodding him to continue. Like cold fingers to a flame, she was drawn to the danger of his warmth.

Never before had she been disappointed by the all-clear signal. To this day, so vivid was the memory she could hear Isaak's voice even now. She glanced over her shoulder. At confirmation of his absence, her spirits sank.

When she turned back to the river, she heard him again.

"There's no other woman. I swear it, Vivian."

She questioned if she was going mad until, past the concrete block, she glimpsed male hands on the railing. She recognized the ridges of his knuckles, the curves of his fingers.

"I have good reason for being distracted. But it has nothing to do with my fondness for you."

It was the start of a likely excuse.

"And? What is that reason?" She meant to sound challenging, but failed.

"My family."

An unexpected answer. "Go on."

His profile edged out from the lamppost. Beneath his flat cap, his skin gained luminescence from the sun's orange glow. "My family lives in Munich," he said, just loud enough for her to hear. "But they're not Nazis. They're good people trapped by a dictator consumed with power and greed."

"By family . . . you mean . . . ?"

"My mother. Yes." His gaze stayed forward, as if borrowing the anonymity of a confession booth. "She lives there with my uncle and aunt. They have two teenaged daughters. Bright, kind girls."

The newsreels. No wonder Isaak took such an interest. With all those snippets of Germans cheering at massive rallies, the films conveyed unity, a whole country bowing to Hitler. She hadn't considered opposition festering within those borders.

Then again, neither had she questioned the tales of Isaak's life.

"But you told me you moved to Switzerland, after your father died."

"It was a wish," he said. "Ever since I was a kid, my mother would describe Lucerne like a magical kingdom. I had planned to gradu-

66

ate from the university and work for my uncle's newspaper, as I told you, but just long enough to save funds. Then I was going to pack up and take her there."

Vivian's thoughts churned as she tried to visualize how all the pieces fit. "So — why can't she go now? If she's a Swiss citizen? Surely it's safer there."

Isaak said nothing, letting the curtain fall free of the entire façade. Here, in the impossible quiet of London, a revelation took shape.

"Your family isn't Swiss," she breathed.

His eyes snapped to hers. "That isn't true. My ancestors are, from my mother's side." He attempted to protest further, but weakened by the flimsy argument, his words trailed off.

"Then it's all been lies. A splendid heap of lies."

Always she sensed a barrier hanging between them, an invisible bridge. Yet she had no inkling of how wide the stretch, or how many deceptions filled the gap below.

If his admission was meant to help, he was mistaken. She had been played a greater fool than she'd realized. The urge to flee overtook her and she did not bother to fight it.

She was several yards from the lamppost when he called after her.

"Vivian, stop." He gripped her shoulders from behind. "Damn it, you're always running away from me."

She was plagued by the truth of this. But then she recalled it was likely his one and only truth, and she tried to break away. "Just let me go."

"I can't do that," he told her. "I love you."

Her body went still.

Weeks ago, as they necked passionately in a secluded park, those very words had escaped her lips. He had smiled in return but replied with merely a kiss. She had managed to hide her disappointment, and ever since refrained from the same mistake.

At last, he had reciprocated in kind. But how to gauge his sincerity?

"Did you hear me?" he said, his mouth beside her ear. He nuzzled the side of her hair. His moist, heated breath sent a shiver down her spine. "I love you, Vivian."

She worked to recover her voice. "We don't even know each other."

"You know that's not true." He relaxed his hold and slid a hand down her sleeve. Beneath her unbuttoned sweater, his fingers settled on the waist of her skirt. He guided her around to face him. His purposeful touch dissolved every layer of fabric.

"Darling, please, think," he said. "Your father fought in the war. Against Germans, for God's sakes."

The Great War. Her father's service. Her mind hadn't yet ventured there.

Vaguely she did recall her father's grousing, back when she was a child, about a local German plumber said to have swindled the neighbors. A *dirty Kraut* was the term her father had used. But it was an emotional slip, and once little Vivian asked him what it meant he never repeated the phrase. Times had changed.

"That was decades ago."

"Yes. But he's still an American diplomat. Political relations are worsening. I didn't know how he'd feel about — how *you'd* feel about me, if you knew." He moved his hand to her cheek, and she cursed her inability to pull away. "Besides, you can't blame me for keeping my guard up."

"Oh? Then who is to blame?"

"You," he said, and Vivian's gaze sharpened.

"Me?"

He arched a brow, as if no answer could be more apparent. "You've made it clear from the start, you have no intention of staying. Sooner or later your father will be transferred, and you'll get what you've always wanted. You'll move back to America and travel from one coast to the other. Bathe in the blue seas of California, pitch pebbles into the Grand Canyon, ride bareback through the Texas plains. You'll live as you please, no one tying you down. Isn't that what you said?"

For Vivian, the memory of sharing those picturesque dreams was somewhat faint. A

69

generous glass of red wine during one of their evening picnics had lubricated her words. Lying on his arm as they gazed at the stars, she had described the places she would visit, each one inspired by tattered, dog-eared issues of *National Geographic.*

It hadn't occurred to her that he would harvest so many of those details.

"Now do you understand?" he said. A look of vulnerability seeped into his deep-set eyes, dissolving the remnants of her will.

She found herself nodding, unsure how the situation had both tangled and untangled in such a short span. All she knew for certain was how much she suddenly needed him close.

She moved forward and delighted in the feel of his arms enfolding her. She rested her head against his neck, absorbing the thrum of his pulse, the scent of his skin. A lavish mix of tobacco, vanilla, and sage. "How did you know where to find me?" she murmured.

"At the end of a long day, your favorite place to go?"

It was testament to existing in another's world, of being greater than a speck of dust.

"I know you, Vivian. And you know me."

She raised her head. A tingling spread through her as she placed her lips on his. He returned the kiss with such intimacy her knees almost gave out.

Once more he held her for a long, wordless

moment. Finally he said, "I suppose you'd better get home. Wouldn't want your parents to fret."

Though reluctant, she agreed. Another lecture from her mother held no appeal.

His arm curled around her shoulder as they walked toward the Underground. They were a pair of the strolling lovers whom only minutes ago she had envied.

Three blocks later, stained concrete stairs led them down to a station platform. Together they waited for her train, bound for Hyde Park, a brief jaunt from her family's home.

Beneath the brim of his cap, Isaak stared off in silence. This time she knew what he was thinking.

Cautious of listeners, she asked, "What will you do? About your family?"

He shook his head and sighed. "I don't know yet. Find out all I can to help them, I suppose. Pray to God we don't wind up in another war."

Without foresight of what was to come, there was little to say.

Too soon the train arrived. A final kiss, a squeeze of hands, and she boarded. She waved through the window as the transport pulled away. "I love you too," she said under her breath and watched Isaak shrink from view.

In the darkness of a tunnel, Vivian fidgeted with her sleeve. Solutions began to form.

They crowded her thoughts, hungry as weeds, until one emerged with promise. The file cabinet in her father's den was the seed of hope she needed.

But where might she find the key?

7

There were no clear answers, only a problem that continued to grow.

Audra sank into the padded stool, a stethoscope looping her neck. Alone in the lab of the clinic, she pulled out the card from that morning. She had only accepted it to be polite. How could she have refused with the man sitting right there?

Dr. Newman Shaw
Licensed therapist
Talk – Trust – Heal

The tagline sounded so simple. Three steps, three syllables. You could almost forget how many years and payments it would take to sustain hope of reaching the goal.

A mix of yips and whines drifted in from the kennel. But it was the melodic whimpers that reminded her of a cocker spaniel she'd once treated. A middle-school boy had abused the puppy for kicks — and this was after extensive counseling for tendencies of violence. Evidently the sessions were as helpful to the kid as Audra's had been for her.

Weeks after Devon's funeral, a friend of a friend suggested a grief counselor downtown. Audra had gone there for one reason only: to garner advice for helping Jack adjust. As it turned out, six appointments with a frizzy-haired shrink who assigned every feeling to a particular shape and color had been six appointments too many.

Maybe Audra had been too hasty. The ability now to decode the shapes and colors in Jack's drawings might have been useful. Obviously, he would never hurt a puppy for kicks; at four, he had even begged her to save a bee from drowning in a puddle. Yet his current behavior seemed a blatant cry for help.

She rubbed the business card between her fingers. The phone wouldn't dial itself. She grabbed the handset from the counter and began to press the numbers.

"You're here!"

She swung toward the greeting.

Entering the room was Tess Graniello. In her signature style, she wore pink lip gloss against creamy white skin, a blond bob angled toward the front, a lab coat over tan Dockers, and a lavender scrub top patterned with tiny white kittens. Basically, if Barbie's countless occupations included a clinic vet and manager, this would be her — but with a suave Italian husband whose local relatives could populate an entire village. In their family, every holiday was just an excuse for daylong eating and, oddly enough, karaoke singing. When Audra was hired here six years ago, Tess invited her to one of the extravaganzas. A plateful of cannoli and a duet, almost recognizable as "I Will Survive," were all it took to forge a lasting friendship.

"I didn't see you sneak in," Tess said.

"Well, you know me and my ninja skills." Audra pushed up a smile.

"Do you have a minute?"

"Yeah, sure." She relinquished the phone, gladly, and tucked the card into her pocket. "What's up?"

Tess leaned back against the counter. She folded her arms, her sass and smile missing. "We ran into a problem this morning with Mrs. Wilfred."

Mrs. Wilfred . . . the original "Crazy Cat Lady."

"Don't tell me she had an issue with me needing to reschedule," Audra said. "That woman cancels on me all the time."

"She showed up for the appointment. When you weren't here, she went on a major rant. And when I say 'major,' I mean she could be heard from Pluto."

Audra would never pass off blame, unless it didn't belong to her. "Tess, I phoned the front desk. They said they'd call her."

"She didn't get the message in time. Apparently, with having to take her cats home, she had to miss breakfast with the Red Hat Society — which for her, as you well know, is earth-shattering. I would've handled the vaccines myself if my morning hadn't already been packed."

Audra groaned. After departing from the school later than planned, she'd hit a deadlock on I-205 and had no option but to cancel. "I'm sorry for missing it, but seriously, the freeway was a parking lot."

"Believe me, I understand. It wouldn't have been a big deal except . . ."

Audra steeled herself before asking, "Except?"

"Hector was here."

A vision of the full scene took shape: Hector Petra, the semiretired Greek vet who'd founded the clinic decades ago, dropped in only on occasion. He had a fairly hands-off style, so long as customer service was up to par.

"And, to make matters worse," Tess went on, "a reporter from *The Oregonian* stopped by just then. He was snooping for info about you and Jack."

Unbelievable. By now the journalistic buzzards should have had other targets to circle.

"What did you tell him?"

"That we had no comment, like you'd asked."

Audra dropped her shoulders and sighed. "Thank you."

Tess glanced toward the hall, a confirmation of privacy. She continued in a lowered voice.

"When Hector asked, I told him you'd been flying out to see relatives. He bought it, but he's still concerned about you being distracted. He said you're welcome to take a few days off if that would help."

If only a vacation were all Audra needed.

"It's really not necessary. I appreciate it though."

"But while you're waiting for your interview —"

"The spot's been filled," Audra informed her, which fully solidified the outcome. "I got the call last night."

Tess paused, taking this in. "I can't say I'm entirely sad about that."

A laugh slipped from Audra's mouth. She was well aware of her friend's hope that the plan to relocate was a temporary phase.

"On a serious note," Tess said. "You doing okay?"

"Yeah. Fine. Just need to look for other options, is all."

Tess tipped her head forward, peering at her. "Sweetie — and I say this with a whole lotta love — you look like doggy doo." The girl was never one to sugarcoat. "For heaven's sake, tell me what's going on. Aside from the job."

The invitation hung there like the crest of a wave. Audra felt the pull of its tide, anchored to the drawings tucked into her purse. A Nazi in an electric chair. Jack and Audra falling from the sky.

77

A twist of angst tightened her chest, along with the need to purge. "It's Jack. He's been struggling with pretty bad nightmares."

Tess nodded, waiting for more.

"The school asked me to come in this morning. That's part of why I was late. They're worried about some pictures Jack's been drawing in class. All of them about death."

A gentle smile played on Tess's lips. "Oh, yeah. I know that meeting. Been to a couple of them actually."

"You have?"

Audra didn't intend to sound so surprised. But the gal was a bionic supermom. PTA President of her daughter's grade school. Fund-raising co-chair of her son's lacrosse team. And when it came to baking, she threw off the curve. If she weren't such a good person, a dozen other moms would have hired a hit on her by now.

"Grace had the same issues," Tess explained, "back in kindergarten, when Russ was in chemo."

"My gosh, of course." Audra should have thought of that.

"She was fascinated by the idea of dying and where we go from here. It lasted quite a while, even after he went into remission. Cooper didn't say much about it. I think as the older brother — he was in fourth grade at the time — and just from being a boy, he wanted to look like the strong one. But eventually I do remember him having some pretty rough dreams. I guess,

78

sooner or later his brain had to deal with all those emotions."

Now, three years later, Tess's husband appeared so healthy, it was easy to forget the challenges the family had faced.

"You know what?" Tess said, a revelation. "That might be why Jack had a problem with flying. Not just from fear of crashing — which tons of *adults* are scared of, by the way — but having so little control over life."

"True . . . I suppose that could've been it."

If the theory was right, Jack had already discovered a reality that had taken Audra more than thirty years to figure out.

"What about the nightmares, though? Were Cooper's ever . . . super vivid? Like with his eyes open?"

Tess waved her hand. "All perfectly normal. Just talk to Jack about it. I'm sure you'll both feel a lot better."

In many ways Audra already did. Everyone could be worrying over nothing.

What was it Devon used to say? *Nuttin' but a scratch.* Blood would be pouring from a cut on Jack's knee, or his elbow swelling from a fall off his skateboard, but hearing that assurance always calmed him right down. Even from the start, whenever Jack took a small tumble while learning to walk Devon would instantly clap and cheer; in response, their son would giggle rather than cry.

Bottom line, for a child the problem was only

big if you told them as much.

"Speaking of kids." Tess regarded her watch. "Cooper's got practice today, so it's my turn to drive Grace to equestrian. I'd better get some charts done. And hey, I almost forgot. Any time you and Jack want to ride my sister-in-law's horse, just say the word. Tracy said you two are more than welcome."

"But . . . isn't that how she shattered her pelvis before?"

"No, no. That happened from a snowmobile. Chestnut is the gentlest creature ever. You should get to know him yourself. Swing by the stable during the summer, or in the fall if it's easier."

Audra noted her friend's insertion of an enticement to stick around. "I'll keep it in mind," she said with a smile.

Tess gave her a look, acknowledging the failed attempt. "All right, back to the salt mines." She started for the hallway but dragged to a stop. Turning back, she spoke with all the enthusiasm of performing a full day of dental cleanings. "A friend of mine works at a pet clinic in Boston. He happened to mention they're hunting for another vet. I could pass your info along if you want."

Audra perked. She'd always thought of Boston as an intriguing city, rich in history and culture and academics. Great benefits for Jack in the years to come. "I'll owe you one."

"More like one million. But yes. You will."

As Tess departed, Audra recalled her earlier mission. She dug into her pocket and retrieved the therapist's card.

Talk – Trust – Heal

She scanned the text once more, and ripped the card in half.

8

When it came to the task at hand, Vivian was on her own. Lying in bed, down pillow scrunched against the white wrought-iron frame, she skirted thoughts of the consequences; they would only apply if she was caught.

The designation *off-limits* applied to many a thing in the James household: the pantry and cookie jar between mealtimes, a china closet full of impractical gifts from dignitaries, any mention of her mother's four o'clock flow of gin and tonic. And the vertical file cabinet downstairs in the study.

Her parents' slumber, however, would soon be deep, allowing her to creep through the house undetected. The waitstaff's nightly absence would also ease her efforts. Over the past three days she had snagged every discreet chance to search for the key by daylight. Under the cloak of darkness, she hoped for a better result.

The most confidential files would be stored

at the embassy. Nonetheless, those kept at home carried enough importance to merit a lock. A memo inside, for instance, might confirm unflagging neutrality by Prime Minister Chamberlain. There could be a proposition for a new non-aggression pact between the United Kingdom and Germany. True, Hitler had reneged on the previous one, breaking the Munich Agreement by seizing all of Czechoslovakia. But the majority of British leaders might still desire peace, just as much as Isaak did. Proof of this could help allay his fears.

Vivian centered on the prospect as she stared at the ceiling, its crown molding trimmed in gold. Lace curtains sieved moonlight across her small but tidy room. With every blink, her eyelids gained another gram of weight. She pinched her leg beneath the sheets. She needed to stay alert. But with fatigue nibbling at her senses, her vision went gray at the edges . . . .

A chiming melody roused her. It floated up the staircase from the grandfather clock in the parlor, marking the hour of one. She had planned to wait until two, yet if she didn't act now another slow blink might tug her into a dream and keep her captive until dawn.

She shook off the dust of exhaustion and planted her feet on the cool rug. In her long cotton nightdress, she tiptoed down the stairs. Beams of light from outside splashed against the arched entry window. Vivian froze, imagining a policeman armed with a flashlight. Instead a vehicle rumbled away, taking its bright headlights along.

Quiet returned to their street lined with virtually matching houses. They stood narrow and three storied, like soldiers at attention. The uniformity of the area was well suited, as many of the residents were employed at the diplomatic hub of Grosvenor Square. When the U.S. embassy moved there a year ago, Vivian had been grateful her family didn't relocate to an apartment in the pillared building. She had barely unpacked from their initial move.

Now she realized the benefits of the alternative. Discarded documents and whispered secrets would have lurked in every corner.

At the closed door of the den, she gripped the ornate knob. She twisted it to the right with painstaking care and glanced cautiously over her shoulder. She pushed the door open, and her heart leapt to her throat.

"Vivian." Her father sat at his desk, working by lamplight. "What are you doing up?"

"I — couldn't sleep."

The last two years had thinned and silvered his hair to the point of translucence. A set of bags puffed beneath his eyes.

"Is there something you need?" he asked.

Insomnia didn't explain why she had intruded into his study.

She feigned a yawn, stalling, and averted her eyes from the file cabinet beside the bookshelves. The coffee mug on his desk spurred a plausible excuse. "I was going to warm up a little milk. Thought you might like some too."

He traced her gaze to the ceramic mug, then peered back at her and shook his head. Did he see straight through her words? Empty as a promise from a crooked politician?

"I'm all right," he said. "Thank you."

"Well, then. I'll leave you to your work." She started to back away, her hand still on the knob.

"Vivian." His tone was unreadable, same for his expression.

"Yes?"

"Your mother and I — we've had a discussion." He reclined in his chair and pressed at his temple, as if to subdue the motion of his thoughts. He still wore his button-down shirt, but with tie removed and collar open.

That's when she spied the couch. Sheets and a large blanket covered the furnishing in the corner, punctuated by a pillow. Something in the bedding, such a neat and tidy arrangement, indicated regular use.

"How would you feel," he said, "about moving back home?"

She stared at him, thrown off. "Back home? To DC?"

85

He nodded.

"It's . . . what I've always wanted."

"Yes," he said. Then silence.

She reviewed his inquiry, its very phrasing so far from the norm. His role had always been that of a quiet judge, stoic but fair-minded. He was sensible and practical long before the Depression. He didn't bother with excess, even in conversation. And he certainly didn't consult over major family decisions, particularly based on feelings.

"When were you thinking?"

"I'm not certain. More than likely, rather soon."

For the embassy to transfer him with little notice meant a significant change had occurred. She thought of Isaak, yet couldn't allow herself to dwell on their separation. Not now. She needed to consider the welfare of his family.

"Is something happening with Hitler?" Cautious of raising suspicion, she added, "I've seen the newsreels. Has there been a development that would affect England?"

He leaned forward, laying his forearms on the desk. Consciously or not, he covered the splayed file of documents. "Nothing to concern you at the moment."

The room was too dim and the print too small for Vivian to read anything from a distance.

"We can discuss the matter later," he said.

"Go on and enjoy your milk." He returned to his work pile. An end to their talk.

What if she simply came out and asked? He had fought the Germans, yes, but on the sea, not in the trenches, and before she was born. His current occupation, in fact, promoted relations among countries. At one time, even Great Britain and America were dogged foes.

"Father?"

He hummed a reply, already consumed by the page in his hands.

"I was wondering . . . ," she began. "Do you think all of these worries over Hitler will eventually die out? Surely there won't be another war."

Still reading, he murmured, "One would hope."

"But — if it does happen?"

Another absent hum.

She pressed on, more daringly.

"What do you think will become of the Germans? Those who aren't Nazis, that is? I imagine a good number of innocent people are there. Just as in any country. They should be allowed to leave, shouldn't they?" She waited for his agreement, any sign that he might help. "Father?"

Finally, he set the paper down. He raised his eyes with weary annoyance. "If the Reich persists in its hostilities, there's no telling how great a catastrophe will result. Hitler will keep every citizen he can at his disposal. All of Germany would be declared an enemy. And I guarantee, they'll suffer for it, in every way imaginable."

"What about the innocent people? What about —"

"No one," he said gruffly, "is innocent in war. Especially not a German."

When she winced at his reply, he let out a breath. He rubbed the bridge of his nose and said, "It's been a tiring day. Run along now. Get some sleep while I finish up."

With the option of his aid eliminated, sleep would not come easily. But she tendered a nod all the same.

9

Moist air seeped from under the door like the passing of a secret. One hand on the knob, Audra rapped twice before opening the door an inch. On the other side Jack sat soaking in her tub. He tended to stay in until he wrinkled into a prune.

"Time to fish you out, buddy. Ten more minutes, okay?"

" 'Kay."

The soft sounds of his splashing were a welcomed comfort. Peaceful and relaxing, they were the precise opposite of her day from the start. She should have known the refrigerator leak was a sign to stay tucked beneath the covers.

Just talk to Jack about it.

Tess's suggestion from that morning had seemed simple enough. But then Audra would see the drawings, each tacked to the walls of her mind, and wondered what frightened her more: crafting the wrong questions or what his answers might be?

She continued down the hall in her faded sweats. Their two-bedroom apartment was located in West Linn, a tree-lined suburb of Portland. Aside from new roofing, the complex was showing its age, as evidenced by the creaking footsteps from neighbors upstairs. The tradeoff was a decent rent that preserved Audra's savings.

Life insurance and wills had long been on her and Devon's to-do list, but naively without urgency. Neither of them had *planned* for an undetected brain aneurysm to rupture while he jogged on a treadmill at the gym. The symptoms had been there, of course, as they often were with disasters. From extramarital affairs to climate change, red flags were obvious in hindsight. As a doctor, albeit for animals, Audra should have seen them waving sooner. The memory loss, the headaches. On his final morning, he'd even mentioned a strain in vision. *Are you surprised*? she'd teased, given his long night of analyzing marketing data, to which he had laughed.

There was so much they had both taken for granted.

Through the open window in Jack's room came a cool evening breeze. A fleet of model planes swayed on strings pinned to the ceiling. An *Avengers* poster rustled over the desk.

As Audra gathered a trail of dirty clothes, a van zoomed by, too fast in a neighborhood with kids. She set the laundry on the foot of Jack's bed and went over to shut the window. The vibrant sky gave her pause. Feathery strips of clouds floated in a sea of purple and pink.

Lured by the springtime hues, she let her eyelids fall. Suddenly she was on their old back deck, the air scented with fresh-cut grass. Devon had insisted on a weekend of camping, but in their own backyard. They made s'mores with a portable gas stove. Jack told ghost stories without including a single ghost, instead starring SpongeBob or ninja warriors. And at midnight, when lightning cracked and a downpour pummeled their tent, they voted two to one to "rough it" by sleeping in the house . . . .

Audra broke from the memory. She shoved the window closed.

This was the reason they needed to move, whether to Boston or elsewhere. Downsizing to this apartment, thought to be a solution, had amounted to a bandage. Ten months here and still the surroundings formed a trap.

Turning, she noticed a stray sock peeking from under the bed skirt. She reached down and uncovered a book. Its sturdy tan covers were spiral bound with thick black wire. At the title, recognition set in: *PIECES OF ME.*

Jack's kindergarten teacher had given him the scrapbook following Devon's death. She suggested it might help, providing an outlet for Jack's feelings. The non-lined pages could double as a journal. He could write, scribble, draw.

Audra's thoughts again circled back to the pictures from school. Her son wasn't *disturbed*. She knew this. Yet doubts had managed to slink into her mind. Flushing them out would be easier if only she could confirm the violent drawings were a fluke.

She knelt down on the woven rug. To encourage him to use the journal, she'd initially assured him that books like this were private, to be read by no one else. Her cracking it open would betray that understanding.

But then . . . as his mother, wasn't she obligated to look?

"Mom?"

She dropped the book onto her lap and raised her head to see him over the bed. Jack stood in the doorway in his Scooby-Doo pajamas. His hair was mussed and damp, a terrier caught in the rain.

"What're you doing?" he asked.

The therapist's card flashed in her mind. *Trust.* A prerequisite for healing.

"Just picking up your laundry." She rose, exhibiting the lone sock from the floor while nudging the journal into place. "Did you brush your teeth?"

He nodded. If he suspected anything, he didn't let it show.

"Hop into bed, then. You've got a big day tomorrow."

For the Saturday of Memorial Day weekend, his grandparents would take him on their annual excursion. At Willamette National Cemetery they would plant mini-flags at the gravesites of veterans, a Boy Scout tradition passed down from Devon.

It would be the first time Audra would see Meredith since their run-in on Monday. To Audra's surprise, their brief phone calls to coordinate schedules had indicated all was forgiven.

Then again, that's how families were supposed to work. Not that Audra would know from her parents, whose forms of contact were limited to postcard updates and two annual calls: Christmas morning and her birthday. They were nice enough people, just not the parental type. Nurturing their latest causes always took priority. They'd started with local issues, trendy ones like clear-cutting and spotted owls — the puppy-mill protest, come to think of it, had inspired Audra's career choice. But then an episode of *Oprah* broadened their scope. Two days after Audra's high-school graduation, the couple flew to Africa to aid villages in need. It was no wonder Audra had debated ever having children. She'd agreed only when Devon promised to helm the family ship, a role he fulfilled with gusto. He was the soccer dad in the minivan, the guy who cooked dinners that didn't come from a box. He was the husband who kept all afloat — but whose absence could leave you drowning.

Jack crawled under the covers. As he flipped

his pillow, Audra recalled the pressing topic. She sat on the side of his bed and took the captain's seat in her mind.

"Hey, buddy, I need to ask you something," she said. "I had a visit today with Miss Lewis."

"It was just an accident," he said before Audra could finish.

The classmate. He was referring to the one he had fended off to stay under the desk.

"Oh, I know it was. And Miss Lewis does too." Audra tried to reassure him with a smile. "But she's still a little concerned about some drawings you did."

He lowered his eyes to his hands, fidgeting with the covers. "She already told me. I'm not supposed to do those anymore."

"That's probably a good idea for now." Audra kept her voice light. She wanted him to chat freely, the way he used to rattle on with his ghost stories. "Could you tell me, though, about the man in the chair? I'd love to know more about it."

He gave a small shrug. No elaboration.

"Did another kid show you something like that? An older boy at recess? Maybe at after-school care?"

He shook his head.

"How about a TV show?"

He paused for a moment, and shook his head again.

The source of the drawings wasn't necessarily important. It was the message behind them.

"If there's ever anything you want to talk about, if you're sad or angry or scared, you know you can tell me. Right?"

"Yeah," he said, sounding a little groggy. A discussion after his warm bath might not have been ideal.

Enough for tonight.

She smoothed the spikes of his hair and kissed him on the forehead. "Don't forget, you still need to tell me what you want for your birthday. It's almost here, you know." Standing, she bent over to grab the laundry.

"Mom?"

She smiled, expecting the name of a toy she'd never heard of. Instead, he gave her a look that deflated any levity. The sadness in his eyes matched the tone of his murmur. "I'm sorry you didn't get the new job."

Her heart turned to gelatin left in the desert. "Oh, baby, it's not your fault." She gingerly squeezed his chin. "Like I said, there might be an opportunity in Boston. That's a much better place. Lots of great things there. They've got some of the best clam chowder . . . and baked beans. And the Red Sox and Celtics play there."

When his expression didn't lighten, it dawned on Audra what might be his greatest concern. "And," she said, "wherever we end up, we can definitely drive to get there."

His mouth lifted at the corners and his covered body visibly relaxed.

On the motherhood chart, Audra felt a small

but distinct plus mark added to her score. Who knew? Maybe that's all the information he needed to change his art — and dreams — for the better.

"Close your eyes now," she said, and kissed him once more.

Then came the scream.

It sliced through the fog of Audra's mind. She was on a couch. The gray couch she'd bought to fit their apartment. How long had she been asleep?

A second shriek tore through the room. Another of Jack's nightmares. She jumped up, fumbling a wineglass. Red sloshed onto her sweatshirt. She had dozed off before even taking a sip. She rarely drank alcohol — the calories were better spent on cake or pie — but the day had called for an exception.

Squinting against the hallway light, she stepped onto something sharp. A LEGO piece, in the middle of her bare arch. The pain snapped her wide-awake, along with another yell from Jack.

"Help meee!"

"I'm coming," she said through gritted teeth, withholding curses at the toy. She forged onward into Jack's room. In his bed, he sat backed up against the headboard. His nightlight cast an eerie shadow, aging him by years. He clawed at a wall of air. His eyes bulged with terror.

"It's a dream, Jack. Do you hear me? It's only a dream." She touched his shoulder gently, an approach that had helped the last few times.

"No!" he exploded with a force that jolted her backward. "Let me out! Let me out *now!*"

"Please. Just listen to my voice."

His gaze, though vivid with fear, placed him in another dimension. A maze in which he didn't belong. If she could visualize it, too, maybe she could guide him out.

"Jack, where are you? Tell me what you're seeing."

He muttered some words she couldn't decipher — except for one.

"Himmel? Is that what you said?" He'd uttered something similar before. She thought of a Hummel. But a collectible figurine made no sense.

He started kicking against the wadded covers, a barricade to destroy.

"Jack," she said, yet remained unheard.

Enough already. She would wake him despite theories to the contrary. A shock of light could break his trance.

She clicked the switch of the nightstand lamp. As the bulb came to life, Jack swung away fiercely and scraped Audra's cheek. In shielding herself, she caused the lamp to topple. The lightbulb popped and plunged them back into darkness. His screams and flailing soared.

"Stop it," she ordered. "Jack, stop!"

His elbow boomed against the hollow wall.

She managed to grab hold of his wrists, to keep him from hurting himself. Within her grip, he twisted and pulled and yelled, fighting to escape. Several minutes of battling slicked her grip with sweat. His left arm broke free and slammed a corner of the night table. The crack alone communicated the damage, even without the wail of pain that projected from Jack's mouth. He retracted into a ball and his body shivered. His cries faded to a soft whimper. The dream had released its grasp.

For now.

"You're going to be okay, Jack." She stroked his back, the motion no steadier than her breaths. "Mommy's right here."

He raised his head and his gaze flitted around the room — to the lamp, his pillow, his comforter, all strewn across the floor. *What happened?* he asked without words.

Because she had no real answer, she simply held him. Her arms trembled, more from anxiety than exertion.

When he agreed to let her, she picked him up with a knowhow for handling scared, wounded creatures. She carried him to the car, a blanket over his body, and drove to the closest ER.

They didn't return until three in the morning.

Once they settled in, Audra's dreams, like Jack's, were so vivid they were hard to discern from reality. She was prepping for surgery, scrubbing her hands and donning latex gloves.

A little girl appeared in the corner. Hair covering her face, she wept into her knees. Audra asked what was wrong. The girl choked out, "You said my dog, Max, would go to heaven. And you *lied*." Audra glanced around the empty room, her technician nowhere to be seen. The clinic ached with quiet. "But how do you know he's not there?" Audra gently challenged the child, who then stopped her crying and lifted her head. Her skin shone pale, thin as a sheet of tissue, but her voice turned hard as stone. "Because I'm dead," she said, "and he's not here."

Audra wiped her hairline, dampened from the dream. She rolled over on her bed and discovered Jack asleep — she'd laid him there after the hospital. Daylight filtered in around the closed white blinds, gracing Jack's face with a peaceful glow, spotlighting the half cast on his arm.

Careful not to wake him, she edged out of the room.

At the kitchen sink, she filled a glass with water. She retrieved her vitamins from the cupboard, and noticed an old container of fish food partially hidden on a shelf. Between Devon's allergies and her full-time job, a dog or cat had never made sense for their family — ironic, considering her profession. They'd once treated their son to a pair of goldfish. When the pets died, Jack grieved for days.

Audra tossed the fish flakes into the trash. Another lesson learned.

She downed the cool water, soothing her roughened throat. Sounds of a televised sports game reverberated from the tenant above. Audra's head felt full of helium, light enough to fly away. When was the last time she had eaten a meal?

A knock on the front door startled her. She hoped it hadn't wakened Jack.

She investigated through the peephole. Meredith stood beside Robert, who wore a Trailblazers cap, both of them in coats. It was Saturday morning. Why would they —

The cemetery. The flags.

Damn.

Audra scrambled to unlock the door before they could ring the bell.

"Hi," she said, letting them in.

"Good morning . . ." Robert's inflection implied more of a question.

Meredith cocked her head, as though rethinking her greeting. Her eyes flickered over Audra.

From a glance downward, Audra recalled her appearance. Between the frazzled hair and wine-doused shirt, she must have been a beauty. "It was a long night. I fell asleep with a glass in my hand." She released a quick laugh at herself.

"Ah," Meredith replied, and smiled.

"So," Robert said. "Is Jack ready for us?"

Audra pictured her son curled up cozily in her

bed. She couldn't imagine disturbing his serenity after the night they had endured.

"Actually," Audra said, "I don't think today's a good day for the cemetery visit, after all."

Robert and Meredith exchanged surprised looks.

"He's actually still asleep. He was having —"

"Grandma?" Jack emerged from the bedroom, rubbing his eyes.

"Gracious. What happened?" Meredith rushed over to him and knelt down. She examined his cast as though it were a futuristic contraption. "What did you do here?"

Jack shrugged, kept his gaze low. He couldn't remember.

"It happened during a bad dream," Audra told them. "He accidentally hit the nightstand with his arm."

"Is it broken?" Meredith asked her.

"It is, but not too badly. The cast shouldn't be on for more than a month."

Robert piped in, "See what a tough nut he is? We'll have to start calling him The Giant, instead of Beanstalk."

Jack's eyes lightened.

"So, whaddya think?" Robert said. "Want to plant flags with your old gramps?"

Jack answered with the start of a smile. "Yes, please."

"Oh, kiddo," Meredith said, and sniffed twice. "Did you have a little accident?"

Audra sighed. After three apple juices in the

ER, liquid Tylenol to help him sleep, and water to wash it down, his poor bladder had hit its max.

"Let's get you cleaned up," Meredith told him.

"Are you sure?" Audra said. "You really don't have to."

"It's no trouble." Meredith was already leading Jack to his room.

On any other day Audra would feel uncomfortable leaving that chore to someone else. But Meredith was family, and honestly, part of Audra's brain was still in sleep mode.

"Can I get you anything while you're waiting?" she asked Robert. "Juice, water?"

"OJ if you got it."

She poured him a glassful that he drank in a few swallows. Then he launched into small talk, about a new construction manager and the unusual weather — springtime in Portland usually meant ten types of rain. Audra followed only half the conversation, her head aching from lack of sleep.

Not long after, Meredith returned with Jack, now dressed in jeans, a rugby shirt, and his favorite hoodie. He slipped on his shoes and Meredith double-knotted the laces.

"Last chance to change your mind about coming," Robert said to Audra. "We can wait if you'd like time to get ready."

Audra envisioned the cemetery, the type of site she hadn't been to since the funeral. So much green in that rolling grass, cultivated by

102

countless tears.

Before she could decline, Robert smiled. "Next time maybe."

"Maybe," she said, grateful he played along as though the possibility were real.

10

Apprehension hung over London, thick as a show curtain preparing to drop. On the train to work that morning, Vivian was shaken by the worry in people's eyes, the pleats in their faces. Not in the children, of course, whose priorities hadn't been swayed from games of marbles and cravings for sweets. Rather, the adults old enough to recall firsthand the blistering devastation of war.

"It doesn't start with an explosion." Mr. Harrington stared vacantly out the shop window. "It bears far more subtlety. A simmer beneath the surface, as if bringing broth to a boil."

He spoke this to no one in particular, though Vivian was the only other person in the store. Customer visits had slowed to a crawl since the startling news broke the day before. The announcement had come mere hours after Vivian's talk with her father, which clarified the tension in the den. Her father had known, or at least suspected, what was headed their way.

A non-aggression pact had indeed been signed, but between the Nazis and Soviets. All this time, even through the *Anschluss,* when Germany annexed Austria, the English had managed to turn a cheek. But now, a hand had been raised to strike the Queen herself. Hitler's march toward domination could no longer be dismissed, at least not by Vivian.

While in the basement that morning, seeking bleach for a coffee stain, she had caught her father's muffled voice. The heating duct projected his phone call from the study. She had balanced her weight between stacked crates and an Oxydol box to bring her ear close to the vent. The words she was able to discern nearly made her tumble.

How she wished today's hours would quicken. Nearly a full workday remained before her date at the theater, where she could divulge her news to Isaak.

At the store counter, she checked her watch, again. A *plunk* alerted her that she had dropped her pencil, again. She swiped it from the floor and resumed transcribing receipts into the tall brown ledger. She erased one line, and another, corrected more entries. For her efforts, the basic equations might well have been algorithms that challenged the likes of Einstein.

"Take the day off," Mr. Harrington said.

"Sir?"

"You heard me, love."

He had never released her prior to closing. Though kindhearted, he was a businessman who lived by the clock. She didn't know how to respond.

"Go and enjoy," he said solemnly. As if, like her father, he already knew.

A campus-wide search posed more challenges than Vivian expected. The staff roster was so large and students so scarce, on account of the summer holiday, she could not find anyone familiar with Isaak. Twice she phoned his dorm, but no one answered.

Admittedly, more than a message delivery propelled her. It was also a longing to see his room. To touch the down of his pillow, to learn in detail how he lived. If only women weren't forbidden from the building. He had often bemoaned this rule in the heat of their kissing, damning his inability to bring her there. For Vivian, it had been a relief, lessening the temptation to compromise her morals. Now she cursed those blasted morals, in light of her family's pending departure — a development of which Isaak wasn't aware.

In the university library, Vivian expanded her hunt to include Professor Klein. Since Isaak assisted the man with research, the two might work in the same vicinity.

"He teaches European history," she explained, inquiring at the counter.

The librarian suggested a jaunt over to the History Department, where Vivian might have more success. She hoped so. If not, she would have no choice but to pine away the hours until the scheduled time of her original date.

After finding the correct building, she wandered the halls, to no avail. She was on the verge on giving up when she peeked through the pane of a door. Two men stood in a large vacant classroom. Even from a distance she knew those golden curls.

Quickly she smoothed her own hair, pinned up at the sides, forgetting for a moment the reason she had come. She grasped the doorknob, discovered it locked. She knocked on the dense window.

The men took no notice. Arms crossed, parked before an enormous blackboard, they appeared intent on their conversation. Isaak was wearing cuffed trousers with the burgundy sweater-vest she loved, and the other gentleman wore a bow tie with his suit. Was that Professor Klein? His chiseled features and ink-black hair, as thick as his eyebrows, came as a surprise. She had envisioned the history professor to be well into his sixties, with a beard like Mr. Harrington's and spectacles low on his nose.

Vivian hated to interrupt but trusted Isaak would be grateful. She gave the door a pound, hearty enough to summon their gazes. She raised her hand in a small wave.

Neither man moved.

Was the window too narrow for clarity from their view?

But then recognition set into Isaak's face, a merging of delight and bewilderment. He spoke briefly to the man, then slipped into the hall.

"What are you doing here?" Isaak asked, shutting the door behind him. "However did you find me?"

"I have news from my father," she blurted.

The lines of Isaak's mouth lowered. He looked around, acknowledging the context, the urgency. "Come," he said, and guided her into another empty classroom.

He closed the door, leaving the fluorescent bulbs off. The mid-morning sky provided ample light through the windows. "You told him about me? And my family?"

"No . . . not yet." She hoped he didn't perceive the delay as proof of her father's disapproval — though it was a stance Isaak had rightly predicted, much to Vivian's shame. "I just thought, from what you said, it would be better to wait. For now."

"It is." He nodded staunchly, to her relief. "So what news did he tell you?"

"He didn't tell me, exactly. I overheard him on the phone. It was difficult to catch all of it, and I could only hear his side."

108

"And?"

"From what I gathered," she said, "Britain is entering into a Mutual Assistance Treaty."

"Another alliance? With whom?"

She quieted her voice, despite their being alone. "Poland."

"My God."

In a game of global chess, he understood what it meant, as did she. If Hitler invaded Poland, the United Kingdom would declare war.

Isaak gazed across the room, lost in his thoughts. "I should go back," he said finally, as if to himself.

It took her a moment to comprehend. He was referring to Munich.

"No. Isaak, you can't do that." On the screen in her mind, she saw the newsreels of British Spitfires, their airmen grinning while loading bombs and ammunition, all of which could soon be headed for Germany.

"What I can't do," he said, "is stay here and do nothing."

"Yes, I understand that. You want to be there to help your family. But don't you see? If you go back, you'll be the enemy."

He squared his shoulders and stared at her. "The enemy. Just as my family is, you mean."

"What? No, of course not. I wasn't saying . . ."

Isaak shook his head, stepping away. He raked both hands through his hair.

No silence could have been louder.

Vivian defied the tension that guarded him by moving to his side. She placed a hand on his arm. A muscle flinched beneath his sleeve, yet he didn't pull away.

"I'm sorry," she said. And she was. Not just for her choice of words, but for the burden he had to carry.

He slid his gaze downward to land on her grip. His fingers followed and layered her hand. "It's nothing you've done, darling. You're the only thing good in this god-awful mess."

Moisture clouded her vision. She felt her heart rising, expanding. "I love you," she whispered. It was only the second time she had dared to say it loud enough for him to hear, and suddenly regretted ever refraining.

He turned to her with a wisp of a smile. As he cupped her cheek, she leaned into his touch and closed her eyes. Teardrops streaked her face. Then his mouth was on hers, and everything but the warmth of his kiss and feel of his hold faded from existence.

At last, he drew his head back. In a matter of seconds, his attention again went adrift.

She debated a suggestion. The solution seemed so obvious it bordered on insulting. "Is there any way . . . for your family to leave Germany? Perhaps it will be easier if they go now."

"Maybe. I don't know. I wish it were that simple."

She sensed it best not to push.

"I'd better go," he said.

The very mention of leaving reminded her of the discussion with her father, his estimation that they would return to the States "rather soon." She ought to tell Isaak. But how could she right now? Such an issue was trivial in comparison. Besides, no plans were etched in stone.

And so, she merely nodded.

"I'll contact you soon," he said. "Thank you, darling, for telling me."

"If I hear anything else, you'll be the first to know."

A partial smile stretched his lips. Then quick as a wink, he was gone.

11

The scene, in another lifetime, could have been a snapshot of war.

It was Memorial Day at Portland's Rose Festival. Bunting of red, white, and blue draped Waterfront Park. Stick flags fluttered in the hands of passing children. Patriotic performances drew listeners to the far outdoor stage as uniformed servicemen threaded through the esplanade. Below them on the Willamette, massive naval ships would soon congregate. Annual Fleet Week would fill the streets with sailors, who these days, to Audra, looked no older than twelve.

But for now, she noted the contrast of elderly veterans being escorted in their wheelchairs. What generational shock they must feel amid the high-tech carnival games and reggae tunes from the band. The Skankin' Yankees were light-years away from the classic styling of the Andrews Sisters.

"Can we do stuff yet?" Jack impatiently scuffed the dirt.

"Hold on a few more minutes," Audra said. "I'm sure they'll be here soon."

He heaved a breath, clearly in doubt. It was actually refreshing to see him excited about any event.

In an attempt to kill time, she revived a game Robert used to lead. "I see . . . Charlie Brown." She subtly gestured toward a stranger who resembled the cartoon character. For each accurate designation, the player earned a point. "Ooh, there's Olive Oyl. And that guy there is definitely Shaggy. I've got three already. You'd better catch up."

"I'm hungry. Can we get one of those?" Too distracted to play, he pointed toward kids with pink and blue cotton candy. The feathery bouquets were larger than their heads.

With dinnertime so close, she imagined the "right" answer was *no*. "Let's have some real food first. Then we'll see."

As a child, Audra had indulged in plenty of treats that were no better; her Fun Dips and Pixy Stix were the equivalent of powdered-sugar injections. Yet that was also in an era when no one locked their doors and sleeping babies rode in cars on the floorboards.

Just then, Tess waved from the entrance. Her daughter, Grace, bounded alongside and submitted their tickets for admission. The eight-year-old had rich olive skin, compliments of her Italian side, and a braid of silky blond hair from her mom. Though the girl's aqua beret was

113

fashionably feminine, the roughened knees of her jeans affirmed a preference for climbing trees over dressing dolls.

"Sorry to keep you guys waiting," Tess said with a grumble. "Cooper couldn't find his mouth guard for practice. We had to turn the whole house upside down. I would've called, but I left my cell on the kitchen counter."

"Not to worry," Audra told her. "We got here a little late too."

"Oh, good." Tess sighed and nudged her daughter. "Gracie, say hi."

"Hi," she said with a smile.

Audra reciprocated, but not Jack, his attention too consumed by their environment. And who could blame him? The scents of every imaginable fried food collided with all the chaos from the amusement park.

"So, Jack," Tess said. "I hear coming out here was your idea. What would you like to do first?"

He answered with a shrug.

"I think he's pretty hungry," Audra supplied.

"Me too," Grace said. "I could eat a horse." She grinned at the veterinary punch line, and Tess tickled her ribs to elicit a giggle.

After brief deliberation, the group decided on lemonades and pizza. In line at the booth, Audra and Tess rattled on about their most notable patients of the week. Among them was a Scottie who was neutered for his extroverted acts. Whenever company came to visit he would drag stuffed animals to the center of the

114

gathering to show off his frisky skills.

"It's starting to rain," Grace interjected. "Can I go find us a table?" She motioned toward the area beneath a huge striped canopy. Her motive was likely more about boredom than being helpful or staying dry, but Audra did feel a tiny sprinkling. Over the city, gray clouds were banding together and dimming the sky.

"Fine by me," Tess said, "if you and Jack stay together." She turned to Audra. "You okay with that?"

Audra hedged. The urge to keep her son close battled the need to let him live and grow. But then she recalled his cast. Though it barely peeked from his raincoat, a tent would provide better coverage should the sprinkling gain momentum.

"All right. But don't talk to any strangers."

"We know." Grace laughed and rolled her eyes, the lesson far too basic for a third grader. "C'mon, Jack. Let's go."

He followed her toward the canopy. They were just out of earshot when Tess switched to a tone of concern.

"You told me about his arm, but you didn't say anything about *you.*"

"What do you mean?"

"Your cheek. I'm assuming that's how you got that."

For a time, Audra had forgotten about the two-inch scratch. An easy oversight for someone accustomed to being scraped, bitten, and peed on as part of a day's work.

She moved forward in the shrinking line. "The ER doc said it's pretty common for kids to lash out when they have night terrors — that's what he called them, by the way."

"Is there anything you can do to stop them?"

"They're supposed to fade on their own." *Supposed to.* How many things in Audra's life turned out as predicted? "Until then, I've at least moved the furniture away from his bed, to help keep him safer."

"How scary. I'm so sorry."

Audra had since read about the affliction online but found no solutions. Nor any connection to flying. She even did a Web search for "Himmel." Most links referenced a park in Arizona, a classical composer, the Dutch translation for "heaven." Nothing that applied. And asking Jack about the word had gone as predicted: He had no idea.

"Next!" the cashier called to them.

As Tess placed their order, Audra glanced back to confirm the kids' whereabouts. She spotted Grace's hat through gaps in the seated crowd, but balloons and tall strangers blocked her view of Jack.

"One pepperoni and three vegetarians," the guy announced in the booth. He handed Tess the slices on flimsy paper plates.

Audra paid for her half and wrapped her fingers around all four drinks. She worked to keep a leisurely pace toward the tent. It was a

116

thin line between cautious and paranoid.

"Hey, I've been meaning to tell you," Tess said. "There's a new partner at Russ's firm. Seems like a really nice guy. They're having a celebration dinner for him at City Grill on Thursday. You should join us."

"Let me guess. He just happens to be single."

"Yeah? So?" Tess raised her volume as they threaded through the noisy dining area. "Is that a bad thing?"

"I've told you a gazillion times, Tess. I'm not interested in dating."

"Who said anything about dating? Just a good old-fashioned roll in the hay would do you some good."

An adjacent table of grizzled men snapped their faces toward Audra and away from their mound of nachos.

"Oops," Tess said.

Lovely.

Avoiding all eye contact, Audra charged toward Grace's beret, a sudden beacon of refuge. But Tess's determination followed.

"You'll come to the dinner though, right?"

"Sorry, can't hear you."

"Please?"

"Too much static. You're breaking up."

Several feet from the table, Audra noticed Grace was waiting alone. She was wearing earphones connected to an iPod in her hand. Audra set the drinks down and scanned the bustling area. "Where's Jack?"

117

Tess tugged Grace's earpieces free.

"Motherrr."

"Where did Jack go?" Tess said.

The girl shrugged. "I thought he was with you guys."

Audra flashed back to his vacant airplane seat, to the terror of not being able to reach him. "Grace, what did he say to you?"

"He just got up and left. I figured he was going back to see you in line."

Oh, God . . .

Audra's gaze zipped from one bystander to another. "Jack!" she hollered across the tent. "Jack Hughes!"

"Don't worry." Tess placed a hand on Audra's elbow. "He probably just went to the bathroom. Do you want me to go check?"

"No. No, I'll go. You and Grace stay here in case I don't see him before he comes back." Audra shot off for the lineup of porto-potties beyond a towering bungee drop.

"Mom, I'm sorry. I didn't know," she heard Grace say before their voices waned.

Audra restrained herself from sprinting in order to view every boy along the way. A short queue of people waited at the blue portable stalls.

"Jack? Are you in there? It's Mom! Answer me."

The doors opened and closed. Strangers exited and entered.

"Has anyone seen a little boy? A seven-year-

118

old, about this high?" She held her hand to her chest.

Heads shook in a stagger of nos.

Audra worked to control her breathing. She sped over the trampled grounds to reach another set of stalls. The results were no different. Panic bubbled beneath the surface, a geyser about to explode.

Then she remembered. "Cotton candy," she said. That's what he wanted. He must have gone on a hunt, too eager to wait.

She bumped past a teenaged couple who dragged their feet as they walked. Next she swerved around a family, their toddler leashed to a backpack.

No sign of Jack at the cotton-candy stand. Same for the one with corn dogs. And elephant ears. And caramel apples on a stick.

A ghoulish shriek wailed from the haunted house.

By now Jack could be back at the table. She fumbled through her jacket pockets to get her cell, before she recalled Tess wasn't carrying a phone. *Damn it all!*

She raced all the way back to reach the edge of the canopy. On the opposite side, Tess was speaking to Security. She caught Audra's gaze, and a look of despair gave the answer.

Audra's thoughts launched into a spin. Round and round they went, like the linked carts of the Red Dragon, clicking and clacking on an oval track, picking up speed with every loop. She wanted to scream. She wanted to sob.

"Jack, please," she whispered. "Where are you?"

12

The simmer had heated to a boil. On September 1, Hitler waltzed into Poland with the confidence of Fred Astaire. In the two days since, herds of civilians had evacuated from London in anticipation of aerial bombings. The German embassy advised all German residents to clear out of Britain; Brits in Germany, Vivian heard, were urged to do the same.

Keeping her promise, she passed along such snippets at her daily meetings with Isaak. While she hated to heighten his nerves, he repeatedly assured her: It was always better than not knowing.

Vivian didn't necessarily agree. A large part of her wished she had not learned of the update over breakfast. *Our plans have been set,* her mother said while buttering a slice of toast. *We'll depart for home next Sunday.*

We, however, did not include Vivian's father. From behind his newspaper and between sips of coffee, he claimed he would

121

follow once affairs allowed. This, Vivian realized, was the reason he had been so grave that night when inquiring about her *feelings* over moving back. She had answered him without knowing what he was truly asking.

After breakfast, on the way to church, she had voiced her wish to stay, to wait and travel as a family. He told her a delay would be too dangerous.

Yet if that was the case, should he not retreat as well? The same went for Isaak. How could she possibly leave him behind?

All morning these were the thoughts that plagued her, through the drone of hymns and now the solitude of her room. The clinking of china and rustling of paper traveled from downstairs, where the maid was busily packing.

Vivian sat at her small desk and flipped her diary to a clean page. She penned her dilemma in hopes of conjuring an answer. Time was running short. Isaak would be waiting by the river at half past eleven. Their frequent meetings had required an equal number of alibis to excuse Vivian from the house. Thankfully today, with political urgency trumping the Sabbath, her father was at the embassy, leaving only her mother as an obstacle.

Vivian scrolled through her options. It had been a while since she and Alice, a British diplomat's daughter, had shared an outing in the city. It was plausible they would have made plans for . . . a picnic . . . or lunch in Piccadilly . . . to say good-bye.

"Vivian, honestly."

At her mother's voice, she covered her diary with a magazine.

The woman appeared in the doorway wearing a yellow sweater and brown A-line skirt. Face powdered and rouged, she posed a cigarette like Greta Garbo. In fact, much about her resembled a film star, but aged from being too long on display.

"We're not waiting until the last minute to pack all of our things," she said. "You haven't emptied a single drawer, have you?"

Vivian's jaw clenched as she leafed through an issue of *London Life.* "Good grief, Mother. We have a whole week." When it came to her parents' marriage, she had never witnessed the slightest spark of passion. But given the current crisis, the woman could at least feign concern.

"Yes, and a week will be here before we know it. Dear, sit up, or you'll ruin your posture before its time."

Vivian obeyed from force of habit. When her mother crossed the room and opened the armoire, she deliberately slouched in her chair.

"You really don't need half of these dresses. A single trunk should be sufficient."

"Most of those are my *work* dresses. And yes, I will need them." Vivian had resigned

123

from the store solely to aid Mr. Harrington's budgetary needs. It wasn't a sign of her conforming to the dull aspirations of a housewife.

Her mother's mouth sank into its standard frown. Smoke from her cigarette plumed past her hair, a brown swoop of proper style. Exasperated, she closed the wardrobe.

"So be it," she murmured. *For now,* her tone affirmed. "I'll be at Mrs. Jewett's for an early lunch. Please, at the very least, pack up your winter clothes before I return."

"You're leaving now?"

"Very shortly, yes. I'd invite you to come along, but the last time I took you there, all you did was pout through their tea and crumpets."

Vivian knew there was relief to be found, not having to craft an excuse to slip out. But it was difficult to celebrate when being treated like a child. More than that, she hated how often in her mother's presence she reverted to exactly that.

"I did not pout."

"You scarcely said two words, Vivian."

"I just didn't have anything to contribute to their snooty gossip."

The truth of it was, her mother's desperate attempts to fit in always made for a disquieting visit. Presumably the woman's pretenses could be traced all the way back to New Hampshire, where a suitable marriage had raised her from mediocrity. The family of Vivian's father was far from the Vanderbilts, but enough successful investments and political ties had lent notable prestige. Then the Crash of '29 took a decent bite out of those funds and, seemingly, out of the love between Vivian's parents.

"Be that as it may," her mother said, "I am in no mood to watch you scowl over lunch, as you did at breakfast and then at church. Heavens. For months after moving here all you could talk about was going home."

"You don't understand."

"Yes, yes," she replied tiredly. "Mothers never do." When she turned to leave, Vivian's frustration sharpened, an arrow of unsaid words. She could hold them in no longer.

"Aren't you worried at all about Father staying here? Or are you secretly hoping something will happen to him?"

Her mother froze, facing the doorway.

Vivian girded herself for a glare, a reprimand. Perhaps even a slap, partly aware she deserved it. Instead, a sheet of silence erected, so brittle it could shatter from a single tap.

When the woman eventually spoke, she did so over her shoulder in a tone cool as steel.

"I was once your age, Vivian. Believed I knew everything about life and love, how the world worked." After a pause, a wrenching mournfulness entered her voice: "Enjoy it while you can."

■ ■ ■

Vivian did her best to shake off the remark. She realized how greatly she had failed while ascending from the Underground, having little recollection of the trip.

On the sidewalk, someone bumped her from behind and shot forward to pass her. No apology. Such rudeness was more typical of a kid in knickers than a gentleman in a suit. Her gaze trailed him to a barbershop, where a group had assembled outside. The presence of women made it clear that something other than a free cut and shave had beckoned the crowd.

Vivian warily approached. The people held in place, still as stone, listening. The stout barber in a white apron adjusted the radio on the counter. The speaker's voice belonged to Prime Minister Chamberlain. Through the crackling static came the formal announcement: Britain had declared war.

War . . .

It was now official. Inevitable, really. The ultimatum had been made; the treaty had been breached. Nevertheless, the surrounding expressions confirmed Vivian was not alone in her shock.

As if that weren't enough, France, Australia, and New Zealand had also joined the cause. Another world war was upon them, all thanks to Hitler and his Nazi regime, dragging with them the populace of Germany.

Isaak. She had to reach him.

She glanced at her watch — eleven seventeen — and made her way toward the Thames. Storekeepers mounted sandbags and crisscrossed windows with fresh tape. Strangers toted boxes stuffed with gas masks on the ready. Optimists would no longer view these as overly cautious measures.

From Vivian's childhood, a nursery rhyme echoed in her memory. "London Bridge Is Falling Down." She dreaded to think the same fate could befall the city. The whole country.

She increased her pace, bordering on a run. When she reached the designated lamppost — no longer *her* special spot, but *theirs* — she checked her watch again.

Eleven twenty-six.

Four minutes to wait, at the most. Isaak was never late. *Punctual as a German train,* he'd once boasted. Though she hadn't considered how telling the phrase was until this moment.

A growing rumble caught her ear. She turned toward the water, where boats had become rather scarce. The image of a German bomber flashed in her mind. She scanned the overcast sky. Patches of clouds were stitched into a quilt, a convenient disguise for the Luftwaffe.

But then she traced the sound. The muffler of an old Ford grumbled down the street.

"Just a car," she sighed. She almost laughed from relief, when a siren wailed. An actual warning. Not a practice drill. A passing mother yelled at her child to keep up. Couples set off in a sprint, retreating to shelters.

Where was Isaak? Vivian searched for his face. Panic coursed through her veins. The siren pierced all thought. She cupped her ears, muting the nightmare, and prayed that any second she would wake.

13

I'll find him, I'll find him . . .

Audra looped the declaration, a flimsy weapon against the images emerging from her memory. They were alerts of missing children — posters and billboards and five o'clock news leads — a collection she had unknowingly accrued since the day of Jack's birth.

"I repeat, we've got a Code Adam," the security guard said into his walkie-talkie. He released the button, and a voice confirmed receipt of the message. He addressed Audra again, his tone and appearance straight from any crime-fighting show. "Do you remember what your son was wearing?"

Jack's entire wardrobe tumbled around in her mind, as if viewed through the window of a clothes dryer. She glanced around the food area, at the outfits of strangers, to jog her recollection.

"He's got jeans on. And sneakers. He has a cast on one arm, but it's covered by his blue raincoat — no, green. It's dark green."

Audra waited as the man relayed the description to the control center. Why hadn't she dressed Jack in something more distinct? For public places, Devon used to put him in bright colors, fluorescent orange and yellow. She just didn't think it would be necessary at his age.

"Did you agree on a meeting spot?"

"We did. The table — I was bringing food. He was supposed to be there with my friend's daughter." She motioned toward Grace, who stood with Tess a few yards away.

"But what about a place for you two to meet up, if he got lost?"

A basic precaution. How had she missed it?

She admitted her negligence by a stiff shake of her head.

"Not a problem." He waved his hand as if to quell her rising shame. "We've already got guys combing the grounds. I'm gonna go check out the carnival booths. Kids wander over there all the time. Those big stuffed-animal prizes are like magnets."

"I'll go with you." She couldn't bear staying idle. She signaled to Tess that she'd be back.

Audra and the security guard traveled past the dart balloons and shooting gallery, the milk-bottle pitching booth. Between the ducky pond and ring toss, a little boy burst into a fit. His father looked to have reached his wit's end.

Would bystanders dismiss any child's screams as a tantrum, even if he was being abducted?

130

Applause soared from the stage, the sound of celebration. A man was talking to the crowd.

A microphone . . . speakers . . .

She asked the guard, "Could we make an announcement up on stage?"

"We've actually got someone about to do that right now."

Audra's mobile buzzed in her pocket. The screen read: *Private caller.* Tess could be borrowing a person's phone.

"Is he there?" Audra demanded.

"Audra? It's Meredith." A quick pause. "Is everything all right?"

The question threatened to break her. *No, it's not all right*! She could hear the sound of her own heartbeat. "It's Jack. We can't find him."

"What? Where are you?"

"The park. At the waterfront. He wanted to sit and he, he left —" The answer collapsed as she caught sight of the river.

She hadn't considered that Jack might wander past the jogging path and down to the docks, baited by the boats and Jet Skis zooming under the bridges. He had taken swim lessons years ago, but only the basics. Not strong enough for a cold, deep river.

"Audra? Audra!" Meredith's voice. "Robert and I will come down there. Tell me where exactly you are."

"Copy that," the guard replied over the airwaves, and turned to Audra. "I think we found him. Over by the stage —"

131

That was all Audra heard before she took off running. She cut around obstacles, the guard trailing behind, until the profile of a boy swam into view. *Jack.* It was definitely him. There he was, talking to a uniformed soldier who had just stepped down from the stage.

"Oh, thank you, thank you," she said under her breath, a chant of boundless gratitude.

Meredith's voice reached out from the phone, held low in Audra's grip.

"We've found him," Audra told her. "I'll call you later." She zipped between people reclined on their blankets, over trampled grass peppered with litter, and through wafting bubbles blown by a little girl with pigtails.

The band returned to the stage and proceeded to tune their instruments.

"Jack!" She threw her arms around him. She wanted to scold him, to shake him, to keep him close forever. "My God, you have no idea how much you scared me."

The security guard caught up and fed a report over the radio.

Audra pulled back just enough to look into Jack's eyes. "You can't wander off like that. Ever, ever. Do you understand me?"

He nodded, and finally her tears dared to fall. She glanced up at the guard, then the soldier whose confusion constricted his features.

"I'm sorry," she said to them both. "I'm . . . so very sorry." She grabbed Jack's hand and briskly led him away, desperate to shed

132

thoughts of *what if.*

With each mile that distanced them from the festival, Audra's relief gave way to aggravation — less at Jack than herself. In a place like that, she shouldn't have let him out of her sight. Not for a second.

She recalled the child at the park harnessed by a leash. She and Devon used to condemn those inventions. Mostly, she now realized, because Jack never needed one. Even as a toddler, he always stayed near, always asked for permission.

So why had he ventured off?

She studied him in the rearview mirror. He stared wordlessly out his window, rubbing his little toy plane. She preferred not to relive the incident, but neither did she plan to let it happen again.

Taking the exit off-ramp, she rolled up to the red light. The ticking of her turn signal compounded the tension. "Jack?"

He connected with the reflection of her eyes.

"You know you're not supposed to walk off without telling someone, right?"

He nodded.

"Then why on earth did you do that today?"

Jack parted his lips to reply, then pursed them and returned to the window.

She reviewed her own tone, firmer than intended. His disappearance had upended her emotions; though it all came out well, the effects were difficult to shake. She exhaled before trying again.

"Buddy, I'm not upset anymore. I just really want to understand why you'd do that."

He didn't respond, just stroked his personal worry stone.

Considering Jack's military interest, like that of most boys his age, the GI at the fair would have easily caught his eye. After all, the man had been a recruitment poster for valor, all spiffed up in an Army dress uniform.

"Did you just want to say hi to the soldier? Is that why you went over there?"

After a pause, he answered softly. "No."

"Jack, I saw you speaking to him."

It then occurred to her that he might be avoiding a confession: that he'd broken a basic safety rule by talking to a stranger.

"Could you please just tell me what you said? I promise, you won't get in trouble if you're honest with me."

He gazed down at his plane, as if the answer lay in the grooves of its wings. He seemed to be growing even more introverted since his nightmares began. When he raised his head, he looked straight into the mirror. "Feel find feel air."

At his altered voice, the tiny hairs on the back of her neck shot up. She twisted to face him, her foot still on the brake. She would have taken the words for gibberish if not for the distinct, purposeful syllables and guttural vowels.

134

"What does that mean?"

He shrugged at her.

"Jack, tell me what that means."

"I don't know," he mumbled.

The phrase had sounded foreign. Yet how was that possible? With the prevalence of Spanish, few kids in America wouldn't be familiar with standards like *hola* or *adios.*

But this was different.

"Do you . . . remember where you learned it?"

He shrugged again, and a honk blared from the car behind. The light had changed to green. Audra scrambled to find the gas pedal and jerked the car into motion. She made a sharp left through the intersection, straining to remain in her lane.

They passed cars and crosswalks and neighborhood blocks. Her autopilot skills led the way as the fingers of her mind shuffled through Jack's drawings. The Army plane in flames. The swastika on the man's chest. And now Jack seemed to be imitating another language. Could it be a European tongue from World War Two?

She'd sat back all this time, not interfering when Robert showered him with fighter planes or reenacted invasions with battalions of toy soldiers, despite their inherent links to violence. She figured it was a normal hobby for boys. Her one condition had been no viewing of programs featuring the glories or brutalities of war.

Once parked in her apartment's lot, she

turned toward the backseat. She did her best not to convey an inquisition. "Jack, I really need you to tell me. Has Grandpa been showing you any war movies? About airplanes blowing up, or soldiers being hurt?"

A crinkle formed on his brow, then he shook his head.

She'd seen that crinkle before, when he tried to keep a secret after a weekend with his grandparents. *They're supposed to spoil him,* Devon had assured her, regarding Jack's overdose of donuts. *It's a perk of the job.* She had let it go, of course, even smiled at the benign tradition.

This, on the other hand, was anything but amusing.

She was about to press harder when her phone buzzed on the passenger seat. This time she had no doubt it was Meredith.

Audra handed the keys over to Jack. "Go on in, buddy. We'll talk about this later."

Jack climbed out of the car. She watched him enter their apartment, only a dozen feet away, before she picked up the call.

"Audra, are you there?"

"Yeah, I'm here."

"I just wanted to make sure Jack was okay."

"He wandered off for a little while, but everything's fine."

"Oh, good. I'm so glad. I know how scary that can be." Her voice lightened, sounding of a smile. "You know, we used to joke that Devon had bloodhound in him. Whenever Robert took him bird hunting as a kid, Dev would always go off exploring —"

The mention of killing animals for sport, combined with such breeziness over a roaming child — particularly after today's scare — was anything but welcome.

"Meredith," she cut in, "has Jack been watching any TV at your house?"

The woman stopped. "Once in a while, I suppose. Why do you ask?"

"Has he been watching war programs? Like on the Military or History Channel?"

"Gracious . . . I wouldn't imagine so." Her air of uncertainty only raised Audra's doubts. "Is there a problem?"

"He's been drawing some violent pictures lately. Then there's the nightmares he's having. I'm just trying to get to the bottom of where he's getting these ideas."

Meredith went quiet, either brainstorming possibilities or sensing the onset of an accusation.

Another confrontation was the last thing either of them needed. The easiest way Audra could handle this was to provide clearer guidelines during their next visit.

"I actually need to check on Jack. But we'll talk more later, okay?"

"Sure," Meredith said. "That's fine. Give him our love."

"I will."

Audra disconnected the call and leaned back onto the headrest. She gazed at the apartment door, home to a son she could have lost. To prevent that from ever occurring, maybe she did need help after all.

She dialed Directory Assistance.

"City and state, please," asked the automated voice.

"Portland, Oregon," Audra replied. "For Dr. Newman Shaw."

14

The name came to Vivian muffled, as if spoken in a dream. She dropped her hands from her ears.

"Vivian!" On the pedestrian walk, parallel to the river, Isaak was hurrying toward her. She set off in a run to halve the distance between them. Upon their meeting, he crushed her to his body, squeezing out her breath, though none of her relief.

The siren continued its warning.

"We have to get to a shelter," he told her.

She nodded against his cheek.

"Come." He grabbed her hand and hastened down the path.

On the sidewalk a torrent of strangers scattered in a panic. They were ants fleeing a storm.

Isaak looked around, assessing, calculating. "The Underground station," he decided aloud. Not waiting for a reply, he towed Vivian deftly through the crowd. They were about to cross the street when two taxis collided. Vivian ducked at the smash of metal and glass, and once more Isaak pulled her close.

For a full second the scene came to halt, like a photograph from the *Daily Mail.* Then all chaos resumed. Isaak led her onward, but a queue had swelled and divided around the immobile cabs. Each footstep ground shards into salt-like crystals. Over the crunching came a shriek. A woman at the corner had toppled from a shove and scraped her knee on pavement. Blood colored the rip in her stocking.

"I have another idea," Isaak said.

Vivian nodded. If their surroundings were any indication, the station staircase could be more hazardous than a German bomber. Then again, in her frenzied state, he could lead her to hell and she wouldn't think to object until waist deep in flames.

"This way," he said.

Changing direction, they zigzagged in and out of the city blocks and into a vacant alleyway. He came to an abrupt stop. A square wooden door lay on the ground at an angle. A cellar. He jiggled the padlock.

"Damn." He scanned the ground as though hoping for a dropped key. He resorted to a pile near the trash bin, discards from a building renovation.

Vivian raised her face toward the clouds. Would Hitler give only a taste of a threat, a chance for Chamberlain to reconsider? Or would he punish them unmercifully to deter other countries?

A sharp clank jostled her. Isaak had sent a gray pipe rolling over the cobblestones. "This'll do," he said, clutching a narrow piece of steel akin to a crowbar with no hook. He shoved the tool beneath the cellar latch and yanked up with a groan. He yanked again, harder. The fastener bent, yet clung to its bolts.

At minimum she ought to ask whose cellar they were invading; they were no doubt breaking the law. But circumstances, she was learning, dictated a separate set of rules.

Joining him, she grasped the end of the tool with both hands. Its rough, rusted surface pressed into her palms. On a count of three, they heaved and tugged until they pried the latch free. Isaak tossed away the steel and lifted the door. She peeked inside and flinched at the ladder. The shoddy rungs vanished into darkness.

He held out his palm to guide her in. "Trust me."

For a slew of solid reasons she would be wise to decline. Yet her trust in him, like the depth of her feelings, ignored all sensibility.

She took his hand and mounted the ladder. The slanted wood bowed under her weight. She was halfway down when Isaak climbed on, and she prayed the structure could hold

141

them both.

At the bottom, she found relief on the packed dirt, just as Isaak slammed the door. The cellar turned dark as a coffin. Her lungs sucked a dusty breath.

"There should be a lantern down there," he said. Creaks marked his descent.

She spread her fingers, inched her shoes by feel. With the siren somewhat muted, she made out a scuffling sound from the side. She told herself it was Isaak, though her ankles awaited the slithering tail of a rat.

Then came the hiss of a match. Isaak used the sulfurous glow to locate a lantern. He returned the matchbook to his trouser pocket and transferred the flame to the wick. Adjusting the knob, he shrank the tall stretch of fire into an orange teardrop.

Shelves covered the walls, stocked with canned foods and dry goods, pickled vegetables and jarred fruit. Barrels of onions and sacks of potatoes huddled in the center of the rectangular space. The air smelled of stale dirt and perishables starting to rot.

Isaak set the lantern on the ground. "The father of one of my classmates owns the general store above us. We'd sneak in here for a snack on occasion," he explained.

"They won't mind that we're here?" Not that it mattered at this point.

"His family evacuated a few days ago." Isaak shook out a pair of burlap bags and laid them out like blankets. "Can't say if they'll ever be back."

The comment struck Vivian as odd. Londoners would return from their rural hideaways eventually.

Then it dawned on her: "They went back to Germany."

He affirmed this with his silence.

Saying no more, Vivian took a seat. A shiver from the cool ground moved through her. She thought of her parents. They would be safe in a shelter by now, her father at the embassy, her mother with her friends.

Vivian hugged her knees as Isaak walked around, scoping the area, fingering the shelves. He shouldn't be so calm and collected. Envy itched at her until his circular stroll revealed itself as pacing from nerves.

"No chance of starving anytime soon." He picked up a jar and wiped the dust to view the contents. "Are you hungry?"

The knots in her stomach gave no hint of untying. "Sit with me." She motioned to the burlap. "Please."

Replacing the jar, he smiled. "Of course."

He settled beside her, his back against the shelves, and she nestled beneath his arm. His cologne smelled of pine, his jacket of a sweet cigar.

"Darling, you're shaking." He rubbed her arm over the sleeve of her sweater, brisk at first, then long and even.

For an eternal stretch, she focused on the rhythm of his breathing. The flow of air, in and out. Anything to drown out the siren's ghost-like cry. Isaak took a few stabs at casual conversation, but the attempts swiftly died.

Lamplight glinted off the rim of his shirt collar. His necklace. She reached for the chain, desperate for a distraction, and followed its path to a golden charm. She traced the grooves of the foreign engraving, as she had done in the past. It was a gift from his late grandmother — his *Oma* he had called her.

A bedlam of voices broke out above. Vivian's muscles recoiled, braced for an invasion. The yelling grew, then dimmed as the stampede passed the door.

"It's all right, Vivian. We're safe down here."

The comment brought scant assurance. Any minute, an explosion could rip through the cellar and blast the jars into pieces. She fended off the image, sharp as razors in her mind.

Sinking into Isaak, she rested her cheek on his neck. How she yearned for comforts of the familiar, a vision of life before war. "Tell me again, will you? All the things back home you used to love."

"In New York?" he said.

She nodded.

"Well . . . let's see. . . ." His subtle German vowels became more pronounced in the dimness. He rested the back of his head against a row of canned soup. "The diners, for one. There was a spot by our house that had the best burgers and fries in town. Probably because they didn't clean the grill very often, so the grease had loads of flavor. And they had the thickest milk shakes you've ever seen. They must have emptied a whole cow to make the shakes that creamy."

A tight laugh slipped from Vivian's mouth. She could almost taste the sweetness of vanilla malt on her tongue. "What else?"

Isaak stroked her hair as he continued. "Yankee Stadium. Pickup games of stickball. Penny candies at Mr. Burke's drugstore — I must have bought a hundred large pickles at that place. After dipping my hand in, my fingers would smell like pickle juice for days." He chuckled, remembering, and Vivian warmed at the idea.

"Then there's the American picture shows — not having to wait for them to make it all the way here. Oh, and those fancy window displays. Better in New York than anywhere."

"Like Macy's," she guessed.

"That's right. They were splendid at Christmas, weren't they?"

"I've actually never seen them during the holidays. Though I've wanted to." Political festivities always consumed her family's calendar, barring any plans that time of year to venture out of DC.

"Then I'll take you." Isaak spoke so decisively, as if Manhattan were across the street, not halfway around the globe. America seemed light-years away.

Suddenly Vivian recalled her pressing news, of her plans to leave in a week. She stamped out the thought, a dried leaf beneath her heel. For the time being, she would allow herself to indulge. She closed her eyes to visualize the scenes, to cling to a feeling of safety.

"What else shall we do while we're there?"

He kissed the top of her head and she could feel the upturn of his lips. "Why, I'll take you shopping, of course. Buy you the loveliest hat in Manhattan."

"Only a hat?"

"A dress — three dresses. A whole wardrobe."

She smiled.

"Have you been to the Empire State Building? It wasn't built when I was there."

"Just a few times." She looked up at him. "Why? Would you like to go?"

He paused. "King Kong doesn't actually cling to the top, does he?"

"Not usually."

"In that case, we'll add it to our list." His fingers moved to her cheek. It was a triangular caress, as though mapping their tour on her skin. "From there, we'll ice-skate in Central Park and take a carriage ride through the city. And we'll have coffee and pastries every week at my favorite café in town."

"Where is that?" she asked.

"It's in Brooklyn, near Prospect Park. Called Café Labrec. It has a small French courtyard with flowers that bloom in every color. Darling, you'll feel drunk on the scent of their croissants alone."

She imagined the smell of baking dough, the chocolate smothered over buttery delights. "How heavenly," she sighed, and that's when the siren stopped.

The air raid was over. The silence was sobering.

"Thank God," he murmured.

Ironically, Vivian felt anything but thankful. She had no desire to leave the virtual world they had constructed.

Isaak shifted, about to stand.

"Not yet." She grasped his arm, and a solution emerged from the cellar of her own mind. She had been so afraid to throw her life off-kilter. Now she knew: What she had viewed as the firm foundation of her future would be but a feeble stage without him.

In the quiet, Isaak cocked his head, questioning. The lantern cast him in shadows.

She rose onto her knees to fully view his face. Her lingering adrenaline emboldened her. "Come to America with me."

His eyes sparked with levity, a continuation of the fantasy, then dimmed as he registered her intent.

"The date's been set," she said. "Just this morning my parents told me. My mother and I are scheduled to leave next Sunday."

"Sunday?" he said. "In just a week?"

She nodded, allowing her suggestion to soak in. He looked away, shoved his fingers through his hair. There was no trace of excitement. But then, it was a large proposition that required more detail.

"Don't you see? It's a perfect idea. After all, you're an American. You belong there," she said. "With me."

He turned to her. Slowly he shook his head. "My life is here, Vivian. My classes, my work. My family."

Concerns over his relatives were a given. She would expect nothing less. All the same, a pang shot through her chest from his low ranking of their relationship, below even schooling and a job. Both of which were doomed in a wartime climate.

She drew back onto her heels. "So what would you do instead? Sit in your classroom and wait for the bombs?"

"Of course not."

"What then? Enlist in the service? Fly with the RAF?" She threw out the exaggerations based on his boyish fascination with newsreels but immediately regretted the scoff. His expression displayed serious mulling of the options.

148

"You'd be fighting against your own family."

"No. I'd be fighting the Nazis."

Incredulous, she blew out a breath. England wasn't even his country.

"Vivian, there's nothing wrong with wanting to do my bit. The evils of what they're doing — they have to be stopped."

She had heard enough political reasoning to last fifty lifetimes. Each conflict, in reality, could be traced to the same distinct villains: male pride and ego. All arguments to the contrary were fluffy justifications.

"The truth of it is," she said, "if you truly loved me, you wouldn't even consider such a thing."

The statement hung between them, bare in the darkness. His lips parted but crafted no reply. Not even a request that she stay in London. No suggestion that they evacuate, like so many lovers would, off to a spot in the countryside. Rather, he would choose war and death over her.

Tears filled her eyes, fed by a pool of stupidity. Falling this hard for a man, much less one on another continent, made her worse than foolish.

She rushed to the ladder, starkly aware she had brought this on herself.

"Now, hold one minute."

When she ignored the plea, Isaak grabbed her by the elbow. She struggled to continue,

149

but he pulled her off from behind and bound her with his arms. "Just calm down and listen."

"Let me go!"

"Look at me," he ordered. He released her just enough to twist her around, and her arm flung free, striking his face. He stood there, stunned.

A budding of fear opened inside her. She recognized the edge in his eyes that had always lured her in. Before she could act, he pressed her back against the ladder. He charged forward to retaliate, but with a kiss. Flared with such hunger, it dizzied her thoughts.

No . . . she would not be manipulated so easily.

She salvaged just enough will to wedge her hands between their bodies and pushed against his chest. Yet he gripped her wrists and raised them to the rungs above. He stilled her head by pressing his cheek to hers and whispered raggedly by her ear.

"I *do* love you, damn it. So much, it's hard to breathe when we're apart. I'd marry you tonight if I could. You have to know that."

She squeezed her eyes shut, told herself not to listen. But the heat of his skin, the raw yearning in his tone, weakened her resolve.

"Look at me," he said again, and relinquished his grip on her wrists. "Darling, please . . ."

She felt his thumb wipe a trail of moisture from her cheek. He leaned into her, his leg touching her thigh, paralyzing her. His mouth brushed her forehead. He stretched slow kisses toward her temple, and the space in her lungs constricted. Every breath took concerted effort.

"I'll go." He spoke almost too softly for her to hear. She expected him to pull away and ascend the ladder, before he added, "I'll go with you."

She digested the words, the full force of their meaning. Her eyes opened and found his face only inches away. "But — you just said —"

"For Christ's sake, Vivian. I think I deserved a moment to take it in. Until a few weeks ago, you had me convinced you were in no hurry for anything serious."

Until a few weeks ago, she had convinced herself of the same. Still, she remained leery of escalating her hopes. "And . . . your family?"

His gaze fell to the side, a long quiet beat. "I don't know. But there has to be a way."

"Of . . . ?"

He looked at her. "To take my mother back to the States. Then I'd know she'd be safe."

Vivian wished her father would help, but his opinions of Germans, particularly after today, would make him utterly inflexible. It was otherwise a wondrous plan. "I'm sure

151

we'll figure it out."

One side of Isaak's mouth hinted at a smile. He tucked away a strand of her hair and again pressed his lips to hers. Vivian's fingers joined behind his neck, drawing him closer. His hand slid beneath her sweater, over her dress, just below her breast. With his other hand he stretched her collar to the side, and his tongue traced over her shoulder in moist, rapturous strokes. Indescribable heat flared through her middle, arching her back, sending a moan from her throat.

Soon, his fingers left her collar, brushed past the side of her waist and hip, and started their way up under her dress. They traveled over her right stocking and beneath her slip. Once at her garter belt, he slowed his pace as if waiting for her to stop him.

This was the boundary they never crossed, despite the pulsing of temptation. Out of habit, her hand indeed layered over his, but this time she surprised even herself by guiding him to continue.

He complied for an instant but then resisted. He peered into her eyes, his forehead creased. "Are you sure?"

A fresh wave of desire surged through her. More than that, the need to prove just how certain she was — not only of their intimacy, but of her commitment to their future. It was just a matter of time before they would trade vows of forever. Perhaps deep inside she had known this the minute they first met.

Reinforced by the notion, she returned to their improvised blanket. She faced him before removing her shoes and sweater. The lantern light flickered over his captivated features, reducing her modesty to cinders. Unbuttoning her dress, she let the garment fall. She did the same to her slip.

Isaak's hunter-like gaze roamed over her figure. She fought the instinct to cover herself, already feeling naked, but then he came closer. He said nothing as he stripped away his clothes, picking up speed with each article.

Acutely aware of his arousal, she felt her entire body flush. He finished undressing her, leaving a trail of sensations over every area he touched, and guided her to lie with him. The ground should have been cool through the burlap cloth, yet she scarcely registered the temperature. His mouth, his fingers, sloped over her breasts and down the tautness of her belly, causing her knees to bend.

"Wait," she said, barely audible. In her mind she felt her toes dangling over the ridge of a cliff, the drop too far to see. She longed for his profession of love, once more, before taking this final step.

But then he raised his head, and the look in his eyes made any pledge irrelevant. No matter the words he crafted, she would follow him regardless.

Fearful though ready, she rose to meet his body and leapt blindly into the void.

15

Nothing fully prepares you for the ramifications of your first time.

From the start, Audra knew that euthanasia was not only a basic part of the job but a merciful one. The terminal surgeries at veterinary school were supposed to have armed her with the required emotional armor.

They hadn't.

The first animal she put down was an old black Lab, deaf and half blind, suffering from liver cancer. It would have been cruel to keep him alive. The family, too, understood this. And yet, after it was over, Audra spent an hour in her office sobbing. Although that inaugural act was the worst of them, to this day an ache would hollow her as she pressed a stethoscope to an animal's chest and confirmed she'd silenced its heart.

She could feel the coming of that ache now as she knocked on the front door.

"We are ready for you," the mother said, "in the backyard." Her soft Hispanic accent held a sullen tone. She escorted Audra through her house and out the kitchen door, back into the afternoon light. Two matching Shih Tzus whimpered from an open window, already in mourning.

Audra's technician, a young sprite of a gal named Jill, was setting up beside the garden. Lush grass led to a serene pond. Here their medical scrubs seemed almost an offense.

The daughter of the family sat on a striped, tasseled blanket. No older than ten, she wore a thin glittery headband over her sable bob. In her arms she cradled a fluffy white rabbit with huge pink eyes. Her parents, clients since the clinic's founding, had made all of the arrangements earlier that week.

"Hi, Isabella, I'm Dr. Hughes." Audra cleared her throat, gravelly from another sleepless night. Jack's dreams had ratcheted up another notch since the festival's excitement the day before.

Isabella looked up with tear-filled eyes.

Audra knelt on the blanket. Her compiled exhaustion would make it harder to control her emotions. "I heard this spot was Snowball's favorite, right here by the carrots."

The girl petted the rabbit's back and eked out a nod.

"I know she lived a very long life, and I'm sure she was really special to you. So don't you worry. I'm going to do everything I can to make this as peaceful as possible for her. Now, I'm

156

just going to take her for a few minutes, then give her right back, okay?"

At Isabella's reluctance, her father stepped closer. "Do what the doctor says, *mija,*" he said gently. She stroked the rabbit's head, her lower lip quivering, before she obeyed.

Jill assisted Audra in clipping fur from the rabbit's front leg to place and secure the catheter. Meanwhile, the mother reprimanded her two young sons for bickering over a light-saber.

Audra attempted to hand the rabbit back, just as promised, but Isabella burst into tears and ran into the house.

"She'll be fine," the father told his wife, and gave a signal for Audra and Jill to continue.

It took Audra a moment to recall her standard script. "First," she said, "I'm going to give Snowball an injection that will literally make her fall asleep. Then, in thirty seconds to a minute, her heartbeat will stop and so will her breathing. Do you have any questions before I start?"

They shook their heads.

After a steadying breath, Audra proceeded as outlined. The rabbit shivered beneath her hand while absorbing enough anesthetic to achieve an overdose. When the time came, Audra held her stethoscope to the animal's chest. It was over. The rabbit's eyes remained open, as they always did, staring back like an accusation.

Usually at this point, owners would share fond stories of their pet. With Isabella hidden away, it wasn't a surprise that the family bypassed a session of nostalgia.

Jill helped Audra pack up the equipment and they headed for their cars. The mother waved to them in gratitude before closing the front door.

"See you at work," Jill said, her tone subdued, before pulling away. If not for an errand Jill needed to run, they would have driven together. Carpooling was efficient and economical, but also safer when one of them was too emotional to drive.

Alone in her car, Audra relaxed into her seat. The normal rush of sadness didn't arrive, and she was relieved for it. She had just started the ignition when a face in her periphery caused her to jump.

Isabella.

Audra rolled down the window and offered a smile. "Hey there."

"Is Snowball gone?" Isabella's voice sounded so small it could have fit in a ring box. Trails of dried tears marked her face.

"I'm afraid so, honey."

The girl nodded. Then instead of walking away, she gazed into Audra's eyes and said, "Is she in heaven now?"

Audra had been asked the same question dozens of times. It had been easier to answer before she knew the truth.

She gathered herself, ready to provide a simple yes. Yet when she opened her mouth, the memory of her own nightmare came rushing back, of another little girl, an apparition in the clinic, confronting Audra about her dog — and the consequence of her lie.

Only when Isabella's face went hard did Audra realized she'd voiced her thought.

There is no heaven.

Audra tried to amend her words. "That came out wrong. I didn't mean that." Which was true; she hadn't intended to hurt her.

But already Isabella was rushing away.

"Isabella!" Audra called out as the girl went into the house.

A pound of shame landed on Audra's shoulders, pressing her to the seat. She should go inside, repair the damage. Or would she merely make it worse? At this point, any contrary statement would be discounted as deception. Even children knew that once you've exposed the Wizard of Oz for an ordinary man, a return to the myth was an impossible feat.

"I'm sorry," Audra whispered. The tears came then, not out of grief but longing, for a time when she, too, believed in magic. What she wouldn't give to have all her problems solved with three clicks of her heels.

Tess announced her entry with a swift set of knocks. She closed the door behind her and shoved her hands into her lab coat pockets. She didn't take a seat.

Audra swiveled in her desk chair to confront

159

the fallout head-on. "I take it you've heard."

"And so has Hector. The girl's parents called him directly."

"Lovely."

"Audra, he thinks you need a break. A chance to . . . get your thoughts together."

Here they went again.

"I told you, Tess. I'm fine." The last thing Audra needed was too much time to dwell — especially now, with Isabella's expression ingrained in her mind. The latest addition to her collection of mistakes. "Believe me, I feel horrible about what happened. I'll gladly call and apologize to the family —"

"Sweetie. This isn't a suggestion."

Audra stared. "What are you saying?"

"I'm saying . . ." Tess took a breath, a grave look in her eyes. "You've been put on leave."

160

16

The announcement was timely, inevitable really, yet Vivian startled at the words.

"You two ought to get onboard now," her father said over the din. His black fedora and trench coat matched nearly every man in Euston Station.

Her mother, shockingly, didn't sprint for the train. Adjusting her white gloves, she conferred over travel details one final time. The netting from her hat reached the narrow tip of her nose.

Vivian checked her watch and begged the minutes to slow.

The cars were bloating with passengers, most of them young children. From open windows they hollered farewells in a clash of thrills and tears. Evacuation tags hung over their travel wear. On the platform, any mother not weeping strained for a portrayal of strength, waiting to break down in private.

On another day, Vivian's heart would sink from the scene. But in this moment her greatest care lay with Isaak, the anticipation of his arrival. She would not dare cross the ocean without him.

It had been seven days since they lay in that cellar, their limbs interwoven like the roots of a banyan tree. A sheen of sweat had glistened their bodies in the lantern's soft light. Breath still heavy, he'd rested his head on her chest. She had stroked his hair and stared at the ceiling, where shadows moved in a watery sway. To her relief, there had been no pain from the joining of their bodies, as rumored from other girls, only initial discomfort fully rewarded by the intensity of Isaak's pleasure. In her arms he'd drifted off for some time, but Vivian had never been more alert. She had given of herself in every way possible, and that vulnerable act left her equally comforted and unsettled.

The next day, she had phoned Isaak from her father's office with specifics of her travels. She withheld objections over Isaak's plans to visit Munich. She understood; he couldn't very well use a telegram to summon his mother across enemy borders. It was an invite to be delivered discreetly and in person. Through the black market he would arrange documents for his mother, his other relatives if possible. *And if they don't wish to go?* Vivian had dared ask, to which he replied without pause: *Then I'll meet you at the station alone.*

But now, here she was, and he had yet to show.

"Travel safely," her father said, catching Vivian's attention. "And don't misplace your luggage tickets." He glanced at the train. "Better not delay now."

"I'm sure we have a little more time before we actually leave," she insisted.

"The conductor already gave the last call."

"Yes, but I'm sure —"

"Vivian," her mother said, "don't be difficult. If we don't make it to Liverpool on time, we could miss the ship."

Steam blasted from the locomotive like a kettle heated for tea. The train would pull away within minutes. Short of throwing herself on the tracks, Vivian could think of no method to stall.

"Wire me when you're safely in New Hampshire," she heard her father say. Until he joined them, they were to lodge with her maternal grandmother, a proper though pleasant woman, beyond her smell of mothballs.

He gave his wife a peck on the cheek. Then instead of separating, they simply stood there. Unspoken messages flowed between them before he leaned in and tenderly kissed her lips.

Vivian felt wholly intrusive, but she couldn't tear her gaze away. She had never seen them exchange more than cursory affection. Dangers of wartime, she decided, inflated even marital emotions. Yet when their mouths parted, the truth of their good-bye became apparent. It held nothing in the way of passion, only a somberness so palpable it thickened the air.

Vivian's mother caught her gawking, a jolt of awkwardness. "Say good-bye to your father," she said, composing herself. She gripped her purse with both hands and strode toward the closest train door.

"Watch over your mother," he said. "I'll see you both when I can."

Vivian nodded, still taken aback.

He took an audible breath and headed down the platform. He was about to veer around a porter, who was hauling a trunk on his back, when Vivian reclaimed her voice.

"Father!"

He twisted to see over his shoulder, and she realized she had no inkling how to fill this moment. Not with words anyhow. She rushed over and embraced him. There was a slight stiffness in his hold, as always, but she took no offense.

"I'll see you before long," he said, and patted the back of her wool coat.

She drew away and discovered on his face a wistful smile. It was a look she would carry with her like a lucky trinket in her pocket.

"Be careful," she said, and he nodded.

Then he sent her off to the train, and she

knew neither of them would look back.

As Vivian neared the coach, her thoughts cleared and anxiety over Isaak returned. For him not to be here, something terrible must have occurred. He couldn't have changed his mind. Considering what they had shared, it simply wasn't possible.

"Are you boarding, miss?" Atop the coach steps, the conductor extended his hand to guide her in.

She was clutching the railing, but her feet would not leave the platform.

"Well?"

"I . . . don't know." She could stay with her father, wait for word from Isaak. Tell her mother she would follow.

"Vivian!" A male voice reached from a distance. "Vivian James!"

Her breath hitched. A plaid flat cap moved through the crowd and a hand shot up over heads. He shouted her name again.

She wasted no time running toward him. "Isaak!" She ignored the conductor's chiding, overtaken by relief and joy.

In her mind she saw it all; together, she and Isaak would marvel at the Grand Canyon, dip their toes in a frothy sea. They would adventure through the plains, resting by campfire, and make love every night until dawn. "Isaak!"

She glimpsed his hat as it passed between people, winking like a star. She could not fathom a grander feeling, though she paused when she lost sight of him. Another man walked toward her, also in a cap, blocking her view. She tried to see around him until he spoke.

"You're Vivian James. Are you not?"

"Well — yes —"

"This is for you." He held out an envelope. Her name was penned across the front in familiar script. Isaak always curled the *V* in such a way.

Vivian was seized by her error. The stranger before her was the man who had called her name, waved a hand over the crowd. Not her beloved Isaak.

The locomotive creaked and hissed, its departure imminent.

"Is Isaak running late?" she demanded. "Shall I wait, take another train? Will he meet us in Liverpool?" Whatever the case, she needed answers this instant, for more than logistics. Prolonging the discovery would be altogether torturous.

The man raised the delivery toward her, an explanation inside.

"Please," she begged. "You have to tell me . . ."

His shoulders rounded downward before he shook his head. "You should go back to the States," he said. "Without him."

■ ■ ■ ■

Part Two

■ ■ ■ ■

In Memory's Mansion are wonderful rooms,
And I wander about them at will;
And I pause at the casements, where
    boxes of blooms
Are sending sweet scents o'er the sill.

I lean from a window that looks on a lawn;
From a turret that looks on the wave.
But I draw down the shade, when I see on
    some glade
A stone standing guard, by a grave.
                    — from "Memory's Mansion"
                        by Ella Wheeler Wilcox

17

Late May 2012
Portland, OR
Contrary to Tess's concern, Audra actually appreciated being put on leave. It had only been two days, but already she was able to focus more on Jack. She just wished quality time together would solve everything, eliminating appointments like these, where his actions and words would be scrutinized.

After school, while driving here, she had kept her explanation simple. "Your school counselor, Dr. Shaw, works at another office part of the week. We thought you might like to check it out. And he's a great listener. You can talk to him about anything you feel like."

Thankfully, little about the room resembled the office of a therapist. At least not the grief-counseling type Audra had endured. There were large picture windows with curtains covered in sunbursts. The love seat beneath her was purple and tucked, with a whimsical curve. Children's décor dominated the space: a wall of painted handprints, colorful kites strung above toy bins, a kitchen play set, and a supermarket stand. If not for the framed diplomas over the desk in the corner, the place could easily be mistaken for a kindergarten classroom.

"Here, let me show you what that does," Dr. Shaw said to Jack. Down on the carpet, the man with swooped bangs and geek-chic glasses pushed a button on the robot in Jack's hands. Lights on the helmet frantically blinked and an automated voice declared the world safe from Veter Man.

At long last, the therapist was interacting with his patient, demonstrating the tiniest speck of earning his fee. Aside from a genial greeting, he had spent their whole session in silence, playing with toys himself. Audra was starting to question the *Talk* portion of his tagline.

"Do you like Transformers?" he asked.

Jack shrugged a shoulder and set the robot down. His interest shifted to a plastic apple and a fake carton of eggs. When Dr. Shaw asked about his favorite foods, Jack moved on to a train carrying circus animals and clowns. He used his cast to knock over the elephant and a trio of brown monkeys.

The man just watched, quiet once again. Audra imagined him scribbling on a mental steno pad. *Shows signs of aggression. Possible attention deficit disorder.*

"Jack actually loves animals," she interjected. "And he's great at concentrating on one thing at a time — when it's a place he's used to."

Dr. Shaw replied with a splayed palm and smile: *Your son's doing fine.*

Audra sat back on the couch and recrossed her legs. Surely the man would base his evaluation on observations from school, not a single hour in an unfamiliar room. Plus, over the phone she had provided other details that could help: the festival scare, the car ride after, and the vividly violent dreams.

Although the old joke about hiring a psychic seemed applicable here — *No need to say much if they're good at their jobs* — she'd share just about anything to achieve a solution, with Dr. Shaw in particular. His input at school could put the principal at ease.

Assuming, of course, this all went well and the plan didn't backfire.

"You know, Jack," he said, "when you first got here, I saw you brought along your toy plane."

Jack recoiled slightly. His hand covered the lump in his jacket pocket.

"Since you like old bombers, I think I've got something you'd enjoy." He dug through a plastic tub, capturing Jack's interest, and retrieved a dark-green aircraft. About a foot long, it was missing one of four propellers. "See that? It's a B-seventeen from World War Two. Like the ones you like to draw."

Jack mumbled something.

"What's that you say?"

Jack repeated himself more clearly. "This

171

one's a B-twenty-four. The Liberator."

"Hmm . . . you sure about that?" Dr. Shaw flipped the plane over to examine its parts. Something told Audra he already knew the answer. "Is there a big difference between them?"

He nodded, though he didn't look up.

"Yeah? Like what?"

"B-twenty-fours are faster and can go farther away. For a longer time too. And they can hold, like, three more tons."

"Wow. That sounds like a better plane all around."

"It can't go as high though. Not with a combat load. It's got the same horsepower as the Fortress, but the altitude ceiling's lower. 'Cause of the Davis wing. And it's heavier too, so the Liberator has to fly faster to take off. . . ."

Audra stared with breath held. Though it was wonderful to hear Jack ramble on again about anything, his advanced knowledge of warplanes left her baffled. Yes, he had model planes in his bedroom, but he'd never described any in such detail.

Jack stopped and tilted his head at the bin. He pulled out a metallic gray object, the body of another bomber. Maybe a ship. He studied it for a long moment, running his fingers over the lines and bumps. A revelation darkened his eyes. With great intensity, he began foraging through the pile of pieces. He assembled two parts together, then added another and another.

"Is that a submarine you got there?" Dr. Shaw asked.

"U-boat." Jack spoke absently, in deep concentration.

"Oh, sure. Hitler used them in the Atlantic. To fight America's Navy, right?"

"Not this one."

"No?"

"This one carried spies."

"I see. And where did those spies go?"

"New York," Jack said. "And Florida."

Audra wrestled down the urge to intervene. She just hoped Dr. Shaw was trying to extract the root of the issue and not feed into an obsession, one clearly formed thanks to Devon's father. Where else would a seven-year-old have learned all of this?

"Florida doesn't seem like a very spy-like place to go." If Dr. Shaw found this amusing, he managed to suppress any sign of it. "Those Germans must've had a tough time, landing there without getting caught. Seems like they would've stood out."

"It's because they weren't just German," Jack said.

"Is that so? What were they, then?"

Jack's hands halted as he pondered this. For the first time since his arrival, he looked straight at Dr. Shaw. "Americans."

A series of beeps shot from Audra's purse. She'd set the timer on her phone for exactly an hour, and was now glad she had. She had

173

heard more than enough to confirm the source of the problem. "Time to go, buddy. Let's put the toys back."

Jack rose right away but showed reluctance in placing the sub in the box.

"You can keep that one if you'd like," Dr. Shaw said. "Another child left it here years ago. I've got too many toys as it is."

Audra didn't see how encouraging Jack with a war souvenir could be productive. If anything, she needed to distract him with another hobby. One glance at Jack's smile, however, and she couldn't bring herself to refuse. "Thank you," she said.

"My pleasure." Dr. Shaw came to his feet and said to Jack, "And thank *you* for sharing all those stories. Glad you set me straight about the B-seventeen."

He nodded before Audra ushered him toward the door.

"Hey, Jack, I forgot to ask," Dr. Shaw said. "How do you know so much about the war anyway?"

Jack turned with a crinkled nose, presenting his answer as the most obvious in the world.

"Because I was there."

18

The mystery continued to swell with time. It had been well over two years, and still Isaak's disappearance trailed Vivian like a shadow. Her telegrams and letters produced no response. She fared no better with calls to his dorm. She had even tried Professor Klein, who she was told had evacuated at the start of the war. She liked to think Isaak had followed him, that in the safety of the English countryside they were biding their time until peace returned.

Most days, though, she simply regretted boarding that train. Whether staying in London would have reunited her with Isaak she would never know, but at least the distance dividing them would not have been so vast.

After arriving in New Hampshire, her mother had instantly melded into the social realm of her youth. Vivian soon learned that

Luanne Sullivan, an old school friend from DC, had relocated to Brooklyn. The girl was receiving room and board in addition to pay for working on a switchboard. The fact that the company was still hiring had struck Vivian as a sign. New York. That's where Isaak would go once he made it to the States.

So that's precisely where Vivian went.

The company's boardinghouse was a lovely brownstone in the center of Park Slope, an affluent section of the borough. Naturally, this reduced her mother's objections, though Vivian would have settled for a shack. Location was all that mattered. Her bags were barely unpacked when she began diligent rounds of Isaak's favorite spots: the shopping strips of Manhattan, the carriages of Central Park, the window displays at Macy's. But with the passing of time and escalation of the war — America, too, had joined the fray — her efforts waned with her hopes.

The single place she sustained any faith was at Brooklyn's Café Labrec.

Once more now she sat in its courtyard. She dropped a sugar lump into her coffee, wishing her feelings would dissolve as easily. If only coming here were not so tempting. Near impossible to avoid, it was a short walk from her residence, enabling these morning visits before the chartered bus to work. Truthfully, even her job as an operator at Fort Hamilton served as a potential link to Isaak.

Catching snippets of military discussions meant uncensored updates on the European Theatre. Which, more often than not, left her in a grievous mood.

Isaak could not have better described Hitler's greed and thirst for power. In June of 1941, he double-crossed even Stalin by funneling 3 million Nazi soldiers into the Soviet Union, and his offensives continued. Across the English Channel, his ruthless bombing raids — the Blitz, they called it — placed all Londoners in danger. Vivian's father remained among them, despite the option to come home. Never was diplomacy more in need, he claimed in periodic letters; his wired messages assured her of his safety. Still, she kept him in her prayers, the same as she did for Isaak.

Perhaps this, above all, was the café's true appeal. It had become like a church, a sanctuary she frequented in search of peace, and answers.

Had Isaak's plans gone awry with the black market and his mother? Was he imprisoned in Munich thereafter? Had he been injured in a raid? Did he return to London and stay to help? Did he join the RAF and take to the skies?

Had he simply changed his mind?

Every Wednesday morning, her usual wrought-iron table served as a personal pew. She relished this semi-cove, thanks to a stone

177

wall behind her and, to her side, a pot of tall, vibrant flowers. Tucked away, she could be left to her thoughts, sometimes her tears. But always she found comfort in the fragrance of blossoms and freshly baked dough, accompanied by Isaak's words.

My Dearest Vivian,

I am writing this letter only hours before departing London. Although I am anxious to see my family and confirm that all is as well as they claim, already I miss you terribly. It has taken every ounce of my strength not to abandon my mission and reunite with you this instant. As you know, however, I could never rest without first settling my personal affairs.

While my hopes are high that my travels will go quickly and without incident, I have arranged for a trusted friend to deliver this letter should I fail to return in time. Your safety, my darling, is of utmost importance. Please do not hesitate in evacuating as planned. Rest assured, wherever you are, I indeed will find you.

Until then, keep this necklace as proof of my promise. Wear it close to your heart, just as I hold my love for you in mine.

Yours for eternity,

Isaak

She fingered her blouse where the charm

dangled beneath. On occasion she would pull the letter from her jewelry box, but merely to touch his scrawled words, not for fear of forgetting them. They were forever imprinted in her heart. Helplessly savoring them now, she continued to block out the city, until a man's voice cut in.

"I said, 'Sure is a swell day, isn't it?' "

Vivian raised her eyes and discovered the question was directed at her. An Army private, roughly her age, smiled from the next table.

"Yes," she said with a glance at the sky. The sun was elbowing its way through the clouds. "I suppose it is." She gave him a cordial look, her standard for these situations, then conveyed disinterest by flipping through her issue of *McCall's*.

"I'm Ian Downing, by the way."

Out of the corner of her eye, she glimpsed his outstretched hand. Since the bombing of Pearl Harbor, military enlistment had spread like a virus. The service in itself was an honorable one, but not the common expectation that all dames lost their marbles over a starched and pressed uniform.

Don't be rude, Vivian. Accept his hand, Vivian. She heard her mother's prodding. A lifetime of drilled decorum was difficult to expunge.

Vivian obliged the greeting but promptly returned to her magazine.

"Mind if I ask your name?" He either couldn't take a hint or chose to ignore it. "Course, I could always figure it out for myself." He tapped his pointed chin as if crafting syllables customized for her face. "It's . . . Alma. No, no — Bessie." He cocked his head. "Cordelia?"

Marvelous. He was going to scroll through the entire alphabet.

"Hmm . . . Irene maybe." Another tap. "Mildred?"

"Vivian," she said, bringing this to an end.

"I knew it!" He snapped his fingers and beamed. "That was definitely my next guess."

An eye roll would have been much deserved — did she really look like a Mildred? — yet the fellow exaggerated such surety Vivian couldn't help but laugh.

She shook her head at him. "You do realize this is a pitiful approach, don't you?"

"Yeah, I know," he said with a shrug. "But if it made you smile, it was worth coming off like a heel."

Vivian would have taken this for the continuation of a practiced pickup if not for the sincerity in his voice, the kind gleam in his greenish-brown eyes. Maybe he didn't deserve the coldest of shoulders. Besides, they were seated at separate tables, affording a buffer of comfort.

"Food sure is great here, don't you think?" He lifted the Danish from his small plate and

180

took a generous bite.

"I enjoy it."

"So, Vivian," he said, after swallowing, "you from this area?" The pastry had stamped him with a yellow mustache that flitted when he spoke. "Or are you just in the Big Apple visiting?"

She tried to keep a straight face, yet found it impossible. "You have . . . some crumbs. Right here." She brushed her own lip to illustrate.

He snatched his napkin and cleaned off the flakes. "Better?"

She nodded.

His eyes lowered, as if shielded by embarrassment. She was only trying to help but somehow wound up the one who felt like a heel. And now she was stuck, forced to soften a conversation she had hoped to avert.

"I . . . take it you're stationed in the area," she said.

"Just across the river, at Fort Dix." He wiped his chin to be thorough and wadded the napkin. "Lucked out actually. I'm from Michigan — that's where my whole family is, back in Flint — but I got some friends from around here. It was nice to already know people in such a big city."

"Sure. I know how that can be."

He crossed his legs, confidence returning. Beneath his dark, close-cropped hair, he had a pleasing oval face and the kind of smile any

181

dentist would gladly take credit for.

"You know," he said, "my buddy Walt and I, we were planning to hit the town Friday. Maybe go to the USO over by Times Square. His girl, Carol, is wild about swing bands."

"Oh?" She knew of the place, mainly from her roommate, who welcomed any opportunity to dance. Vivian had yet to go, despite Luanne's urgings; an evening of laundering socks had more appeal than a hall packed with servicemen in heat.

"How 'bout it?" he asked.

"How about . . . ?"

"Golly, you sure don't make it easy on a guy, do ya?" he teased. "About going out with me? Making it a double date?"

How dim-witted of her. Of course. A date. They were strangers, though.

As she mulled it over, a flutter formed in her stomach. She barely recognized the sensation. Could she really accept? He seemed like a keen fellow. Luanne might even be willing to come, for both safety and decency.

Vivian straightened in her chair, invigorated by the offer, just as Isaak's image barged into her thoughts, and with it a feeling of betrayal.

"I — I can't."

"All right," Ian said. "Then how about Saturday?"

She shook her head.

"Sunday?"

"I'd love to, but . . . I'm engaged."

"Sorry. I didn't realize." Ian glanced toward her hands resting on the table. Too late she recalled the absence of a ring. She curled her fingers under, yet already it was clear: He viewed the decline as a brush-off.

"Well, I'd say he's one lucky man."

She sought a way to explain. The engagement wasn't formal, but a promise had been made, without expiration.

Ian rose from his chair. "Guess I better shove off. Hate to sit around goldbricking all day." He gave her a smaller version of his perfect white smile and tossed a crinkled dollar next to his plate. "It was real nice talking to you, Vivian."

"Likewise."

When he started away, she focused on her magazine to avoid watching him leave.

Her beloved sanctuary suddenly felt isolated rather than secluded.

"Bonjour, chérie." The manager of the café seemed to magically appear. He wore his signature gray vest, loose on his aging frame, and a pin-striped bow tie. "You are enjoying your coffee, yes?"

"It's splendid. Thank you, Mr. Bisset."

He began to clear the soldier's table, his usual waitress out with a cold. "You have the day off, I see."

With the way she was feeling, she wished that were so. "Not today," she said, before it

183

dawned on her why he would assume as much. She glanced at her watch. "Oh, criminy! I'll never make the bus." With operators to deliver to two other locations, the chartered bus waited for no single person.

Vivian gathered her belongings and jumped to her feet before remembering she hadn't paid. She fumbled through her purse for change.

"Allez, allez." He waved her off. "You pay me next time."

She would not have agreed, but her stodgy supervisor deemed tardiness a cardinal sin. Vivian's last infraction had induced the firmest of warnings. She thanked Mr. Bisset with a peck to the cheek, inducing a chuckle.

"I won't forget!" she called out, and scurried toward the street.

Block after block every taxi was taken. Up ahead the streetcar dinged. She sprinted in a flourish, propelled by benefits she refused to lose. Beyond wartime scoops, her job allowed her financial independence, a counterargument to her mother's matrimonial crusade — not to say the woman didn't supply plenty of other reasons her daughter required a husband.

Vivian still had her special savings, of course, stored in the back of her closet. But she had sworn not to squander those funds on anything mundane. They were for her and Isaak, their excursions from coast to coast, the honeymoon she had envisioned too many times to count.

In the event that would ever happen . . . .

Tears pricked her eyes. She blinked them back and picked up her pace, as if ample speed could outrun her doubts.

19

Audra needed this job like the air in her lungs. She needed this change for her son.

After yesterday's session with Dr. Shaw, Jack's nightmare gained new ferocity, spanning almost an hour. The proof lay in Audra's eyes, still bloodshot despite half a bottle of eyedrops. She just hoped her interviewer's computer was set low on the brightness scale.

Why did their call have to be on video? At least she still had an hour until noon, giving her ample time to practice.

"Please tell me my last answer didn't sound overly rehearsed."

On Audra's laptop, set on the kitchen table, Tess responded from her office. "It didn't."

"But how about the one regarding splenectomies? And dental radiographs?"

"Nope and nope."

"Did you think —"

"It was perfect. All of it. Personally, I'd hire you," Tess muttered, "back."

Audra pressed down a smile. "Thanks."

They both knew it was unfair to keep staff at the clinic short-handed, given her full intention to move. By resigning, she now had no choice but to focus on the goal.

"I'll call you tonight and let you know how it went," Audra said, but Tess wasn't yet done.

"You do know Boston gets about a hundred inches of snow, right?"

"I'm pretty sure you've mentioned it."

"And the cost of living there is almost as high as San Francisco? Then there's also the crime rate —"

"Tess," she said. "You were the one who hooked me up with this contact in the first place."

"Yeah, well. Moment of weakness."

"Wish me luck."

A pause. "Can you imagine what a city known as 'Beantown' must smell like in the summer?"

"I'm hanging up now."

"Whatever."

Audra ended the video call and softly laughed.

She double-checked her computer settings and confirmed they were in order. Then she reviewed her outfit, a royal-blue sweater and charcoal slacks, a step up from her usual. She'd even flatironed her hair, wearing it long over her shoulders, and applied lipstick and mascara. Though no curling of the lashes. She had to draw the line somewhere.

Now, with Jack at school, there was nothing to do but wait.

And think.

About Jack.

After leaving the therapist's office, she had asked him what he meant by saying he'd been there during the war. He hadn't answered, and it seemed best not to push him. Maybe his nightmares were blurring the line between what was real and not. But how to stop it?

This was the question that gnawed at her.

Audra needed a diversion. She despised deep cleaning, but tidying — with its distinct before and after states — always gave her satisfaction.

In Jack's room, she tossed his pajamas into the hamper. She threw away tiny paper scraps and cracker crumbs from his desk, put his kid scissors and glue stick back in a drawer. As she made up his bed, she thought of the book hidden beneath.

His journal.

What would a kid his age write inside? About his feelings, more pictures? What if he did recall his dreams but, when told to draw "happier things," had lost the courage to share? The key to his night terrors could lie in something he was suppressing, and that discovery would be worth a minor infringement.

Before she could change her mind, Audra grabbed the book. She sat on the bed and flipped open the cover.

On the first page was a drawing. Again smoke plumed, but only from a chimney. The house was two stories high, like the home they used to own. A grassy yard, billowy clouds, and a ball of sun comprised the scene. No planes or signs of death.

Relieved though still searching, Audra continued on. The doodling and handwriting developed with his age. And then he shifted to collages. Ticket stubs and candy wrappers overlapped various strips from the Sunday comics. Newspaper photos and magazine ads had been trimmed to fit the pages: an amusement park ride, a baseball stadium, a picnic in the park. Together, they formed a compilation of Jack's favorite things.

The Eiffel Tower, though, surprised her. As did the cruise.

She studied them closer, until the connection became achingly clear: He wasn't featuring the places in the scenes; it was the people. All were families, smiling and laughing, hugging, holding hands. They were the unbreakable units that had once created the security of Jack's world.

The doorbell rang. Audra flinched, and a tear broke free, catching the journal's edge. She dried it with her sleeve and tucked the book away.

A rapping on the door followed. The maintenance guy from the building wasn't due until two. He must have squeezed her in early to keep her leaky fridge from forming another lake. Either that or he wanted a head start on his weekend.

Regrouping, she made her way to the door and swung it open.

The man wasn't one she recognized. He had no coveralls or box of tools.

"You're here," he said, sounding relieved. "I wasn't sure if . . . that is, well, I hate to bother you, but I was hoping you could help me."

At the pause, she said, "I can try."

An unreadable smile formed on his lips. "The questions I've got will probably seem un-usual . . . ."

The remark tipped her off, and she bristled. He had to be a journalist, likely the same one who had aggravated her situation at work. His unassuming attire — a rust-hued button-down shirt and jeans — was clearly a strategic move.

"If you're the reporter who came to the clinic, I can tell you right now, you've caused me more trouble than I needed. Now, I'm asking you nicely, please leave us alone." She reached for the doorknob.

"No, wait." He stepped forward. "That's not me. I'm not a reporter." His mix of sincerity and urgency prevented her from closing the door. Still, she remained cautious.

"Then who are you?"

"I'm Sean Malloy. At the festival, I heard the security guard say your name on his radio. I apologize if I'm intruding, coming here like this, but you took off so fast."

The soldier. From the stage.

In the chaos of finding Jack, she had barely

given him a glance.

"The thing is," he explained, "we hit a roadside bomb, over in Afghanistan. My team was on patrol. Part of my memory was wiped out. I've been trying everything I can to get it back. Visiting old places and people I knew. When your son came and talked to me, I figured somehow we must've known each other."

Audra tried to keep up, the conversation so unexpected. She had assumed his uniform alone had reeled in her son.

She studied the man's face, hoping to solve the mystery, not just for his sake, but Jack's. In the soft natural light, Sean's eyes were the color of topaz. His hair was sandy-brown, worn short on the sides, longer on top. Around his late thirties, he had a strong jaw and his complexion promised a tan from the smallest rays of sun.

All were nice traits but none of them familiar.

"I'm afraid we'd never met before." She hid her disappointment that felt selfish given his situation.

"But your son," he said, "how else could he have known?"

"I . . . don't know what you mean."

With a quizzical look, Sean pulled a necklace from beneath the collar of his shirt. He dangled the round golden charm for her to see. An inscription of tiny letters appeared on the aged trinket.

"*Viel Feind, viel Ehr,*" he read aloud. "An old German saying. It's what your son said to me

191

that day."

An icy shiver rippled through her. Was that the phrase Jack had recited after she'd questioned him in the car? It sounded similar enough, but that didn't make sense. Even if he knew the adage, the coincidence of repeating it to a stranger who owned the same engraving . . .

Of course. The engraving.

It was so simple, so obvious.

"He read your necklace," she realized. "He must have, when he saw you wearing it."

Sean shook his head. "I was in Class A's, ma'am. I wasn't wearing any jewelry."

His certainty struck her as a challenge. "Well . . . maybe you forgot to take it off."

"I don't think so."

"Then, you must've misheard him."

Sean's expression mirrored the doubt she felt, yet she refused to let hers show. With every passing day, her logical reasoning and understanding of Jack drifted further from her grasp.

Just then, a trill sounded from behind.

Her laptop.

The video call. She had forgotten the interview!

"I have to go get that."

He responded with a nod, but the plea in his face halted her. In that frozen moment, with her future plans at risk, she had to make a choice.

"I'm sorry. I wish I could've helped." She

infused her voice with all the kindness she could, then closed the door and rushed inside.

20

Once on base, Vivian hurried into the building that housed the switchboard room. She smoothed her hair and dress and punched her time card in the hall.

Fourteen minutes late.

Perspiration on her scalp threatened to streak her face. No time for blotting. Through the pane of the door she spotted her chair at the end, waiting vacant beside her roommate. Luanne snatched up a cord as fast as she'd dropped it, connected the call, and moved on to the next. The two other operators were working at the same swift pace.

Vivian opened the door to an immediate greeting.

"Miss James." The surname was spoken with the sharpness of a sneeze.

Vivian slowly rotated to the right, where her supervisor scowled from her desk. Her appearance was meticulous as always. She wore her light silvering hair in a tight French twist and a suit jacket with shiny brass buttons. When Vivian had first learned she would be overseen by a woman, she was pleasantly surprised — until they became acquainted.

"Good morning, Mrs. Langtree."

"Afternoon — wouldn't you say?"

"Yes, ma'am. I do apologize. I missed the company bus and had to catch a streetcar —"

"In other words," Mrs. Langtree said, "it wasn't a dire emergency that caused your tardiness." The woman could sniff out a lie like a bear hunting sweets.

"No — well, not exactly." Just then, Vivian remembered that the woman, widowed from the Great War, was rumored to have one particular soft spot: her son, an airman stationed in Georgia. "You see, I'd encountered a rather young soldier. And he was telling me about how his family lives in" — she racked her memory — "Michigan, all of whom he surely misses a great deal. Particularly as he adjusts to life in such a large city. So I'm sure you can understand why I found it difficult to leave."

Creases in Mrs. Langtree's forehead relaxed a fraction, in turn relaxing Vivian. But after a moment, those lines snapped back deeper than before. "In that case, Miss James, you had no excuse to forget your duties here. Need I remind you, our country is at war. The work we do is vital to keeping our troops safe, and therefore requires operators who

195

respect that fact."

"Yes, ma'am."

"Furthermore, if I recall correctly, I have already given you a final warning." Mrs. Langtree rose from her chair. Evidently she wished to be at a superior height for her next statement, which could only mean one thing. She raised a crooked finger just as an Army officer entered the room, authoritative in stature.

"Pardon me," the man said.

Mrs. Langtree dropped her finger, shifting her tone. "Colonel, how lovely to see you."

"May I speak with you?"

"Why, yes. Certainly." As the man turned for the hall, Mrs. Langtree gave Vivian a pointed look. "We shall continue this shortly." She then swiveled on her heels and shut the door behind her.

"Psst," Luanne said, twisting in her chair. Strawberry-blonde curls framed her round face. She was Shirley Temple aged by a decade with a personality to match. Her lips pursed into a question: *What's the scoop?*

Vivian dreaded to supply the prediction. It was through Luanne she had been hired at all — well, through the girl's brother at any rate. Gene Sullivan was a first lieutenant assigned to Army Intelligence, spending much of his time at Fort Hamilton. He tended not to say much, same as in high school, but had spared enough praise in a recommendation to secure Vivian her job.

Today, after her firing, he might regret he had said a word.

She glanced through the window at the back of Mrs. Langtree. If the discussion took a good while, perhaps the woman would lose interest in resuming the previous one. She might even decide training a new girl wouldn't be worth the trouble. War dealings, after all, took priority. With American troops battling fiercely in the Pacific, it would not be long before they invaded Europe. This would require support of every kind, including skilled operators.

Vivian hustled to her chair to exhibit her worth. She adjusted her headset and mouthpiece, its horn-like receiver curving up from her chest plate. She inserted a rear cord into an illuminated jack and threw the front key forward.

"Number, please," she said, and connected the line.

"I hope that went better than it looked." Luanne's natural lilt always projected the warm, patient tone the rest of the operators had been trained to learn. "What happened to you? I thought you were only going for coffee."

"I just lost track of time."

There was no reason to elaborate. Luanne would undoubtedly call her batty for turning down a perfectly enticing date, given that her own beaus came and went. Besides, all Luanne knew was that an old steady in London had left Vivian reluctant to court. Nothing else. Preserving the details seemed a way to keep Isaak alive, if not in reality, at least in Vivian's mind. She snagged another call to avoid saying more.

"Number, please . . . Thank you." She plugged in the front cord as a scream belted from the hall.

"I told you, there's been a mistake!"

All four operators snapped their attention toward the door. On the other side of the glass, their supervisor raged. The colonel's mouth moved around his words. He reached forward, but Mrs. Langtree pulled away.

"It's not him, it's not!" She covered her ears and frantically shook her head. Her meticulous hairdo sprouted loose.

Luanne touched Vivian's arm. "Her son," she said.

The lights of the switchboards receded into the background.

Mrs. Langtree yelled again, not in words but a howl. The sound was so mournful it echoed off the walls of Vivian's heart. Then, without warning, the woman collapsed into the colonel's arms. His forlorn expression implied he had been a friend — of her son or late husband or both — and, as such, would not have allowed a piece of paper to present the news.

The personalized delivery, however, did not improve the result. For Mrs. Langtree now sobbed as though the last fibers of her world had unraveled, leaving barely a memory to grasp.

Vivian covered her mouth in an effort to withhold her tears. She managed to succeed, save a few strays, until later that night.

In the still of darkness, as Luanne slept deeply in the next bed, there was no escaping reality. Not every loss was confirmed by an officer at the door. Nor a telegram with the power to sink a fleet.

Loss, often the worst kind, also arrived through the deafening quiet of an absence.

Vivian sat down on the cold tiled floor with her back against a wall. From the lower compartment of her jewelry box she retrieved Isaak's letter. Along with the wrinkled page came a season-old clipping from the *Brooklyn Eagle.* It drifted, light as a feather, onto her lap. The article reported that a year had passed since a little girl had vanished; an FBI agent sought out clues long after police ruled it a dead-end case and now every lead had been exhausted.

Vivian wasn't entirely sure why she had saved the piece. Maybe she was drawn to the father's quote, testament to his unrelenting faith: "We'll never stop searching. No matter what, we'll never stop." A grainy photo captured weary determination in the faces of both parents.

Vivian touched the picture that typically embodied hope. Tonight, she saw only fervent denial. Denial of a truth that to everyone else was glaringly evident.

She pulled the golden chain out from the top edge of her nightgown. Moonlight through the window glimmered off the charm. She thought of the strolls, the kisses, the day in the cellar. Images she once recalled with the vividness of a feature film had become gray-toned snapshots of a previous life. How long before they faded to nothing?

Though difficult to imagine, at one time her parents, too, could have shared such a passion, gradually leeched by time and duty. Perhaps only in picture shows did that type of love survive. Everything else, she was learning, came to an end.

Slowly Vivian unclasped the necklace, accepting what she had been dreading since the day she left London. She bowed her head to meet her knees and soundlessly wept until her tears ran dry.

21

For a full day since the soldier's visit, the engraving on his necklace never left Audra's mind. If she had conveyed even an ounce of coherence in her interview, it was only from rehearsing beforehand. How else could she have asserted her abilities to treat and nurture and solve when she was failing to do those for her son?

Desperate for a remedy, she was grateful Dr. Shaw had a last-minute cancellation. She left Jack in Tess's care, so she could see the therapist alone. Their last appointment had done nothing to improve Jack's nightmares. But the fact remained: At Dr. Shaw's prompting, her son had spoken more in ten minutes than he had in ten months.

Perhaps the escalation of his dreams indicated they were closing in on the core of the issue. The same applied, Audra realized, when diagnosing the cause of physical pain; the most discomfort arose when pressing down on the ailing spot.

She certainly felt that discomfort now, if that was any sign.

At his desk, facing her chair, Dr. Shaw made notes from her update on Jack — about the German inscription and Sean Malloy. A connection still seemed ludicrous, but without a rational answer she was willing to consider anything.

Within reason.

Heater vents on the ceiling stirred the opened sunburst curtains. The windows served as frames for the Saturday morning grayness. In the play area, a tea set and doll clothes were strewn over the floor, remnants from a prior session.

Dr. Shaw pressed up his glasses. He crossed his ankles below his plaid pants and flipped through the pile of Jack's drawings. Though the man had asked to review them again, he had yet to detail the purpose. He had yet to say much at all.

Every minute accrued a billable charge. Wasn't he financially obligated to speak?

Finally, he exhaled, pen over his notepad. "So, Jack's added nothing about all of this when you've asked him?"

"That's right."

"And that word you heard during his nightmares?"

"Himmel." A few times now he had repeated it in his sleep. While serving pancakes one morning she'd revisited the question. "He says he doesn't know what it is or where it's from. I also

asked him again about the German adage, but says he doesn't know that either."

"And you believe he's telling the truth?"

"Honestly? I'm not sure what to believe. The only thing I can figure out is he may have seen some things on TV, like you suggested." During a visit with Robert and Meredith tomorrow, Audra planned to reiterate her request that they not subject Jack to military shows. Of course, she would ask them kindly and at the end, to avoid dampening the celebration of Jack's eighth birthday.

Sadly, with the burdens her son carried, he already seemed much older.

"That still doesn't explain everything else though," she admitted. "Which is why I'm here."

Dr. Shaw scribbled some more. He glanced up at her, then down, as if debating on expressing a thought. "How about . . . birthmarks?"

"What about them?"

"Does he have any you'd describe as unusual?"

Although puzzled by the relevance, she scanned Jack's body from memory. On the backside of his shoulder was a small hemangioma, a common enough mark. It was flat and smooth, and the majority of its red hue and strawberry shape had faded over time. Devon used to say it was proof they had originally picked Jack in a berry field and taken him home to make cobbler.

"Nothing unusual that I've seen," she replied in truth.

Dr. Shaw nodded. "When he was younger, did he happen to have imaginary friends?"

"I don't know. Maybe. I don't remember."

In a room set for the Mad Hatter, Audra was being lured down a rabbit hole. She'd had her fill of trudging through the dark without direction.

"Dr. Shaw, if you're going somewhere with this, I'd appreciate if you could tell me."

After a quiet moment, he closed Jack's file. He walked toward the door in a distracted manner.

Audra started to wonder if clothing wasn't his only indulgence that trended in the seventies.

But then he stopped at a shelf and slid out a book. "I know this might seem unconventional — and it's not often I would suggest it. But with everything about Jack I've heard and observed, I think it would be worth taking a look."

"What is it?" she said eagerly.

"An old professor of mine wrote this, based on interviews with literally thousands of children." Dr. Shaw handed over a paperback titled *From Beyond.* Smudges of fingerprints tinged the glossy black cover. Its corners were curled from use. A sprinkling of stars implied a book of . . . astrology.

Perfect. Just what Audra needed: a summary of Jack's celestial traits. Combine that with his lucky numbers from a fortune cookie at Chow

Bello, and their problems would be over.

"So you're saying, you want me to read about children's Zodiac signs?"

"Past lives, actually."

Even better.

Now her son was — what? A German pilot who died in a crash during World War Two?

She came here for guidance, yes, but not the Ouija-board variety.

"I'm sorry, Dr. Shaw. But I don't believe in reincarnation. Not any more than I believe in voodoo dolls or psychic hotlines." She tried to give the book back, but he gently refused.

"What you or I believe isn't important here. What matters is what Jack believes, and finding out why."

The point was difficult to argue. Borrowing anything from the man, however, would guarantee another visit, and she strongly doubted she would return.

As though sensing this, he said, "If I don't see you again, drop the book in the mail. But before then, for your son's sake, please give it a try."

22

The solution was clear. Vivian would start with a new outlook. Granted, she had no misconceptions when it came to her heart; part of her would always yearn for Isaak. So much so, she could not fathom loving so fiercely again. In fact, she flat-out refused to allow it. But that wouldn't stop her from recovering at least a semblance of happiness. Life was too brief to waste.

Nothing had clarified the point more than the death of Mrs. Langtree's son. The casualty of a training exercise, he hadn't even left the States. He was supposed to be safe. But that word, *safe* — like innocence, according to Vivian's father — did not apply to wartime.

She sat on her coverlet now and gazed about her room, at the walls painted buttery yellow. Since the addition of blackout curtains, the place resembled a hive. And Vivian felt the restlessness of a bee.

"I have an idea." She tossed aside her magazine as Luanne came through the door.

"We," she declared, "are going out."

"Out? You mean, tonight?"

"Not just tonight. Right this very minute."

Luanne laughed, setting her toiletries down. "Then I hope it's a pajama party." She made an obvious point, with a pink scarf binding her hair and a robe on her small frame. Her evening soak in the claw-footed tub had cleansed her of powder and lipstick. In this state, she looked no older than the day she and Vivian met in home arts class. It was only from Luanne's help, with sewing and cooking and diapering a doll, that Vivian had passed that tedious course.

"I suppose we do need to spiff ourselves up first," Vivian said, noting her own work attire. She charged over to the closet and began to undress.

"What on earth's gotten into you?" Luanne smiled from the vanity stool. She blotted lotion onto her hands. "I thought Fridays were your laundry nights."

Sadly the remark was not an exaggeration.

Vivian deplored the thought of how dull she had become. "Not anymore," she replied simply.

Weekends were hereby reserved for adventure. She was through eking out her days like a widow, cautious and passive and wallowing in grief. With Isaak's necklace and letter forever stored away, she would behave as any spirited twenty-two-year-old should.

"Ooh, I've got it," Vivian said. "How does roller-skating sound? It's been ages since I've done that."

"Sounds horribly painful. I'm awful on those things."

"Don't be silly. We'll do it together." Vivian plucked out a peach skirt and modeled it over her slip.

"Even so, I really should stay in tonight. I need to finish packing."

"Packing?" Vivian glanced up.

"For the morning train. Remember? I'm helping a friend in Poughkeepsie with a bond rally this weekend." Luanne paused from applying lotion and sighed. "Have you truly forgotten?"

"Of course not," Vivian tsked, although she had. Her mind had been much too preoccupied. "Tell you what. We'll just catch the first half of a double feature. It'll be good for us to get out, even for a little while, after being cooped up all week."

The lingering bereavement in the switchboard room, despite Mrs. Langtree's temporary leave, had made their workspace even more confining.

"Now," Vivian said, riffling through blouses, "which outfit shall I grab for you?"

"I wish I could say yes, Viv. But with traveling, too, I'd be useless tomorrow."

Orchestral notes of a drab classical tune reverberated through the hall. The landlady's radio would be stuck on that station all evening.

Vivian had no choice.

"Okay. Dancing," she said. "We can go dancing."

Luanne slowed the rubbing of her elbows. "Mmm, that *is* tempting," she cooed, and Vivian knew it was settled. "No. No, I really shouldn't. I don't want to show up looking like a hag tomorrow. Nobody will want to buy bonds from me."

Vivian didn't return her friend's smile. She felt like a child finally permitted to swim, only to discover the pool had been drained.

Defeated, she dropped down on her bed. For certain, she would bring this up the next time Luanne begged her to go dancing at some servicemen's club . . . .

The thought jostled Vivian's memory.

"The USO at Times Square," she said, remembering.

"What about it?"

Vivian pictured the soldier from the café. He planned to hit the town tonight. It wasn't quite eight o'clock. If she hurried, she might be able to catch him.

"You're not going by yourself," Luanne implored.

Vivian was already back at the closet. "Not to worry. I'm meeting someone." After a few more hangers, she honed in on a cherry-red dress with tiny white polka dots. Flared and sleeveless, it would make a snazzy number for the jitterbug. The plunging neckline on its own would regain Isaak's attention.

Ian, rather. Ian's attention.

"And who is this someone?" Luanne demanded as Vivian wiggled into the fabric.

"Just a GI I met at the café. He'd asked me on a double date, but I turned him down. Anyway, he's a dandy fellow."

"Are you sure he still plans to be there?"

"Absolutely." Because he had to be — so Vivian could make right by her mistake. She quickly brushed out her hair, pinned a white silk flower by her temple, and retouched her makeup. With the seams of her stockings reasonably straight, she buckled the straps of her shoes.

"I don't know," Luanne murmured. "Maybe I should go after all." She untied her scarf, exposing a head of pinned curlers.

"Nonsense. You're practically ready for bed." Vivian dabbed her neck and wrists with her Californian Poppy perfume. "I can get along just fine. Don't you fret."

Luanne met her gaze in the mirror, clearly torn. "Please, be careful. And wake me when you get home, so I know you're safe."

"Yes, mother hen," Vivian playfully agreed. Though if all went well, she would be frolicking away until dawn.

A dozen catcalls later, she felt the impact of

her mistake.

Going to the club alone would have been just fine in her usual wear, but the brazen red dress invited more attention than Vivian had bargained for. The initial gawking of men was admittedly flattering, and she wove through the crowd with both chin and chest lifted. But as their gazes became like fingers, roaming up and down her body and hovering over her cleavage, she regretted not bringing her sweater.

I'll hardly need one, she had told Luanne before heading out the door. *I'll be too warm from dancing all night.*

Obviously, she hadn't considered other benefits it offered.

"Hey, angel. How's about cuttin' a rug?" A sailor with a wide forehead and crooked teeth grabbed her hand.

"No, thank you," she said, pulling away. "I'm here with somebody."

After all this trouble, Ian Downing had better be here tonight.

She continued to scan the room. Fort Hamilton was a major embarkation center, and every serviceman awaiting deployment appeared to have congregated in this dance hall. Uniformed men outnumbered the dolled-up ladies tenfold. Cologne clung to the curtain of smoke. Through the haze, band members onstage tapped their keys and blew their horns while a woman at the microphone sang

211

"Chattanooga Choo Choo."

"Sakes alive, ya sure are a looker." She traced the comment to a red-haired marine with freckles spanning his nose.

"Sorry, I'm here with somebody," she said, the response now a reflex.

"So am I," he said. "Ain't she a beaut?" He held up his date of a silver flask. "Care for a personal intro?"

She shook her head and turned away, and that's when she spotted the private. In his starched khakis, Ian Downing stepped out from one of the room's large white columns. He was speaking to a couple: his buddy with a steady, she guessed. Walt and . . . Carol, was it? Even halfway across the room, Vivian recognized Ian's sparkling white smile.

She adjusted her posture, conjuring the air of Jean Harlow. The starlet, even in a silk nightie, would feel sensual, not bare. As Vivian strode through the teeming area of tables and chairs, she prepared her explanation. How she had fibbed about a fiancé, leery of dating a stranger. How after careful thought, she had reconsidered his invite.

Vivian was ten feet away when a buxom blonde appeared. She brushed Ian's nose with her finger and giggled. He leaned down, planting a kiss on her lips that implied it wasn't the first. Then his friend pointed to the exit, and the two couples headed that way — directly toward Vivian.

She spun around, frantic, and veered to the right. Again she moved around the tables and chairs and returned inadvertently to the grinning marine.

"See that? Knew you'd change ya mind!"

A peek to the side confirmed Ian was gone. She felt ridiculous over her error, followed promptly by irritation. She was here to have fun. With or without a date, that's precisely what she was going to do.

The marine swirled his flask around. "It ain't gonna bite ya."

Hard alcohol had never appealed to her, but if partaking meant shedding the title of a prude or old biddy, so be it. She accepted the container but held it low as she unscrewed the top. To her knowledge, the USO prohibited booze. She downed a hefty swig, igniting a blast of white heat. A Roman candle had exploded in her chest. Her lungs objected with a series of coughs.

"Better take it easy with that stuff." She knew that voice — and it wasn't the marine's.

Vivian turned to find Luanne's brother. In an Army uniform, Gene Sullivan stood with his arms folded, his buzzed black hair free of a hat. Running into him here seemed an odd coincidence, particularly since he disliked these places even more than Vivian did.

But then she realized: "Luanne sent you." The sentence came out hoarse, no smoother than a croak.

"She thought you might need help getting home."

"Yes, well —" She cleared her throat. "I appreciate the concern. But I don't plan on leaving anytime soon."

He lifted a shoulder. "Whatever suits you."

The remark clashed with his manner. For he continued to stand there, eying the flask in her grip. This was his standard bearing — more of a subtle brooding than razor coolness. The only difference between now and in high school was his thickened jaw and broadened build, reinforcing his role as a protective brother. If permitted, he would likely even stay Stateside to keep watch over Luanne.

But Vivian was not his sister. Nor was she a damsel to be rescued.

"I'll be fine on my own, thank you."

He nodded toward the band. "I'm just here to enjoy the music."

She squared her body with his, irked by the challenge. After years of appeasing others at stiff formal functions, she deserved a single night without judgment. An evening without greetings, curtsies, or bows. No ankles crossed, head leveled, pinkies up, eyes down.

In a defiant toast Vivian raised the flask — presumably whiskey, undoubtedly cheap — and threw more gulps down her throat. These went down easier, only a series of low flames. She withheld her grimace, acutely aware of

Gene's scrutiny, and returned the drink to its owner.

"I believe I'm up for that dance now," she said, hooking the marine's arm.

Clearly unsure when he had asked, the man hesitated for a second before escorting her off. They found space among couples in the midst of the Lindy. In an effort to mimic, the marine twirled her in circles, not catching the beat, and flung her in haphazard patterns. Several times she had to apologize for stepping on other people's toes. At one point, she suspected a different song had begun, though she couldn't be sure of a thing. Faces were blurring and the room was spinning. Her stomach roiled with liquor.

"I need . . . to stop," she told her partner. But he continued to toss her about, oblivious to all but the tempo in his head. She struggled to break free, his grip holding tight. "Please," she said louder. "I don't feel well."

Trumpets assaulted her ears and smoke polluted her lungs. Then, on a dime, the movement stopped. Gene had his hand on the man's shoulder and spoke to him in a hush. The marine nodded and ventured away. Had Gene slid him a bribe, made an officer's threat?

Vivian's pride resented the intrusion. Unfortunately, with the sway of the room she found the need to clutch him for balance.

"Still wanna stick around?"

She shook her head, a bit too quick, and the whole place tilted at an angle.

"C'mon, twinkle toes."

Her gaze, like her hands, didn't budge from his forearm as she followed him through the mass. She stumbled once along the way, but Gene prevented her fall.

"The floor," she said, "it was moving."

"It does that sometimes." She heard a smirk in his voice.

Finally, they were outside. The night air was crisp and clear. Like drinking water in the Sahara, she couldn't take in enough.

"So," he said after a bit. "You well enough to walk?"

Salvaging her composure, she nodded without looking his way. She plodded beside him on her own, determined not to stagger. Headlights from passing cars stung the backs of her eyes. They were five blocks from the club — though who was she to keep count? — when a huge swish rolled through her belly. She stopped, hoping to still the motion. But it rolled again, with an added tide of nausea.

"I think I . . . need . . . to sit." Just then, thank God in heaven, she spotted stairs to her right. She lowered onto the concrete steps, an apartment building above. The music still ricocheted in the caverns of her mind. Every note felt like a pebble adding weight she could not uphold. Her brain became a boulder. She needed to lay it down.

Her head was almost to the step when a hand netted her cheek.

"Whoa, whoa, whoa. Not on that." Gene flung something aside that clattered when it landed. A tin can? A metal lid?

"Okay," he said. "Go ahead."

She relaxed her neck and landed on a . . . soft . . . surface. Not concrete. More like fabric. Trousers. Gene's leg.

The position was too intimate, even for a non-prude, nonbiddy. But her limp form refused to shift, both too heavy and too comfortable. Vivian decided she would sleep here, until her bare arm caught a shiver.

"You leave a coat back there?" he asked.

She tried to shake her head, unsure if she succeeded.

After a moment, Gene patted her upper arm. The tentative gesture transitioned into short yet gentle strokes. The heat of his skin contrasted against the coolness of her own. She let her eyelids drop, lulled for an instant back in time, back to when Isaak, too, had soothed her in such a way. She had missed this more than she realized — not just Isaak's presence, but the sheer wonder of being touched.

Vivian released a shuddered breath. With it came flashes of her behavior. What a spectacle she must have been. She curled her hands beneath her chin, her knees up to her chest.

217

How foolish she was acting, and long before tonight.

"I just wanted to forget," she whispered, wholly wishing that she could.

Gene's hand paused on her arm, and for a second she expected a reply — a mock, a chiding, a suggestion they continue home. But he simply resumed his strokes, and for the first time in years she didn't feel so alone.

23

Audra flipped her pillow to its cool side, and a shiver ran down her neck. Five minutes passed. Then ten. The digital screen glowed like a taunt: 1:22 A.M.

She rotated the clock on her bedside stand to make it face the wall. Through the gap in the doorway, left open so she could hear Jack when needed, the night-light shone in yellow. It sliced a beam down the middle of her bed, dividing the vacant half and "hers."

She pondered potential sleep aids: hot bath, warm milk, a book. No doubt, thanks to Dr. Shaw, the discussion about a book today was the source of her insomnia.

Finally giving up, she kicked off the comforter. If she wasn't going to rest anyway, she might as well be entertained by the author's preposterous theories. Who knew? Maybe she would learn the Queen of Sheba had come back as a poodle. Worst case, the text would be dry enough to knock her right out.

In the living room, she clicked on a lamp. She

plopped onto the couch with the book.

From Beyond.

"Beyond what? Sanity?" She bit off the sneer, told herself to keep an open mind, to stop being so cranky. She was reading this for Jack, to gain even a dash of helpful insight.

Starting at the beginning, she skimmed the introduction. Memories from reincarnation, it stated, typically faded by age six or seven.

The tidbit punched a small but distinct hole in Dr. Shaw's theory.

Still, she forged on to the first account, in which a five-year-old Ukrainian boy often rambled about needing to practice for a large performance. He played no instrument, didn't dance or sing. But during a visit to his aunt's, having never touched a piano, he sat down at her Wurlitzer and poured out the *Moonlight Sonata.*

Supposedly.

In Prague, a young boy suffered from a phobia of blades. If even a small butter knife was set out for dinner, he would break into wild hysterics. Eventually, he described being murdered in another life. He cited the birthmark on his rib cage as the place where he'd been stabbed. A transcendental scar. On a similar note, several other kids described having phantom pains, indicative of wounds that had ended their previous lives.

The next chapter featured an Australian girl with asthma. After recovering from a severe attack, she recalled being strangled in an alley. She named specific landmarks, all verifiable yet absent from modern maps.

A couple in India spoke about their daughter and her claims of being a courier in the French Revolution. They chalked it up to imagination until she suddenly spurted phrases in antiquated French.

The stories went on and on, testaments to another realm. Effects of tragic deaths sometimes carried over, they said, while other souls sought closure to unfinished business.

Before Audra knew it, she had sped through half the pages. She couldn't deny goose bumps had risen from each similarity to Jack — birthmarks, phobias, and foreign speech. But how much was lore? Were they tales created just to sell a book, or to draw attention to families starved for the spotlight? That's not to say nuggets of truth weren't there. Even the *National Enquirer* based many articles on fact before distorting or exaggerating to craft alluring headlines.

But Audra had no interest in those. She had come to revere the provable. What she could hear, smell, and touch were the nuts and bolts of her world. In fact, with decent effort, she could derive explanations for every factor of Jack's case. Except for one.

His knowledge of the engraving.

Odds were low that she and the soldier had both misheard the phrase. She should have

221

studied the necklace closer to properly investigate. The more she learned, the more she could eliminate. And that elimination, she decided, would lead her to the actual cause.

Audra moved over to the kitchen table. She opened her laptop and launched an online search. This time she would be more thorough.

Using anything Jack had mentioned, she entered a series of keywords. They led to a wide range of sites: historical time lines, military tributes, veterans' memoirs, memorabilia collections, World War Two reenactments, and more.

She had no idea there were so many people these days who enjoyed dressing up as Nazi officers, accessorized with authentic Lugers and even German shepherds, to spend their summer weekends playing war.

Shaking this off, she reworked her keywords. She added, deleted, and changed their order, seeking the right mix of ingredients for a recipe that worked. She skimmed numerous accounts of saboteurs and spies. They were men and women on both sides of the war, including Nazi agents captured on the East Coast. This one piqued her interest, especially since many had been sentenced to the electric chair for their crimes. A disturbing link to Jack's drawing.

In the end, however, there was nothing her son couldn't have gleaned from a PBS documentary. More important, there was nothing connecting the combination of words with the crash of a plane.

Once again, she reviewed her search.

WWII aircraft German U-boat Nazi spies New York Florida electric chair

She reinserted *Himmel,* this time at the front. Upon her pressing *Enter,* the top of the screen restated all of her words but with a question: *Did you mean: Hemel*?

The search engine was suggesting she had misspelled a name. A slight tremble settled in her hand as she clicked her agreement, refreshing the results. *Jakob Hemel* jumped out in snippets from the content of two different sites. She followed the first link.

After a good amount of sifting, she located the name in a long list of servicemen. He had served in the German air force! But . . . during the First World War. There was no relevance she could see to Nazis or swastikas. No indication he was killed in action.

She reversed to her prior search. Breath held, she clicked on the second link, only to face a message: *Server cannot find the page.*

"You're kidding me," she said.

She tried again, and again, but her efforts failed. She sought out the home page of the site with the link, to no better result. A separate search for *Jakob Hemel* produced nothing remotely related.

Frustration piled inside, layer after layer. She was probing for other options when a muffled scream jarred her.

Jack. Another nightmare.

For a moment, she had forgotten their grueling routine. At least she was already awake. She hurried down the hall and found him thrashing around on his mattress.

"We're gonna crash!" he hollered.

"Jack," she ordered, "you need to calm down." She grabbed hold of his wrist and cast. "Listen to me. You're just dreaming. It's not real."

"We gotta get out!" Eyes open, unseeing, he shook his head with vigor. What she wouldn't do to take his fears away, gather them in a ball, store them in her own soul.

"Wake up for me, buddy. Just wake up. *Please.*"

"Help me!"

He fought against her, and she did her best to maintain her strength. But after two weeks of nights like this, she was tired. Mentally, physically, emotionally. How much longer would this go on? Months? Years? What if he only got worse, no matter where they chose to live?

Hit by a spate of exhaustion, she felt tears mounting behind her eyes. "You're all right, baby. You hear me?" Her voice cracked. "You're safe in here, Jack."

That's what she had intended to say. Yet instantly a calm swept over him, like a power cord had been disconnected. The stillness was so sudden, so shocking, that she reflected on her own words.

The name she had called him was Jakob.

24

A noise yanked Vivian from the depths of sleep. Something tapped the window. The room was dark and curtains blocked her view. A branch must have brushed the pane.

No — no, that wasn't possible. She lived in a brownstone, a corner room on the third floor, not a single tree within reach. Oh, these thoughts were too straining. Her skull felt packed with sand. She glanced at Luanne's bed lying empty and disheveled. The girl must be sneaking in late, using the fire escape to avoid a lecture from the landlady.

But wouldn't Luanne be taking the train soon? She had made mention to that effect while Vivian was getting dressed for —

Where had she gone tonight?

More taps came, growing loud as a hammer on nails. She pressed her pillow to her ears, but not fast enough to prevent her head from throbbing. She envisioned a woodpecker assaulting the glass. The need to cease the sound crushed any other thought.

She pried herself from the cocoon of her sheets and rounded Luanne's bed. When she pushed away the curtains, sunlight blasted through the glass. Her headache bloomed in full. Squinting against the rays, she discovered . . . Luanne's brother?

Befuddled, she slid open the window.

"Morning, twinkle toes."

In that instant, flashes of the prior night assembled in chunks. The dance. The flask. The stairs. She had kissed him. Or he'd kissed her. Had she only dreamt it? Oh, Lord, what had they done?

She pressed her fingers to her temples, dizzied from the unknown.

"Yep. That's about how I figured you'd feel," he said, then abruptly averted his gaze. "You might wanna . . ." He motioned toward her body, which further confused her until she looked down. Her red dress hung in a crooked mess, half of her brassiere exposed.

Her mind snapped to attention, as if by a whiff of smelling salts. She covered her chest with a pillow, terrified to imagine just how much she had already shown him.

"Last night," she said, "I didn't — I mean, I think it was . . . a mistake."

"Yeah?" he said, now looking at her. "Which part?"

"I just — you know. With what happened."

He raised a brow, waiting. An obstinate tack. A decent man wouldn't demand an

226

admission, much less take advantage of a woman in a vulnerable state.

Gene suddenly snickered. "If you're referring to something between you and me, you've got *nothing* to worry about."

She would have been relieved if not for the implication that any temptation would be absurd. Then again, she was hardly his type, based on the bombshell he had dated throughout high school. Paired in photos, the sprightly cheerleader and quiet quarterback were a yearbook editor's dream.

Vivian swallowed, her saliva like a layer of sap. "In that case, would you care to tell me what did happen?"

"Nothing to alert the cavalry over. We took a walk, you fell asleep. I flagged you a cab and delivered you home to Lu, safe and sound."

It must have been past curfew, which meant he couldn't have made it inside. Not without creating a scene. She dreaded to ask: "So, at that hour, how did you . . ."

"I maneuvered you through this window here. And the ladders were no picnic, let me tell you."

She nodded, his answer a light balm. "Well. I appreciate all your help."

He didn't reply, just handed over a paper sack.

"What is this?"

"A plain breakfast roll and two aspirin.

227

You're gonna need them. Oh, and chug a gallon of water or you'll be sorry tomorrow." He spoke as if he had been in her condition many times before. It wasn't behavior she admired, but in this case, it reduced her embarrassment.

"I will," she said.

For a moment, his gaze drifted off to the side. He nodded at nothing in particular. "All right, then," he said, and turned to leave.

As he navigated the metal grates, she sieved the sand in her head to find a suitable parting. If he hadn't been at the dance, she hated to think where — or with whom — she would have landed.

"Gene!" she called out, too loud for her own brain. She dropped her volume. "If there's anything I can do to thank you . . ."

He halted mid-descent. A look of consideration played over his face. "Actually, yeah. There is."

The words had spouted from her mouth as a courtesy. Already she sensed she would come to regret her offer. "O-okay. What is it?"

"I'll pick you up at noon. Wear something you don't mind ruining."

"But — what are we doing?"

"Noon," he said, and continued downward.

She sank against the window frame. Every fiber of her body wanted to soak in a tub and sleep the day away. "Should have kept my mouth shut," she said under her breath.

"Noon," Gene repeated, and strode off without looking up.

The morning flew by in a snap.

Food, water, and aspirin, plus a much-needed nap, had molded Vivian into something resembling a human. Unfortunately, the creaky rumble of the truck — a vehicle Gene had borrowed from the base — threatened to reverse her progress.

"Are you planning to tell me where we're going?" she asked.

"A house," he said.

"A house."

"Yep."

"To do . . . ?"

"A project."

This was far from revelatory. His cuffed jeans and white tee told her as much. As requested, she had dressed similarly despite the undisclosed purpose. She was about to press him for more, but extracting details felt like tweezing invisible splinters. She rested her head on the side window and focused on the road, staving off a recurrence of nausea.

A few minutes later he pulled over to the curb below a gray Victorian house. Located in Ditmas Park, it had a turret, bay windows, and a wraparound porch.

Vivian followed Gene to the rear of the truck, where he released the tailgate and climbed on up. He handed her a large-bristled brush and two buckets of paint. As he lowered a ladder from the flatbed, she stared wide-eyed at the row of remaining cans.

"Surely we're not painting a whole house," she said. Then added, "Are we?"

"Nope."

She blew out a breath. It wasn't a monstrous mansion, like many of the homes in the area, but still that would have taken them days.

"Just the porch and columns," he said. "And the lattice below. The stairs too. Oh, and the fence."

Twinges of exhaustion set into her limbs. She recoiled at the thought of ingesting paint fumes for hours. "Marvelous."

He hopped onto the ground.

"Any particular reason we're painting here?" she asked.

"Yeah." He threw an old sheet over his shoulder. "Needs a new coat."

Weathered with cracks and dirt, the place was indeed due for a touch-up. But obviously that wasn't her point. She wondered if the side job would earn him a fee. If so, using her as free labor would be unethical.

On account of the previous night, however, she was in no position to protest.

Gene hefted the ladder and headed for the house. "You comin'?"

The question was presumably rhetorical.

Over the arch of blue sky the sun traveled its course. Done with the latticework, Vivian started on the low white fence. Gene went from columns to railings with military precision. Other than whistling various show tunes — a surprise, as he didn't seem the type — the guy made not a peep beyond necessity. It was no wonder he had been assigned to Intelligence.

Twice he delivered drinks from inside, the only indication somebody was home. The glasses of chilled lemonade were a luxury given the new ration on sugar. For lunch he carried out sandwiches: bologna and Swiss on rye.

After devouring her last bite, she said, "You do realize this is a cruel form of punishment."

Gene was kicking back on the porch steps above her. He smiled without pity, like the overseer of a chain gang on an allotted break. He swiped a rag over his hairline and the base of his neck. The muscles in his arms rose and shifted. Small patches of sweat caused his shirt to cling, accentuating the firm breadth of his chest.

Vivian turned toward the street. She pressed her glass to her forehead, its coolness fleeting.

"We better get back to it," he said, and none too soon.

■ ■ ■

By the time all the paint had been set to dry, the neighborhood glowed like a string of lanterns.

Vivian waited in the truck, body slumped, her limbs limper than yarn. She felt no trace of guilt for leaving Gene to repack the supplies. She had, without question, repaid her debt.

She rolled her head toward the side window and spotted him on the porch. He stood at the front door, face-to-face with a shadowy woman. She touched his arm as they spoke, Gene now with words to spare.

Vivian sat up.

The woman gave him a small basket, a token of thanks. Perhaps a trade in a blossoming courtship.

Could all of the day's work, slaving in the sun, withering from fumes, have been done to impress a girl? He had been vague about details for a reason.

"Incredible."

If the lovebirds wished to carry on, they could do so on their own time. Vivian pushed on the horn, yielding a glance from Gene. Then he angled toward the woman and accepted a kiss. It was only on the cheek but, had they been in private, would undoubtedly have been meant for the lips.

He trekked down the steps, revealing a full silhouette of the woman. She moved backward to close the door. Light from inside swept past her face before she disappeared. Her features were familiar, though hard to place out of context.

The aroma of bread, from Gene's kerchief-covered basket, billowed as he drove. A block down, Vivian's mind snagged on the recognition.

"Mrs. Langtree," she said. "Was that . . . her house?"

He gave a nod, his gaze locked on the street.

She had almost forgotten the two were acquainted. It was from his recommendation that Mrs. Langtree had hired Luanne, and later Vivian as well. His motivation for today's chores now became clear. A widow without a son would have few helpers to maintain her home, thus Gene's actions had assured her that she wasn't on her own.

Vivian cringed at her prior assumptions, namely those pertaining to the scene on the porch. In Gene's company, Mrs. Langtree had appeared so very different.

"I had no idea you two were close," Vivian said, stricken by how little she knew of them both.

Gene steered in silence. Finally he replied without turning. "Neal and I met at basic. Became buddies right off the bat."

Neal Langtree. The airman.

"Oh, Gene . . . I didn't know. I'm so sorry."

"He was hell-bent on getting those fancy pilot wings. We could've done it together, you know, if I'd wanted to. . . ."

He trailed off, leaving Vivian to fill in the rest. Whether he was regretting not being there or questioning his own survival — perhaps simply mourning the senselessness of it all — the moisture rimming his eyes did not require words.

No freedom comes without a price, people would say of the pilot's honorable end. The adage was far more palatable when those sacrificed were distant strangers.

Vivian reached past the basket and laid a hand on Gene's arm. He didn't grasp her fingers, didn't glance her way, but somehow the gesture felt welcome.

Once at her brownstone, she slowly drew back. Gene exited the truck and opened her side. "Thanks for your help today," he said, guiding her out.

"It was my pleasure." And she meant that, in more ways than anticipated. "Well, then . . . good night."

At the absence of a response, she departed for the stoop stairs. She was halfway to the door when he called to her.

"You — have any plans tomorrow?"

She twisted around. Tomorrow would be Sunday. No work, no roommate. But she caught herself before answering. "That would

234

depend."

He cocked his head a little.

"Is this for some other *project*? Because if it is, I'd like to negotiate a rate up front."

The corners of his lips tugged into a smile. He shoved his hands into his front pockets and said, "I just thought, our trade — it didn't seem quite even. Figured I owe you a decent lunch at least."

Lunch, her mother would say, did not constitute an official date. All the same, heat rose to Vivian's cheeks, hopefully concealed in the dimness between street lamps. "Let me guess," she said. "Noon?"

His smile widened. His dark eyes glimmered. "Sleep well, twinkle toes."

The following hour drifted by as hazy as a dream. Vivian nestled into her bed, washed and warm, on the cusp of sleep. Only then did she realize: A full day had passed without a single thought of Isaak. His grip on her heart had loosened at last.

She rolled onto her side, blanketed by a sad sort of relief, and envisioned possibilities of tomorrow.

25

Out on the deck, Audra studied her son from across the table, visualizing the impossible. She added a dozen years to his face, put pilots' goggles over his eyes, dressed him in a flight jacket marked with a Nazi patch.

Jack looked up at her curiously. "Mom? What is it?"

She squashed the image, outrageous in every way. "Sorry, I was just zoning out."

"Got the chef's special for two here," Robert announced, delivering a plate of veggie patties. His timing was impeccable.

"Wonderful," Audra said. "Thanks for making those."

"You betcha." He wiped his hands on his apron, the caricature type that transformed his torso into that of a bodybuilder. "Buns will be right over." He swooped back to the barbecue, where he plated the meat patties for him and Meredith and the toasted bread for them all.

Audra was grateful the weather allowed them to celebrate outside. Helium balloons were tied around the deck, adding a rainbow of color to her in-laws' backyard. Special occasions of any kind could be rough after a loss; that's why Audra was determined to make this a bright and cheery event.

"Are you excited to see your cake?" she asked Jack.

"Uh-huh." He took a gulp of his fruit punch, staining his mouth with a joker's grin.

She stage-whispered, "I hear Grandpa got you something super special this year."

"Really? What is it?"

"I don't know yet. Apparently it's Top Secret."

He smiled and bounced his legs dangling off the seat. Audra reveled in his delight until he snagged a baby carrot from the veggie tray. Combined with the setting, the sight reminded her of Isabella and her rabbit on a blanket by the garden . . . .

Audra brushed away the thought to make room for anything light. Like an old favorite game.

"I see . . . Geppetto," she said, indicating Robert as the target.

Jack twisted his lips, thinking. "Super Mario."

"Hmm, good one. How about . . . Elmer Fudd with a mustache."

"Papa Smurf."

Tied, two to two. Audra was pondering more mustached characters when Meredith returned from the house. She joined them at the table with a bowl of potato salad.

"This one's a new recipe, so I hope it's okay."

"I'm sure it's great," Audra said.

Robert brought the last of the items over and settled in his chair. "I say we have at it. Okay with you, Mama?"

Meredith hesitated only a moment before nodding. "Let's dig in," she said with a smile. She was skipping the blessing on account of her guests. While part of Audra found this refreshing, the rest of her sank with guilt. Her commentary about harps and wings must have spurred the change.

Jack, on the other hand, didn't seem to notice. Though he was accustomed to prayers before meals here — as Audra never discouraged him; he would discover the truth on his own — he appeared just as pleased to dive into his burger.

"Careful now, Jack," Audra said. "Try not to get ketchup on your cast." She took care in articulating his name. Ever since last night, when calling him Jakob had distinctly soothed him, she feared making the same mistake — almost as much as she feared the reason it had worked. On the drive over, she had asked him about the name, undeniably similar to his own. As usual, he shook his head.

Whose idea had it been to call him Jack in the first place? Hers or Devon's, she couldn't remember. It wasn't a family name. No specific actor or athlete or character in a book sprang to mind as the inspiration.

Not that it mattered.

"So, Robert, how's business going?" she asked while scooping up fruit cocktail.

"Pretty well," he said. "They tell me no walls have fallen down this week. So far."

"That's always good news."

Meredith said, "What about you, Audra? Any word from your interviews?" She seemed more interested than investigative, a welcomed difference from before.

"There might be an opportunity. Nothing set yet." In actuality, as of this morning, a solid option had materialized. But she would save that for a private discussion. She diverted the subject, perpetuating small talk as they all enjoyed their lunch.

To Meredith's credit, her mentions of Devon were limited, her efforts for levity clear. Always a teacher, she entertained Jack with fun facts that ranged from the formation of Multnomah Falls to squirrel-proofing her garden with mothballs and cayenne pepper.

When the time came, the couple went inside to prepare for the finale. Audra transferred gifts from the car to the back deck, where Robert assembled a mound of presents. On this day above any, Audra saw the value of a grandparent's duty to spoil.

They all sang "Happy Birthday" as Meredith carried out the cake. It was shaped like a moon, with candles surrounding a big wax *8.* A sign protruded from airbrushed craters: *Happy birthday to our shooting star*!

239

Robert snapped his camera. "Make a wish, Beanstalk."

Jack's concentration rivaled that of a surgeon. The candles dripped into puddles of color. He blew out the flames and the group applauded. It seemed they all shared a common wish, based on the quiet that set in like a low-lying cloud. The tearing of wrapping paper helped hide the tension, as did Jack's pleasure over his toys, books, and clothes.

Audra had just finished her cake, chocolate with raspberry filling, when Meredith rose to clear the table. "Audra, would you mind grabbing the bowls?"

"Not at all."

As Audra assisted in gathering, Jack salvaged crumbs from his plate. He chuckled at the frosting that fringed his grandpa's mustache. The sound, though brief, was powerful enough to make Audra contemplate her plans; there was much to gain from a drastic relocation, but there also would be loss.

"Holy Toledo, I forgot to bring out the best gift yet," she heard Robert say as she stepped into the house.

In the kitchen, Meredith rinsed off plates and cups for the dishwasher. Without being asked, she shifted away from the sink, giving Audra access to the trash can below. Audra deposited a wad of dirty napkins and closed the cupboard with her foot. The routine here, together, filled her with a rush of the familiar. A choreography she missed.

"Looks like Jack's still having bad dreams," Meredith said, without turning from the sink.

"Yeah. He is."

The drooping of his eyes, or Audra's, must have given them away. After all, she had provided few updates since the festival. She hadn't deliberately avoided the woman's calls, but neither had she raced to return them.

Meredith's demeanor told her this hadn't gone unnoticed.

"I'm sorry we've been out of touch lately," Audra said. "There's just been some issues with Jack, and I've been trying to figure it all out."

"Well, you know Jack's welfare always comes first for us."

"I do."

Meredith scrubbed at a grill spatula, the charred pieces not budging. Her skin grew splotchy from the intensity of her efforts.

Soaking the tool in suds would be better, letting the grime ease gradually rather than forcing it clean. But who was Audra to say as much? The same advice could apply to her own life.

Maybe Meredith was right; distance from family could prove more damaging, and not just for Jack, but Audra too. Her parents were prime examples.

"Meredith," she said softly. "I could really use your help."

At this, Meredith shut off the faucet and

241

turned. Her expression underscored how long it had been since Audra had confided in her about anything.

Meredith nodded, encouraging her to continue.

"I got a call this morning from the interviewer in Boston. I guess he wanted to tell me before he went on a trip tomorrow. Anyhow, it's unofficial until they can sort out some details when he gets back, but basically, they're offering me the job. If all goes well, I'd start in August."

Meredith's look of concern grew dim. She seemed to have aged ten years since their last visit. She picked up a kitchen towel, wiped her hands. "And . . . you're going to take it."

"I am — was. I'm not sure. There's been a lot going on. More than you know about."

A pause. "I'm listening."

Audra heaved a sigh, too tired to filter her words. "All right, then. Here goes."

Once her internal gate opened, the details rolled out in a long, breathless string. The drawings, the therapist, the book, the soldier. Nazi spies and wartime subs, plane crashes and electric chairs. A German phrase and inscription, the name of a man who remained a mystery.

Even if she wanted to, Audra couldn't stop purging. Every admission was a burden lifted, a shackle unlocked. When the entire summary had run its course, Meredith leaned back against the counter, her shock betrayed only by

242

her eyes.

"And you believe . . . Jack has been reincarnated?" Her tone dragged with the same disbelief Audra had initially directed at Dr. Shaw. The word *reincarnated* in itself conjured visions of infomercials reserved for airings at three in the morning.

"I know it sounds crazy. To be honest, I first thought it was all from Jack watching war movies at your house — even though you said he didn't." In hindsight, Audra wasn't proud of those doubts. "But now, given everything that's happened, I think there's more to it. There has to be. I just don't know what."

Silence expanded between them, filling every cranny of the room.

Meredith stared at the dishcloth in her grip, as if waiting for it to crawl away. Finally she lifted her gaze. "I need to ask you a question," she said, and Audra readily nodded. "Has this man . . . this soldier . . . when he comes over . . . has he had anything to do with Jack getting hurt? His bruises and the like?"

Audra was so startled by the question, her voice faltered. "Of course not. Why would you think that?"

"You said he's been to your apartment."

"He has, yes. But only once." Nothing about the guy conveyed a con man or serial killer. "He was just looking for our help."

"So Jack's injuries," Meredith went on, "they're all from you, then."

"Yes, I told you that. I . . ." The realization came slowly at first, then hit with the force of a grenade. "Meredith, are you accusing me of something?"

Meredith struggled to answer.

That alone said it all.

Just then, Jack ran into the room. "Mom, look!" he exclaimed, raising a rifle in the air. "Check out what Grandpa gave me."

Now it was Audra's turn to be shocked. "That was the surprise gift?"

Robert entered with a prideful grin and ruffled Jack's hair. "It's just like the one I grew up with. Mere and I happened across it at an antique store in Sellwood last week."

Audra kept her voice neutral in front of Jack. "I thought I made it clear that I didn't want him hunting, for birds or anything else."

"Oh, well, sure. But it's only a BB gun. Harmless as pie."

Audra had removed enough BBs from the bodies of defenseless cats to know this wasn't the case. Besides, the last thing Jack needed was a weapon to amplify his wartime confusion. At the very least, Robert should have asked her first.

"You know what, Jack?" she said. "It's getting pretty late. We should get going."

"But Grandpa said we could go shoot at soup cans."

"Another day."

His shoulders dropped along with his smile,

tempting her to give in. But a single glance at Meredith eliminated the notion.

It went without saying that Audra had made her decision about moving, and now there would be no delay.

She immediately packed up Jack's gifts, except for one. "We'll keep the BB gun here where it's safe. Okay, buddy? Now, say good-bye to your grandparents."

He obeyed without protest and followed her to the car.

While driving away, Audra looked at Jack in the rearview mirror. How could anyone, much less a family member, believe she would ever abuse her son?

A single thought tamped her outrage: the chance that Meredith wasn't alone in her suspicions.

Audra's craving for a solution had never been greater.

She had lost her chance to save Devon. If she'd examined each of his symptoms to uncover the truth, the outcome could have been different. She wasn't about to repeat her error, not with Jack. If necessary, she'd search the earth, the sea, the sky for the answer.

26

More than two hundred feet hung between Vivian and the ground. As the ascent continued, she shut her eyes tight. She had made a mistake. She wanted to get off. Yet with the ferocity of her grip, removing her from the ride could prove impossible without pliers.

"This was a horrible, awful idea," she said to Gene, who was harnessed beside her on the canvas seat. She only vaguely recalled that the idea had been hers.

Created for the World's Fair, the Parachute Jump had always appeared a thrilling ride with a partner. The open-air steel structure possessed all the sturdiness of the Eiffel Tower. This had been her claim whenever trying to sway Luanne, whose aversion to heights had prevented the adventure.

Vivian now recognized her roommate's sensibility. Confidence came in greater supply when at the bottom gazing up.

"Focus right here," Gene told Vivian. "Not down below, just on me."

At first, she suspected pliers might be needed to lift her eyelids too, but the warmth in his tone lured them partially open. Her vision moved over his khaki tie, his collar, his face.

"That's my girl." He issued a casual smile, as if sharing a booth at a diner, not dangling in midair. "We're almost at the top."

She appreciated his efforts, and most of all the withholding of mockery, but a flimsy, overused chute couldn't possibly slow their fall. A few faulty metal rings could send them *splat* into Steeplechase Park, flat as a strip of gum. It didn't help that the scruffy men operating the cables were less interested in their jobs than the shapely females on Coney Island.

"Will it help if I hold on to you?" Gene asked.

She replied with a tiny nod, though internally the motion was vigorous.

He navigated his hand around the straps behind her. Over her pedal pushers, he wrapped the side of her waist. "I've got you, see?"

She did, and a small part of her relaxed.

Gene glanced up toward the release mechanism. "Remember, now, don't look down."

Vivian nodded again, a split second before they dropped toward the earth. She sucked in a breath, the air thin from altitude and fear, and buried her face in Gene's shoulder.

His firm hold braced her for a jerk of the straps. A sudden weightlessness followed, breezy and soothing — hopefully not from a trip to heaven.

"Wow," he said. "Would you get a load of that."

The sheer awe in his voice gradually lifted her head. Their parachute had mushroomed, enabling a dramatic, bird's-eye view. Afternoon sunrays had formed the fingers of a wizard, turning canals into gold, softening buildings made of brick. All the bustling stilled and noises ceased, as if the world took a moment to rest.

"Sure is somethin' else," he said. "Feel like you're seeing all of New York from here, don't ya?"

"No," she said in amazement. "More like the whole country."

It was hard to fathom that at this very minute, on Pacific shores and European borders, young men were engaged in battle. Although Vivian lacked the naivety to believe so, way up here — above bridges connecting islands, the grand statue affirming liberty — even perpetual peace seemed possible. In fact, with Gene at her side, a sense of safety enfolding her, anything seemed possible.

They rode the Parachute Jump three more times in a row. Each went off without a hitch, thanks to Gene tipping the operators. Passengers otherwise risked getting stuck halfway — much too long for the "mishap" to be romantic, just an amusing pastime for the workers.

Powered by adrenaline, Vivian continued the charge for adventure. Together, they laughed and hollered while conquering every ride in the vicinity. They dipped on the Tornado, wound through the Cyclone, and zipped down the Thunderbolt, seizing each other's hands or arms when needed. By the time they broke for a meal — a couple of Nathan's Famous hot dogs — their physical interaction felt like an old hat.

It wasn't until they were out on the pier, the sun retiring over the sea, that his touch caused her to tense. Gene's thumb brushed her cheek and followed the slant of her jaw. The salt-scented air mingled with soap and pine from his skin.

Could a kiss come so soon?

They had known each other for years, but not like this. Always she had considered him handsome, but in a different way: as the brother of a friend, with a manner more reserved than her usual taste. In two short days, her perspective had pleasantly broadened.

At his second stroke to her face, she held her breath, anticipating the next step.

"You missed some," he said.

She stared, confounded, as he dropped his hand.

"There was paint on your cheek. From yesterday."

"Oh. Yes." Blindly she rubbed at the spot. "Thank you."

He nodded and angled toward the water.

Inside, she flamed with embarrassment. She had sorely mistaken his intentions. After her episode at the dance, maybe his care was only the protective, brotherly kind.

But that couldn't be right. His side-glances all day had affirmed his attraction. True, he hadn't poured with conversation, yet she had found the trait refreshing. There was no pressure for idle chatter. Already they were so familiar, as if his arm were a shawl she was always meant to wear.

Until now.

With only waves lapping the quiet, she sensed that comfort receding. For a reason she could not pinpoint he had begun to pull away.

"So," he said. "You ready?"

Ready to leave, ready to part ways?

She smiled and replied, "Absolutely."

Awkwardness solidified with every stop of the streetcar. Vivian willed its pace to quicken. Any eye contact from Gene amounted to a flicker. He appeared deliberate in allowing strangers to divide them, though he had

250

insisted on escorting her home.

After disembarking, they wound through the moonlit streets, trading only the sounds of their footsteps. At the sight of her brownstone she imagined his relief.

"Here we are," she said at the base of the stoop.

He looked up at the building, as if surprised by the destination.

"Well," she said. "Thank you for the day."

"Yeah. It was fun." He extended his hand for a formal shake, which she accepted while gritting her teeth.

"It was certainly memorable."

Not bothering with a good-bye, she wheeled around and headed up the steps.

"Vivian."

She grasped the banister. Against her irritation, she forced herself to face him. "Yes?"

"On Tuesday," he said, his hands in his jacket pockets, "Ringling Brothers will be in town. I was wondering if you'd like to go. To see the circus."

For years, uncertainties of the heart had left her emotions in a frenzy. As if riding the Cyclone, they had been twisted and turned, raised and dropped. She had no desire to revisit the turbulent ride.

"Before I answer," she said, "I have to know why."

"Why . . . ?"

"Why you're asking."

251

The corners of his eyes creased. "I'm not sure I follow."

She was aware of how brash she sounded, possibly neurotic, but the need for self-preservation trumped all else.

"Gene, the truth of the matter is, I like you. Very much. But from one minute to the next, I can't tell what you're looking for. If it's only friendship, that's perfectly fine. I'd just prefer to be clear from the start."

He said nothing as he stood there, as one would do while strategizing an escape. But then he slowly climbed the stairs and stopped when their eyes became level. As he leaned in, her breath hitched in her throat. He hovered an inch away for a torturous, wondrous second before placing his mouth on hers. He tasted of butterscotch, or taffy, from penny candies at the pier. It was a perfect match to their kiss. Rich, smooth, and sweet.

"Does that answer your question?" she barely heard him say.

She dragged her eyes open, and nodded.

"Good." He smiled at her. With the side of his broad hand, he caressed her cheek. "I've had eyes for you for a long time, Vivian. Just didn't think you were ready for anything — with what Lu mentioned, about some old steady. And what you said after the USO. I sure wasn't going to push if —"

Her finger gently touched his mouth. No reason to hear more. She slid her hands onto his shoulders and brought him in for a kiss. Though more intimate than the first, it had all the warmth and patience of lazing in the sun. All the comfort of a heated bath.

When they finally drew apart, his hands light on her hips, she reflected on the day, such an unexpected path. She could not keep from grinning.

"Pick you up on Tuesday?" he said.

Vivian agreed, reluctant to let him go. But he kissed her hand before descending the stairs and fading into the darkness.

Once he had disappeared, she turned for the door. Her hand was on the knob when a chill skimmed her spine. Not from the air, not from Gene. She surveyed her shadowed surroundings.

Somebody, she swore, was watching.

27

The journey to find Sean Malloy had Audra feeling like a stalker. To her relief, only a handful of people with his name were listed online in the Portland area. An age range for each one had aided her deduction. Except for an outdated phone number, the search had been easy — until she reached the address.

It was located in northwest Portland, specifically the Pearl District. Over recent years, like polishing a grain of sand into a lustrous white gem, a tide of visionaries had transformed the old industrial area into a prime cultural hub. Modern art galleries, trendy martini bars, and culinary shops selling fifty-dollar colanders now inhabited what had once been rugged, abandoned warehouses.

Audra found herself at one such building, comprised of renovated high-end lofts. At the entrance, an elderly male resident informed her that nobody lived there by the name of Sean but that a Judith Malloy did and, who knows, they just might be related. He kindly directed her to a nearby art gallery where at noon on a Wednesday the woman would be working.

Following his instructions, Audra turned left by the yoga club. Several blocks later she discovered a wide black awning sandwiched between a Zen store and gelato shop. An arc of white letters on the window read: *The Attic.*

She paused at the door, debating on how to present her mission. What if Judith wasn't a relative but a bitter ex-wife? Any mention of the guy might earn Audra an earful of choice words.

A series of beeps blared from half a block down. A delivery truck was reversing direction. Audra fought an urge to follow suit. Jack's school bus would drop him off at two forty. No time for delay.

She strode inside, where a waft of mint tea greeted her from an entry table. The recordings of an airy flute floated into the rafters. Burgundy carpet ran beneath moveable and permanent walls, all exhibiting original artwork.

"Now, remember," said the lady at the counter, "when you go to unpack it, just slide the piece out from this side." She handed the man a large rectangular box. "I hope your wife enjoys it."

"I guarantee she'll be thrilled."

"You two have a great anniversary."

"Thanks a lot, Judith."

Sure enough, the elderly tenant had steered Audra right.

Thankfully, Judith appeared a little old to be Sean's ex. Well into her sixties, she possessed an elegance befitting her classic look: fair skin, soft angles, and a short hairdo that few women, outside Audrey Hepburn, could pull off as well. Her sole modern touches were dangly copper earrings and a matching necklace, all with an African flair.

As the customer turned to leave, a FedEx gal rolled a hand trolley over to the counter. She requested a signature on an electronic device before discussing a delivery issue.

Judith glanced over at Audra. "I'll be right with you."

Audra smiled. Not wanting to hover, she busied herself by exploring the nearest collection. The multi-media creations were grouped on a wall. Iridescent jewels, dyed ribbons, and metallic paints composed surreal worlds of fays and fairies. Not childlike versions often printed on calendars and in picture books. These were sophisticated. Mysterious. Dark.

"I apologize for the wait." Judith approached from the side. "My manager had a dental emergency this morning, leaving me a bit scrambled."

"No problem," Audra said, a split second before the initials on the art — *JM* — sank in. "You created these." Spoken aloud, her tardy realization felt idiotic and, in front of the artist, partially insulting. Even more so when you were planning to request a favor. "What I meant was, these are really beautiful."

"Well, thank you. I'm glad you like them."

"I especially love how you . . . made the wings."

Judith groaned. "The bane of my existence. Half the time, those darn things make me want to quit altogether, switch to a more sane career. Like lion taming or alligator wrestling."

Audra smiled as she surveyed the moonlit swarms. Their three-dimensional wings, delicate and veined, appeared crafted from rice paper.

"Besides, there'd be no point," Judith sighed. "Eventually, I'd stumble across something that inspires me, and that obsession would pull me right back to my studio." She flicked her paint-stained fingers behind her.

Audra's gaze followed to the referenced spot, a room set back in the corner. In doing so, she scanned more works on display, easily viewed without the obstruction of patrons. Featured in various pieces were hummingbirds and dragon-flies, lightning bugs and dandelion seeds, all of them objects of . . . flight.

The correlation was unnerving.

She swallowed before asking, "Have you always focused on flying?"

"Flying? Oh, as a theme," Judith said. "For the most part, I have. I suppose I've been fascinated about it ever since I was little. But then, what child isn't, right?"

Fascinated wasn't the word that Audra would have chosen, but she nodded as Judith continued.

"I used to wonder about that, actually — why

kids love it so much. I spent years trying to figure out why we're drawn to things like kites and butterflies and rockets. Then there's unicorns and dragons. Paper planes and balloons."

Audra had never considered reasons for the universal attraction. She had to admit it was an interesting observation. "And? Why do you think that is?"

"Personally?" Judith said, and regarded the closest art piece. "I think it's the magical idea of floating above everything. Being untouchable, not knowing where you're going to land. Just the pure freedom of it." She drifted briefly into her thoughts before shifting the frame to hang a quarter inch lower. "Now, then — before I bore you with more of my philosophical analysis — are you looking for something in particular?"

Audra had to stop and reset her thoughts. She hoped it wasn't offensive that she didn't come to shop. "The truth is, I'm actually looking for someone."

Judith's sleek eyebrow rose, either intrigued or wary.

"His name's Sean Malloy. He's a young Army vet. We . . . happened to cross paths at the Rose Festival last week. And I'd heard you might be related —"

"You're that woman. The mother of the boy who'd gotten lost."

Not Audra's proudest distinction.

"I'm Sean's mom," Judith explained, "so I was there with family, to see him being honored by the mayor. I only caught a glimpse of you that day." She lowered her chin with a compassionate smile. "I've thought of you and your son quite a bit. I'm so glad everything worked out."

"Thanks. Me too." An understatement.

Judith patted her chest. "Anyhow. Sean mentioned you two might know each other . . . Aubrey, was it?"

"Audra. Hughes." To avoid complicating the situation, she bypassed the details. "I'd love the chance to catch up with him, if that's possible."

"Oh, yes. You definitely should. The doctor said anyone from his past might be helpful. Here, let me jot down his address for you. Sean mentioned he'd be there all day." She snagged a pen from the reception counter and scribbled on a notepad. "He's staying with my aunt, on her farm up in Vancouver. You'll love meeting her. She's ninety-three going on eighty."

Audra didn't expect such eager cooperation. She checked her watch. Vancouver. It would take at least fifteen minutes to reach southwest Washington and another forty to get home.

"I'll let them know you're coming." Judith passed along the paper, before a serious look took hold. "You do know about his accident, I assume?" Her tone suggested Audra should know more prior to the drive over.

"He just said there was a bomb, while he was on patrol."

"A roadside bomb, that's right. It broke a few bones that thankfully have healed well. The

259

hearing in his left ear is still damaged, though, which you might have noticed."

"I didn't. I'm glad you mentioned it." Audra hadn't noticed much of anything during his time on her doorstep.

"Since Sean was the only one in the vehicle who made it through, we don't know much else. Just that it's been hard on him, not remembering what happened. Of course, as his mother, I'd prefer he not remember any of it — though that probably sounds selfish."

"Not to me," Audra said.

Judith smiled.

"How much of his memory has he lost, do you know?"

"Almost three years in all. Four months being his deployment, and about two and a half years before that. He gets bits and pieces now and then, so I'm sure the rest is locked in there somewhere. The doctors say it's all pretty minor, compared to other traumatic brain injuries. But for Sean, it's still made a big difference."

Memory loss wasn't anything Audra would ever dismiss as minor, not ever again. "I can imagine."

"Now that he's been back for six months, I've nudged him about getting a job. About getting out and reconnecting with friends. But I think my nudging is sounding more like nagging." She smiled again, gave a shrug. "I guess I was hoping that . . . maybe you could help him out."

Audra looked at the address in her hand, these days appreciating any clear destination. Careful, however, not to make an empty promise, she replied, "I'll see what I can do."

28

Intent on reaching her destination, Vivian hurried into the brownstone. She went straight up the stairs toward the safety of her room, unnerved by a sense of being watched. She felt it in the air after bidding Gene good night.

And those suspicions were confirmed when she opened her bedroom door.

"Luanne," Vivian said, noting her friend's knowing look. "You're . . . back from your trip."

"So I am." Parked on her bed, Luanne held a knitting project on her lap that she seemed in no hurry to finish.

At the window facing the street, the curtains gapped just enough for an incriminating view. "When did — how long have you been home?"

"For a while."

Vivian caught a glimpse of herself in the vanity mirror, lipstick faded and cheeks flushed. After a day on the rides, her tangled hair and disheveled clothes could spell out more than a kiss.

She retreated to the closet. "So, how did it go? Did you have a good weekend?" She slipped off her crimson sweater, a hue matching her face.

"I did."

"Really? That's marvelous."

"Evidently you enjoyed yours too."

Vivian fumbled with a hanger. She felt the bashfulness of a little girl, her fingers slicked in oil. "It was all right, I suppose."

How foolish of her not to consider Luanne in all of this. Vivian needed to collect herself before making things worse. "I think I'll take a bath. Did you see anyone using the tub?"

"It's okay, Viv."

"You mean, it's available?"

"I mean about Gene. That is, you and Gene."

Reluctantly Vivian turned to face her.

"As a matter of fact, it's beyond okay." Luanne broke into a grin. "It's magnificent."

"Honest?"

Luanne nodded heartily and said, "He's been so afraid to date anyone since Helen. After all, it didn't end well and — oh, never mind that." She waved it off. "I do have to admit, I've suspected for some time now that Gene was secretly mooning over you. I just didn't feel it was my place, especially if you weren't looking for a relationship —"

Relationship. Hearing the word caused Vivian to bristle. This was to be the adventurous phase of her life.

"Luanne, please," she interrupted, "keep in mind, we've only just started dating." Her mind had scarcely processed even that much. "Besides, there's no guarantee it will work out. We're just . . . enjoying each other's company."

"Yes, yes, of course! I completely understand." Although her voice conveyed sincerity, her eyes glinted with a scrapbook of wishes: throwing rice outside a chapel, hosting Sunday family barbecues, nieces and nephews playing games in the yard.

Could it be that Gene shared the same vision, that casual courting wasn't part of his makeup?

"I'm going to whip up some hot cocoa," Luanne said, as if a celebration were in order. "I'll be right back. Don't go anywhere."

For Vivian, it was a superfluous directive. Wherever would she go?

Yet from this thought she recalled her special savings. Her tin of distant dreams.

Not for the first time, she longed to grab those funds and run.

As it was, the urge for extremes lasted only until Tuesday. For that's when Gene returned for their next date. He had an aura about him that always salved Vivian's worries, a

264

presence that made her feel safe.

At no time was this more apparent than during the circus at Madison Square Garden.

To amuse the crowd, a prankster of a dwarf sprayed a tramp clown with a bottle of fizzy water. The clown in turn chased him helter-skelter with a huge sloshing bucket. Just as the clown flung the contents in revenge, the dwarf hit the ground, leaving the audience to take the soaking.

Vivian had barely ducked when Gene, on instinct, launched his arms over her in a protective dome. Soon everyone realized the clown had swapped his bucket of water for one of white confetti.

"Sorry," Gene said afterward, referencing his overreaction.

"Don't be," she insisted, and kissed him on the cheek.

Even during the trapeze numbers, in which scantily clad ladies stretched their bodies in impressive shapes, he appeared conscious of Vivian alone. And not just at the circus, but at movie palaces and restaurant booths, during strolls on the Brooklyn Bridge. She felt it when he touched her elbow or the small of her back, guiding her through a doorway or down a set of steps.

And so it went, week after week, one outing following the next. After three months together, it could have been three years.

Her mother was delighted even prior to

meeting Gene. "How's that dashing officer of yours?" she would ask Vivian during visits to the city. Her approval was so ardent, in fact, Vivian regretted not keeping him a secret. She needed to be cautious to avoid another mistake.

To reduce the pressure early on, Gene, too, agreed they ought to date freely. And yet Vivian knew he had no desire to do so. Nor, in truth, did she. Like a ride on the Parachute Jump, she was falling and floating and secure all at once.

So immersed had she become in this idyllic foray she had forgotten all about Café Labrec until she spotted it from the bus during her morning commute. Already the first Friday of June and her bill remained unpaid.

"Criminy." She cringed at what Mr. Bisset must think. Her father had instilled in her the value of keeping her word.

Anxious to reconcile her debt, she anticipated the workday would slog until clockout. Fortunately, she was wrong. Every officer on post suddenly had an incoming call. The switchboard blinked with the incessancy of a pinball machine.

Name, please. Name, please. No time to say, *Thank you.*

At one point, Luanne tapped Vivian on the shoulder, announcing their shift was over. Vivian was astounded. It seemed the day had just begun.

She shed her equipment and ambled toward the door, where her supervisor sat at her desk. "Have a good evening, Mrs. Langtree."

"Hmm? Ah, yes. Good evening." Although the woman had recently returned, her vigilance had lessened, her thoughts often wandering. Part of Vivian missed the staunch figure who appeared to have passed with her son.

The bus rolled its way through the borough.

On the path of their evening loop, Vivian kept watch for the Brooklyn Botanic Garden and the famed museum of art. After being cooped up in a room all day, she welcomed the sites she and Gene liked to frequent. Sometimes Luanne would join them, calling herself a third wheel, to which Vivian would remind her that without one any tricycle was doomed to collapse.

This evening, the missing wheel would be Gene. A work assignment required he stay overnight at Pine Camp, up in the North Country.

Bemoaning this, Vivian disembarked from the bus. She followed the group toward the stoop of the brownstone as they discussed plans to leave at six. Several of the girls had sweethearts stationed at faraway bases. A distractive evening was much needed. It was opening night of *Yankee Doodle Dandy,* and bowling or a diner would be sure to follow.

The idea sparked a memory. Vivian had almost forgotten the café again.

"Good grief," she muttered.

"What's wrong?" Luanne asked.

"I have a quick errand to run. But I'll be back in plenty of time."

Luanne smirked. "Viv, your errands are never quick."

"Oh, shush," Vivian said lightly, and hurried down the steps.

"If you're late," Luanne warned, "James Cagney and I will be spending the evening without you."

Vivian waved her purse in acknowledgment.

Minutes later, she spotted the glass window of the shop. The bell jangled as she entered and a sense of nostalgia surprised her. The aroma of baking dough was so warm and inviting, she felt reunited with an old friend.

"*Bonsoir,* Vivian." Mr. Bisset set down his newspaper and emerged from the cashier's counter. He wore the same vest and tie from her last visit, making it seem as though no time had passed. "I was beginning to worry, *chérie.*"

"Yes, well, it's been rather busy these days."

"No, no. You must never be too busy for the desserts of life, my dear."

"I'll try to remember that," she said with a smile. "Have you been well yourself?"

"I cannot complain." He smiled in return, but in a manner reminiscent of Mr. Harrington. The kind tinged with concern for loved ones, and for good reason. Nazis had occupied Paris now for almost a full year. "*Allor,* your seat is waiting outside. I shall bring you a fig tart, new to the menu. Soft and sweet, warm with butter."

"I do wish I could. But I came by just to pay my last bill." She retrieved the coins from her sweater pocket. "I'm truly ashamed of how long it's taken me."

He raised his palm in refusal.

"Mr. Bisset, you have to accept. I'll feel terrible if you don't."

He mulled this over and said, "We will trade. I shall take these" — he scooped up the change — "and you sample the tart, on the house. Now, go, go."

Between his quiet worries and her inexcusable delay, she saw no way to decline. What's more, his description of the pastry caused her stomach to grumble. She had eaten only half of her lunch due to the flood of calls.

"I'm not sure how this comes out fair for you," she pointed out.

"In times like these, Vivian, it is more than fair."

As he moved toward the display case, she admired him wistfully. She could always skip changing clothes for tonight, even meet the group at the theater if necessary. Luanne would understand.

■ ■ ■

Out in the courtyard Vivian treaded toward her table. An old somberness returned, as if released from the cobblestones by the weight of her steps. Two couples at separate tables dined nearby, their faces dappled with light from the setting sun.

She lowered into her seat, tucked away by the wilting flowers. A graveyard of memories. This, she knew, would be her last visit. Closure would come from this final indulgence. It was the ending of a chapter, the relinquishing of grief. She closed her eyes to wholly absorb the sounds and scents, etching them into the recesses of her mind.

" 'Scuse me, miss?"

A boy no older than six appeared nearby. He approached her table with cap in hand. His threadbare clothes and dirt-smudged cheeks tugged at her heart. She glanced past his head on the lookout for Mr. Bisset. Though kindhearted, the man would not approve of beggars troubling his patrons.

She signaled for the boy to come closer, then dug through her purse and produced two dimes. "Here you are," she said in a hush.

He gave a nod and slipped the money into the pocket of his trousers. His gaze darted around before he asked quietly, "You *is* Vivian, ain't ya?"

"Why — yes. But, how did you —"

"This here's for you." He handed her an envelope from the inside of his hat, folded in half, edges curled over.

"What is this? Who is it from?"

"Some fella in the alley. Gave me a whole dollar to deliver it right to ya."

A dollar would be a fortune for the child. She unfolded the envelope to examine both sides. It bore not a single marking.

"How did the man know I'd be —" She looked up and found the child halfway through the courtyard. Thoughts swimming, she tore open the casing and pulled out a note. The handwriting, printed in block letters, had a messiness that appeared rushed.

VIVIAN,
MEET ME TONIGHT ON BINNEN
BRIDGE AT 10.
TELL NO ONE. COME ALONE.
ISAAK

Her chest cinched. An ancient grip squeezed out her air, the hand of a ghost reaching from the soil. It wasn't possible. Isaak was gone.

Or was he?

She snapped her head up to locate the messenger, now out of view. Whoever had employed the boy — she needed his description.

Vivian sped through the courtyard and out

271

to the sidewalk. Her gaze combed the area in frantic sweeps, from cars to shops to alleys, but the child had evaporated like mist. He left no proof of existence. Save for the missive in her hand.

29

A half hour later Audra sat alone on a stranger's couch, the slip of an address still in her grip. Upon arriving she'd barely said hello when Judith's aunt ushered her inside. The compact lady with silver-blond curls introduced herself as Luanne, the sister of Judith's father, Gene.

"Go on and make yourself at home. I'll let Sean know you're here," Luanne had said, her smile as warm as the eyes behind her glasses. Then she shuffled out the front door.

Perhaps Sean was helping out in the barn. Audra had passed the brown wooden structure when coming up the drive. Two donkeys were grazing in a fenced-in field. The whole property looked to be two or three acres with trees scattered like freckles.

Only after parking did she pause to wonder what the heck she was doing here.

Skirting the thought, Audra scanned the cozy living room. The interior of the house conformed to the charm of its powder-blue exterior. Porcelain collectibles and framed photos sat on end table doilies. Cookbooks and craft books filled shelves flanking the fireplace. Hunched in the corner was a floor model radio, like Rip van Winkle in a decades-long sleep.

A song rang out from the mantel clock. "Westminster Chimes" marked the one o'clock hour.

She and Tess would usually be on lunch break. By now, at a restaurant near the clinic, they'd have devoured a veggie bento or spinach-and-cheese crepe. Already Audra missed their routine. More than that, she missed her regular clients and the animals she had treated and saved. And now another vet had taken her place. Just like that. Nothing to it. Wham-bam, you're hired.

"Stop it," she muttered to herself. "You're the one who quit."

"Audra?"

She flew to her feet and turned as Sean entered the house, his great-aunt right behind.

"Sean. Hi."

"Hi . . ."

Audra couldn't tell if his curious tone came from questioning her monologue or from surprise over her presence. Based on his scruffy jaw, wrinkled T-shirt, and dusty jeans, she went with the latter.

"I hope I'm not bothering you. At the gallery, your mom told me I should stop by. That she'd tell you I was coming."

Luanne patted Sean's arm. "Oh, dear, that's my fault. Your mother did phone, but I didn't re-

274

alize your friend would be here so soon." She shifted her attention to Audra. "I'm afraid I don't move as fast as I used to."

"Neither do I," Audra assured her.

Luanne smiled. "Well, I'll put some water on for tea. Better yet, I could make some hot cocoa if you'd like."

Audra suddenly felt like she was younger than Jack. "Sounds delicious."

"Sean?"

"Huh? Uh, yeah. Thanks."

Luanne winked at Audra and padded through the dining room, presumably on to the kitchen. The quiet left behind was the type that followed a shove off a cliff.

He gestured to the couch with the pair of work gloves in his hand. "Want to sit down?"

Audra nodded and reclaimed her seat. She stored the address in her jeans pocket to prevent fiddling with the paper. As Sean settled on the sofa chair, he set the gloves down and briskly smoothed his hair, appearing to realize his tousled state.

She thought of their last encounter, how she'd all but slammed the door in his face. An apology seemed in order. "I'm sorry I —," she began, just as Sean began to talk. They both stopped short.

"You go," they said, again in chorus, which caused them to laugh. A crack spread through the tension, loosening the air.

She tried again. "I just wanted to say I'm sorry

275

if I was rude to you before."

"It's okay. It was my fault. I must have seemed like a crazy stalker hunting you down."

"No. Not at all." It didn't seem necessary to point out how they paralleled in this respect. "From what your mom said, about what you've been through, I can understand why you wanted to find us."

Now who was the scary one? It sounded like Audra was interviewing his relatives.

"I only talked to her, by the way, because I went to her home first." That didn't sound any better. "The address listed online was under your name, but a guy at the building said it was hers, and he told me about her gallery. I went, since it was close by. Otherwise, I really wouldn't have bothered her . . . ."

Sean laughed softly, making clear she was rambling.

"And," she said, "I'm going to quit now."

"No worries. It makes sense. I used her address for forwarding while I was away, after I sold my condo."

"Oh, sure. Of course," Audra said.

Chimes again rang from the clock, snapping her back to her mission. She had come to uncover answers, not for a leisurely chat.

"Sean, the reason I'm here is about my son — Jack. The German phrase you quoted, when you came to see me —"

He shook his head, lowering his gaze. "Look, you were right. If you're saying we'd never met,

276

I obviously just misheard."

How many hours had the guy spent evaluating the lunacy of his claim, that a little boy, a stranger, had somehow memorized the foreign engraving on his necklace?

Straightening, Audra rephrased. "I really need to know what that adage means."

A question knitted his brow.

"Please," she said. "It's important."

Though hesitant, Sean nodded. He pulled out the charm from his shirt, a show of proof to eliminate speculation. *"Viel Feind, viel Ehr,"* he said, just as he had before. "A friend of mine works with a guy from Hamburg. Told me it's basically: 'The greater the risk, the greater the reward.' "

Audra realized, right then, she had no idea what she'd expected.

"The literal translation," he went on, "is a little different. From what I could gather, it means 'Many enemies, much honor.' "

Enemies.

Like Nazis in electric chairs.

"Do you mind if I ask where you got the necklace?"

"It belonged to my late grandma," he said. "My mom's mom, Vivian. I found it while going through Aunt Lu's basement. I was making room for my things to keep here during my tour. I'm pretty sure of that anyway. I have some flashes of it in my head. Other than that, all I know is I was wearing it when I woke up in the

277

hospital in Kabul."

He gave the charm a wry glance and shrugged. "I must've figured if it survived a world war in one piece, it might help me make it too. Now I just wear it, hoping it will spark more memories, I suppose."

Audra nodded along, though her mind had latched on to two words. "When you say 'world war,' I assume you're talking about . . ."

"World War Two," he said, placing the necklace back under his shirt. "It may be older though. I'm not sure."

"So, your grandma was German?"

"Not that I know of . . . but I'm guessing the man who gave it to her must have been."

"You mean, it wasn't from your grandfather?"

"Nah. It seemed like a first love kind of thing, years before they got married."

A name suddenly drummed in Audra's head. It pounded in her ears like a caller who refused to leave until someone opened the door. "Was the other guy — was he Jakob Hemel?"

Sean studied her as if deciphering where this was headed. "Don't think so."

"Are you certain?"

"It was more like . . . Isaiah. Or Isaac, I think . . . but with a k."

Relief swept through her, colliding with an illogical surge of disappointment — all of which ceased when he added, "The necklace came with a letter from him — that's how I figured it

278

was wartime. But I haven't looked at it in a while."

It was a clue. Or another element to eliminate. Either way, she needed to read what the man had written.

"Is there any chance I could see the letter?" she asked.

Sean paused, his expression clouding. He had complied long enough without knowing her purpose. Tit for tat, it was her turn to share.

A kettle whistled from the kitchen. Luanne would be joining them soon. If her views were anything like Meredith's, the whole conversation could end just as poorly. There was no time to waste.

"The thing is," Audra said, "I'm not sure you misheard my son."

At this, Sean looked dubious. But then he leaned forward, hands clasped, elbows on his legs. She had forgotten about his hearing.

She controlled her pace, despite a desire to speed through. "Everything started a month ago. See, Jack's always had a fascination with planes, so I thought he'd love riding on one for a trip to Philadelphia. But then we took off . . . ."

Sean listened intently as she stuck to the relevant highlights. He gave no impression of the need to find a straightjacket. In fact, his topaz eyes conveyed genuine interest that paved the way for her summary to flow.

Audra had just finished when Luanne entered the room with a tray of steaming mugs, cheese

279

slices, and animal crackers.

"I wasn't sure if you wanted marshmallows, dear, but I took the liberty of adding them. I hope you don't mind."

"It's perfect," Audra replied. "Thank you."

Luanne distributed the drinks and parked the tray. She eased herself onto the far end of the couch, where she took several sips. Audra blew on the surface of her cocoa, aware of Sean's distracted state.

"I'm sorry," Luanne said. "Did I interrupt something?"

"No," Sean said abruptly, as if coming to. "We were just talking about Audra's son. It's 'Jack,' isn't it?"

Audra looked at him, afraid he was about to request she repeat the whole story. "That's right. It's Jack."

"He sounds like a great kid," Sean said.

"Yeah. He's . . . amazing."

Sean gave a small, rigid shake of his head — *Don't say anything more* — and drank his hot chocolate. Grateful, Audra did the same.

"So you're married, then?" Luanne said with a tinge of disappointment.

"Actually, I'm not anymore."

"Oh, I see."

This was Audra's standard for the topic: let the answer hang there, let people assume what they'd like. Divorce was the natural assumption, given current statistics, and one that didn't create an awkward exchange, a dutiful condolence over someone they had never met.

But for some odd reason, the words spilled out of her. "My husband died two years ago."

"Ahh, yes." Luanne lowered her mug, held with both hands. "I'm sorry to hear that." There was no discomfort in her tone, no pity in her face. Just an empathy that, in an instant, explained why she lived alone. No wonder Sean had taken up residence on the farm, even temporarily, providing help as well as company.

All the same, Audra had said enough. She downed more of her drink and observed the clock. "Gosh, it's getting late. I should probably get going."

"Already?" Luanne asked.

"I'm afraid so. Jack will be home from school soon." Audra set her mug aside as Luanne nodded in understanding.

"Whereabouts do you live, dear?"

"Just down in West Linn. We're staying at the Forest Side Apartments, but only until —" Once again she was sharing too much with the woman. "Until we find something permanent," she finished while standing up. "I'm sorry I can't stay longer."

"Here, I'll walk you out," Sean said.

Luanne waggled a finger at Audra. "Be sure to grab some eggs in the barn. We only have three chickens, but those fine ladies have fully honed their craft."

Audra laughed. "I appreciate that, but I'd hate to risk missing the bus."

281

"How about a rain check?"

"I'll look forward to it."

Sean escorted Audra into the serene landscape. The donkeys were still chomping away, a goat now too, and birds trilled from the branches of an apple tree. It was refreshing to see animals so happy and healthy and out of cages.

"I can definitely understand why you're staying here," she said. "It's nice. Really nice."

"My mom doesn't agree though. Right?"

Audra shrugged, not wanting to cause problems. "I think she's just concerned about you."

"Yeah." He gazed off as they walked. "I know."

"Well, maybe . . ." She stopped herself. Why was she acting like an old family friend? And who was she, of all people, to dole out a map for the road to recovery? "Never mind," she said, and smiled as they reached the car.

"Hey, I almost forgot," Sean said. "I'd be happy to show you the letter if it'll help, and anything else I come across. Might take a couple days. I'd have to figure out which box it's in."

"That'd be wonderful. Thanks." She climbed into her seat and glanced back at the house. "Also, thank you for not saying anything to Luanne. I know how hokey it all sounds."

"No worries. It's not a time in history she likes to talk about anyway. Dredges up a lot of tough memories."

Audra should have realized the detour wasn't

only for her. The woman could have lost her husband, or any number of loved ones, during a period of such massive tragedy.

Sean went to close the car door as Audra noted her oversight. "Wait. Should I write down my phone number?"

He tightened his lips to squelch a smile, suggesting he'd already found it on his own.

At the red light two blocks from her apartment, the cell phone buzzed in her purse. Audra felt a flutter of excitement before reminding herself that he wouldn't call this soon.

As she scrounged for her phone, she thought of another person. Meredith. They hadn't spoken since the party three days ago. Audra couldn't blame her entirely for questioning Jack's bruises, his cast, his not remembering how they happened. Still, Audra looked forward to her mother-in-law's call of apology.

Those hopes fizzled from the name on the screen.

Audra answered on speakerphone. "Hi, Tess."

"Where have you been all day? I left messages on both of your phones. You *know* you're not allowed to have a social life without me."

"Sorry. I had some things to take care of." The light turned green, prompting Audra forward.

"Things, huh? That sounds cryptic." Tess barely paused before pressing, "And?"

"And . . . it was nothing. I was just out . . .

seeing this guy . . ." Audra didn't know how to continue unless she told her friend everything.

Tess gasped. "You're seeing someone?"

"What? No. That's — no."

"Oh, my word. I can't believe you've been holding out on me. Who is he?"

"Nobody."

"Nobody, my tush." The woman even cursed like a perfect mother. "Don't make me skip my appointments to go find you."

Audra tried to argue, but a laugh escaped instead. The whole idea was ridiculous. Besides, in two months, barring a horrible twist, she and Jack would be moving to Boston.

"Seriously, Tess. I'm not dating anyone."

"In that case, who is this guy you're *not* dating?" Tess clamped down like a pit bull.

Audra fended off the inquisition as she steered through the parking lot and into her spot. "I've got to meet Jack at the bus stop. I'll call you later."

In the midst of her friend's objection, Audra hung up and laughed again. She couldn't recall the last time she had enjoyed her day this much.

She hopped out and headed for the apartment. The yellow transport would be rolling up soon. She could sort through the mail, even pay bills, while she waited.

"Are you Audra Hughes?" A lean man in a navy windbreaker stepped away from her door.

"Can I help you?"

"Are you Audra Hughes?" he repeated as if

284

robotically programmed.

"Yes. Who are *you*?"

He handed her a thin packet of papers and walked away.

"Hold on a second. What is this?"

He straddled his motorcycle, threw on a helmet, and started the engine. As he zoomed away, Audra regarded the document.

IN THE CIRCUIT COURT OF THE STATE OF OREGON

"A summons?" she read.

She skimmed the pages, first not understanding, then in disbelief. Every word was a brick, every line a steel beam. Yet she continued on to the end. As comprehension bore down, her arms nearly gave out.

Meredith and Robert had filed a petition.

For sole custody of Jack.

30

Nothing about the note reflected the person Vivian had once loved. No term of affection. No resemblance in handwriting. To be certain of this, she compared the letter from Euston Station. While cursive and print structurally differed, not even the *V* in her name matched the style of Isaak's hand. Moreover, there was no logic in the secrecy.

TELL NO ONE. COME ALONE.

It could all be a cruel prank. A glass of spring water could not be clearer. Still, here she was in Prospect Park, on Binnen Bridge in the dark of night.

Bringing company would have been wise, but whom? Even if Luanne or Gene had been an option, their presence might have kept the caller away. In which case, Vivian would never know for sure. And she had to know. Simply for answers, if nothing else.

"Awfully late for a stroll, young lady." The policeman, barrelchested with a double chin, appeared by the far railing. He waved his nightstick like a reprimanding finger. "You should be at home where it's safe."

"You're absolutely right, Officer." Vivian issued her most compliant smile. "And that's exactly where I'm headed. Just as soon as my brother arrives to walk with me."

Any allusion to a romantic rendezvous, based on the policeman's presumed code of morality, could end up spurring him to lurk in the area.

"How soon you expecting him?"

"Any minute now, sir."

In an assessing manner, he looked over at the patches of forest, the boathouse down below. Light from the full moon cast shadows over his heavy-lidded eyes and broad nose. "I'm just getting off my shift," he said, "but why don't I wait till your brother gets here."

"That's so kind of you, though truly not necessary." She caught sight of the man's ring, a traditional gold wedding band. "I'm sure you're anxious to see your family after a long day. And in your line of work, your wife probably frets enough without your running late."

After a moment, his head bobbed a little in amused agreement. He twisted the nightstick in his hands as if seeking an answer by feel. "You sure you're comfortable out here?"

"Oh, certainly. I appreciate your concern, of course. As I said, he'll be here any time."

He exhaled heavily through his nose. "All right," he said. "You have any trouble, just give a yell. Another officer ought to be right in the area. Understand?"

"Yes, sir. Thank you. I will."

He nodded, then strode off into the blackness.

The rushing of a small waterfall helped to drown unwelcome sounds, the snapping of twigs and cooing calls from creatures in the trees. The air smelled of dirt, faintly of stagnant water.

She angled her watch to view its hands by the moon. It was a quarter past ten. For more than a half hour she had waited in this sprawling park, a maze of archways and tunnels, foreboding sculptures with leering eyes. She felt them closing in.

Waiting longer would be fruitless. It was a joke, or a mistake. If the person was really her Isaak, he would find her at home, reunite with her in daylight. To believe in his existence, only to be crushed by another loss, could leave her in too many pieces to recover.

Taking her cue from the officer, she surveyed the area before stepping off the bridge and continuing on to the pathway, along the curving river and dense forest. She hugged her arms against a cool breeze that rustled through the branches.

A footfall came from behind.

She spun around, went still as a park statue.

No one there. No other noise. Just the jagged cadence of her own breathing.

It was only her imagination, she contended. Yet her inner child went unconvinced, still afraid of monsters lurking in the closet. Her legs insisted she run, not to halt until secure in her room.

She turned to do just that, an overreaction or not, when something reached from the trees. A hand grasped her arm. She recalled the officer's warning and opened her mouth to yell. A hand muzzled her attempt. Her fingers flew up to pry the grip away. She sensed the body of a man behind her.

"Don't scream," said the husky voice, before he whisked her into the shadows.

31

The world went quiet, frozen on its axis.

"Mom, are you okay?"

Audra detected the faint sound of her son's voice. It echoed through the long, dark cavern of her mind, where confusion and hurt and shock had pooled.

She gripped the steering wheel like a hammer. The urge to swing grew with each passing mile.

"Mom?" Jack said from the backseat.

She supplied a reassuring answer, though the words might have been jumbled. Her brain was still whirring from the loop of accusations, the formal outline of grounds to steal Jack from her life. *Get in the car,* she'd told him the instant he stepped off the bus.

Robert and Meredith, one way or another, would reverse what they had done.

Audra parked along the curb at the base of the couple's driveway. The charming shutters and vibrant flower beds suddenly appeared a façade.

How else could she have missed this coming?

Yes, there had been ongoing tension. And yes, it had reached a new high at Jack's birthday, when Meredith made her suspicions known. But what kind of relatives file for custody without giving a hint of warning?

A guy in the next driveway sponged suds over his windshield. Across the street three women sat on a porch, all sunglasses and drinks, while children played tag on the lawn.

Audra had a sudden urge to alert them all, to expose Robert and Meredith for the people they truly were.

She told herself to calm down. No good would come from making a scene. She would be smart about this. She would reason it out once she'd thought everything through.

"It's Grandpa!" Jack said.

Down the driveway came Robert Hughes. His strides were those of a seasoned commander headed into battle.

A flood of betrayal returned; it fueled Audra's anger to a combustible level. A solitary spark and she just might explode. She needed to leave right now.

With great effort, she placed her hand on the key to restart the motor. But in a final glance over, she noticed Robert's eyes connect with Jack. A target to be captured.

Audra's restraint snapped in two. Again, she was on the Philly-bound plane, determined to protect her son. Primal instinct took over and sent her charging from her car to block Robert's path.

"Audra, listen," he said. "I know you must be upset."

"Upset? Are you kidding me?" Her voice spiked to a boom she didn't know she possessed. "Just because you want to destroy what's left of my family?"

"Hang on, now. We're not trying to destroy anything." He showed his palms, a false show of innocence. His name, too, was on that petition.

Past his shoulder, there was movement in the window. Meredith was spying from the curtains. Bold enough to hire a lawyer but too cowardly to face the accused.

"How long have you been planning this, Meredith?" She aimed her fury toward the house. "How long?"

"That's enough," Robert said, low but gruff. He motioned discreetly to the car.

Jack. Jack was watching. Fear and bewilderment contorted his small features.

The heat in Audra's veins dropped ten degrees, cooled by a shot of remorse.

What was she thinking? How could she have brought him here?

Sounds of splashes pulled her gaze. The man washing his car held the nozzle of a hose, his attention locked on the drama. Water missed its mark and streamed toward the gutter. The mothers and children had also stopped for the show.

"We just want to work out what's best for Jack," Robert said to her. "Please know, that's our only intention."

Audra didn't reply. She couldn't without saying something she might regret. She rounded the car in a composed manner and lowered into her seat. Her hand quaked as she drove away. She focused on the road, striving to keep Jack safe, a priority she had just trampled.

Paused at a stop sign, she dared to look over her shoulder. Jack firmly rubbed at his plane, a distant haze in his eyes.

"Jack, I am so, so sorry. I shouldn't have lost my temper." At the break in her voice, the rising of tears, she turned back around. Her first goal was to get them home, her second to fix this mess.

In the entry of their apartment, she apologized again. She gave him a hug, which he didn't return — not that she blamed him. "Baby, why don't you go run a bath? Let me know when it's ready and I'll put a bag over the cast. Then we'll have some dinner. Okay?"

He nodded, shoulders toward his ears, and treaded away.

The apartment never felt so small.

Audra geared up before retrieving the phone. In the privacy of her room, she called the last person she could count on.

"Tess, it's me."

"Hey. I hope you're calling to fess up. Because you are so not off the hook."

Audra cut straight to it. "I need to know — could your husband take on a new case?"

Tess went quiet, changing gears. "I'd have to ask him. Why? Who's it for?"

Her answer stalled, hindered by the memory of Devon's old saying: *nuttin' but a scratch.* The problem was never bad until you acknowledged it aloud. But this was more than a scratch; it was a gash through the heart by people she loved. Family she trusted.

"Audra?"

"It's for me," she managed to say. "I need a lawyer, in order to keep Jack."

32

Arms pinned to her sides, Vivian shuddered from a cold rush of helplessness. The man behind her tightened his hold, one hand on her mouth, the other around her chest. Trees surrounded her like bars of a prison.

Again, he sent hushed words into her ear, but she deciphered none of them. Her internal screams wailed too loudly as she struggled to break free. Not a single soul knew where she had gone. The note from the café, stored in her jewelry box, would not be found in time.

The horror of it all slowed the scene to a crawl. Her thoughts stretched out, long and thin, the strands of an endless web.

She had become the missing little girl, the one from the paper, leaving loved ones to grieve with few clues and no answers. She saw her own mother weeping, her father distraught. This would be the tragedy to revive the couple's bond, or sever it forever. She pictured Luanne and Gene, dazed by a swarm: officers and detectives, rookie reporters. In the midst of world war, the abduction of a diplomat's daughter would barely make a headline.

Could it be for a ransom? How long had the man followed her?

How did he know of Isaak? The thought of exploiting that memory, the malice of such bait, altered Vivian's fear. It boiled and mounted into an eruption of anger, doubling her will to escape.

She shoved her shoulder downward and wrestled an arm loose. With every ounce of her strength, she jabbed her elbow into his gut, causing him to moan. She pushed through his grip and started to run.

"Stop," he said.

She swerved around a tree before the roots sent her tumbling. She scrambled to rise, wanting to bellow at full volume, yet her throat, constricted by terror, blocked any rise of sound.

"Darling, please!" His tone resembled a plea. But it was the familiar rasp and endearment that forced her to glance backward.

Moonlight illuminated the man in his overcoat. He was reaching out, but not chasing. The sway of branches caused a flicker over his face. Like the flashing of a time machine, it transported Vivian across the Atlantic. Once more, in the velvety seats of the London cinema, she watched the black-

and-white images of a newsreel reflect and dance across . . .

Isaak.

This man was Isaak.

"Are you hurt?" he said.

She could only stand there. The whisper of his name swirled in her head. *Isaak.* His golden curls had been snipped away, but she recognized the deep-set eyes, the dimple of his chin. The handsome lips that so often — more in her dreams, regrettably, than in life — had laid trails over her skin.

"I didn't mean to frighten you." He approached with tentative steps. "I'd have met you on the bridge, but the policeman was circling around."

His accent was stronger than she remembered. She could be dreaming, hallucinating, encountering a ghost.

Guided by hope, she hazarded to touch his sleeve. She rubbed it between her fingers and confirmed the reality of fabric. The reality of his existence.

"It's you —" She covered her mouth, withholding a sob that sprang from a buried well.

His lips slanted into a smile. It was the very one she had feared she was doomed to forget. He wiped a tear from her face and clasped her fingers tight. His hands were warm and smooth, like mittens lined with silk.

"My God, how I've missed you," he said. Emotion burned in his gaze.

Whether by his effort or hers she could not say, but suddenly she was in his arms. The thumping of her heart formed a drumbeat against his chest.

"Vivian, Vivian," he said over and over, as if to hypnotize her with the word. His mouth brushed her cheek. Her neck tingled from the heat of his breath. Could this really be happening?

She closed her eyes, savoring the feel, the scent of him. She inhaled the sweetness of tobacco and sage, or was it the forest? No. There was no forest, no passage of time. They were back in a dank cellar, the air electric from the gliding and joining of their bodies, and a song played out . . . .

But the song was not there; it was here. Here in the cursed present.

Isaak, too, must have heard, for he ceased any movement.

Beyond the labyrinth of trees, an unseen person whistled "Shepherd's Serenade." The second officer must have been making his rounds.

Vivian considered the traits of such a duty, the honor and righteousness. The heroism embodied by the uniform. And from the thought came the memory of another man. A fellow whose kind and caring nature had not only fractured the shell over her heart but seeped through the hardy cracks.

Although Gene had agreed to a casual

courtship, a budding of guilt opened within her.

The whistling drifted away.

She edged backward from Isaak, her loyalty torn. Her gaze slipped from his face and fixed on a discovery. In the gap of his coat was a neckerchief. She followed the sailor's tie to an insignia she recognized from newsreels and propaganda ads, an eagle perched on a wreath.

Inside the wreath was a swastika.

"What is this?"

He traced her attention. In a frantic sweep, he cinched his coat closed. Their bout of struggling had exposed his uniform. "I can explain," he said, reaching out.

Vivian instinctively stepped away. The heat of her skin had dissolved, the fluidity of her limbs gone rigid. "All this time . . . I thought . . . I thought something horrible had happened to you."

"Please. Hear me out."

"Instead, you were serving for the Germans?"

"It wasn't my choice."

Truth gathered like a cloud, threatening to empty in a downpour of stones. She revisited the option of screaming for the police.

But Isaak's eyes locked her in place. "I went to see my mother, as I told you I would. I wasn't there more than an hour before the Gestapo pounded on the door. They took me in for questioning."

From the angle of his face, the moon highlighted a line on his cheekbone, a scar Vivian hadn't noticed until then. The inch-long mark bespoke an interrogation that had entailed more than words.

"What did they want from you?"

He was about to reply yet stopped. Without more, her imagination would supply the worst.

"Isaak. I deserve to hear it."

He took a breath. "They wanted details . . . about us."

"Us?"

"Our relationship. More than that, any political information you'd given me."

Vivian recalled the old basement, the tidbits that had floated through the vent and onto a platter she so eagerly delivered.

"What did you say?"

"I told them I knew nothing. I said that you had no interest in politics. That we never discussed your father's dealings. But they didn't believe me." He shook his head, his jaw muscle flexing. "I thought they were going to kill me, Vivian. I was lying there on the floor, murmuring prayers in my head. Then another man came in, a senior lieutenant — though at the time I could barely make out his boots. My eyes were swollen shut. But I knew his voice."

The memory of the scene played across

Isaak's face. For a fraction of a moment, he was back in that room.

"And you knew him — how?" Vivian said, and he again met her eyes.

"It was Professor Klein."

Despite the reeling in her head, she visualized the man's features. The chiseled lines and beardless face, the thick eyebrows and jet-black hair. At last, the incongruence became clear; he was more suited to a Nazi uniform than a teacher's garb.

"You'd told him about me," she realized. "That's how they knew."

"When I first mentioned our dating, he discouraged it. I didn't know he was trying to protect me. Maybe both of us. He just said that any distraction from my studies could jeopardize my funding. That Mr. Mueller wouldn't approve of wasting his money. But I couldn't stay away from you. As much as I tried, I couldn't."

"So you kept us a secret."

He affirmed this with a solid nod. "Then you came to the campus looking for me, and it became obvious to him that I hadn't heeded the advice. In some ways, putting the truth out there was a relief. I knew he had family in Germany, so I told him of the news you'd shared. He and my father had been friends since childhood. For years, with my father gone, he looked out for me like a son. But I had no idea he was a retired officer."

The full picture was taking shape, including the real reason she couldn't reach the professor by phone. He hadn't evacuated for the purpose of safety; he had been called back into service by Hitler.

"At first, he was compelled by his duty," Isaak went on. "But he assured me, he never meant for me to be harmed. I truly believe, darling, if he hadn't come in and stopped them, I wouldn't have lived through that day."

The gratitude in his voice encircled her like a net. She felt herself drawn in until skepticism pushed back.

Something didn't fit. The equation was off-balance.

"You're saying they arrested you. Used brutal force for a confession that you wouldn't make. And yet, they trusted you enough to let you join their military?"

"I know how it sounds. I swear, it was all the professor's doing. He convinced an old comrade, an officer in the SS, that the report about me was mistaken. He told him my loyalty remained with the Fatherland. The home of my parents. In the end, they decided that my English skills, and my ability to blend in here, could make me a strong asset for a special assignment."

"But if you wanted to blend," she pointed out, "you wouldn't be wearing a German uniform."

He regarded his collar and agreed. "I was

302

instructed to wear this only until I made it ashore, so if I were caught I'd be treated as a POW. I was then to bury it and change into civilian clothes. But in doing so, I'd be labeled a spy."

"And that isn't what you are?"

"I was sent here as a scout." He said this firmly, desperately, as if trying to convince himself there was a difference. "I'm only to confirm data and contacts before meeting at a rendezvous point."

Part of her insisted that the less she knew the better. But after years of unanswered questions, she could not rest without the full story.

"Who is it you're meant to meet there?"

He glanced around in a precautionary manner. Evidently what he was about to reveal was more incriminating than all that preceded it.

"A week from now, or shortly after, eight agents will be delivered by U-boat, just as I was. Half at Long Island, the rest in Florida. They were trained at the German High Command for Operation Pastorius. For two years, they're to sabotage waterways and canals, magnesium and aluminum plants. Anything to delay war production, but also to demoralize citizens. They'll target train stations and Niagara Falls. And department stores too — though just the ones owned by Jews."

Her thoughts stumbled, attempting to keep

303

up. "Why?" she breathed.

"They want German Americans to be blamed. The Führer is convinced Roosevelt will turn on them, just like he did to the Japanese here in the States. Then those with German blood will retaliate, bringing more power to the Reich."

The magnitude of the mission far surpassed Vivian's comprehension. The details soaked into her with the power of acid. She strained to salvage a shred of reasoning.

A week, he had said. They still had a week.

"It's not too late," she assured him, and herself. "You have plenty of time to let authorities know what's coming."

"And I plan to," he said, yet a stipulation resounded in his tone.

"However . . . ?"

He moved a step closer. "First, I have to know my family is out of Germany. They need papers — exit visas, new identities — so they can cross the Swiss border. Which is why," he added slowly, "I need your help, darling."

"My help?"

"Through your father. With all of his connections, surely he can arrange this. There are only five of them. I brought a list of their names for you."

As he delved into his pockets, Vivian mentally grasped his request. What followed was the impossibility of fulfilling it.

"He can't," she said. "That is — my father isn't here."

Isaak looked up, the folded paper in his hand. "Where, then? At the Capitol? Wherever he is, we could —"

"Isaak," she said, "he never left London."

The lines on his brow deepened. "I thought that by now, your father would have come . . ."

She shook her head.

Another ill twist of fate had befallen them. Isaak rubbed at his hair — his buzzed, military cut — as if to stimulate new ideas. "There has to be a way. I can't turn myself in until they're safe. I simply can't."

The repercussions were woven into his voice, his eyes: As relatives of a traitor, his family would never be granted the luxury of a formal interrogation. One knock at the door and they would vanish into dust.

"I'll find someone," she heard herself say.

He gawked at her, a series of wordless questions.

Her mind scraped for the answers. "Who knows, maybe my father can still help. He also has colleagues in DC, men I've known through the years." Whether she could trust anyone in regard to Isaak, she would determine as she went. "I'll just . . . tell them I'm friends with your family. Nothing about you for now. And that they're in imminent danger and have to be saved."

305

Isaak paused before nodding. Through a layer of dimming hope was the need to believe. All of his faith, the fate of his family, he would place with her.

He spoke softly as he came closer. "I despise dragging you into this. My God, I never should have left your side, darling. Never."

When he lifted his hand to touch her cheek, it took all of her will to stop him. Innocent lives were at stake, both on the home front and abroad. For now, these would take priority over the sorting of her heart, and her feelings for Isaak Hemel.

■ ■ ■ ■

PART THREE

■ ■ ■ ■

Here, where the world is quiet;
Here, where all trouble seems
Dead winds' and spent waves' riot
In doubtful dreams of dreams
          — from "The Garden of Proserpine"
                by Algernon Charles Swinburne

33

Early June 2012
Portland, OR
The water feature in the corner, a huge sheet of glass atop smooth white stones, was surely meant to relax clients but only added to Audra's frustration. She needed to be sharp and clearheaded, and the sounds of a gentle brook were causing her eyelids to droop. Though she was growing accustomed to fractured nights of sleep, the court summons from yesterday had left her tossing and turning until morning. Now, during waking hours, her body wanted to doze.

Go figure.

She kept herself awake by picking at a thread on the black leather couch. With checkered pillows and an amoeba-shaped table, the waiting area looked more like an LA nightclub than a legal firm in Portland.

At the reception desk, a twenty-something gal with large hoop earrings answered the phone with a long string of surnames. She was transferring the call when Russ Graniello appeared in a charcoal-gray suit. He wore his black hair neatly slicked to frame his olive complexion.

"Good morning," he said to Audra. "Sorry to have kept you waiting."

"Oh, gosh, not at all. I appreciate you squeezing me in so fast." She grabbed her purse and stood, expecting a friendly hug. It had become their usual greeting after sharing potlucks and birthdays and more than one off-key duet of "Islands in the Stream."

Instead, he offered a handshake.

"Come this way." He guided her down the hall and into his office.

The room was smaller than she had imagined for a nice-sized firm. Aside from a few file folders and a single lawbook, his desk appeared too tidy for an attorney. Not one who rolled up his sleeves, anyway, and dug deep into his cases.

"Please, have a seat," he said, and lowered himself into his tufted rolling chair. As he flipped through a folder, Audra sat down, now fully alert.

From conferences with the school principal to sessions with Dr. Shaw, these scrutinizing reviews had become regrettably familiar.

Russ began to pen notes on the documents she had faxed over the night before.

On the lateral file cabinet by the window was a framed photo of his family, exuding love and smiles. A stark reminder of what Audra stood to lose. She had dressed in tan slacks and an emerald V-neck, wanting to look nice for this meeting, but wondered if a suit would have been wiser.

"So, it appears," he said, "that your in-laws' primary grounds for seeking custody are based on suspicions of abuse."

She would have presumed his inflection on *abuse* would communicate even a hint of incredulity. Yet from his tone, he could have substituted a thousand trivial words — *stone, bowl, log* — and they would have conveyed equal emotion.

"I love my son more than anything. I'd never in a million years try to hurt him."

"Of course," Russ said assuredly, but proceeded in work mode. "Now — just so I understand the whole situation — have Robert and Meredith ever addressed their concerns with you?"

"No," she insisted. "They never said anything about filing a petition. Ever."

"Sure, that's not surprising. But what about the issues they've outlined? Jack's injuries, his reclusive nature, and so forth."

"Well . . . I suppose some of it. They brought up the bruises on his wrists once. But I told Meredith, those were from Jack's struggle on the airplane." Audra wasn't sure how much Russ knew about the flight. "You see, he panicked a bit during takeoff . . . but I thought he'd enjoy flying, because he's always loved planes —"

Russ gently interjected, "It's okay. You don't

311

have to explain. I'm aware of the incident."

Audra sat back and nodded.

"What about your son's birthday barbecue? Did they ever ask you about the bruises they noticed at that point?"

Audra recalled the distinct change in mood, after she'd returned from her car with Jack's gifts. She had assumed Devon's absence was the cause, unaware — until the petition — that Jack's sleeves had slid up just enough to expose his marks.

"Meredith did say something while we were doing the dishes. She made a comment about it looking like Jack was still having nightmares. But that's it." Once more, Audra wasn't clear how informed Russ was on the topic. "Tess might have told you, but Jack suffers from night terrors. They can be extremely violent. *That's* the reason his room was in shambles when Meredith saw it." Contrary to the woman's allegation. "Sometimes I even have to hold him down to keep him from hurting himself."

"Like the fracture to his arm?"

"Yes. Like his arm."

This seemed sufficient enough to move on from the cast issue. But then Russ asked, "Do you know why your in-laws think alcohol was involved?"

Alcohol. The merlot she had spilled before taking Jack to the ER.

"I'd fallen asleep on the couch, holding a glass of wine. I was still wearing the stained shirt the

312

next morning when they saw me. I hadn't even taken a sip of it."

"So, you didn't pass out from inebriation."

"God, no," she said. "I don't drink."

Of course, if taken literally, the statement would be viewed as false; over the years, Russ himself had seen her enjoy margaritas and martinis firsthand. "What I meant was, I don't have a drinking problem."

Fabulous. Now she sounded like an alcoholic in denial. She tried again.

"Jack and I had been in the ER through most of the night. Otherwise, I would've been showered and dressed long before Meredith and Robert showed up."

Russ nodded while writing down more. "This was on Memorial Day weekend, correct?"

At last, a simple objective question. "Yes."

He proceeded to locate the pertinent section. "It says here you tried to cancel their pre-planned outing with Jack, just before they discovered he'd wet the bed. Is any of that right?"

In her short time with the petition, she had already memorized each claim. As indications of abuse, Robert and Meredith had cited age-inappropriate urination, his sudden interest in violence, and the physical outburst at school. Supposedly, at the Rose Festival, his running away from Audra was another telling sign. Either that or a direct result of her dictatorship. Not only had she banned her son from "normal

313

and healthy" children's activities, she'd robbed him of any positive spiritual influence and made a concerted effort to erase Devon from his memory.

Was it any wonder that reading this heinous list had caused Audra to drive straight to their house to confront them in person?

Unlike then, however, she would now control her tone. "Jack just drank too much juice in the ER. Before then, he hadn't had an accident since he was little. As far as me almost canceling on them, I was worried Jack would be too tired after such a long night. I was actually *trying* to be a good mother."

She wanted Russ to chime in, to contend that any judge would agree she was exactly that. But he merely nodded while taking more notes.

"I also see here," he said, "that your in-laws feel you've been attempting to distance them from Jack. Not just with phone calls and visits, but also moving cross-country."

The accusation was almost as appalling as the other ones!

"Our move has *nothing* to do with them." Her brusqueness raised Russ's head. She returned to calm reasoning. "Since Devon's death, Jack and I have been through a lot. We just need to start a new life somewhere else — for us."

No question, she had made mistakes. But when it came to this case, there was only one crime to which Audra would admit her guilt: confiding too much in a couple she believed she could trust.

"I'd like to add, the only reason I ever told Meredith so much is because I was trying to keep her in, not out, of Jack's life. I actually wanted her advice about his nightmares and his interest in . . . military . . . things."

Russ suddenly turned to the next page. "I assume you're referring to the reincarnation issue? Your theory that in another life Jack died in a World War Two accident."

"Yes — no. It wasn't *my* theory. It was just *a* theory."

She cringed as the words tumbled out. Were these seriously the best arguments she could formulate? Keep this up and a custody battle would lead to a commitment hearing.

"Please, Russ, believe me. I am not delusional."

He responded with an unreadable smile. After all, crazy people never accepted they were crazy. A second case of denial.

Audra unclenched her hands and folded them in her lap, an attempt to resemble the rational client who would accompany him into court.

If he took the case.

After a quiet beat, Russ set down his pen and steepled his fingers. His voice reclaimed a touch of the warmth she recognized. "Rest assured, Audra — regardless of these claims — taking a child away from his or her biological mother is exceptionally difficult in Oregon. You don't have to be a good mother to keep your son, just not a blatantly abusive one. Frankly, a crack whore can maintain custody, so long as she doesn't shoot up in front of her kids at the breakfast table."

The example, lumping her in with an addicted prostitute, didn't exactly boost Audra's confidence.

"What's more," he added, "grandparents in particular are hardly ever awarded custody."

"You're saying it does happen though." An important point to clarify.

"On occasion," he admitted, "yes. But it's remarkably rare."

Rare. The adjective grated her nerves raw. She had grown well acquainted with the word even before losing Devon. She'd often used it herself when informing clients of the unlikelihood that the worst would befall their pet — only to later diagnose a fatal infection, second tumor, or failing organ that couldn't be saved.

Rare, for Audra, couldn't hold a thimble of water.

"So, how long do cases like this usually take?" she asked, turning to the pragmatic.

"That depends. A few months after the initial filing, the courts frequently start with what they call a 'housekeeping' hearing."

"And what is that?"

"That's where the judge tries to get a gist of how long the evidentiary hearing will last. It's also a chance to sway both parties toward a settlement. This is assuming the petitioners are serious enough to pursue the case even that far."

That much, if nothing else, was abundantly clear. "What happens in the meantime?"

"There could be depositions scheduled. And your in-laws will probably request an evaluation of you and Jack. This would be on their own dime unless you wanted the court to appoint a psychologist, which I'd personally recommend; it could mean you'd have to split the costs, but I wouldn't be surprised if the judge made the petitioners fully responsible."

Evaluations. Depositions. The details swam in Audra's head and delivered her back to her earlier question. "About how long could all of this take?"

"The standard," he said, "is twelve months."

She gaped, hoping she had misheard. "A whole year?"

"That said, given your circumstances, I would say nine months isn't at all out of the question." He stated this as though he'd delivered a platter full of relief, rather than a bin of burning dollars.

Assuming he was right about her chances of maintaining custody, that still meant a large depletion of her savings. Those funds were for her and Jack to start fresh in —

Oh, no. Boston. It hadn't dawned on her before.

"I've accepted a new job on the East Coast. We're supposed to move before August."

317

"I'd heard that was the plan," he said, "and it might work out just fine. But if the case does move forward, I'm afraid you won't be permitted to relocate until it's over."

Just like that, the gate leading to Audra and Jack's future had been slammed shut. She squeezed her eyes and rubbed her temples, wishing away the entrapment.

"You know, Audra," Russ said with a sigh, "although you might not be up for this at the moment, there *is* another option you should consider."

With barely the energy, she lowered her hand and inclined her head.

"You could talk to your in-laws. Come to an understanding without a judge involved. Often-times, open and direct communication can make legal action unnecessary. Perhaps, on some issues, you could even reach a suitable compromise."

The solution sounded so easy. A key to the gate, dangling within reach. She could picture herself grasping it.

But then a memory surfaced from Jack's preschool days. A larger boy, to pillage a scooter in the playroom, had given Jack a hefty shove. Jack pushed back in defense. When Devon learned both kids were made to apologize, he delivered a staunch objection to the school director. Defending oneself didn't warrant a "sorry." Or an appeasing compromise.

The same principle applied here — even to

Devon's parents.

"I'll talk to them," Audra said, "when we go to court."

34

June 1942
Brooklyn, NY

At Ebbets Field, on a deceivingly pleasant Sunday, Vivian avoided conversation by looking engrossed in the game. The Yankees, in the first half of a doubleheader, had lost by a run to the Cleveland Indians and were charging back with a vengeance. She cheered and clapped on cue, all the while averting her attention from Gene.

Postponing the date had appealed to her for many a reason, but canceling at the last minute could have raised suspicion. She wanted desperately to come clean, to ask for advice. From his experience in Intelligence he could offer ideas and insight. But given her history with Isaak, asking Gene to help him seemed wrong. More than that, it would put Gene in direct conflict with his duties as an officer.

And so, all weekend she had barely slept, scarcely ate, as she racked her brain for alternatives. She had quickly ruled out her father; even if he were receptive to her plight, communicating by telegram or phone would be unwise. A letter, too, risked interception and could take months for delivery. The same obstacles prohibited her outreach to politicians; any she adequately trusted had been transferred due to war demands.

Starting tomorrow, Vivian's eavesdropping on the switchboard would serve a new and urgent purpose: to find sympathetic contacts, preferably in the upper echelons, while sifting for any hint that Isaak's mission had been detected.

No progress. Still trying.

This was the update she had penned the previous day, without mention of names, and left for Isaak in the café courtyard. The underside of the flowerpot had become their nightly mailbox.

He would not say where he was staying, on what means he was living, which activities filled his hours. Though he withheld these details to protect her, such maddening unknowns nibbled at her like moths upon wool.

"Vivian." Gene's voice snapped her to the present. He seemed to be repeating himself.

"Yes?"

"Game's over."

It took her a moment to decipher the meaning as literal.

Tiles on the scoreboard affirmed she had

missed the Indians' efforts, pummeled by the pinstripes thirteen to one. All around, the crowd was rising, shuffling up the stairs and out of the stadium, as if rushing to evacuate before an explosion.

"Sorry," she said lightly. She went to stand, but his hand stopped her.

"I'd like us to talk first."

Despite the gravity of his tone, she retained her smile. "Sure," she said.

"Vivian, I know there's something you're not telling me."

Her body stiffened in the seat. Had she been as transparent as she felt?

With the confrontation upon her, while undoubtedly inevitable, she had no inkling where to begin.

"It's your father, isn't it?" he said. "You're worried about him. That's why you've been so distant."

The excuse hung between them, inviting her to latch on. Concern for her father did, in fact, line the edges of her thoughts. And yet she could not bring herself to agree.

"I just . . . have a lot on my mind, is all."

"You can say anything to me, doll. You know that." He spoke in such earnest, beckoning her like a winter quilt ready to wrap her in its fibers.

Ironically, it was this warmth that increased her reluctance to tell the truth. Trapping him in this awful predicament would be unfair.

Nevertheless, she could not ignore the need for help. With so much at stake, she had to try.

"I've been worried for my father too, but, you see . . ." Any spectators were far out of earshot. "I have friends I made back in London, when I was traveling around. We struck up a correspondence. It's a family that lives in Germany — not Nazis, mind you. As you can imagine, I've grown terribly nervous about their safety."

He shifted in his seat, though his expression didn't alter. At the absence of dismay, Vivian continued.

"It's crucial they leave right away. They're hoping to make it to Switzerland, but as you know, they'll need special papers to go that far. I've been trying to figure out a way. There simply has to be something I can do."

"How many are in the family?" he asked.

"Five. There's a woman and a couple and their daughters. They're extremely lovely people, just stuck on the wrong side of the border. They have no desire to be there any more than you or I would."

Vivian stopped there, careful not to say too much or to push too hard. Gene gazed out at the field and nodded to the rhythm of his thoughts. A good sign.

But then the motion morphed into a shake of his head. As if to himself, he said, "I don't know that anything can be done for them."

Her stomach sank, although it shouldn't have. He was only affirming what she already knew.

"All the same," he added, "I'd be happy to find out. Give me a day or two to snoop around. See what I can come up with."

She brightened inside, a kindling of possibility. "Oh, Gene. You'd do that for me?"

"Of course," he said, and drew her hand to his lips. "Why wouldn't I?"

Enduring a pinch of guilt, she smiled without a reply.

The next day, as Vivian connected one call after another, she did her darnedest to keep her hopes in check. Gene could certainly come back empty-handed. As for her father's colleagues, her dismal streak had not improved. If she arrived at no other solution, Isaak could be sacrificing his family in order to surrender.

He would do that, wouldn't he? Surrender regardless if necessary? *I can't turn myself in until they're safe,* he had said. But it was an emotional statement, not a resolute vow. Going through with the mission would be incomprehensible . . . .

The blinking of her switchboard diverted her from doubt.

"Number, please," she answered. The gentleman sounded official as he asked for a colonel's line. "Thank you, sir." She plugged in the corresponding cord, rang the officer, and connected the call. But before disconnecting herself, she noted Mrs. Langtree lost in her thoughts, the other operators preoccupied.

Vivian let the curtain of her hair fall forward. Hiding her hand, she covered the mouthpiece to mute sounds of the room. She listened carefully as the men traded greetings and celebratory remarks over the victory in Midway. The naval battle was sure to be a turning point, all the newspapers had raved. These men, too, concurred on this, then proceeded to chat at length about a recent night of . . . poker.

The freedom of major nations hung in the balance and these Army "brass" were reminiscing over a queen-high flush.

A flick to her ankle gave her a start, a warning from Luanne.

Vivian switched the toggle. She rushed to the next call as shoes clacked in her direction. Mrs. Langtree moved closer, ever closer, but continued on to the last operator. A new girl sought assistance with a long-distance charge, wanting to confirm she had drafted it properly.

Vivian expelled a quiet breath. The engraving from Isaak's necklace reinforced her motivation: *The greater the risk, the greater the reward.*

Mrs. Langtree was still handling the bill

when an Army officer summoned her to the door. "Might I have a word with you, ma'am?"

Muscles in the woman's neck visibly tightened, an aftereffect of a request all too similar, much too recent. She nodded and left the room.

"What the devil are you doing?" Luanne whispered to Vivian, less a question than a charge of foolishness.

"Just getting an inside scoop," she whispered back.

Luanne rolled her eyes, though the edges of her lips lifted. It was the second time this morning she had saved Vivian from being caught. "You'd make a terrible spy, you know."

Vivian did not disagree.

Granted, usually she would wait until Mrs. Langtree set off for the ladies' room before listening in on a line. But today was different. In a matter of hours Vivian would be meeting Isaak. How direly she wanted to present a significant find in person. As usual, however, she needed a higher security clearance for anything of great value. She had plenty of knowledge about troops and training, weapons and bases, even tanks, planes, and ships — yet none of this would do him much good.

She glanced at her wrist, forgetting she had left her watch at home. She swiveled toward the wall clock posted by the exit and halted at the sight. Framed by the door's window, a stern-faced officer stared directly at Vivian.

Or did it just appear that way?

Mrs. Langtree said something to the man, then pointed in Vivian's direction.

Vivian whirled back to the switchboard, her pulse in an instant gallop. Her hands shook as she struggled to connect a call. She felt the officer's gaze on the back of her head. It burned through her hair and seared her skull.

"Miss James?" Mrs. Langtree was now in the room.

Vivian turned her body halfway and found no clue in the woman's eyes. "Yes, ma'am?"

"The major needs to speak with you," she replied. "In private."

35

There was nothing surprising about the statement, only the way it suddenly applied to Audra's life.

Energy is neither lost nor gained, only transferred.

It was a fundamental law of physics — more scientific than spiritual. Maybe that's why her mind kept revisiting the quote since the day she finished the book. And to think, when Dr. Shaw had forced the thing into her hands, she had no intention of even cracking the cover. Now select passages were imprinting themselves on her brain like galactic secrets on an ancient scroll.

In Jack's bedroom, she placed his laundered shirts in a drawer. When she pushed it closed, she imagined storing her mystical theories inside. There would be ample opportunity to obsess over them at the next session with Dr. Shaw, after his return from a conference in Vegas.

Audra smiled at the vision: hundreds of suited shrinks parked around poker tables, analyzing each other for tells.

She just wished their festivities hadn't been planned for this particular week. The result was six days of waiting until Jack's next appointment, a delay intensified by today's meeting with Russ. For that's when she had learned of the race they were in: a sprint to uncover the source of Jack's behavior before a judge and evaluator presented speculations of their own.

She closed the curtains over the darkened windows, just as Jack appeared in his pajamas.

"Hey, buddy. You finish your routine?"

"Yep," he said softly, and climbed into bed.

"Brush, floss, and flush?"

He nodded. He had covered it all.

"You sure? Because if you did happen to skip the toilet flushing, I'll have to sentence you to . . ." She twisted her lips, deciding. "Five full minutes of severe and merciless tickling."

He smiled widely, as if recalling the tickle attacks he used to love. He'd giggle and wiggle even before being touched, just from clawed fingers near his sides, toes, or tummy.

But the memory didn't last. His expression retracted and lips went level. All throughout dinner he appeared to be wrestling with a thought, yet each of her inquiries had met a dead end.

"Remember," she said again, "I'm here if you want to talk. Okay?"

He scratched the skin at the edge of his cast and simply said, "I know."

When it came to Jack, she was becoming one

of those old Chatty Cathy dolls that spewed the same few sentences over and over.

With an internal sigh, she pulled up the covers, leaving the sheet loose enough for his feet to burrow free. He used to sleep cocoon-style, blankets drawn snugly under his chin. These days he required more space, as though ensuring the option to escape.

"Just one more day till the weekend," she reminded him.

"Yep."

"You know, on Saturday, Tess and Grace wanted to join us for a picnic. How's that sound?"

"Good," he said, but nothing else.

Audra nodded. "Good." She smiled and kissed his forehead. "Sleep well," she told him, consciously opting against bidding, *Sweet dreams.* It would be enough to see him rest through the night without an episode of terror. After three straight weeks, one could only hope.

She clicked off the nightstand lamp. The hall's gentle beam cast shadows over Jack's face, giving a glimpse of his future stages. Junior high. High school. College.

Life was suddenly moving too fast.

Needing to slow it down, she sat on the side of his bed. She stroked the fine strands of his hair, and an ache throbbed beneath her ribs. It was the area where loss tended to settle. Saying good-bye ten years from now would be difficult enough; she couldn't fathom the day coming sooner.

At this very minute, a private investigator could be hunched over a computer, gathering any dirt possible to strengthen the case against her. He wouldn't have to dig far. Laws in Oregon might traditionally favor the mother; but what about one with no current income? Depending on the court date, her offer in Boston could easily vanish. As for her last job, the timing of her resignation, within days of being put on leave, looked like she'd been allowed to save face while actually being fired.

It wouldn't be tough to believe. After all, she was the woman who had gone on a rant before an entire neighborhood. A woman who rarely heard from her own parents. A woman who, in the beginning, never wanted to be a mother. Yet now, faced with a chance of losing that privilege, she could think of nothing she wanted more.

"Mom? What's wrong?" Jack's groggy question alerted her of the tears slipping down her cheeks.

She wiped them away and smiled. "Nothing, baby. I'm just tired. Just very, very tired."

Between his heavy blinks, he peered at her with eyes of a bottomless depth. *Old-soul eyes.* That's what a nurse in the maternity ward had called them. Even as a baby, Jack had scarcely cried. He was too busy gazing around in a serene yet eager way, as if reacquainting himself with his surroundings.

331

She had forgotten about that. The recollection had been buried in the shuffle of life's more pressing issues, none of which mattered now.

"Is it because you're sad," he said after a pause, "from your fight with Grandma and Grandpa?"

Oh, boy.

She had brought this on herself, of course. Confronting Robert while Jack sat there in the car was a reactionary mistake with a long ripple of consequences.

"I guess we're all kind of sad about that," she admitted. "But we're trying to work it out."

"It's about the BB gun, isn't it? 'Cause if it is, I really don't need one."

Why hadn't she connected that before? She should have, in order to prevent Jack from feeling responsible. "The BB gun has nothing to do with it. And you've done nothing wrong. I promise."

Relief passed over his face, but just a thin shade. "You . . . still love each other, don't you?"

Although odds of reconciling had become immeasurably remote, she was mindful in choosing her words.

"Sometimes grown-ups have disagreements, just like kids do. In our hearts, we still care about each other. The most important thing is, we all love *you* very much." She touched his round nose with her finger. "Okeydokey?"

He smiled halfway and nodded.

"Good. Now, close your eyes and get some rest."

She stroked his head again until he drifted into a peaceful sleep. As his breathing rose and fell, ebbing him further from wakefulness, she caught the gaze of a man. Captain America stared from the *Avengers* poster across the room. The same character was plastered across Jack's latest backpack.

A hero, she realized, of World War Two.

Her attention moved to the model planes in the corner. She'd always attributed Jack's fascination with bombers and other aircraft to his stuffed 747, a favorite gift from his third birthday. But what if it was the other way around? Maybe the plush toy had become his favorite because of interest that already existed.

A mumbled phrase drifted from Jack's mouth. Nothing she could make out. Typically she would let him be, but now she couldn't afford to ignore it.

She spoke just above a whisper. "What'd you say, Jack?"

"Yeah, yeah . . . ," he said, resembling a three-beer slur, like the day he'd ingested laughing gas before having a cavity filled. On the car ride home, he had rambled on and on, sharing every thought that entered his head.

Perhaps once more she could benefit from his narrow interim of consciousness.

She leaned closer to his ear. Against her dwindling skepticism, she pushed out the name

333

that consistently eased his nightmares: "Jakob."

Not seeing a reaction, she tried again, more pronounced. "Jakob Hemel."

Jack didn't answer, but his breath hitched.

"Buddy, is that who your dreams are about?"

A hum indicated agreement and sent Audra's mind spinning.

Vivian's necklace. Isaak's letter. Was it possible Jakob and Isaak knew each other? Served as pilots in the war?

She tempered her volume, so as not to wake him. "Jack," she said, "do you know who Isaak is?"

He shifted onto his side, angling his face away. But she couldn't let up. She sensed a window open between them. She would have to hurry before it closed.

"Could you tell me why he —" Not *he.* To make progress, she would have to buy in fully. As Dr. Shaw had told her, what she believed didn't matter right now, only what Jack did. "Why are *you* here? Is there a reason you've come back?"

At that, he resumed his mumbling.

She held her ponytail aside and hovered her ear over his mouth. The response came in jagged pieces: "So . . . finally . . . she can . . . be with him . . . ."

When he trailed off, Audra pressed, "Who is *she*?"

No reply.

"Jakob? Please, tell me who 'she' is."

334

A long exhale confirmed his deepened level of sleep, leaving Audra to review her approach.

This was ludicrous. She was speaking to him like a psychiatrist treating a patient with split personalities. She needed air, needed to ground herself in reality.

Quietly she retreated to the kitchen and opened the window over the sink. She inhaled crisp breaths through the screen, wishing the netting could filter her thoughts.

None of this could be real. If it was, it meant an afterlife existed. That a higher power, too, could exist. That something touted as good and holy stole lives on a whim, inflicting pain on those left behind. And for what purpose? There wasn't one — which was why Audra had taken the reins of their lives into her own hands.

How quickly those reins were slipping from her grasp.

"No!" Jack bellowed from his room. "Let me out!"

He was peaceful only minutes ago. Rarely did he start so early.

Audra raced to his bed to find him wildly flailing. She called him Jakob several times, but he just screamed with renewed intensity. She clasped his upper arms, taking care not to press too hard. Repeatedly he broke free.

Which would be worse? Incriminating bruises or another trip to the ER — where, incidentally, a nurse might recall their previous visit, wine-stained shirt and all? None of these factors

335

would help keep Audra and Jack together . . . .

Wait.

That was it.

The figures in his drawing, the couple who held hands while falling toward the waves — they were never Audra and Jack. But they, too, wanted to be together.

"I'll bring them back to each other," she said over his yelling. Distantly, something about it made sense. "I don't know how, but I'll find a way."

Just like that, he went eerily silent. The fright left his eyes, his muscles gone lax. She guided him to lie down and offered the usual assurances until his eyelids lowered again. Another dream he would forget by morning.

"It's all right," she soothed, rubbing the back of his shirt. She felt both clearer and more confused about what was happening. "Everything's all right."

His pajama collar, misshapen from the struggle, exposed the birthmark on his shoulder. Or rather what remained of it. Originally bright and solid red, the hemangioma had once been a perfect strawberry. Over the years it had faded to pink, gone soft around the edges. Yet only now did Audra notice the shape.

His birthmark had become a heart.

36

Vivian sat on her bed, writing fiercely in her diary. Her heart still thudded as she described the torturous walk from her switchboard chair to the Army major. Only a march to the gallows could have felt longer. Her legs had prickled with a thousand needles as Mrs. Langtree shut the door, confining the three of them in the hall.

There was no arrest, however. No interrogation. No accusation of treason, a crime Vivian hadn't fully realized, until that second, that she was committing. Rather, due to the prestige of her father's work, backed by Mrs. Langtree's surprising endorsement, the major was offering Vivian a job. The newly formed WAAC, or Women's Army Auxiliary Corps, would soon overtake the base's switchboard, requiring a uniformed staff of operators.

Vivian's initial stammering and flushed cheeks had passed as delight. "I would love a chance to help out, of course," she'd managed to say. "But I'd need to make sure my parents are comfortable with my serving in the military."

"That's quite understandable," the major had replied.

Evidently, Vivian struck them as far from someone who, an hour from now under the dome of night, would be conspiring with a soldier of the Reich. No doubt, that's how her meeting with Isaak would be viewed. A wiser person would call it off. Yet she couldn't. She needed to see in his eyes that no matter the outcome for his family, he would still betray his mission.

Monday — same time, same place.

Decoded, her invitation specified Prospect Park at ten. Last night at the café, she had slid the message beneath the clay pot just minutes before closing. It was the soonest she could get there after returning from the ball game with Gene.

"*Chérie,* you come here again so often!" the café manager had exclaimed, spotting her in the courtyard. "You see? The fig tart, I knew it brings you back." He beamed with such culinary pride, Vivian gratefully played along.

A knock interrupted the memory. It was a rapping on glass from the curtained window.

Without seeing, she knew it was Gene. He often entered from the fire escape past curfew.

338

She suddenly recognized her awful bind.

"Criminy," she murmured. He was supposed to work late tonight. How was she to meet Isaak in an hour at Binnen Bridge?

The tapping became insistent. Fortunately, it was muted by orchestral music drifting up from the floor below.

Then it dawned on her: Perhaps Gene had come bearing news of Isaak's family. A solution could be within reach. Vivian had no choice but to answer. Besides, if she pretended to be out, she would need an explanation of where. With Luanne gone on a date, Vivian hadn't bothered to prepare an alibi.

How she despised this need for deceit.

She calmed herself before parting the curtains. As she raised the window, she caught sight of his face.

"Isaak."

"May I?" He motioned toward her room.

Utterly relieved, she scuddled out of the way. He had added a fedora to his outfit, but as he crawled inside, the same German uniform peeked from his coat.

Struck by the altered plans, she whispered, "Did you not get my note?"

"The Army is using parts of the park for training exercises." He looked outside before closing the window. "I wouldn't have come here, but I couldn't think of another way."

She had never told him where she lived . . . .

But then she recalled his specialized training, his ability to furtively track her to the café and who knew where else.

"You have news for me," he said. His voice vibrated with such hope, she regretted the ambiguity of her message.

Vivian cleared her throat, realizing they could speak at a normal level. For once, she appreciated the intrusion of the landlady's RCA. "I haven't had luck with acquaintances of my father, I'm afraid. But I do have someone else trying to help. A person in Intelligence. We should know more soon."

Disappointment set into his features. He said nothing while laying his hat on Luanne's bureau.

"I'm sorry, Isaak. I'm doing everything I can think of."

He took this in. Regrouping, he shook his head. "I've no doubt about that. Believe me, darling, I'm terribly grateful."

From a female voice in the hallway Vivian recalled the door. She hurried over and turned the lock. The measure was solely a precaution, but when she twisted to face Isaak she registered the connotation — securing them in her bedroom, alone.

"I have a Luanne," she blurted, and caught the misstatement. "I meant roommate. I have a roommate. That's why . . . the lock . . ."

He moved closer, a seductiveness in his gray-blue eyes. He was a stranger and a lover

340

all in one. She wanted to step away, but her legs defied her. Soon his fingers reached her cheek, sloping to her neck, and the proximity of his body launched a shiver down her arms. Would he always affect her in such a way?

Gene . . . she had to think of Gene. Pressure mounted as Isaak leaned toward her.

"There's another fellow," she told him. "A fellow I've been dating." She waited for Isaak to pull back. He only raised a smile.

"I know that, Vivian."

He knew?

Yes. Yes, of course he did.

"But I also know you wanted to see me as much as I did you. There's nothing you've told me tonight you couldn't have put in writing." His low rasp fogged her mind. Even if she disagreed, she had no ability to refute him. "I swear, Vivian, I'd be with you every minute if it didn't put you in danger."

She strained to collect her bearings, to address the issue at hand. "We should . . . really talk. About a plan. We need . . . a plan."

As she curbed her gaze from his lips, she noted the clothing on the vanity. A diversion. Her salvation. She forced herself to break away.

"I bought these for you." She scooped up the pile, nearly dropping the shoes. She had intended to bring it all to the park. They were plain men's garments, meant to blend: black trousers and socks, a button-down shirt and a tie. "In case you didn't keep the civilian outfit you were given. With what you have on, you're begging to be caught."

"Vivian," he said, "I told you already —"

"There's a reason you were instructed to bury your uniform. At least take these with you and consider it. Soon enough you'll be speaking to authorities and it won't matter what you're wearing. Until then, we need every day we can get." She held out the clothes. "Am I wrong?"

He looked at the stack, and slowly at her. It appeared he knew what she was asking, the confirmation she was seeking. "No, darling. You're right." He relieved her of the items and walked toward the window.

Her chest tightened at the imminence of his departure. There was no guarantee she would see him again. How many times could two people say good-bye?

But then, to her surprise, he set the garments on her bed. He removed his coat and loosened his neckerchief.

"What are you doing?" she said, barely finding her voice.

"What you asked for." His gaze on hers, he continued to undress, sending a rush of blood to her face.

She swung to face the wall. Classical notes from violin strings mixed with the rustling of his navy pullover. Out of the corner of her eye, in the vanity mirror, she saw him toss the shirt aside. Lamplight accentuated the lines of his shoulders, the V of his naked back. His muscles had gained strength and tone. She watched, mesmerized, as he unbuckled his belt. He raised his eyes and connected with the reflection of her stare.

Vivian jerked her head away, feeling like the one exposed. Then came the dual thunking of his boots, the whooshing of his trousers. And her mouth went dry.

An eternity lapsed before he declared himself fully dressed. "Better?"

Composing herself as best she could, she reviewed his dapper appearance. Since their parting in Europe his jaw had thickened and the area around his eyes had wearied. But at his core, he was still Isaak — the man with whom she had shared picnics in the park and strolls by the Thames, kisses under a London moon.

A rattling shot from the door. The jiggling of its knob.

"Viv, are you in there?"

Luanne. To keep her from danger, she could know nothing of this.

As if understanding, Isaak scrambled to collect his uniform. Vivian handed him his boots and ushered him toward the window.

"Vivian?" Luanne said, knocking.

"Uh, yes?" Vivian called groggily. "Who is it?"

"It's me. Who else?"

343

"Be right there." Vivian helped Isaak climb out and went to lower the window.

"Tomorrow night," he whispered. "Altman Movie Palace, seven o'clock."

"What?" she said in a hush. "No — I — we shouldn't."

"I'll wait for you in the balcony. The very back row."

Luanne knocked again, yanking Vivian's attention. When she turned back to Isaak, he was descending the first ladder.

She slid the window shut.

Heading for the door, she tousled her hair and rubbed at her eyes. "Sorry about that," she said, letting Luanne in. "I must've locked it by accident, before I drifted off." She shuffled away and flopped down to sit on her bed, as if it had been a chore to abandon it. "You're back early, aren't you?"

Luanne closed the door. Her questioning look ended with a shrug of her brow. "Not early enough, as it turned out."

"That bad?"

"Only the first date and he's already talking about how many children he wants to have the minute the war's over."

"It's probably because he sees what a great mother you'd be." Among the differences between her and Vivian, this was a distinct one. Even in passing on the street the gal had a knack for making kids smile.

"Maybe so." Luanne shrugged out of her

cardigan, its daisy appliqués sewn by her own hand. Further proof of her natural domestic skills. She hung the garment in the closet and her eyes gained a gloss.

Vivian didn't have to ask why. It was merely a matter of time before American troops were deployed on a massive scale. As a young Army private, the fellow had a high chance of landing on the front line, which made any plans past tomorrow a wishful notion.

"Anyway," Luanne said. "What about you? How was your evening?" She padded over to the bureau to change into her nightgown.

"Fairly uneventful." Discomfited by the fib, Vivian aimed to busy herself. She flipped open her diary, as though resuming the activity that had taken up her night.

"Have you decided about enlisting yet?"

All things considered, Vivian wasn't exactly an ideal candidate. "Not yet," she said, attention on her book, unseeing.

"Might be worth it, you know — just to see your mother have a conniption."

A valid benefit to consider, but later.

"Hey, Viv. Whose is this?"

Vivian raised her head and found Luanne with a hat.

A black fedora.

Isaak's.

In an instant, Vivian's thudding heartbeats returned.

"Oh, yes. That." An explanation rushed to

345

mind and quickly tumbled out. "I bought it today. For your brother."

Luanne inspected the item. "Really?" she said, uncertain.

"Of course. Why wouldn't you think so?"

"It's just that . . . well, it doesn't look . . . new."

Vivian honed in on the dust marks, the bent brim. She replied as if the reason were obvious. "That's because it isn't, silly. It's from a secondhand store."

The lies were pouring out faster, like grains of quicksand, sure to drag her under. "I thought it was best to conserve, with the war on and all."

Luanne contemplated a thought as she glanced to the side — was she looking at the window?

"What did you think?" Vivian pinned on a smile. "That I was hiding another man in here?" She felt herself sinking, past the ankles, up to the knees.

Luanne hesitated, then snipped off a laugh. "I don't know what I was thinking. I know how deeply you care for Gene. After the mess with Helen, I just get a little protective sometimes."

It took Vivian effort to connect the name, given the settling of her pulse. "The cheerleader," she remembered. A discussion on the girl he dated through high school was a welcomed shift. "Why? What happened between them?"

"He didn't tell you?"

Vivian shook her head.

After a pause, Luanne gave a shrug that said her brother wouldn't mind the divulgence. She leaned her back against the bureau. "They stayed together even when Gene went off to college. I think Helen was hoping he'd propose before then, but he wanted to wait. Eventually, he found out Helen had stepped out on him — if you know what I mean." Her inflection and lowered eyes alluded to much more than a kiss.

No wonder Gene, too, had bypassed any mention of former loves. It was for Vivian's sake as much as his. "I take it they didn't stay friends," she guessed.

"Not for lack of trying — by Helen anyway. She truly wanted a second chance. She even came to me in tears, looking for advice. She was so desperate to fix things. But it was too late. She'd broken his heart, and for Gene, there was no going back."

His value on loyalty and trust certainly fit within his character; still, testament to the fact caused Vivian a stirring of dread.

"Well, enough of all that," Luanne said with abrupt lightness. She walked over and handed Vivian the fedora. "As I said, I know you'd never do anything like that."

Although the assurance came with a smile,

threaded in her tone was a message resembling a warning.

37

"And why, may I ask, has it taken you this long to tell me?" From Audra's kitchen table Tess shot a light, accusatory glare.

"Umm, because I didn't want you to think I was crazy?" Audra said. A statement of the obvious. At the counter, she spread peanut butter on another slice of wheat bread.

"Yeah, well. Too late for that."

Audra smiled, though inside she longed to hear — from someone not being paid to say so — that she still appeared a sane, suited mother. For a second, she was tempted to tell her friend as much, but it was too much like requesting a hug. The response didn't seem genuine if you had to ask.

She simply continued with the sandwiches by adding a layer of strawberry jam. Meanwhile, Tess steeped her tea, sweetening the air with orange spice. In the adjacent living room, afternoon sunlight wove through the vertical blinds. Perfect weather for a picnic. With Audra's recent abundance of free time, a distraction was never more welcomed.

"So, have you tried talking to Jack?" Tess said. "At bedtime, like before?"

"I have. But he hasn't said anything else."

Last night, Audra had approached him during his "golden hour" — a term Dr. Shaw used in his reply e-mail, describing a child's common openness while on the groggy ridge of sleep. This time, Jack didn't so much as mumble.

"The therapist said we could always consider hypnosis. He does it sometimes with kids for other issues . . . but I don't know."

Tess nodded slowly. "Could be worth a try."

"Or it could make things worse."

"Maybe," Tess said, and sat back with her tea. "At least it explains why Jack ran off at the waterfront."

Audra paused while resealing the jam jar. She had forgotten it was actually Jack's idea to attend the festival.

Was it possible his search for Sean hadn't been a coincidence? That Jack somehow sensed the soldier would be there?

A loud engine sound shook the walls. Jack and Grace were watching a cartoon in Audra's bedroom. Days ago, the TV in the living room had fallen into a coma, as if a plague were spreading among the appliances.

"Jack, will you turn that down?" Audra called out.

Grace yelled back, "We're looking for the remote! Oh — there it is! We found it!"

The volume dropped to a human decibel level.

"Wow," Tess said. "Back in our day, we actually had to stand up and walk three whole feet to adjust the television."

Audra typically would have laughed, but her bundled thoughts smothered the sound. At the core of those thoughts was pure, unspeakable worry.

She finished packing the sandwiches and grapes before realizing that Tess had gone silent, a rare occurrence unless an issue was troubling her. Maybe she had an opinion she was afraid to voice. Maybe, upon review, Russ had predicted an unfavorable outcome.

"Tess, please tell me what you're thinking."

"Huh? Oh, it's nothing." She smiled. "My mind just veered off."

"No, really. I want to know."

Tess fiddled with the handle of her mug and said, "Honestly? I was thinking of Tiger Woods."

Audra blinked. "You were . . . thinking about golf?"

"I just remembered a story about him. Apparently when he was a baby, his parents used to turn on the Golf Channel and he'd instantly stop crying. He could watch the sport for hours. So, it got me wondering if Tiger's fascination was left over from a past life. Like those kid prodigies who were on *Oprah.* Their feet couldn't even reach the piano pedals, but there they were, playing insanely advanced pieces from Bach and Beethoven."

Oprah. The defining show of Audra's life.

While she appreciated the input, few judges would be that broad-minded. "On the other hand, maybe their parents made them practice every waking minute since the day they were born." She wiped the counter with a paper towel as Tess mulled the argument.

"Yeah. Probably. All I'm saying is, now that I think about it, I can see lots of evidence from kids who might have held on to things from a past life."

Evidence implied proof. Proof suggested fact. This wasn't fact, only debatable interpretation.

"As I told your husband, I'm not saying I actually believe in any of this. What I care about is getting to the bottom of what's causing Jack's issues."

Tess offered a smile. "Sure. I understand." She went to add something, but then sipped her drink instead.

Audra wadded the paper into a ball, again unsettled. "What is it?"

Tess sighed as though to downplay the point. "I just wish you had told me earlier. I could have helped out if I'd known, with Hector and your job . . ."

"What do you mean?" Audra said. "You've been great. Tess, you're the one who set me up with the interview in Boston." Examples even relating to the case sprang to mind. "You also hooked me up with Russ. And when I told you about Jack's drawings and nightmares, you were a huge help."

"If you say so."

There was more than regret adding an edge to Tess's voice; it was a question of trust. She didn't think Audra trusted her enough to confide in her. But that wasn't the case.

"Okay, fine. You really want to know why I waited?"

"Yes," Tess said. "I do."

"Because you're a superwoman."

Tess gazed back at her, surprised.

"Somehow you find a way to manage the clinic *and* your clients, run your kids to lessons and games, plus volunteer for every school activity that exists — and all without breaking a sweat. I have no doubt, at your husband's work events you'd even be voted The Perfect Hostess. So please understand, that's the reason I wasn't super eager to tell you how much I'm screwing up when I only have a fraction of that list."

There. Audra had finally said it.

Yet it was a decision she wished she could reverse as a slow grin overtook Tess's face. This wasn't the kind of support Audra was hoping for.

"Sweetie, not everything is how it appears." Tess folded her arms and lowered her chin. "For your information, Grace's gymnastics coach hates me for no apparent reason, but since Grace loves her, we stick around. Last week, at

353

the equestrian center, I stepped in a fresh pile of grade-A horse poop. In open-toed shoes. Cleaning them off caused us to run late for gymnastics class, which made the coach an even bigger fan of mine. Shall I continue?"

The appropriate answer would be *no.* But Audra found herself nodding.

"Let's see," Tess said. "Oh, yeah. I hate those stuffy legal dinners, almost as much as attending PTA meetings. Trust me, you don't know misery until you've sat through two hours — seriously, *two* hours — of women arguing over the shape and color of confetti we should sprinkle at a fifth-grade graduation picnic."

Audra fought off a grin.

"Feel any better?"

Audra couldn't deny that she did. "Why on earth haven't you ever said any of this before?"

"I don't know. I suppose, with everything you've been through, I felt like my problems were nothing to whine about."

Ironically, even selfishly, Audra had found that hearing other people's hardships could be somewhat therapeutic. "In the future, please don't hold back."

Tess lifted her mug, as if to seal the pledge with an invisible clink. "Deal," she said, and gulped down the rest. "Now, what do you say we all go to the park? That way we can show off our awful parenting skills in public."

Audra laughed. "Perfect."

■ ■ ■ ■

Rounding up the kids took the same effort as herding a litter of cats. Audra and Tess alternated orders like two sergeants sharing a post.

Put your shoes on. Go to the bathroom; try to go anyway. Yes, I've got bread for the ducks. Did you wash your hands? No, you can't go without socks. Because I don't want to hear complaints about a blister. I thought I told you to wash your hands.

A century later, they were all heading toward the door. Grace, her light hair in double braids, trotted over the threshold. Jack had retrieved his scooter from the laundry room. He was walking it out, wearing shorts and a long-sleeved Timbers shirt. It had been over a year since Audra had encouraged him to ride. He insisted he could steer just fine with his cast. Though with reservations, she agreed.

"Jack, wait," Audra said. "You forgot your helmet."

"I'll be fine," he said, anxious to go.

Tess piped in, "But your brain won't be if it rams the pavement."

"Exactly my point." Audra smiled. "You guys go on out. I'll grab it for him."

Tess ushered them onward, hugging a grocery bag of their picnic food, as Audra went to Jack's room. The place looked like a hurricane had hit. Pajamas and toys were strewn on the floor. The covers on his bed were half off and twisted. Her request that he tidy before company arrived had clearly gone unheeded.

Oddly enough, she didn't mind all that much. It was nice to see him act like a typical boy.

The inside of the closet wasn't much better. It took serious scrounging to locate the helmet, streaked in blue and yellow, amid his old cleats and shin guards.

Maybe it wasn't the worst idea in the world to see if he wanted to play soccer again — at some point. Once his arm healed.

They would try the scooter first.

She closed the closet and her sandal landed on something sticky. Dabs of glue were adhering paper scraps to the carpet. "Jack," she grumbled.

She cleaned up the pieces, evidently from a school project, and threw them away before they could dry. After washing her hands, she hurried outside with the helmet. She was locking the door when she heard somebody speaking to Tess.

Audra followed the concrete walkway around a heap of overgrown bushes and discovered a guy crouched down beside Jack.

"Oh, there she is!" Tess said. "Audra, we just ran into your friend."

The man stood up with a smile that halted her steps.

Sean Malloy.

"Hey," he said. He wore faded jeans and a

black cotton shirt, just snug enough to highlight the broadness of his chest and shoulders. His face was clean-shaven, but his hair, while not disheveled like before, still had a relaxed, finger-brushed style.

"What're you doing here?" That hadn't come out right. "I mean, I didn't know you were stopping by."

"I was just running errands in the area." He slid his hands into his front pockets. "Sorry. Guess I've been making a habit of showing up unannounced."

"No, it's okay. I did too. Or — have, anyway. Made a habit." That wasn't right either; a habit required more than her single house call. "If I were to visit you again. At your aunt's house, that is. Without warning."

Too bad Jack's helmet was too small to crawl into. She pictured her tongue as knotted as a leash.

"Actually," Tess said, saving her, "we were all out here, trying to adjust the scooter. And —" She turned. "It's 'Sean,' right?"

"Yes, ma'am," he said.

"Well, Sean was kind enough to help us raise the handlebar. Apparently he and Jack had already met." Tess gave her a discreet look that not only acknowledged Sean's identity as "the soldier" but also demanded to know why his physical description had been omitted.

"Mom, can we go?" Jack posed a sneaker-clad foot on the scooter, ready to push.

357

Grace was swinging the bag of bread heels around like a lasso. "Yeah, I wanna feed the baby ducks."

Tess widened her eyes at Audra, nudging an invite for the unplanned guest.

Clumsily, Audra asked him, "Would you want to? Join us?"

Sean perked at first but shook his head. "I'd hate to intrude." He picked up a manila envelope on the ground beside him. "Why don't I leave my number so we can talk . . . about things, when it's a better time?"

He seemed to choose his words carefully, with no offer to leave the packet. Over the past several days, perhaps he'd unearthed information best delivered in person.

"Shoot, you know what?" Tess interjected. "I just remembered, I need to swing by the dry cleaner before they close."

At only one in the afternoon, the excuse couldn't have been more transparent.

"Are you sure?" Audra asked, an auto reply.

"Yeah. Cooper's got a game later, so we actually need to be back for that too. You all go to the park though. Grace and I will join next time."

"But Mom," her daughter protested. Her bread bag now hung limply at her side.

"Sorry, Gracie. If you hurry and get in the car, I'll swing through Dairy Queen on the way home."

That one did the trick. Duck feeding was nice, but sundaes were a gold mine. With the power and speed of an F-4 tornado, they handed off the food bags and jetted away, leaving the group behind like a pile of debris.

38

"Well, look who's here," Luanne announced, alerting Vivian of their unexpected company.

In the hallway, Gene strode over to where they stood, just outside the switchboard room.

"Gene," Vivian said. "What a surprise."

"Are you joining us for lunch?" Luanne asked.

"Sorry, Lu. Another day." He turned to Vivian. "Could we go somewhere and talk?" With his officer's hat in his hand, there was no shielding the grimness in his eyes. "I won't keep you long."

"Yes, of course," Vivian said, and told herself not to read into his words.

"I'll save you a seat," Luanne said to her, then bid good-bye to her brother and continued toward the civilian mess hall. Her expression gave away nothing.

Gene gestured for Vivian to go first. She led him outside, focusing on her steps, navigating the minefield that had formed around her. The torture of waiting for the blast could not be worse than enduring its aftermath.

Two doors down, with a tally of fewer words, Gene guided her to the backside of a building. A handful of enlisted men were indulging in a smoke break. One of the privates glanced over. At the recognition of Gene's rank and towering build, he pitched his cigarette and snapped to attention. The others followed, a few of them striking salutes, bodies straight as rods.

"You boys clear out," Gene growled. It was a voice Vivian didn't recognize.

"Yes, sirs" overlapped as the guys scampered away like mice. Smoke lingered in their wake.

Gene hitched his hands on his hips. His gaze settled on Vivian. "I need to talk to you," he said, "about the friends you're trying to help."

She nodded, not missing the way his tone dropped on the word *friends*.

"Are you sure . . ." He paused, started again. "Are you sure the names you gave me were right?"

At the unforeseen question, she stared for a moment, reshaping her focus. "I believe so." The list of names. From Isaak. She had copied them directly. "Yes. Yes, I'm certain they were."

"The reason I ask is, I did some checking.

361

Turns out, these people were already in the files."

She would have taken this for a promising update, a prerequisite to a swift solution, if not for his demeanor.

"Sweetheart, your friends probably seemed like real nice folks. But they're not the sort you ought to worry about."

"Why? I don't understand."

He appeared to be weighing how much to confide. "Vivian," he said, "they're all Nazis."

She shook her head, correcting him. "No. I told you —"

"They're officially registered as members of the Party. Not just that. They're devout, active members. One of the daughters, the older girl — Gertrud — she was even in the Lebensborn program. That's when they send them to a special maternity house. It's for birthing pure, Aryan babies."

"Gene, no. That can't be right."

All of this was absurd. There had to be an explanation.

She raked her mind for possibilities. Quickly she realized: "It's the names. The names I gave you, they must be the same as another family's." For all she knew, the surname of Hemel could be the German equivalent of Jones.

"It's them, Vivi."

"It can't be. There's just a mix-up."

"No. There isn't."

"How do you know that?" she demanded. He should at least consider it. Only God Himself could possess such certainty.

"Because all five of the names matched. Two I could see as a coincidence. On an off-chance, maybe three. But not all five."

To this she had no answer.

"Also, you were right about the man in the family, about him running a paper. One of the issues he'd printed came in from Europe with a batch of intelligence, some propaganda. It's probably what first put them on the radar. I brought a picture for you. It's all I could manage." From a shirt pocket he unfolded a photo slightly larger than his hand. He presented it as one would evidence in a trial. "See for yourself."

She rushed to accept, propelled by the scantest hope that all of this was in error. Due to the size of the image, most of the newsprint was too small to read, but the headlines appeared to be in German. Confirming this was a pair of symbols that flanked the title of the publication; they were solid black swastikas.

Instinctively she moved her thumb from the marks. With how easily they seared her thoughts they should have been in red: blaring and molten.

"Back in the files," he continued, "there were some translations of the articles. Mostly praising Hitler, exaggerating German victories. But some pretty hateful stuff too, condemning Jews and whatnot. One of the worst pieces I saw was actually written by the publisher's own nephew."

Her throat quivered at the mention, at the idea of who that might be. There were only nieces on Isaak's list. It took everything in Vivian to keep her voice steady. "Who is the nephew?"

"His name was Jakob. Jakob Hemel."

A tiny part of her relaxed. "I hadn't heard of him," she admitted as Gene tucked the photo into his pocket.

"His mother's one of the people you know, from your list." He provided this as if merely to jog her memory. "Anyway, his father served as a pilot for Germany in the Great War. As it so happens, you and his son might have passed each other on the street."

She shook her head, not following.

"In London. He went to the university there — paid for, incidentally, by a Nazi war profiteer. This nephew, Jakob, majored in journalism. Probably so his anti-Semitic articles would actually sound intelligent." Gene laughed at this without humor. "And the best part? The creep was born in America, if you can believe it."

The university.

Journalism.

An American.

In her mind, the pieces intertwined like the

wires of a switchboard. They sparked and buzzed on the verge of an overload. Through the din, a single word emerged.

Lies.

The lies she was told. The lies she believed. Those for which she had given every part of herself.

Even now, by hiding her knowledge of Isaak in New York — or whoever the man really was — she was committing treason against her own country. She was jeopardizing her future and that of her parents too. Not to mention the scandal and suspicions that could befall Gene and Luanne.

And what of the conspiracy, the alleged espionage? If there were indeed other agents, they might have already arrived. Maybe it had always been a solo mission. Either way, there must have been reasons for involving her, a true purpose to moving Isaak's family. Assuming that was ever the goal.

"Point is," Gene went on, "you'd be wise to forget all about these people. Clearly they're nothing but trouble."

Vivian looked up at him and he paused. His expression softened. Tenderly he squeezed her hand. "Sorry, Vivi. Probably said too much." He had switched from informational to personal. "I know it wasn't what you wanted to hear."

"No. Please," she said. "Don't be sorry. You did the right thing." Which was much more than she could say for herself. If anyone should apologize, it was she, for believing there was ever a choice to be made between the two men.

"You sure you're okay?"

She nodded and smiled. "I just feel foolish," she said, though this was only a partial truth. *Foolish* didn't do justice to the stupidity, the hurt, rising in her like a tide. One that in mere hours — at her secret meeting at the cinema — could come crashing down on them all.

39

Audra's apprehension rose as she waited to hear the information Sean had uncovered. At an empty picnic table, he took a seat across from her and set down the manila envelope. For the three-block walk from the apartment, he had carried it close to his side. Jack had rolled along on his scooter, just as he did now around the paved loop of the park, fully in view. The air smelled of bark chips and freshly cut grass.

"So, here's the letter I told you about." Sean pulled out a small envelope, yellowed from age, and handed it over. "It took a little work to remember which box it was in."

"I appreciate you doing that," Audra said.

The top edge was jagged from being ripped open. No postage. No address. Just a name inked in cursive: *Vivian.*

"My grandma's father was a diplomat," Sean explained. "He was stationed in England before the war broke out. So I'm pretty sure this was written right before they came home."

Bracing herself, Audra unfolded the page from

inside, yellowed, too, and wrinkled. She began to read.

My Dearest Vivian,

I am writing this letter only hours before departing London. Although I am anxious to see my family and confirm that all is as well as they claim, already I miss you terribly . . . .

Audra paced herself, despite eagerness for any clue that would end her family's troubles. She felt like a kid again, decoding a secret message from the bottom of a cereal box.

The author wrote of traveling to settle "personal affairs," on what sounded a tenuous journey, and urged Vivian to evacuate in the event he failed to return. He vowed to reunite with her one way or another and described his necklace as proof of that promise.

He signed the letter:

Yours for eternity,
Isaak

"Audra? You all right?" From Sean's tone, she wondered how long she had been staring at the page.

"I'm . . . yeah. I'm fine. It's . . ."

Nearby, Jack zipped past the swing set, riding another lap on a runway of sunlight. Over on the jungle gym, girls in pink squealed gaily while their mothers chatted on a park bench.

"What is it?" Sean said. "Was there something familiar in there?"

"I don't know. I guess it's something Jack said the other night. He was half asleep and told me the reason he came back was" — she blocked out how ridiculous this could sound — "so that finally she can be with him. Jack didn't give any names. But in the letter here, there's so much about, well . . ."

"The two of them reuniting," Sean finished.

"Exactly."

He raised his eyebrows and blew out a breath that conveyed precisely how she felt. If subscribing to any of these theories classified Audra as looney, at least she wasn't alone.

Now to find out more about the couple and what had divided them.

"Did you know your grandma very well?" she asked.

"Never met her, unfortunately. She died before I was born."

"Oh, I didn't realize." The women of the Greatest Generation always seemed made of Teflon, enduring and strong, the kind who lived to be a hundred. "Did she die during the war?"

"Nah. It was after that. Here, I actually have some info about that too." He emptied the manila envelope. Peeking out from a thin stack of papers was an old newspaper clipping that he slid out for Audra to read.

An obituary. Absent a photo, it gave a basic

report of the deaths of both Vivian and Gene Sullivan. During a fishing excursion, they had perished in a boating accident off the coast of Cape Cod. They were survived by their parents and young daughter, Judith. A memorial service was to be held at St. Augustine's in Brooklyn.

"This is terrible," Audra said, starkly reminded that family tragedies traced back to the beginning of time. "What happened to them, do you know?"

"They rented a motorboat for the day and got caught in a nasty storm. Thankfully my mom was back home, staying with my aunt. After that, Aunt Lu and Uncle Fred raised her. And I think my grandma's parents helped out quite a bit too."

Audra recalled what Sean had said about Luanne and suddenly realized: "So, that's the reason."

"What's that?"

"You told me Luanne doesn't like talking about that time in her life. I figured it was about the war, but now I get why."

"Ah. Yeah," he said. "Apparently, she and her brother, Grandpa Gene, were really close. He was an officer in Army Intelligence. I think all three of them had gone to high school together. Aunt Lu and Grandma Vivian were roommates in New York later, worked as phone operators — or something like that. Got most of this from my mom. Aunt Lu's never wanted to say much about it, so we don't push."

"I can understand that."

Sean nodded. A wistful smile indicated he recognized her personal view. "Anyway, after I moved to the farm, I was settling in and going through my old boxes, and that's when I found the letter. Same for the obituary and some other stuff that belonged to my grandparents. I remember first finding the things, like I told you, but can't say why I'd personally hung on to them."

As Audra listened, she threw a glance toward Jack. He was still speeding smoothly around. "Have you ever asked your mom about all of this?"

"I don't think she knows much more than I do. Said she's always wanted to learn about where she came from and who her parents were. When she was a kid, she went through a phase of drilling my aunt for details. Aunt Lu would give her little nuggets, but always wound up getting emotional over it, or at least really quiet. So after a while, my mom dropped the subject. Also, 'cause I think she didn't want to give the impression that my aunt wasn't a good enough mother, because she was. She was great."

"Seems like she would have been." Audra smiled at the thought of the woman serving hot cocoa and marshmallows. The only thing missing from her snack tray had been a plate of grilled cheese sandwiches cut into mini-triangles. "Did your aunt and uncle have kids of their own?"

He shook his head. "Just my mom. Not sure if that was by choice, after all they'd gone through. Or if there were . . . other reasons."

The small hitch in his answer gave Audra pause; a couple's potential fertility issues were, first off, none of her business and, second, a far leap from any relevance to Jack.

Guiding the discussion back, she asked, "Do you have any idea at all who Isaak might've been?"

"Not a clue. I wish I could ask Aunt Lu about him. But I doubt she'd be up for chatting about my grandma in a relationship with another guy."

"Sure. Of course." Audra couldn't blame the woman; her loyalty belonged to her brother. Still, any obstacle at the moment was disappointing. She tucked the letter into its envelope and remembered the other pages Sean had brought. "Do you have something else in there?"

He didn't respond. He'd turned his head to gaze at Jack, still rolling in circles. It was an analytical gaze, the kind she, too, had used to examine Jack's features and behavior, envisioning him in a different era. In Sean's case, maybe he was even searching for a distant family resemblance.

"Sean?"

"Huh?"

His hearing, she kept forgetting. Audra could only hope she hid her own weaknesses as well as he did. "Are those for me too?"

He looked down at the papers, refocusing.

"Sorry, yeah." He slid them across the metal table. "I did some digging around about Jakob Hemel. Had the same luck you did online. But a research librarian helped me find this."

Audra started with the top page of the stapled packet, impressed he had gone to so much trouble. She quickly realized, however, the photocopied article featured a subject she'd already covered: the Nazi spies who were captured on the East Coast.

Sean added, "There's a name in the article I think you should see. It's on the third page."

Anticipating a reference to Jakob, she rushed to the last sheet. Attached with a paper clip was a folded newspaper article, yellowed like Isaak's letter. She tugged it free and scanned the story of a child who went missing in 1940.

"What is it I'm looking for?"

"This." He moved the clipping aside and tapped his finger on the photocopied page, at the name underlined in pencil: *Daniel Gerard.* "He was an FBI agent involved in both of these cases."

Audra glanced back at the aged clipping and verified the connection. But she shook her head, unsure how this pertained.

"The article about the missing kid," Sean said, "was in a box with my grandma's things. I can't think that's a coincidence." He had a point, yet the link remained muddled.

"I wish I understood how this all fit together."

Sean nodded, also at a loss.

Just then, she spotted Jack cutting a corner by some boulders. His scooter started to tip. He caught himself, but his leg grazed one of the rocks. He dusted off his knee and carried on as before.

"I should've made him wear jeans," she muttered.

"Ahh, he's fine," Sean said, and she supposed he was right. "Hey, I almost forgot. There was a sergeant I met at the VA hospital, a real nice guy. His wife collects old wartime keepsakes that have gotten lost over the years — like letters and photos from Korea, World War Two, Vietnam. She tracks down the families of the vets they belonged to and returns the stuff. Anyway, I got ahold of her through her Web site. Just told her you were doing a genealogy project, and that you were looking for information about a distant relative with Jakob's name. I only gave her a few other details. Don't know if she'll find anything, but figured it couldn't hurt. I could send her your contact info if you'd like."

"That'd be great." Audra smiled, again touched by his efforts. Under the circumstances, few people, much less a virtual stranger, would offer this much support. "Thank you, Sean."

"It was nothing."

"No, really. Thank you — for all of this." She gestured to everything he had brought along.

He shrugged and reciprocated the smile. "It was good for me too. Gave me an excuse to go through my old things. Even had a few memories pop up because of it." He began to gather the papers, letter, and articles. "You're welcome to keep these, by the way. For however long you need."

"Are you sure that's okay?"

"My family's not doing anything with them." He slid the contents back into the manila casing. When he handed it over, she found herself wishing details about Sean, too, were inside.

"The memories that came back to you," she ventured to ask, "were they helpful at all?"

"I don't know," he said after a pause. "They don't seem like it."

"Your mom mentioned that you're still feeling . . . out of sorts."

"That's one way to put it." His clipped laugh made Audra wince.

"Sorry," she said. "I didn't mean for it to sound like a small issue."

"No," he insisted, "you didn't."

She nodded, deciding to leave him to his privacy, already in awe of how much family history he'd been willing to share. But he surprised her by continuing.

"The best way I can describe it . . . is a bad night with a fifth of tequila. You blink and everything blacks out. Except the next day, you don't wake up in your frat house to hear about how you did keg stands, or danced on a table naked. Instead, you wake up in a hospital, and when you get home everyone is suddenly three years older. You find out you not only joined the

Army, but you fought in a war — where, incidentally, you were the one person in your vehicle who made it out."

Audra tried to imagine the shock of it all. Assembling the pieces would seem horrifically surreal. She wasn't certain how to respond. "Do you at least remember wanting to be in the service? Earlier in your life even?"

"I guess I'd thought about it. But it was way back in high school." He half smiled. "Probably because I thought the uniform would help me get more dates."

Based on his looks now, she couldn't imagine his needing a uniform for that. "But you went to college instead?"

"Yeah. Made my mom a lot happier."

"Your dad too, I'd bet." Audra caught herself, once more speaking as if she and Sean were old friends.

"Actually, I wouldn't know," he said, then appeared to realize the ambiguity of the remark. "He and my mom got divorced when I was three. He moved to Ohio and started another family. So I always knew him, but not well."

Audra could relate to the nature of the relationship, with both of her parents, but on a lesser scale.

"Anyhow," Sean went on, "my mom says she came unglued when I enlisted. Apparently, as a news producer, I told her I was tired of watching from the sidelines. Wanted to make a difference." He shrugged. "Whatever the reason, I

376

quit my job. Sold my condo. It's like in a single day my whole life turned upside down."

Audra could relate yet again, this time to the fullest degree.

"What do the doctors say, about the memories you've lost?"

"That it could stay this way. Or I could get little things here and there, maybe chunks once in a while. Or one day it could all come rushing back. Basically, it's anyone's guess. I suppose that's why I've been dragging my feet in a lot of ways. Hard to move forward when you're not sure exactly who you are."

Audra recognized the irony of this. To her, moving forward had appeared the best way to reestablish an identity. What's more, there were times over the past two years when amnesia would have seemed a gift; now, given Sean's story, she wasn't so certain.

"God, listen to me," he said under his breath. "Talking nonstop. Whining about my life when I should just be grateful I survived, right?"

"I don't think it's ever that simple."

"Yeah, well," he sighed. "At least now you know, when a reporter wants to call me a war hero, it's a bunch of bull." He laughed at the farce of it all. "To be honest, that day at the Rose Festival, for the ceremony with the mayor — I almost flaked out at the last minute. I only went through with it because my mom and aunt were so damn proud."

Audra smiled. "I'd say they deserve to be."

He brushed this off by looking away.

"For what it's worth," she said, "I'm really glad you went."

He turned back to her, and from her eyes he seemed to understand: It was the only way they would have crossed paths. "Me too," he said.

The answer sent a surge of warmth up her neck. It continued over her cheeks and widened her smile.

"Mom, can we eat?" Jack had rolled up to the table.

"Um, yeah," she said, flustered, as he hopped off his scooter. "Grab a seat." She had almost forgotten about the picnic she'd packed.

Jack sat down but, to her surprise, did so on Sean's side of the bench.

Audra unloaded the grocery sack and gave Jack his sandwich. He dove in, still wearing his helmet, before she could hand over his juice box and bag of grapes.

She scrunched her nose at Sean. "All I have are PB and Js. If you'd rather pass, it's totally fine."

"Are you kidding? That's my favorite." He snagged a sandwich, adding, "And lucky for me, since Aunt Lu makes them for me *all* the time."

Audra laughed. "I have no doubt."

For several minutes, the three of them quietly enjoyed their lunches.

Then Jack, with another surprise, asked

Sean: "Did you see how good I'm steering with one hand?"

The question was slightly garbled from a mouthful of food, but Audra wasn't about to correct him. His tone, though at a gentle volume, held the most enthusiasm she'd heard in as long as she could remember.

"I saw that!" Sean said. "Pretty impressive there."

Jack slurped down his juice. "You know, I used to steer with no hands too."

"Wow. Seriously?" Sean replied between bites. "That's awesome, buddy."

Audra paused at the nickname. More aptly, the way it drifted from Sean's mouth, soft and natural as a leaf from a branch.

Jack wiped his mouth with the long sleeve over his cast. "After eating, wanna see me do it?"

Barely catching the reference, Audra cut in, "No. We don't."

"But, Mom," he pleaded, "it's easy."

She hesitated, not wanting to dampen his mood, nor to be a "strict dictator."

But Sean jumped in. "Better listen to your mom. She's a smart woman. Knows what she's talking about."

The claim almost made Audra laugh. Boy, if he only knew.

"Besides," Sean added, "you wouldn't want to end up with two casts, right? How would you hug all your girlfriends?"

379

"Uh, Sean." Audra looked at him. "He's eight."

Sean cleared his throat. "As I was saying, your mom's a smart woman."

She rolled her eyes, unable to stifle her smile — even more so when Jack giggled. The sound was so light and sweet she feared she had imagined it.

Hoping to sustain the momentum, she hazarded to bring up some of Jack's old favorites: SpongeBob and ninja warriors.

"Who the heck is SpongeBob?" Sean asked.

Jack gaped as if the guy had never heard of air.

Audra doubted a former media producer was unacquainted with the famed cartoon. If he posed the question to keep her son talking, it worked. Jack, with the patience of a retired grandfather, launched into biographies of colorful characters from the underwater city of Bikini Bottom. The show's humor, while not always the most appropriate, was admittedly very funny.

When Sean moved on to the ninjas, the conversation fizzled. It seemed Jack had used his allotted words for the week in one fell swoop. He did listen closely, however, to Sean's insider tips on dealing with casts, the itching in particular.

The only other discussion Jack prompted was at the pond while feeding ducks.

"Is that real?" he asked, referencing Sean's

armband tattoo. "Did you get it for being in the Army?"

Audra, too, had noticed the black Celtic design peeking out from the edge of his shirtsleeve, but she'd averted her eyes from his upper arm to prevent giving the wrong impression. Now her attention bounced between the tattoo and Jack's fascination. And she wondered what specifically had drawn her son out today: his interest in Sean as a soldier, or if a spiritual familiarity connected them.

She was ruminating on this thought when a dog barked. She reflexively glanced up but honed in on a stranger. A man sat in the driver side of his SUV, alone in the parking lot, his face angled in Audra's direction. The tree shading his windshield lent his eyes a hooded look. Atop his steering wheel an object glinted in his hand. Whether a phone or a camera, either one could be taking photos.

Could her in-laws have hired a PI? What would the evidence he'd collected here show? *Just look at her poor judgment, bringing into Jack's world a mentally troubled war vet, a guy who actually believes he's somehow linked to her son's past life.*

"Daddy!" a little girl hollered, playing by the slide. Beside her, a woman made "come here" motions toward the same SUV. The man smiled and pointed to his cell phone, an illustration of finishing a call.

Though relieved, Audra had been sobered by

her nerves. She turned to Sean and Jack, who were pitching the last of the bread crumbs. "Sorry, guys," she said, "fun's over for today."

They soon collected their things and headed for the apartment. Almost there, Sean asked to use the restroom before he left. Naturally Audra agreed, but part of her — unjust as it was — felt anxious to see him go.

In the meantime, she helped Jack store his scooter in their laundry room. "Why don't you wash up in the kitchen," she said, "and I'll slice you an apple?"

Jack hung his helmet on the handles. "Is Sean having dinner with us?"

"Not this time, baby." A knock came from the front door. "I'll get that. You get cleaned up."

He nodded with a dash of disappointment. As he shuffled away, Audra went to the door and checked the peephole. Two policemen stood outside.

She told herself not to be paranoid, like she had been at the park. And yet there was no ignoring the callers' demeanors. The way they anchored their hands on their gun belts, facing the door without talking, not smiling.

The officers weren't here for a friendly house call.

382

40

Vivian worked to calm the jittering of her pulse. Any second now the projector's beam would blink to life. From the balcony of the movie palace, alone in the far back row, Vivian assessed the room yet again. For a Tuesday evening, attendance was lower than usual. With all but a few people opting for the main floor, vacancies surrounded her like a moat. Including the seat meant for Isaak.

At last, a newsreel flickered onto the screen. Parade music blared from the speakers. Boasting steadfast skill, fresh-faced GIs wove through obstacle courses and under wires, heaved themselves over slatted walls. They charged invisible enemies with bayoneted rifles. Airmen with equal zeal strapped on parachute packs to simulate jumps over cushioned mats. In a wisp of levity, they painted dedications on the canvas of bombs — *Delivery for Tojo, Greetings to Hitler* — the enemy so clearly defined.

Enviously so.

Then came the planes. Propellers whirred on P-38 Lightnings. The pilots roared down the runway, machine guns at the ready, and a revelation came to Vivian: Isaak's craving for wartime reports originated not from concern for his mother but from his father's military feats. Bedtime stories would have described the man donning a German uniform before zeroing in on Allied targets.

Could Vivian's father be among those targets now? Isaak had appeared genuinely disappointed that her father remained in London. Had there been a plan involving his connections, his knowledge? Perhaps this was the true reason Isaak had summoned her to Prospect Park, the only reason he had courted her from the start. It would make sense why he had been secretive, about both their romance and his past.

Even their initial meeting could have been the product of a scheme. At the outdoor market, where he had covered her debt and whisked her off in the air raid, he might have been following her already when the opportunity arose.

How useful she had been, an indirect line to confidential, prewar updates. Until now, she had actually believed it was her idea to seek out the file-cabinet key and eavesdrop on her father. A brilliant manipulation.

Come to think of it, on the university campus she had not found a single acquaintance of Isaak's. A spy would keep to himself. Except, of course, when it came to collaborators, like his professor Herr Klein, or fellow spies with whom Isaak would have met covertly — in such hideaways as the store cellar.

It was a plot befitting a Hollywood film, too outlandish for reality. But then what else was she to believe?

So many deceptions. Too many to count.

All day long they had accumulated in the pit of her stomach. They now began to churn. To keep from retching, she channeled her focus to the cinematic images. Sailors stood at attention on a massive Navy ship, straight as perfect rows of teeth. Churchill and FDR shook hands in united display. "The Axis powers will soon see their error," the narrator asserted. "They have woken a sleeping giant that will not rest until the fallen heroes of Pearl Harbor are avenged."

Not long ago updates of the like were a nuisance to Vivian, pesky gnats to shoo away. But those updates had since materialized into something inescapably real. Without warning, they had enveloped her entire world.

A noise boomed.

She jerked and looked over her shoulder. The technician in the projector room, a cigarette hanging limply from his mouth, appeared to have dropped a reel.

Vivian uncoiled herself to face forward, and

she gasped. At her side, Isaak sat in the shadows. He had slinked in undetected, like the phantom he had always been.

"Sorry to keep you waiting," he said near her ear.

Through the tunnels of her mind, one of his old sayings echoed. She stared at the screen and recited dully, "More punctual than a German train. Isn't that right?"

"I just wanted to be cautious," he explained.

"Ah, yes. Cautious." She had been that too once, with her future, her heart. She mourned the day he had convinced her to discard them both.

"Darling, what is it? You seem upset."

Upset. The concept applied to many a circumstance: wine spilled on upholstery, a favorite goblet dropped in the sink. "No," she replied honestly. "I am not upset."

The suggestion was so trivializing it struck her as laughable. Quite literally. In place of rehearsed words, a throng of giggles gathered in her mouth. She did not possess the power to withhold them.

"Vivian?" His voice poured with bewilderment.

For a moment she felt the irrationality of her outburst, but then the reasoning gained clarity. Her body was laughing to keep from screaming or, worse, from shedding another tear over this man she never knew.

Someone in the balcony sent out a *shush.*

The reminder of an audience stifled her momentum. Yet, above all, it was Isaak's hand on hers that fully stomped her amusement.

She pulled her arm away. *"Don't."*

Suddenly Isaak's gaze shifted past her. White pinpoints reflected in his eyes.

With a brisk glance, Vivian traced his attention to the silhouette of a man standing in the far aisle. The fellow was combing the rows with a flashlight at his shoulder. A policeman-like hat topped the outline of his head.

Isaak clutched the pocket of his jacket — perhaps a pistol stored inside. He shot Vivian a look that bordered between panic and uncertainty: an ironic question of betrayal. Then he slumped far into his seat, as if the furnishing, with enough pressure, would give way to a secret passage.

All at once it hit her. The mistake she had made coming here, playing this dangerous game. She should have told the police. She should have told Gene. It would have been the sensible step. She just didn't want to confess until she had confronted Isaak herself. She needed the truth firsthand, for her own personal reasons, possibly to redeem herself for being so easily swindled.

Now, though, the chance for any of that might already be lost.

The man aimed the flashlight toward the balcony's front row, where a couple shielded their eyes. They groaned in annoyance before the beam moved on. Vivian felt anxiety oozing from Isaak's pores as he deliberated whether or not to flee. Only then did it occur to her that to evade her own arrest she had no choice but to follow.

Once more she imagined Jean Harlow, and the ways her characters might solve this dilemma. No doubt, kissing the fugitive was standard fare to create a façade. But before Vivian could act, the authority with the flashlight — not a policeman, she realized, but an usher — snatched a lone man by the collar and guided him to the aisle. Based on the reprimand, the viewer was a drunkard who had made a habit of sneaking in for naps.

Vivian fixed her eyes on the screen, catching her breath, and Isaak regained his composure. Jimmy Stewart saluted the camera in his Air Corps uniform, the epitome of chivalry and sacrifice. Women did their bit by working in American factories, like the ones — supposedly — on the Reich's list to destroy.

The thought directed Vivian back to her purpose. Lingering adrenaline empowered her to charge on.

"Were you scared I had given you up?" she said in a low, quiet tone.

"Don't be silly, darling. I know you wouldn't do that."

She turned toward him, pleased his hand had moved from his pocket to the armrest.

"And why is that, *Jakob*? Because we know each other so well?"

He gazed back, his surprise nearly undetectable. "Yes," he said.

"How can you say that," she spat in a whisper, "when you've lied to me all along?"

"That's not true."

"You told me your name was —"

"I was born Jakob Isaak Hemel. Jakob was also my father's name. I've gone by 'Isaak' since I was a kid, only to avoid confusion." He squared his shoulders to her. "What else would you like to know?" It was more of an invitation than a challenge, but she still treated it as the latter, undeterred by a technicality.

"Since you brought up your father — is it true he fought for the Germans?"

Following a pause, Isaak nodded. "He was discharged early on, after being wounded. It happened before I was born. He rarely spoke of it. All I know is that he'd experienced enough of the German cause to want to leave the country for good. To seek out a better life somewhere else."

Vivian gritted her teeth. The excuse sounded almost scripted. "If that's the case, if America was so grand, why didn't you stay?"

"Had it been up to me," he insisted, "we would have. After my father died, my mother didn't want me quitting school in order to

389

work. A few months later we moved in with her sister's family, back in Germany, just as I told you."

"No," Vivian reminded him, "you said it was Switzerland."

He conceded with his silence, and added, "Vivian, you know why I was afraid to tell you that. I swear, I have never lied to you about anything else."

"Is that right? You would swear it to me?"

"Yes."

"On what? Your father's grave? The lives of your family? Of course, I'm referring to the family you had vowed *weren't* Nazis."

He hesitated for a second, then peered straight into her eyes. "And that was the truth."

On the contrary, according to Gene's report, it was a flat-out lie, now told directly to her face. It took concerted effort to keep Vivian from shouting her retort.

"I'm afraid your file disagrees. It says they're officially members of the Nazi Party. 'Devout members,' I believe it said. And that your cousin was even part of some Aryan birthing program." She fisted her hands on her lap, unsure which component disgusted her more. "Then again, with the articles you've written, about your superiority over filthy Jews, you were probably the one who convinced her to join."

Isaak's expression hardened. The scar on

his cheekbone gained a menacing air. He exhaled heavily several times through his nose, a valve ready to burst.

She had gone too far.

"Let's go," he said, seizing her elbow.

Internally she shrank; outwardly she froze.

Another *shush* traveled across the balcony, a reminder of potential witnesses.

"If you have anything to tell me," she said in an undertone, concealing the crack in her voice, "you can say it right here." She readied herself to scream, but Isaak released his hold. His anger deflated and his body sank into the seat. His face turned to the screen.

When he spoke, it came as a ragged whisper. "An SS officer came to the house. He claimed to want information about *me.* It was the duty of the Gestapo, but Gertrud let him in. She was the only one home when he forced himself on her."

Vivian remained silent as the pain, the guilt, of this rippled across Isaak's face.

"As the mother of a bastard child, she would have been disgraced. But as the mother of a pure Aryan baby by a leader in the Reich, she was a national treasure. Just days before I came home, my relatives decided they had no choice. They finally gave in and joined the Party. They did it to reduce suspicions on all of us, but mostly for Gertrud. To help secure her admission into the Lebensborn program."

Reflections from the projector mottled

391

Isaak's skin — but did not hide his opinion of the human thoroughbred system. "After all that, the baby was stillborn. I suppose, in some twisted sense, that was God's way of showing mercy." He glanced toward Vivian. "You know what 'Lebensborn' means, don't you? The 'Spring of Life.' Ironic, don't you think?"

With a look of disgust, he didn't wait for her to comment. "Before long, my uncle was ordered to publish only articles approved by the Party. Stories that showed the Nazis in a favorable light, of the Wehrmacht gaining ground, winning the war."

Vivian couldn't deny it: The more Isaak shared, the more her skepticism waned.

She straightened with a shudder, wary of being fooled again. "I saw one of your articles," she broke in. "It was your name on it. Your words."

Isaak solemnly met her eyes. "My name, yes. Not my words. After I was arrested, my uncle wrote several articles that he printed as being mine. He presented them as evidence that I was a good, loyal German. He told everyone I secretly despised America ever since my father died in a factory there, a result of mistreatment and carelessness. Best of all, my uncle blamed the accident on a Jew. None of that was true, of course. But he was willing to say anything to protect me, and apparently so was Professor Klein."

From the reference to the instructor, Vivian recalled details of Isaak's benefactor, a war profiteer whose reichsmark were soaked with blood. "What about your ties to Mr. Mueller? And the source of his money?"

Isaak gave a helpless shrug. "He was a businessman, a steelmaker. He paid my tuition. I only met him twice. Professor Klein had arranged it all . . . ." He trailed off, and shook his head. "I know how all of this must sound, Vivian. But I swear to God, I'm telling you the truth, about me, my past, the mission. About everything at stake." Underlying the desperation in his voice was inarguable sincerity. He shut his eyes, shoved his fingers through his hair.

It was useless to fight what she felt to her core. Denying this — to him, or herself — would only waste valuable time.

"I believe you," she told him. "Granted, that could make me the most foolish person on earth . . . but I do."

He looked up and his lips edged toward a smile. Not the charming, slanted grin that existed in her dreams. Rather, the one in real life, which had changed over time — as they both had.

"I presume," he said at last, "that the person with the file was the one you were counting on for help."

Reluctantly she affirmed this. "I'm sorry, Isaak."

He nodded and murmured something too soft to hear.

She waited a moment before asking him, "What are you going to do?"

Gaze lowered, he clasped her fingers. She might have retracted them if not for the tally of a thousand days spent wishing for his return.

"What I've always suspected would happen," he said as if accepting defeat. "I'll turn myself in. If I don't, they'll continue to train more operatives and keep sending them over."

Seeing sheer resignation in a man who was once larger than life was almost too much for Vivian to bear. Her mind fell back to an image, a photo from the newspaper that for some inexplicable reason had captured her interest. Beside the article of the missing little girl was a picture of her parents in grainy gray tones. Despite seemingly insurmountable odds, their faces wore an enduring veneer of hope.

In Vivian's memory, she reviewed the photo again, and halted at a thought. As if viewed through a camera lens, the idea gained focus. It would be a gamble, yes. But with no other options, the solution called to her.

"Do you trust me?" she said to Isaak, whose brow sharply dipped.

"Of course."

"Good," she said. "Because you'll need to."

41

At this point, all Audra could do was hope. She assured herself that the worst wasn't yet to come. But she knew better, even before she opened her front door to the two uniformed men.

"Good afternoon," said the one on the right. He was pale skinned, with a slight crook in his nose. "I'm Officer Hall and this is Officer Ramirez." The sturdy Hispanic-looking man tipped his hat.

"Hello," she said.

"Ma'am, are you Audra Hughes?" Officer Hall continued with the lead.

"I am."

"Ms. Hughes, we're stopping by today because a citizen called, saying they've heard a child screaming from your residence on several occasions."

A neighbor. It had to be — though Audra could only guess which one. Their encounters had never surpassed a trade of courteous smiles.

Why hadn't she thought of it before? There would be no basis for anyone here to presume

395

Jack's frequent screeches of "help me" and "let me out" merely resulted from his dreams.

"That's totally my fault," she admitted. "My son's been having horrible nightmares. The walls aren't the thickest here. I really should've let the residents around us know."

"Could I ask who's in your apartment today?"

Thrown off, Audra took a moment to reply. "Just me and my son, Jack. I'm a single mom."

"Is your son around right now?"

"Well, yes. He's in the kitchen."

Officer Ramirez looked past her shoulder and spoke for the first time. "Afternoon, sir."

Audra turned to find Sean approaching. "What's going on? Is everything okay?"

Oh, God. She'd forgotten he was here.

"I'm sorry," she said to the officers. "I should've remembered — this is Sean Malloy. He's . . . a friend of ours. He's just visiting. For the day." Although she had told Sean of the night terrors, having this unfurl in his presence magnified her embarrassment. Unfortunately, inviting him to leave could suggest to the policemen that she'd been hiding him on purpose.

Officer Hall resumed his mission in a distressingly genial tone. "Ma'am, we'd just like to check on your son real quick, make sure there's no concern. Then we can get out of your hair and let you enjoy your weekend."

"Sure. That's — fine." She tried not to stammer. "Jack? Could you come over here, please?"

"Would you mind if we came inside?" Officer Hall asked.

"No. No, please do." She backed up to let them through and closed the door, right as Jack arrived in the entryway. His sleeves were pulled up a few inches, the cuffs dampened from washing at the sink.

The second officer angled toward Jack. "Hi there. I'm Officer Ramirez." Beneath the warmth of his smile, he had to be scanning, assessing. "Is your name Jack?"

Jack nodded.

Officer Ramirez then looked at Audra. "Would it be all right if I talk to Jack in his room for a moment while you talk to Officer Hall?"

"Yes. Of course." She put on a smile to help ease Jack's puzzlement. "Baby, these policemen are just here to make sure you're safe. Why don't you show Officer Ramirez your room . . . so he can . . . see your bombers?"

She was trying to keep things casual, and immediately regretted the mention of an armed weapon. "I just mean your old warplanes, the models. Like in your dreams." Now she sounded as if she was prompting his answers, demanding he confirm her claim of nightmares.

No doubt Officer Ramirez, too, was considering the possibility, but his animated tone masked the thought. "You've got model airplanes in your room?" he said to Jack. "You know, I used to paint them with my grandpa. Ships too, but the planes were my favorites." He exuded the

397

experience of a father, making clear that in these situations he was the one assigned to the kids. "How about we take a look, little man?"

Jack paused for only a second before nodding again. As he led the officer away, Audra recalled the state of Jack's room. The explosion of toys and clothes and bedding didn't suggest an ideal environment. Small quivers reverberated in Audra's knees.

"Would you care to sit down?" she asked, and was relieved Officer Hall agreed.

Sean gave her a look and motioned to the door: *Do you want me to leave*?

She tightly shook her head.

Though still confused, he nodded and followed.

In the living room, Audra and Sean sat on the couch with appropriate space between them. The officer sat on the sofa chair and pulled out a small notepad. He jotted down the names and birthdates of everyone there, formalities required for a report.

"Ma'am, I noticed your son's got a cast on his arm. Could you tell me what that's from?"

"I'd be glad to," she said, eager to explain. She also sensed that volunteering too much too fast could come off as scripted. "You see, a few weeks ago, he was having a night terror — that's what the doctor at the ER called them." She hoped the term had been recorded in Jack's medical file. "The dreams cause him to flail around a lot, and that's how his arm hit the dresser. Since then, I've done a better job of holding on to him to keep him from hurting himself. But he does get some bruises that way."

"Excuse me, Officer," Sean interjected, appearing to comprehend the nature of the exchange. "If you're trying to find out if Audra's an abusive mother, I can tell you right now, there's not a chance. The kid really does have physically violent dreams."

"Have you seen these yourself, sir?"

"Well . . . no. I haven't."

"Have you spent much time with the family?"

"No, not much. But we just met recently."

The officer nodded, wrote on his pad.

"Sean, it's all right," Audra said quietly. He was trying to help, a former news producer taking the lead, but could end up making things worse.

Officer Hall again addressed Audra. "Is there anyone professional you're seeing, to help your son with these episodes?"

She perked at this. "Yes. We've been seeing the counselor at his school. His name's Dr. Shaw." Never had she been more grateful for sessions with any therapist.

"That's good to hear. I'm sure that'll be helpful."

The topic led her back to evaluations for custody. She debated on bringing up the case, afraid the officers might somehow find out and make a note of her omission. But then Officer

Ramirez emerged from Jack's bedroom — without Jack.

"Ms. Hughes," he said, "I was wondering if you could tell me where your son's injuries came from?"

Officer Hall had heard everything yet didn't say a word.

She swallowed, realizing what was happening. They were comparing stories, looking for discrepancies. She calmly repeated her explanation. When she finished, Officer Ramirez asked, "Would you mind if I took a peek at your son's chest and back? Just to be thorough."

His request held all the lightness of a search for freckles, not signs of parental cruelty.

"That'd be fine."

"Great. Could I also snap a few photos of any injuries? The more detailed we are, the less chance we'll need to come back again."

She nodded her consent. Would any wise person actually say no?

He turned with a half smile and proceeded to Jack's room.

Officer Hall went on with basic questions, perhaps a way to fill the time. Audra answered each one, all while imagining the scene beyond the wall. She saw the birthmark that could be viewed as a scar from a cigarette burn. She saw the scuffs on Jack's knee from the boulder at the park. And in her head, she could hear the explanation she had suggested he relay at school.

My mom told me to say I got hurt from my nightmares, if any of my teachers ask.

Mandatory reporting might otherwise have led staff members to call a child abuse hotline. Audra had encouraged Jack's answer as a pro-active measure, to prevent any more suspicions. A measure that now could backfire.

Finally Officer Ramirez returned, this time with her son. "I think we're all set, ma'am."

Officer Hall stood, putting the notepad in his back pocket. "Thanks for allowing us to take up your time, Ms. Hughes."

"Of course." She and Sean simultaneously rose, although only Audra walked the officers to the door. Once they were gone, the quivers in her knees moved to her hands. She placed them on Jack's shoulders and knelt to eye level. "I am so sorry about that, Jack."

He scrunched his brow, not seeing a reason for her apology.

For that alone, an urge to cry mounted inside. She drew Jack into her arms, holding him tight, and resisted the notion of ever letting go.

401

42

On the phone with a receptionist, whose evident duty for the FBI was to screen for credible callers, Vivian had been right to anticipate resistance: "What *specifically* is this regarding, ma'am?"

Her "urgent" request for an appointment with Special Agent Daniel Gerard was not to be granted blindly. Foreseeing this, and unable to sleep after leaving Isaak at the cinema, she had spent much of the night mentally rehearsing her approach: *I need to speak with him about a private matter of national security.* Yet when the time came and her lips parted to voice the words, she envisioned the receptionist fighting a yawn, unmoved by the hundredth call of its kind that week.

And so, in that instant, Vivian conjured an alternative. It was a wide step from the truth but somehow rolled off her tongue with the smoothness of buttercream. The woman paused before replying, "One moment, please." Shortly after, she returned to the line and offered Vivian a mid-morning slot.

On the upside, the lies were compiling too quickly to accrue guilt. Her latest, to excuse her from work today, was an imaginary toothache that required a dentist's visit.

Then again, given the nervous clamping of her jaw, a real ache was destined to follow. Fortunately, it would all be over soon.

She clung to this assurance now while trailing a secretary through the New York Field Office of the FBI. Her grip held tight to the handles of Isaak's satchel.

In case they want proof, he'd explained as he handed her a key. It led her to Grand Central last night, where she opened the corresponding locker, expecting maps and documents to corroborate his tale. What she discovered in their stead left her short of breath.

"Here we are." The receptionist, a tall woman with beady eyes, gestured to the open door.

"Thank you," Vivian said, her voice suddenly hoarse. Clearing her throat, she stepped inside and flinched at the rattling of glass from the door closing behind her.

"Miss James." The man rose from his desk and came around to meet her. His dark features were the same from his photo in the paper. In his mid-thirties, he had a lean build, a neat but crooked tie, and the start of a receding hairline.

"Thank you for seeing me." With great reluctance she released her hand from the bag, but only long enough for a handshake.

Agent Gerard seemed to sense this, giving the satchel a look. "Please, have a seat."

She smiled and obliged by lowering onto one of the visitors' ladder-backs.

As the fellow returned to his chair, Vivian examined the pillared files that littered his desk. The signal of a hard worker — or merely a messy one. The same could be said of the ashtray containing a knoll of cigarette butts, one of them wending gray smoke into the confined space. Posters of *Wanted* criminals hung on a corkboard with an array of illegible notes. Beside a map of America, tacked up with pushpins, was a daily calendar with no dates torn off since March 3.

"So," he said, settling back in, "I understand you have some information for me."

"That's correct. Yes."

In spite of his controlled manner, a product of either his training or callousness from prior cases, his brown eyes betrayed him. For they exuded a tiny gleam of hope that now caused her shame.

"I think I should begin," she said, "with a confession. You see . . . I'm actually not here about Trudy Beckam. It was all such a tragedy, the disappearance of that little girl. I do so wish I had a new clue that could help, but . . . I don't."

The man remained stone-faced, though his eyes notably dimmed.

"I'm very sorry to have deceived you. But I was afraid you wouldn't agree to see me otherwise. That you'd think I was some paranoid woman who'd listened to one too many episodes of *Miss Pinkerton.* Or perhaps somebody who was just looking to stir up —"

Agent Gerard raised his hand to halt her, a worrisome sign. "Why don't you tell me why you are here."

Vivian straightened in her chair and nodded, recalling her practiced account. "Agent Gerard, I have knowledge of an impending threat to our national security. In just four days — no, three — as early as this Friday, that is — a group of Nazi spies is scheduled to be delivered by submarine to the East Coast. On the shores of Florida and New York. Their primary goal is to sabotage war production plants, but also to demoralize citizens by blowing up places like department stores and train stations. Ultimately, they even hope to rally German Americans against our own country." She paused to gauge his reaction, which thankfully showed no trace of humor.

"You mind telling me how you came across this information?"

She took care not to mention names quite yet. "I learned it from a scout assigned to the

405

mission."

"A scout, you say."

"That's right. He's an American, born and raised in upstate New York. And he would very much like to turn himself in."

"But . . ."

"But?" she echoed.

"I assume there's a reason *you're* here, rather than him."

"Oh. Well, yes." She was grateful the man had brought this up. "There's a slight complication, I'm afraid. It involves his family."

"His family."

"There are five of them still in Munich. From what I understand" — a preemptive disclosure — "they're doing their best to put on a front of supporting Hitler's efforts. But I believe wholeheartedly that they'll be in grave danger if they're not relocated before my friend exposes the operation."

Agent Gerard reached into his desk drawer and shuffled around, as if searching for a notepad and pen. Instead, he retrieved a fresh cigarette and a matchbook. "So this friend of yours," he said, between puffs igniting the tip, "he asked you to come here?"

"Yes — or no, rather. It was my idea."

"You sure about that?"

The question revived doubts from her past, over who had truly initiated the plan to gather political news from her father. Again, she brushed them aside.

"I'm sure of it," she said.

"Mmm." More puffs on his cigarette. "And these targets you mentioned, I take it you — or this scout — know specifics about dates and locations of these attacks."

She figured Isaak to be well informed of such details, though she hadn't explicitly confirmed it. "I-I think so," she said. "He does have a list of contacts on a handkerchief. I do know that for certain."

"Because you've seen the names?"

"Well, no. Not yet. The list is written in invisible ink." In her own ears, she heard how naïve that sounded. For credibility, she needed to recall which chemical would make the writing visible. What did Isaak tell her? Ammonia, was it?

The desk chair creaked as Agent Gerard reclined several inches. Arms folded, he exhaled a ribbon of smoke from the corner of his mouth. "Miss James, you seem like a nice, smart girl, so I'm going to be real honest with you. If I had to guess, I'd say this gentleman friend of yours was inspired by the Sebold case."

She stared, unfamiliar with the reference.

"William Sebold. The German-American snitch. He helped us take down the Duquesne Spy Ring. Surely you read about the trial last year."

Her interest in politics had only lately reached respectable heights. Admitting her ignorance, she shook her head.

"Well, it sounds to me like your buddy knows all about it. Thanks to Sebold's co-operation as a double agent, thirty-three spies were rounded up and put on trial right here in Brooklyn."

Vivian's mind whirled, seeking a connection, as the man leaned forward with his elbows on the desk. "Look, I don't doubt for a minute that your friend's got family in Germany. If I were him, I'd want them the heck out of there too. But the rest of it, this East Coast spy business, it sounds like a bunch o' bull to me — if you'll excuse the expression."

"But . . . it's true, though," she said, and caught her own halfhearted tone. She girded herself, battled against her doubts. "My father works for an American embassy. I would know if he were lying."

Agent Gerard's brows arched in slight surprise, then lowered. "Maybe your father can lend a hand then, to help you out."

"He can't. He's in London. And we don't have enough time."

"I see." After a quick glance at his watch, he crushed out his cigarette and came to his feet. "I do wish you luck, Miss James. And make sure, if this friend causes you any real trouble, you take your concerns to your local police station. You hear?"

Vivian went to stand, unclear what else to

do, and only then remembered the evidence in her lap. How could she have forgotten?

She jutted her chin as she rose. "I have proof."

Agent Gerard shed a small sigh. "Is that so?"

"He was given funds for their contacts, and also to aid their tasks. The majority of the stash was to be hidden until the other spies arrived safely onshore." With that, Vivian unlatched the satchel. In a series of small shakes, she sent the contents tumbling onto the desk.

The agent gazed wordlessly at the bound stacks of cash, an uneven mountain of green. No training had prepared him for this kind of moment.

"What is this?" he breathed.

"A reason you have to believe me."

In a slow, tentative motion he picked up a bundle, as if hastiness might prove it a mirage. He fanned an edge of the bills, each of them a crisp and clean fifty, perfuming the air with forty thousand dollars.

"Now will you help me?"

He was engrossed in thought. Vivian's summary suddenly required focus, measurement, dissection. "Three days isn't much time," he said. Not a critical remark, a reflective one.

"I know," she told him with regret. "With the article, I wish I'd thought of you sooner. I should have."

He looked up at her. His eyes narrowed into a question.

"That's what brought me here," she explained. "The article about Trudy Beckam. It said that aside from her parents, everyone gave up. Except for you." She lightly shrugged. "So, that's how I knew . . ."

"Knew what?" he said, a tad leery.

"That you're willing to fight impossible odds."

His gaze lingered on her before returning to the money in his hand. He didn't speak but gave a nod, just perceptible enough to sustain Vivian's hopes.

43

In the dimly lit office, Audra barricaded her thoughts to keep doubt at bay. She needed this to work. She sat by the desk in the corner to observe the session without interfering. A combination of curtains and darkening blinds eclipsed the Wednesday afternoon light.

Reclined on the whimsical couch, Jack followed each verbal instruction. He breathed in and out while focusing on the floral sticker on the ceiling. Dr. Shaw, on a neighboring chair, guided Jack into a mode of relaxation. The man swore it to be thoroughly safe.

He had further explained: If Jack were younger and his "veil" were more open, he could have regressed with casual prompting. In this case, hypnosis could serve as a nudge. Since children pass through trance-like states on any given day, induction would be relatively simple.

Hypnotherapy. One more concept Audra had previously scoffed at.

After the officers' visit four days ago, she was

411

willing to try even this. She had since contacted other apartment tenants, apologizing for the noise from Jack's dreams. Most residents had been gracious, but a few had skepticism in their eyes.

Russ had assured her not to worry; if the policemen weren't satisfied by the "welfare check," Karly's Law would have required them to arrange an immediate medical exam for Jack. The fact that they'd refrained implied acceptance of Audra's claims. This, Russ had said, could help her on the custody front. Or, on the flipside, serve as proof that her in-laws weren't the only ones reporting suspicions.

Dr. Shaw continued, slow and soothing. "Remember now, Jack, you're the one in complete control of our journey. I'm going to paint you a scene, but it's up to you to make any choices. Let's start with a beautiful house. Imagine you're inside that house, standing at the top of a staircase. The space around you is filled with warm, yellow sunlight. You can feel it on your hair and your face. Everything around you is quiet and peaceful."

Audra pictured the setting herself. She felt the sun's warmth, the room's tranquility. Her tension dissolved as she sank comfortably into her chair.

"At the bottom of the stairs is a door, and beyond that door is another quiet and peaceful place. It's full of light and love. But to get there, you'll need to walk down the stairs. With each step, you're going to become even more relaxed. Would you like to go, Jack? Good, let's take a step. Ten, that's the first one. Your body is already getting heavier. Do you feel how heavy you're getting? In your arms, your hands, your legs, your feet. Now, we're going to take a second step. Nine . . . ."

Audra's eyelids started to drop. She strained to keep them open. Jack's latest night terror hadn't come until four in the morning, allowing her just enough sleep to leave her too restless to go back to bed.

She straightened her posture. Listening closer, she hoped for any hint of how to bring the pieces together: Jakob, Isaak, Vivian, the FBI and Nazi spies, the reunion of a couple divided.

Dr. Shaw was on the seventh step down . . . now the sixth . . . every limb growing heavier.

Audra's eyes continued to fight her, every blink like the fall of velvety drapes. She could no longer hold them open.

Then her head jerked up. Her chin had dipped to her chest and startled her awake.

Dr. Shaw was standing beside her, his hand on her shoulder. He had adjusted the lighting. The room was slightly brighter.

"Mrs. Hughes, we're all done." He wore his practiced smile as he released his hold.

"But — we just started." Across the room Jack sat on the floor, sifting through the bin of mismatched toys. That's when she realized it

413

was Dr. Shaw's hand that had woken her. "You're kidding me. I fell asleep?"

"Not to worry. I've recorded the session, so you can play it back at home."

She rubbed at her eyes to clear her vision. In doing so, her wrist discovered a trail of saliva by her mouth. She swiped the moisture away as Dr. Shaw settled into his desk chair.

"Could you . . . tell me what happened?" she asked quietly, conscious of Jack's presence. "After the stairs and the door."

Dr. Shaw pleasantly obliged. "When your son was ready, I guided him into a boat that drifted into a fog. As I mentioned before, past life regression isn't a specialty of mine. But what I've found is that patients who did regress well used the mist as a transitioning point. From there they were able to access memories from a past life."

Audra still couldn't believe she had dozed through all of this.

"And," she said, "what did Jack say?"

Dr. Shaw sighed, shook his head. "I'm afraid he didn't see anything. That's not to say those lives didn't exist. It could simply mean that for one reason or another he wasn't willing to revisit them. At least not today."

Discouraged, she sat back. She didn't have the luxury of unlimited time and money. There had to be a solution they just weren't seeing. She gazed over at Jack. He pushed a button on a robot, triggering its deep automated voice:

"Together, we shall use our secret weapons to defeat Veter Man once and for all."

Dr. Shaw said to her, "During the next session we could certainly try again. We might have more success with a second attempt."

Audra nodded, though her thoughts had already seized another option. Specifically, another person. And that person was hiding something. Audra realized this now, looking back. She had missed the connection before today's mentions of boats, the past, and secrets. Most of all, one's willingness to access memories.

Now, she just had to figure out which button to press to obtain the information needed.

44

It was a place where people didn't ask questions.

Vivian perceived this the instant she entered the hotel. Stacked chairs and an old mattress lined the walls, creating nooks and crannies to shelter guests' secrets. Down the stairway, a suited man escorted the type of female who provided company by the hour.

An orange sunset spilled muted hues through the lobby windows. It was too dark for the sunglasses over Vivian's eyes, too warm for the scarf enwrapping her hair and neck. Yet for now, she would retain her semi-disguise.

As she crossed the chipped tiles to reach the caged elevator, the grizzled man behind the counter never once glanced up from his newspaper. In fact, he appeared to deliberately drop his head. No wonder Isaak had chosen this place as his hideout for the duration. With the funds he had been given, he could have stayed at the Martinique or the

Hotel Governor Clinton, but here, tucked away on a side street in Queens, he had optimized discretion while minimizing use of dirty Nazi money.

She rode the creaky lift alone, glad for the uninterrupted transport to the fourth floor. So close now to voicing her declaration, she could barely contain her smile.

In the vacant hallway, she gave the area a quick scan before knocking at 42. "Isaak," she said quietly, "it's me."

Seconds later came the rattle of a chain sliding and screech of a bolt turning, and the door opened halfway. Isaak stood with his shirt unbuttoned, tossed on haphazardly, as if he had been undressed only a moment ago.

She slipped past him, concentrating on her news. The air held a musky scent, corralled in the room by the closed curtains. Food wrappers, empty Coke bottles, and half a loaf of bread crowded a table in the corner.

The instant Isaak finished resealing the door, she announced: "Everything is done."

He turned to face her.

"It wasn't easy, but Agent Gerard pulled it off. Somehow he did it. Documents, travel arrangements, IDs. All of it in just two days. Your family should be crossing the border into Switzerland within hours."

Isaak responded with only a nod. No trace of the elation she had envisioned since her latest stop at the FBI office. Perhaps relief was overwhelming him.

She removed her sunglasses to connect with his eyes. "Isaak. Did you hear what I said?"

"The Gestapo would've been watching them. Now more than ever."

"Well, yes. Likely so. But the FBI took this into account. That's why they've taken precautions. Their contacts there —"

"Which ones?"

"I'm . . . not sure who they are exactly."

"Which *precautions*?" His sudden impatience caused her to draw back. Her impetus to smile had fallen away. But so had Isaak's, she reminded herself, long before today, his worries justifiable.

She sat on the foot of the bed with purse and glasses on her lap. "What I've been told is, they've created a fake order from German Intelligence. It calls for your family's relocation to Berlin as a reward for your service. And for their loyalty to the Third Reich."

"Berlin?"

"This is only to get them on the first train. Once they're in transit, someone will guide them to switch routes to travel south, using other papers. Their new identities."

"Nazi officers will be patrolling every stop. Where will they be detouring?"

She shook her head. "Agent Gerard couldn't tell me. He said it's best that we not know all the specifics."

"Of course it is — for him." He huffed a

dark laugh. Then he rubbed his hair and started to pace back and forth over the threadbare carpet.

Vivian wondered how much of the floor's wear had been caused by his shoes alone.

"How do we know this agent of yours isn't a spy for the Nazis? They could have infiltrated the FBI. That's how the arrangements could have been made so quickly."

"That's absurd. Agent Gerard is not a German spy."

"How do you know that?"

"Because he's not," she said. "He was handling a case of a missing child before this. Isaak, please. Come sit down."

He continued his laps, not hearing her. The bedside lamp flickered its amber glow, as if tension in the room carried an electrical current. "So, my family's documents," he said, "how much proof did he show you?"

Timid but honest, she answered, "He . . . couldn't exactly."

Isaak stopped. His eyes darted to her face.

"But the man did give me his word."

"His word?" Isaak said. "What the hell were you thinking?"

She felt like a gullible child who had squandered the rent money. She began to second-guess her actions, of where she had gone wrong — but no. No, that was nonsense. She didn't deserve a scolding of any kind. She had done her best with what she was

419

given. What more did he expect of her? Did he really believe he could have done better?

She shot to her feet. "If I had demanded proof, Agent Gerard could have easily created false evidence. Either way, I wouldn't have known the difference. And neither would you."

He paused, his shoulders lowering. "Vivian —"

"I never asked to be pulled into the godforsaken mess. I've risked everything — endangering my parents, people I care about — in order to help you." Pressure from all the lies, the anxiety, the flip-flopping emotions, at last reached a tipping point. "So, no, Isaak. There is no proof. There is no guarantee. But I have faith Agent Gerard is telling the truth," she said. "Just as I had faith in you."

He said nothing as she collected her purse and glasses from where they had fallen to the floor.

Moisture rushed to her eyes. She kept them down, unwilling to satisfy him with a show of caring. "By tomorrow morning, they should have confirmation of your family's safety. Once they do, you're to report to Agent Gerard's office."

"Vivian," he said again. When he reached for her, she angled away. She was hanging over a chasm with a fraying rope in her hands. His touch was a blade that would send her plummeting.

420

She stated her final message: "I'll send word to you through the front desk."

With that, she headed for the door, where she briskly released the bolt. The chain caught halfway. She was struggling to slide it free when Isaak's arm reached past her. He braced his hand against the door to prevent her escape.

"Forgive me," he rasped. "It's my fault, all of it. Darling, please don't leave."

She told herself not to listen. But his chest brushed her back, and as always, the warmth of his skin, the feel of his breath, weakened her resolve.

"Look at me," he told her. "Please."

She did not fight him as he guided her around, though she managed to avert her gaze. He loosened the scarf from her head, threading his fingers through her hair, and she cursed the tingling of her skin. Soon he leaned forward. She prepared to defy a kiss. Instead, his forehead gingerly rested on hers. He closed his eyes and whispered, "Vivian, I'm scared."

It wasn't just the words that captured her but the ache in his tone, a helplessness she, too, had once endured. His soul lay before her, raw and open like a wound. She could not bring herself to walk away.

"Everything will be all right," she told him. "You'll see."

He tilted his head and smoothly, slowly

nuzzled her cheek. A familiar but foreign sensation. "I love you so very much," he said. "All this time, I always have." He covered her lips with his before she even noticed their approach. What started out brief and tender — an apology, a token of gratitude — gained the charge of something greater.

It was a yearning, deep and buried. A grieving for years past. It was for every touch and smile and kiss they were promised, stolen by the grips of war. It was a need, for even a moment, to be in control yet swept away by an emotion too vast to describe.

Above all, it was freedom. And like a plucked string, that feeling reverberated to Vivian's core as Isaak laid her on the bed. His hands and mouth rushed over her, fulfilling wants of their own. A distant voice whispered in her mind, a reminder that no freedom came without a price. But that voice swiftly faded at the sound of Isaak's breathing, the clank of his loosened belt. Flames chased his fingers as he moved under her dress and a moan slipped from her throat.

The last sight Vivian caught before closing her eyes were wiry cracks on the ceiling, the markings of a structure on the verge of crumbling.

45

Audra's hopes had been whittled to fragments, but a sizeable one remained. The revelation had come to her yesterday, after the regression attempt had failed. Her focus on their session had quickly turned to "First Thursday."

The monthly art walk in the Pearl District was known for beckoning hordes of people, many of whom, like Audra, had little knowledge of art. They came for the cultural experience. Galleries on practically every block showcased the newest exhibits. Amid the sculptures and paintings, wineries served complimentary tastings and musicians played jazz and blues.

Dressed up for the evening, Audra had worn a touch of makeup, her hair long and styled, but only to fit in with the trendy mass. Her attendance at The Attic held a singular purpose.

"Audra!" Judith greeted her. Her voice barely carried over the surrounding murmurs and cellist's performance. "I told Sean to invite you, but he didn't tell me you were coming."

Audra smiled. "It's not his fault. I didn't let him

know until this morning."

"Well. In that case, I'll let him off the hook *this* time." Judith laughed, then gasped with delight. "My goodness, this must be your son."

"Yep, that's him. Jack, this is Sean's mom, Ms. Malloy."

"Hi," he said with a wave. He even gave a congenial smile.

"Please, call me Judith. Oh, Audra, he's even cuter than I remember from the festival." Judith patted the lime-green scarf that draped her like a cowl-neck. The rest of her outfit was elegant and artsy in flowy black silk. "Wow, I can't get over how much he looks like you."

The remark would have seemed a mere courtesy if not for the genuine awe in Judith's tone. Maybe with age Jack finally resembled Audra more. A nice notion.

Audra winked at him. "That's meant as a compliment, you know."

He didn't respond, distracted by the guests milling about, many using their wineglasses to point at various pieces.

"Feel free to roam around, you two," Judith said. "I'm afraid I haven't seen Sean yet, but he should be arriving soon."

"Actually," Audra said, "he insisted on driving us. He dropped us off at the door so he could go find a parking spot." Parking in northwest Portland was never scarcer than on First Thursdays, which had made Sean's offer to chauffeur them difficult to resist. The added benefit for Audra had been the chance to privately thank him for his support after the park.

"Well, how about that," Judith clucked. "Sounds like a bit of the chivalry I tried to drill into his brain managed to get through."

"I would say more than a bit."

It was an honest comment, but the intrigue on Judith's face made Audra wish she had refrained. She didn't want anyone — especially not Jack — to mistake this for a date. "So," Audra said, reverting to her task, "I hear Luanne will be coming tonight."

"Yes, yes. In fact, she's already here."

Audra was amazed that Luanne, even at her ripe age, still loved to drive herself around town.

"If you don't see her anywhere, she's probably over there in my studio. The joints in her knees were bothering her earlier, so she might be resting them."

"I hope she's okay. Would you like me to check on her?"

"Oh, you're so sweet. But Sean can handle it." Judith flitted her hand, clinking her copper bracelets. "You and Jack should enjoy your evening."

"It's no problem. Really, I'd be happy to." For more than one reason.

Judith was about to answer when her gaze shot past Audra. "I think I recognize this handsome gentleman. I was starting to worry about you."

Sean made it through the entry, looking like

he had a story to share. "It is seriously vicious out there."

"Why?" Judith said. "What happened?"

"I got back in my car, just to put my ticket stub on the window, and this elderly lady was waiting in her van. So I signaled I wasn't leaving. She actually flipped me the —" He stopped to glance at Jack, who was suddenly captivated, and finished with: "A very . . . not polite sign."

Jack chuckled a little, as though well aware of the censored word. Audra didn't want to imagine what other off-color phrases had made it into his repertoire. All the same, she couldn't help laughing along with Sean. It was encouraging to see Jack in a happy mood, which admittedly came more easily when Sean was around.

"Sorry to interrupt," a woman broke in. She wore cat's-eye glasses trimmed in blue rhinestones. Presumably the gallery manager. "Judith, there's a customer in the back interested in one of your new pieces. She'd like to discuss it with you if you're free."

"Sure thing. If you'll all excuse me." About to dash off, Judith turned to Sean. "Oh, I meant to tell you, honey. There's a guy here who says he's a friend of yours. I didn't catch his name, but told him to keep an eye out for you."

"Great. Thanks."

Audra heard the subtle dread in his voice, and she understood. A reunion with anyone lost to Sean's memory would make for an awkward exchange, or at best require a convincing

426

façade. Audra knew how it felt to stumble across old acquaintances who sought a friendly update, having no knowledge of your latest news.

"So, what do you think, Jack?" Sean motioned to the closest wall. "You like this one?" The spotlighted piece was a multimedia creation of fairies.

Jack scrunched his nose. "Tinker Bell's kinda girly," he said, though he did admit to liking the darker, more mysterious butterfly painting. As Sean guided him to the next wall, Jack pulled his toy plane from his pocket and stroked it with his thumb, as if detecting the common theme of flight.

Luanne was nowhere to be seen.

"If you two are okay for a while," Audra said, "I'll go see how Luanne is doing. Jack, do you mind?"

He shrugged. "That's fine."

"Do you need help finding her?" Sean asked.

"Your mom says she's resting in the studio. I thought I'd see if she needed anything."

Sean smiled in appreciation, causing Audra a twinge of guilt. "Come on, buddy," he said to Jack. "We got some art to see."

Watching them venture off, Audra assured herself that confronting Luanne alone, without anyone knowing, was the right approach. As Vivian's roommate and longtime friend, the woman must have been privy to details of Vivian's life prior to Gene. But Luanne's reasons for secrecy were yet unknown.

At the refreshment table, Audra filled a glass with water. She took a breath before poking her head into the studio. "Care for some company?"

Luanne looked up, seated by the worktable against the wall. "Well, aren't you a sight for sore eyes." She returned a small frame to a lineup of photos.

"Sore knees too, I hear."

"Ah, yeah." Luanne swatted the air above her legs. "Live long enough, you need replacement parts for almost everything."

Audra stepped inside and closed the door, muffling the chatter and music. Shelves of art materials covered a full wall: foils and gems and wires and paint. Works-in-progress reclined on easels, their fumes wafting from drying acrylics.

"For you, madame." Audra presented the drink, which Luanne gratefully accepted. As Audra pulled up a stool, Luanne took a sip that caused her to scowl.

"What in heaven's name did they do to this water?" Luanne studied the pink-tinted liquid.

"I think they soaked rose petals in it. Would you like something else?"

"No, no. It'll do. Just don't be surprised if I start sprouting leaves." Luanne grinned and set the glass down by the photo she'd been studying. A man with salt-and-pepper hair and a bright smile had his arm around Judith at a younger age; beside them hung a landscape painting in an array of vibrant hues.

"That's my Freddy there," Luanne said, observing Audra's attention. "It was the first time a buyer put Judith's art on public display. By the fuss we made, you'd have thought it was at the Met, not a bar and grille."

Audra smiled, taking a moment to recognize the natural segue to Luanne's past. "Sounds like you were great parents to her."

Behind Luanne's bifocals, a tinge of somberness entered her eyes. "Yes, well. We weren't the real thing. Just did the best we knew how." She wiped a smudge from the frame, and a pensive smile warmed her face. "Freddy was a good man. And strong. Eight years ago, the doctors diagnosed him with colon cancer, gave him six months to live. But that stubborn fool fought for three more years."

Audra was suddenly tempted to postpone the pending talk. But then she thought of Jack and his nightmares and her longing to care for him until her own graying days.

"Luanne," she began, "I need to talk to you about something."

The woman turned to her, tilting her head a fraction. "What is it, dear?"

"It's about . . . well, it's about Vivian."

The name clearly came as a surprise. "Oh?" Luanne said.

"I know this might be a strange question. But I was hoping you could tell me about her and Isaak, about what happened between them during the war."

At this, the wrinkles lining Luanne's mouth deepened. She dropped her gaze to the lap of her floral dress, as if contemplating. "His name doesn't sound familiar," she said, and picked at invisible lint. Her hand appeared to quiver from a cause other than age.

Audra had no desire to interrogate the sweet lady, but a remedy for Jack could be an arm's length away. She couldn't give up without reaching.

"I understand how painful it can be, talking about loved ones you've lost. I genuinely do. But I'm begging you — as a mother who loves her son, just as much as I know you've loved Judith — I'm asking for your help."

Slowly, Luanne raised her eyes. They were bewildered and heavily guarded, but she was listening. And that was all the prompting Audra needed.

Without reservation, perhaps from repetition, she delved straight into the major highlights. One event after the other, she recapped her skeptical journey. All along Luanne said nothing, not a single act of acknowledgment, yet Audra didn't stop. She barely took breaths between sentences until she reached the end, at which point silence draped the room, far thicker than any paint fumes.

Luanne stared at her distantly. A flush resembling a rash had crept into her cheeks.

"I wouldn't blame you at all for thinking I'm

nuts," Audra added, hoping to dispel the idea. "Either way, the fact is, I don't know how to help Jack without knowing more."

A long quiet passed before Luanne went to speak. When she did, the words came even but firm. "I wish I could help you, but like I said, I don't know anything about it."

Audra's spirits recoiled. Outside of crawling on her knees, she could think of no other way to ask.

All of a sudden, music and chatter from the gallery rose in volume. From the opened door Jack shuffled over. "Mom, what took so long?"

"Sorry about that." Audra tried to smile. "I just had to talk to Luanne for a while."

Sean declared from the doorway, "We need to leave early." From his cool demeanor, it was clear he'd surmised the gist of the conversation and didn't approve. He had, after all, warned Audra that dredging up the past would upset Luanne — and based on the woman's expression, he was right. "Are you feeling well enough to drive home, Aunt Lu?"

Luanne hesitated before nodding. "Yes . . . I'll be fine." She said this while looking at Jack, who was surveying the shelves, absently rubbing his toy plane.

"Come on, Jack," Audra said, standing. "Let's go."

"But, Mom" — he pointed at Luanne — "it's Miss Muppet."

This was his personal nickname for Miss

Piggy, created from reruns of the *Muppet Babies* cartoon. He was playing their usual game, noting Luanne's curly hair and now pinkish skin. But this wasn't the time.

Audra held his hand to guide him out.

Sean had already disappeared into the crowd.

At the doorway, Audra glanced back into studio. "Good night," she said to Luanne, but the woman didn't answer.

46

Afterward, neither of them spoke. The only sounds came from movement in neighboring rooms, murmurs from the hallway, cars on the street.

Reclined on the hotel bed, Isaak watched Vivian replace her clothing. When she was ready, he walked her to the door. The word *good-bye* hung between them, though they knew better than to verbalize a thing so final. There was much unknown, with as many feelings unclear. They merely traded smiles before she departed into the hall. She rode the elevator with sunglasses on, scarf snug around her hair.

Again, the grizzled man in the lobby did not look up.

Through the dusty window, sunset was yielding to dusk. She strode out the door and down the street. For several blocks she suc-ceeded in avoiding all thought. But her senses noted something behind her, perhaps Isaak gazing at her from his room. Unable to resist, she glanced over her shoulder and spied a man with a rifle.

She removed her glasses to confirm the view. He and another man stood outside the hotel. Fedoras covered their heads. Trench coats layered their suits.

Vivian slid behind a newsstand and craned her neck to keep watching.

Before long, four other men emerged from the entrance. Among them was Agent Gerard, guiding Isaak by the elbow. In the manner of a captured prey, Isaak's hands were bound behind his back.

"No," Vivian whispered. She was astounded, aghast. This wasn't the agreement. He wasn't a criminal. He had done nothing wrong.

She launched into a sprint, dropping her glasses, not knowing how they had found him.

But then she realized. Oh, Lord. She had led them here.

The man with the rifle opened the door of a black Ford. Agent Gerard helped Isaak duck inside.

"Stop!" she yelled, spurring one of the others to draw his sidearm. Agent Gerard, seeing her, reached over and directed the gun skyward.

"She's okay," he announced to the others as Vivian stopped to confront him.

"What do you think you're doing?" she implored.

"Calm down," the agent told her, and ushered her aside. "The deal's the same. His family, the whole bit. The big guys at the top just wanted to be careful."

"Isaak doesn't need to be handcuffed. He was turning himself in."

"Look," the agent said. "You remember that Sebold case I told you about? Thirty-three Nazi spies who were rounded up here?"

"I . . . Yes, I guess, but —"

"Well, there was another espionage case before that. Back in '38, we caught a Nazi agent named Rumrich. A German American, same as your fella here. He gladly cooperated and we wound up with a list of more than a dozen spies. In the end, though, all but two of Rumrich's buddies got away, including the ringleader. The FBI came out looking like a cage of buffoons. We can't afford to bungle a case that badly again."

"Hey, Gerard!" one of the men called out. Engines of the two Fords were revving. "We set to go?"

"Yeah, yeah."

Vivian peered through the car window and caught sight of Isaak. He shook his head at her, a tender smile on his lips: *Everything will be all right.* Her own assurance had circled right back to her.

"Go on home, now," Agent Gerard said. "I'll take care of your friend."

She grabbed his sleeve and looked him in

435

the eye. "You promise?"

The man blew out a breath, his hand on the car door. Before climbing in, he nodded. "You got my word."

47

The drive home from the gallery had worn Audra's strength to the nub. If not for tunes on the radio, silence in the car would have swelled like helium, the pressure growing until something burst.

Behind the wheel, Sean had trained his eyes on the pavement. Audra had hoped there was another cause for his glacial mood, but his two-word answers suggested nothing else. With Jack in the backseat, she had no opportunity to voice how and why she'd approached Luanne. When they rolled up to the apartment, Audra thought to invite Sean in; they could speak in private once Jack went to bed. But she simply said good night, figuring it was better to let everything settle.

Two days and three voice mails later, however, he hadn't responded. Though his reaction seemed excessive, she at least wanted to explain. She considered calling the house instead of his cell, but she refused to bother Luanne. Plus, by now he and his great-aunt had probably conferred over the police visit and custody case, further justifying his avoidance.

On the other hand, maybe he had just been busy.

The swirling thoughts were making Audra neurotic. At some point, couldn't sleep deprivation literally make a person insane?

She readjusted her bed pillow and rolled onto her other side. She wished her brain had an off switch. Tess and Grace had come by to steal Jack for an afternoon outing, first to a bookstore, then to ice cream, allowing her a much-needed nap. But now here she was, on a quiet Saturday, and her body wide awake.

Finally she gave up.

Needing an activity, she went to the kitchen for a snack. She had just reached the fridge when the phone started to ring. The cordless was missing from the charger.

"Fabulous."

The ring trilled again and she froze, listening to trace its location. It was in . . . Jack's room. She jetted in there, and on the fourth ring she found the phone on his dresser — right where she had left it. She was definitely losing her mind.

"Hello," she answered, and was relieved the person hadn't hung up.

"Hi, Audra, it's Russ. Did I catch you at a bad time?"

Her relief ended there.

"No, not at all."

438

"Great. Because I have good news for you."

For a blissful instant Audra imagined that the case had been dropped, that the other attorney had convinced Robert and Meredith to withdraw the petition. But then Russ announced, "Our court date has been set."

Audra's silence must have communicated her failure to view the development as "good," since Russ went on to elaborate. "The 'housekeeping' hearing will be in just two months. Depending on how it goes, there's still a chance you could keep your plans in Boston."

All things considered, that chance wasn't a strong one, but she aimed for optimism. "You're right. It's possible."

"Would you like to hear the details? Or I can e-mail them over."

"Um, now is fine. Let me write them down." She went to Jack's desk and snagged a pen from the plastic cup that held markers and kid scissors.

"Are you ready?" Russ asked.

"Almost. Just need some paper."

"No problem. Take your time."

She opened the top drawer of the desk to discover a chaotic mound of old homework. The first two sheets were writing assignments with *Super Job* stickers at the top. She opted for a half sheet of pink paper — just a library notice from the school. She flipped to the blank side and said, "All right. Go ahead."

Russ rattled off dates and times and locations.

439

When she had finished transcribing, she read them back for confirmation.

"I'll be in touch with more soon," he said, and she thanked him before they hung up.

A court date.

A judge.

This was actually happening.

She sat on the foot of Jack's bed, letting the handset tumble free. The page, though, remained in her hand. She gazed at the note unseeing.

After a while she folded the paper half, putting the thought away, and a printed word leapt out at her: *OVERDUE.*

It was an overdue notice for a book, checked out by Jack in March. According to the warning, if it wasn't returned by the third week of June, he would owe the school a replacement fee. The final due date was this coming Thursday, the last day of the school year.

What book would he have kept for three months?

She unfolded the note to read the title: *Incredible Moments of World War II.*

Any book about war would be intended for older students — unless it contained only snapshots of the glorified aspects: Rosie the Riveters, victory parades, and patriotic banners.

Then she remembered. She had seen a book in Jack's closet. Last weekend, while scrounging for his helmet, she'd spotted an oversized paperback among his things. It was just before she'd stepped on the shreds of paper . . . .

As the elements collected in her mind, an indescribable dread seeped through her. The world went portentously still, an eerie calm that precedes disaster.

Audra flung open the closet. She tore through the piles of clothes and toys. Beneath the tattered box of Monopoly was the book she recalled, edges worn and corners curled. A scrap of paper dangled from the inside pages.

She flipped to that section, where various photographs had been cut out. He had never done such a thing before, destroying a book like that. What use would he have for the pictures? As a second grader, he'd have no school projects involving world war. Even if he did, the principal would have mentioned it during their last —

Suddenly it came to her.

The journal.

She hurried to kneel by his bed and pulled out the book. *PIECES OF ME.* The title accurately described a life once whole, now shattered into jagged parts.

She leafed through the collages she had already seen, the comic strips and candy wrappers, the magazine ads featuring families. This time she noted that the cruise ship was bound for Europe, and recognized the symbolism of the Eiffel Tower as the heart of the continent. She had gained a new perspective on these images, but they still fit the equation, just in a different way.

Now to reveal the pictures beyond them.

Fear expanded, encompassing her like a fog, as she turned to the next page. Thankfully, she discovered only more of the same. The London Tower, the Colosseum, remnants of the Berlin Wall. For several more pages the theme continued.

And then it all changed.

48

Vivian startled from her semi-conscious haze. A rapping on wood. Her bedroom door. She was about to plead for Luanne to answer but recalled her roommate's absence, out for a late appointment at the beauty salon.

"Miss James?" The voice of the landlady.

"One moment." Vivian maneuvered herself upright on her bed, noting her nightstand clock. Nearly six. After work she had dozed off while resting her head, which continued to throb from three weeks of harbored worries — over not only the FBI's case but also her maddening indiscretion. With such compromised morals, she had needed no other reason to decline joining the WAAC.

Her one saving grace was the military assignment that had kept Gene out of town, hopping between bases. The separation should have enabled her to unsnarl her mesh of feelings. But how could she even begin without an update on Isaak's case?

"Miss James."

"Yes, I'm coming!" Vivian called out, rising to her feet.

"A gentleman is on the phone for you."

Vivian halted.

Agent Gerard. The call she had been expecting all week.

In an instant, the haze dissipated. She scrambled into the hall, bid her thanks, and flew down the stairs. The man had repeatedly affirmed that the Hemel family had been moved to a safe, undisclosed location before all eight spies were apprehended. But there were no developments regarding Isaak. Only that visitors were prohibited until legal formalities were complete. Growing antsy, Vivian had recently left numerous messages at the New York Field Office, where a slew of meetings, according to the receptionist, had occupied the agent's schedule.

At the entry table, praying for good news, Vivian snatched up the handset. "Hello? This is Vivian. Hello?"

"Hi ya, twinkle toes."

Her chest constricted, stealing her breath. Her lungs refused to function.

"Sweetheart? You there?"

"Gene." She hefted a smile into her tone. "You surprised me."

"I know. Didn't think I'd have a chance to ring you till this weekend. They got me running so ragged here. But turns out, I had time to spare and the phone was free. So, how have

444

you been? You get my last letter?"

"Letter? Oh, yes. A couple of days ago." She couldn't bring herself to read more than half of it. She didn't deserve his kind and doting words. "I'm sorry I haven't written back. It's been terribly busy around here too."

"Sure thing. Not to worry. I just wanted to —" He stopped. "Vivi, hold on." He spoke off the phone, muffled, and returned with a groan. "Sorry about that. Looks like they need the line already."

"It's okay. I understand."

"Ah, doll. It's swell to hear your voice anyhow. I hate that I can't be there for the holiday."

Vivian had nearly forgotten. Tomorrow was the Fourth of July. With gunpowder needed for the war, she doubted it would feel much like a celebration.

"At any rate," he said, "should be just two more weeks. After that, how about I treat my girl to a fancy night on the town? Even kick our heels up if you want. What do you say?"

She swallowed down the shame, the turmoil, rising in her throat. "Marvelous."

"It's a date, then. I'll call again when I can."

"Good."

"Oh, and Vivi?"

"Yes?"

His voice dropped to a hush. "I love you."

It was the first time he had verbalized the phrase. Her chest tightened even more. The reverent words formed a vice inside her, each crank the result of another deception.

That's when she realized: With the saboteurs in custody, she could at last tell Gene the truth. How much he could bear to hear she didn't know. Considering what Luanne had said about his former steady's betrayal, the odds of his forgiveness were slim, the chances of hurting him guaranteed.

"Vivian?" He sounded tentative, fretting over her silence.

The confession gathered on her tongue. Like a cluster of pepper, it stung her senses and begged for release. Yet she couldn't. Not over the cold, impersonal wires of a telephone. No matter how daunting it was, she owed him the admission in person.

"Me too," she heard herself say, and detected his easement in a small breath.

Soon the line went dead, but the handset stayed in her grasp. A pair of female tenants entered the house and tossed out greetings in passing. They carried bags and hatboxes from an array of department stores. Sunshine had brightened their noses with rosy hues of summer.

Envy for such normalcy swept over Vivian. Good or bad, she needed to know where matters stood. Anything was better than this state of uncertainty.

On the phone, she summoned the operator and requested the FBI. The receptionist, even

446

at this hour, cited a meeting for Agent Gerard.

"Would you care to leave another message, Miss James?"

Vivian refrained from her standard agreement. "That won't be necessary," she decided.

After all, there was no need to leave a message when she could confront the man in person.

49

His eyes stared back from the grainy pixels of a black-and-white photograph. At the top of the page, halfway into Jack's journal, was a Nazi commander in uniform. A flag bearing a swastika hung in the backdrop. None of this, in particular, was the cause of Audra's angst. It was the caption beneath the picture.

Heinrich Himmler, Reichsführer of the SS, delivering a speech.

Not Himmel. Not Hemel.

Himmler.

The entire collage represented World War Two. Prominently displayed was another disturbing image: a bomber plane diving toward the ocean with smoke pluming from its tail.

Audra rolled off of her knees to sit on Jack's bedroom floor. She needed a solid foundation before turning the page. A snippet of an article appeared on white paper, like the various Web pages he had printed during computer class. Except this one was educational in a much darker way. It featured the account of Nazi spies who were caught on the East Coast and sentenced to the electric chair.

Audra had barely digested this when she plodded onward and found a Rose Festival calendar. *Upcoming Events on Memorial Day.* Included in the listing were small head shots of the soldiers being honored — including PFC Sean Malloy.

The journal slipped from her hands as she tried to make sense of it. Jack had checked the book out in March, months before the night terrors began.

From a place deep in her memory came the scene of a movie. The title eluded her, but she could see the actor's face. It was Kevin Spacey, playing a character who was pretending to be someone he wasn't. In an office at the police station, he recounted his life to an investigating detective. But the story he told wasn't real. He had made it all up by combining photos and fliers and names that surrounded him. And the detective had swallowed it whole. Why? Because he was so hungry for resolution he would have believed anything.

Audra glanced around her. She saw the model planes suspended from the ceiling. She saw Captain America, the hero on the poster, his face on Jack's backpack. She saw the toy plane on his nightstand, its paint rubbed thin from . . . deception? Confusion? Desperation?

As the old saying went, the simplest answer was typically the right one.

449

Perhaps Jack, in his seclusion, had invented a fantasy world aided by his collage. And those images, embodying the darkness of wartime, had gained a realism that now consumed his days and nights.

She had questioned him on every element; always he'd replied with a shrug or *I don't know.* After all, if he'd admitted the source of his knowledge — of the people or words or pictures — it would have meant confessing to a journal crafted from a vandalized book. More than that, his imaginary realm would be over.

Which it was, from this minute on.

Audra marched to the kitchen, grabbed a trash bag, and returned to do what she should have long ago. She blamed herself more than Jack for creating this disaster, for seeing things that weren't actually there.

In his drawings, the people falling from the plane were her and Jack. Nobody else. The photo from the library book, of the bomber in a fatal dive, must have left him terrified to fly. It was no different from a child watching *Jaws* and becoming fearful of the ocean.

Sure, while half asleep he'd responded to being called Jakob. Swap out a few letters and the name would be Jack. As for the inscription, a few German words from a TV program would have sounded close enough to convince a poor combat vet that the puzzle of his own past could be solved.

In other words, there was never some spiritual

450

message in need of decoding, no unsettled soul seeking a reunion. But Audra had bought into everything — perhaps unconsciously craving her own fantasy world — and dragged others down with her.

Enraged at herself, she stood on a chair and yanked down Jack's model planes. She shoved them into the trash bag and added the poster from the wall. Next she grabbed his backpack, emptied its contents on the bed, and threw the casing away. She would replace them all with better ones. Harmless and normal, they would feature robots and athletes and dinosaurs. Things that didn't drive her and Jack to the brink of insanity or deplete their family savings. They wouldn't draw policemen to the front door or pry open an elderly woman's tomb of memories.

Most important, they wouldn't jeopardize Audra's right to keep her son.

Her hands trembled as she pitched the toy plane into the trash. She scoured his desk for anything more and found the submarine from Dr. Shaw.

No surprise that the hypnosis had failed. If the man were astute enough, he would have known why. Jack needed someone who recognized what this was from the beginning.

That someone should have been her.

It wasn't too late. She would start over and do it right. Together they would clear out mistakes of the past. To that end, she picked up the journal, its pages splayed in her hands.

She would take Jack to the store and let him pick out a new one, any design of his choice. A journal that couldn't be used as evidence of what a gullible mother she had been.

"What are you doing?"

Audra swung toward the doorway. Jack stood there in front of Tess and Grace. He scanned the room in a panic, over the bare wall and ceiling, and halted at the open journal in her hand. The look he gave was of sheer betrayal.

In defense, she reminded herself what had driven her here. This wasn't all of her doing. "I found the library book you destroyed, the pages all cut up. Jack, why would you do that?"

He stared at her, not answering.

"Jack? Tell me why."

Still he was silent.

"Please, say something," she demanded. Frustration returned and her eyes pricked with tears. "Don't you realize what you've done to us?"

"Audra," Tess broke in. "I think that's enough."

Jack curled his fingers, his chin crinkling, fighting back his own tears. The sight was a stab to Audra's heart. She was trying to protect him, and all she was doing was making things worse.

"Baby . . . I didn't mean that." She moved toward him, but he vehemently shook his head. He pushed past Tess and ran toward the front door. Audra instinctively went to follow, but Tess touched her arm.

452

"You stay, I'll go."

It was either a kind gesture from an experienced mother or a message that Audra had done enough damage. Whichever the case — perhaps it was both — Audra managed to nod. When Tess hurried off, Grace followed.

Alone, Audra surveyed the room. In the aftermath of an explosion that she had largely created, she couldn't deny that if it were up to her, if she were the judge at this very moment, there wasn't a chance she would rule in her own favor.

50

Encircling Foley Square in Lower Manhattan were tangible, solid structures of age-old justice. A granite pediment, Corinthian colonnades, and broad, sweeping steps adorned a trio of courthouses. The relevance of this symbolism was not lost on Vivian as she approached the FBI's office.

She had a block to go when two suited men exited the building, one with a briefcase, the other with a cigarette. Brimmed hats shaded their features from the early evening light. From this distance either one could be Agent Gerard. If not, they just might know his whereabouts.

"Pardon me!" Vivian called out. Though they continued on, she tried again over the motors of passing cars. "Agent Gerard!"

They turned to her, exposing their faces, and rewarded her attempt; the gentleman smoking was indeed the one she sought. He uttered something to his companion, sending him off, before meeting Vivian halfway.

"Miss James —"

"I'm sorry to come unannounced, but I've been trying to reach you."

"Yes, I know . . . . I was going to call when I had more information."

"When is Isaak going to be released? Are they allowing him to defect, or will he be sent back? Please, I need to know what's happening."

Agent Gerard pitched his cigarette at the pavement, ground it beneath his shoe. He appeared to hold his breath even as he replied, "There's been a trial."

A trial?

She shook her head, certain she had misheard. "When you talked about legal formalities . . . that's what you were referring to?"

"When we started, it was just a possibility. But FDR pushed for a military tribunal."

"What is — what does that mean?"

"It's an armed services court of law. Closed-door. No press, no jury. Just seven generals on a panel."

She visualized the daunting scene. "You never said anything about this."

"It's not the usual. They haven't convened one since the Civil War. But the President wanted to move things along, keep it out of the media. Plus, with a war on, he didn't want civilian rights getting in the way." At this, the agent gazed toward the street with a slight look of distaste.

"So you're saying the trial is over," she realized, still trying to process the update. It didn't seem possible in the span of a few weeks. She fought to keep her voice level. "What was the ruling?"

When he didn't respond, she followed his attention to the string of courthouses. Their grand colonnades suddenly resembled the bars of a trap.

"Agent Gerard. What was the verdict?"

He dragged his eyes back to her. "Isaak wanted proof about his family, that they'd been relocated safely. When we coughed up documents, he was convinced they were fake. He refused to give us any details about the operation. As a result, he was found guilty of treason and espionage."

"That — no — that can't be right."

"One of the others, a guy named George Dasch, called our office a day after arriving near Amagansett. The next week, he coordinated a meeting in DC, where he handed over a bag of eighty-four grand. He provided all the intel we needed to arrest his three buddies, along with four others who came ashore near Jacksonville. That's how we ended up getting all eight."

"But Isaak surrendered first," she insisted.

"He was still considered an enemy spy."

She went to argue the point when she recalled Isaak's clothes. He was captured out of uniform. Oh, God. He had listened to her when he shouldn't have.

She would fix this. She would explain.

"It's my fault he wasn't wearing his uniform. I didn't think it would matter, once he came forward."

"His clothes weren't the issue."

"But — I should speak to someone to be sure."

"I'm sorry," Agent Gerard said, "but it's too late."

"It's no such thing," she burst out. "It can't be. All of this just happened. Now, tell me whom to speak with."

"Miss James." He spoke with such solemnity she wanted to scream. "This was a military tribunal. Which means there are no appeals. The judgments are final." He reached into the breast pocket of his suit and produced an envelope. "Isaak asked me to give you this."

The familiar script of her name wrenched her stomach. She brought herself to accept the offering but had no intention of reading its contents. Isaak could convey the message in person, when they met to discuss his options.

This time, she would go to anyone, including her father, for help.

"I have to see Isaak. Where is he?"

"The past few days, I did everything I could. Meeting after meeting, trying to help." Agent Gerard removed his hat. He held it to his middle, as one might offer condolences. "The other eight are going to be tried by a military commission in DC next week. FDR wants to make an example of them all, so the Germans won't send over more —"

"I don't care about that!" She was far beyond logic, beyond compassion. "Tell me where they're keeping him. Or I'll . . . I'll march through those doors over there and find out on my own."

He parted his lips, giving way to an interminable pause. Did he think she was bluffing?

Vivian started off toward the building.

Only then did the agent yield: "This morning, just after eleven, Jakob Isaak Hemel was put to death."

She flipped back around, and stared.

"By the time I'd heard, it was already over." The agent held there, shook his head. "I'm very sorry. About all of this."

You're lying! He's alive and you're lying! These were the words she wanted to yell, but all she could do was stand there.

"Rest assured, since we helped his family before he backed out, the FBI will want to keep a pretty tight lid on your friend's case. So no one will ever know about your involvement." Finally he said, "Listen, why don't I take you home?"

She watched his hand settle on her arm, bare below the sleeve of her dress. Yet she couldn't feel the contact. She couldn't feel anything at all, except panic and a budding of anger. With scarcely a voice, she said, "How did he die?"

"Miss James, let's just —"

"How?"

He released her and answered in a quiet tone. "The electric chair. Then they put him to rest in a cemetery."

Again, the vice on her lungs cranked tighter. "Where?"

"He's in an unmarked grave within the prison walls. It's the standard for this type of situation."

Standard. What a vile description for an execution. She was tempted to strike the man down. In fact, she wanted to take out everything in sight. But then, what would that change?

She looked him in the eye. "You gave me your word."

"I told you I'd help him the best I could, and I did that. Believe me, it was out of my hands." The defense flowed out as if prepared for the accusation. His voice, however, seemed to waver from lack of confidence.

"He trusted you," she said.

Agent Gerard added nothing as Vivian backed away. It appeared that he, too, recognized the waste of any effort.

From Foley Square Vivian traveled the streets on an aimless path that dimmed and cooled around her. Hours floated by without meaning. Somewhere along the way, she recalled the inscription of Isaak's necklace and recognized its lie. The risks she had taken were great, yet this was the ghastly reward.

Eventually she found herself standing at the Brooklyn Bridge. The water below looked strikingly like the Thames. It was at that moment, without a single tear spent, the sealed envelope in her hand, that she realized the error of her statement. What she truly meant was: He trusted *me*.

■ ■ ■ ■

PART FOUR

■ ■ ■ ■

So from our dreams my boy and I
Unwillingly awoke,
But neither of his precious dreams
Unto the other spoke.

Yet of the love we bore those dreams
Gave each his tender sign;
For there was triumph in his eyes —
And there were tears in mine!
                    — from "The Dreams"
                        by Eugene Field

51

Mid-June 2012
Portland, OR

"You can do this."

Audra savored the encouragement from Tess, who sat behind the steering wheel of her parked minivan. In the distance, Mount Hood loomed like a caretaker of the grounds. River View Cemetery was set on the west bank of the Willamette River in Portland, known as a burial site of legends ranging from famed pitcher Carl Mays to the Wild West's Virgil Earp.

But Audra had interest in only one person here and he wasn't a national legend.

"For some stupid reason," she said, gazing out the passenger window, "I actually thought that once I made it onto the property, the rest would be easier."

"Sweetie, nothing about it is going to be easy. That's why I came with you."

A sprawling expanse of green grass and trees created a serene view that failed to grant serenity. For twenty-five minutes now, Audra

463

had been unable to leave the car.

She turned to Tess. "This is silly, making you sit and wait. You should be at work."

"No. I should be right where I am," she said. "Besides, playing hooky meant I got to assign Crazy Cat Lady's appointment to Cheyenne." Any joke about the clinic's new vet should have amused Audra, but not today.

After all, this wasn't just any Tuesday morning in June. It was Devon's birthday. Consumed by the roller coaster she had been riding for more than a month, she had barely noticed the coming date that normally approached like a countdown to the apocalypse.

Months ago, nothing on earth could have lured her here, but that was before the dilemma with Jack had come to a head. After Tess had coaxed him back to the apartment, Audra addressed him calmly. She apologized for overstepping — it seemed she was always doing that nowadays — and invited an open discussion that went nowhere. Although she'd since purchased him a new journal, which still remained on his desk encased in its plastic wrapping, she did rehang his poster and planes. This was more than a peace offering. With the help of rational thought, she had realized those objects weren't the cause of his issues, just a means of expressing them.

Nonetheless, for the three days since, Jack had notably regressed. No smiles or laughter. Not a word beyond necessity. Except in his sleep, of course. Although his night terrors hadn't worsened, they showed no signs of improvement.

One would think, with her renewed skepticism, she would be even less inclined to visit a cemetery, a place renowned for its ghostly connections. But she needed Devon's advice. Lately the whisper of his guidance had faded to an all-time low. She didn't expect his voice to come from anywhere but her own memories, obviously. She just hoped a site like this, where others claimed to have felt closer to him, might rejuvenate those memories and more.

"Thirty minutes," Tess said suddenly. "Time's up." For a second Audra expected her to restart the engine. Instead, she opened her door and climbed out.

"Where are you going?"

"I'm walking you over there. Oddly enough, the grave markers don't come to the car."

It was one of Audra's quips flung back at her — though typically used for much lighter topics. Tess's support through patience and compassion had decidedly shifted direction.

"Let's go, my dear." Tess held up her keys. "Can't lock the van with you in it."

"Did I forget to mention I wasn't necessarily looking for tough love?"

Tess winked at her and closed the driver-side door. Left with few choices, Audra pried herself from the car. As soon as her door clicked closed, Tess locked the van with two beeps, removing any opportunity to retreat.

They walked in silence past other cars parked along the curb. The long paved road wound through the cemetery. The air smelled of pine and the bloom of flowers. Clouds covering the sky were as white and fluffy as freshly fallen snow. Not until July would sunshine be a daily constant.

Audra followed Tess's lead in stepping onto the grass, as she otherwise would not have recalled where to turn. The day of Devon's funeral had been a spinning kaleidoscope of flower sprays and eulogies and condolence offerings that her brain scarcely absorbed.

"We got lucky, no doubt about it," Tess said. The remark came out of nowhere, as if continuing a conversation.

"With . . . ?"

"That February, when the driveway iced over and Russ slipped and fell."

Audra only grew more confused. "Tess, where are we going with this?"

"I don't think I ever told you, but if he hadn't hurt his shoulder from that, he never would have gotten a CAT scan. The symptoms were all there, looking back. The indigestion and heartburn and nausea. We wrote it off as a stomach bug. That, and stress from work. My biggest fear was that he'd been developing an ulcer."

Audra saw the angle of the discussion now and resented the timing. It was hard enough to

466

come here without an accompanying lecture. "We don't need to talk about this here."

"Why? It's the perfect spot."

Audra stopped walking. "Tess."

"If there's any place you have a chance to finally unload your guilt — none of which you deserve, by the way — this is it."

"I never *said* I felt guilty." Not a lie. Technically, it wasn't anything Audra had verbalized.

"Are you saying that isn't a major part of why you've never come back here?"

Lacking a defense, Audra looked away. She wished she could discount Tess's reasoning. But that reasoning, she realized, held truth. Her avoidance of this site derived less from her ban on spiritual beliefs and more from an inability to stand at the grave that she had indirectly helped dig.

"Listen, I'm not an expert on the subject," Tess said, no longer challenging. "I'm only being a royal pain in the rear because it's exactly what I'd need you to do if our roles were flipped. Like I said, our family was lucky. But if we hadn't been, I'd have blamed myself for the tumor in Russ's stomach — which would've been flat-out ridiculous."

Audra's emotions, already on edge, were rising to the surface. She focused on keeping them inside. "So, you believe it's about luck, then. Not that everything is somehow meant to be." The last sentence emerged without the sarcasm she had intended.

"I don't know . . . I guess I believe in a little of both. What I do know for sure, though, is you have every right to a great life. You really do, Audra."

No doubt, Audra wanted to believe that. She wanted a great life for Jack even more than herself. The way Tess described letting go of guilt, however, made it sound as easy as dumping rotten fruit in the trash. And it wasn't going to be that simple.

Tess appeared ready to say more. Before she had a chance, Audra interjected lightly, "Please, whatever you do, don't start with the whole 'Devon would've wanted you to be happy' thing."

Tess scrunched her face. "Oh, jeez, no."

That much was a relief.

"He definitely would've wanted you to be as miserable as possible." Tess flaunted a smirk, and Audra couldn't help but smile.

"You *are* a royal pain, you know."

"I'm well aware. And you, my friend, are heading over . . . there." She directed her finger farther down the row.

Delaying the task any longer wouldn't make it easier.

You can do this, Tess had asserted, and she was right.

"Here goes," Audra said. She bolstered herself with a breath and resumed her strides. The plaques lay evenly spaced and flush with the ground. A married couple . . . a devoted teacher . . . a mother taken too soon . . .

468

When it's someone you love, wasn't it always too soon?

At the sixth plaque, Audra halted.

Devon Walker Hughes
1976 – 2010
Beloved husband, father, and son

A wave of feelings passed through her. The epitaph once more solidified reality. It was strange and surreal to be standing here again, this time refreshingly alone. There was no circle of mourners in black. No shiny, body-length coffin hovering over a rectangular hole. It was just her and a plaque and a distant scattering of strangers.

As fate would have it, the grave marker to the right of Devon's was for a veteran of World War Two. She could laugh at this — but wouldn't.

Unsure what to do now, she noted a lady on her knees in another row, placing roses in a receptacle. Audra followed suit by kneeling in her jeans and brushing some dried blades of grass from Devon's name.

"I guess," she said quietly, "this is when I'm supposed to pretend you can hear me." Speaking to a slab of granite seemed ridiculous, but then, there weren't many things she had done this past month that didn't fall into that category.

"Let's say for the sake of argument that you're listening — just so I don't feel like I'm talking to myself. Which I am. But all the same, I'm hoping this will help stir up some ideas. As you might know, Jack has been having a rough time. We both have, actually." Tears gathered in her eyes, a downfall of expressing the words aloud. She tried to blink them back, but a few blatantly defied her.

She picked up her pace. "I feel like I just keep screwing up. I want so badly to help Jack, but I don't know what he needs. Is it more attention? What am I not doing right?"

After soothing Jack from his dream the night before, she had curled up in his bed and held him as he slept. But any bond of closeness had vanished by breakfast.

Again, she thought of another kid, the boy who had deliberately wounded a cocker spaniel. Perhaps attention, of any kind, was all he'd been after. Audra just wished she knew what Jack yearned for, beyond the usual praises and smiles and hugs.

" 'Talk — Trust — Heal,' " she said. "That's the motto for the therapist Jack's been seeing. Sadly, I think I've broken the second part of that in a pretty big way." Absent of trust, she feared talking and healing were gone as well. "Bottom line, Devon, I could really use your advice right now."

There was no reply of course. She closed her eyes and listened for the memory of his voice. But still, nothing came. No whisperings of wisdom.

Then again, who's to say he would have

tackled the issue any better. For two years now, while far from perfect, she had managed as a single parent. Her husband wasn't ever coming back, regardless of anyone's hopes or prayers. Rather than asking what Devon would do, maybe she ought to start trusting in herself.

From the soft chirping of birds and clean scent of grass she absorbed the peacefulness of the grounds. Out of this, a recollection came to her: of their family on a camping trip.

This time, she deliberately held on to the vision instead of pushing it away, and more images rolled over the tracks of her mind. She recalled Devon's specialty of breakfast-for-dinner, and how at the movies he would finish his popcorn before the film even began. On one of their early dates, she'd laughed hysterically over his shocking realization that the Kenny Rogers song was about four hungry children, not four *hundred.* Then there was Devon's amusing infatuation with marshmallow PEEPS and how he'd make Jack giggle by transforming candy corns into vampire fangs.

When at last Audra opened her eyes, she registered tears hanging from her chin. They had spilled from a bittersweet pool of sadness and joy. She dried them with her shirtsleeve, surprisingly not bothered by their existence. For they signified both a parting and reuniting in one.

So finally she can be with him.

The phrase had persisted in her mind, but

471

suddenly with a different perspective. Could it be, subconsciously, that this visit — this reunion — was what Jack wanted all along?

Maybe Meredith was right. Maybe in an effort to evade the bad, Audra had blocked out all of the good, and that goodness was what Jack needed more than anything.

"Audra," Tess said.

Nearly having forgotten she was there, Audra twisted around to find Tess close behind, motioning at an angle. Audra's eyes traced the gesture and discovered a couple standing three rows down. It was Robert and Meredith with a bouquet of lilies. Naturally they would pay their respects on their son's birthday and with his favorite flowers.

That's when it dawned on Audra. This could be the place to make amends. Their commonality of love and loss over Devon could surely bring them together. Same for their care of Jack.

Meredith appeared to read these thoughts.

Prodded by hope, Audra took a step forward, yet just then the woman pursed her mouth and cut her gaze away. An unmistakable message.

It was time for Audra to leave.

472

52

Late July 1942
Brooklyn, NY

The message arrived on a Saturday morning. Vivian had just made her way down the stairs for breakfast when the courier arrived with a telegram. After assignments at three bases for a total of six weeks abroad, double the length first expected, Gene was taking a train ride home.

Vivian would have attributed her sudden nausea solely to anxiety over their impending discussion if not for news from the day before. Her fainting spell at work, along with fatigue and absentmindedness, had led her to see a doctor at Mrs. Langtree's urging. Given that July heat and humidity were likely culprits, it had seemed an excessive chore — until the white-haired doc, with his deductive line of questioning, jarred Vivian with the truth.

She was pregnant.

Months ago, a revelation of the sort would

473

have struck with the force of a wrecking ball. Yet since learning of Isaak's death, perhaps due to familiarity of the loss, or maybe a shell erected of guilt, she instead gained a numbness that enabled her to function. Like moving underwater, it was a slow, surreal, muted existence. She had become a spectator of another's woman's life.

If you want to talk, I'm here, Luanne recently offered. It appeared Vivian's mood had been taken as an effect of Gene's absence. Still, Vivian couldn't help wondering if it was true what people said, about the telling signs when in the family way. Was it plain on her face, in her eyes?

Vivian feared this now as she caught her own reflection in the polished silverware on the table. She averted her gaze from even the waiters gliding by at the Waldorf Astoria. It was her mother's preferred hotel during periodic stays such as this. In a corner of the restaurant, a harpist plucked chords beside a large topiary fashioned after a genie's bottle.

"You're not eating your lunch," Vivian's mother observed across the span of white linen.

Vivian glanced at the citrus salmon she had but pushed around on her plate. She should have interjected an alternative when the woman ordered on her behalf. The smell of seafood was making her queasy. "I'm just not very hungry."

"Are you certain you're feeling all right?" It was the second time her mother had voiced the inquiry. "You look . . . a bit off."

"I'm fine. Really. A smidge tired, is all."

A commentary about Vivian's job requiring too much energy would typically follow. Instead, her mother appeared on the verge of issuing a statement of import. But suddenly, as if to drown the words, she drained her gin and tonic. Then she set down the glass and resumed idle conversation between labored pauses and cigarette puffs. Her unspoken syllables screamed in Vivian's ear.

Ask me! Vivian wanted to say. For the more her mother fidgeted — with a fork, her lighter, the brooch on her burgundy dress suit — the clearer it became that, somehow, she knew.

Regardless of the consequences, Vivian felt a growing need to share her plight. She understood there were alternatives: giving the baby up for adoption, or a secret appointment with a willing doctor. But both of these were unthinkable. Hence, it wasn't advice she yearned for as much as an assurance she would not endure this alone. Such a comfort might even shed the numbness encaging her.

"Well," her mother said, an abrupt conclusion. She crushed out her half burned cigarette in the beveled ashtray. "I'd better fetch my belongings from my room."

"Already?" Vivian said. "I thought there

would be more time."

"I've decided to take the earlier train, departing just past two. It's unfortunate I'll be missing Gene by just a few hours." She waved her fingers at the waiter, a request for the check.

Perhaps she had altered her schedule in order to avoid the man presumed responsible for Vivian's condition. After all, who else would it be?

Restaurant staff cleared the serving ware and settled the bill. All the while, Vivian mentally willed her mother to stay. But the woman closed her handbag and prepared to rise.

Vivian felt the world closing in. If she stayed silent, it would crush her into nothing. "Please," she said, "if you have something to say . . ."

Her mother crinkled her brow as if at a loss. Quiet stretched the air, padded only by the harpist's chords and surrounding chatter. At last, Vivian's mother lowered her gaze and straightened in her chair.

"Very well," she said, "though I don't know exactly how to phrase this." There was a stiffness to her jaw, adding a clip to her words. "It's certainly not a lifestyle I'd foreseen. I suspect your grandmother will have plenty to say on the subject."

Simple as that, the reality of disapproval crystallized into shards, each one aimed at

Vivian's heart. She couldn't help questioning her decision to speak up. In the end, maybe she was destined to manage all on her own.

"The situation, you see," her mother went on, "is that your father . . . should be returning by month's end."

Vivian's thoughts came to a halt, derailing. "Sorry?"

"He'll be coming home. To DC, that is. We agreed, however, that it would be better — for us both — if I remained in New Hampshire."

Absorbing this, Vivian flashed back to the couple's parting at Euston Station. She recalled the way he had said good-bye even to Vivian. Messages she could not decode. She considered the makeshift bed in his study, his choice to stay in London. All were signs she had noticed but ultimately discounted. "So, you *are* divorcing," she said.

Her mother's eyes darted around them, a reflexive alertness of strangers. "Heavens, no." She gave a nervous laugh and continued in a hush. "We just won't be living under the same roof. Of course, whenever we can, we'll all be together for the holidays. Thanksgiving, Christmas. But really, with your being out of the house now, making your own way in life, I imagine there will be little difference for you."

Vivian mined for a reply without success. She was stunned as much by the development as the sudden support of her own independence. It took her a moment to realize her reaction was perceived as a demand for explanation.

"The truth of the matter is, we got married on a whim," her mother said. "We had been courting for less than a month. But the Great War, it amplified emotions, and he was so handsome, particularly in that gallant uniform. And we were very, very . . . young." Her focus drifted to her cocktail glass and held there. She seemed to view her memories in the melting cubes. "When he came back, after a few weeks, I told myself the war had changed him, and that with time he would revert to his old self. He was so serious and logical. Not at all how I remembered. It wasn't until months later that I finally recognized the truth — the truth being we never actually knew each other."

Vivian nodded slowly, comprehending the situation all too well.

After a pause, her mother finished off the watery drops in her glass. "Anyhow. I've wanted to tell you for a while. But frankly, I was worried what you'd think." She smiled awkwardly. "Silly, isn't it? With my being the parent and you the child."

The maternal reference spurred the recollection of Vivian's own dilemma. Someday soon she would share it with her mother, but not now.

Vivian reached across the table and grasped her mother's hand. "What I think," she said, "is that I want you both to be happy."

Her mother looked back at her, eyes welling. It was a moment of gratitude, of support and understanding. Vivian only hoped, when she most needed it, she would receive the same in return.

In the meantime, the impending reaction of another person would take greater priority.

Every minute between her mother's departure and Gene's arrival passed simultaneously too fast and too slow. On the platforms at Grand Central, servicemen of all branches reunited with their loved ones or traded good-byes with tearful sweethearts.

Vivian waited in the center of the bustling scene, attempting to remain calm.

The instant Gene stepped off the train, his face beaming bright as the sun, she felt a joy that conquered all dread. But the triumph didn't last. His hug wrapped her waist and instantly reminded her of the secret that had taken root — one that, in all likelihood, would soon divide them.

Even so, she would plea for forgiveness and hold on to hope. It was thin as a petal and just as fragile, but she cupped it with care and smiled when he touched her face. She savored his kiss from start to finish, knowing it could be the last.

"I say we go for a walk," he said.

While a delay of the conversation had distinct appeal, she had not foreseen the detour. She caught sight of the bulky duffel at his feet. "But what about your things?"

"I can carry it. Need to stretch my legs from the long ride. C'mon." He gestured his chin down the platform. "After working so hard, I deserve to parade a pretty girl around town, don't I?"

There was no argument to be made. Gene deserved much more than he knew.

Together they headed out of the station and through the balminess of the city. The scents of roasting nuts on vending carts provided relief from exhaust fumes and wafts of sunbaked trash. Gene used both hands to grip the bag over his shoulder, and thankfully so. Had he linked with her fingers, the nervous sheen on her palms would have made itself known.

He talked a great deal, seemingly more than usual, covering highlights of his tasks and travels. He glanced her way now and again, but his attention mostly roamed over the tall buildings and construction sites, the sea of cabs and pedestrians. Time away must have allowed him to experience the city anew.

"How about a quick break?" he said. Perspiration dotted his hairline. "Stuff's getting a little heavy after all." He dropped his Army-issue bag at the base of an apartment stoop.

Across the street, a woman with a kerchief around her hair was shaking out a rug. Dust motes in the late afternoon light drifted like snowflakes. A ways down, kids were drawing with chalk on the sidewalk while others played in water spraying from a hydrant.

Vivian realized this was where she would tell him. No amount of waiting would cushion the impact. She took a fortifying breath before bending to sit.

"Hang on," he said, and gently tugged her hand, keeping her upright.

She expected him to point out something to be avoided on the step — a wad of chewing gum, a splinter of glass — but he merely stood there, his hand around hers.

"Vivi, every day we were apart — every hour, for that matter — it became clearer to me that you're the girl I want to be with."

She stared, trying to follow the aim of his declaration.

"If anything, I'm a dumbbell for not seeing it right from the start. I just feel like I've wasted so much time. With my job, the war, there are a lot of regrets floating around out there, and — well, the point is." He wet his lips as if to slicken his pace. "The first time we were really alone together was here on these stairs. It was that night after the USO, remember?"

Her gaze shot to the steps as her mind raced to keep up, his intentions latching on.

481

"I didn't know what was hurting you then, or who. All I knew was I wanted to hold you and protect you. I guess, ever since, I've never stopped feeling that way." He gave a small shrug, and his Adam's apple shifted. "I'd planned on taking you out for a fancy night on the town. Dinner, candlelight, all that business. Maybe I'm a royal heel for not doing it properly. It's just that once I got on the train, this spot came to me and . . . it all seemed right." With that, he looked into her eyes and lowered onto one knee.

"Gene," she said on a gasp.

"Just hear me out," he told her. "Sure, we haven't been dating all that long, but when a fella knows, he just knows. There have been times in my life I was afraid of something like this, but I'm not anymore. Not with you. I want to have a family together, and spend my life with you. If you'll have me, Vivian."

He reached into the pocket of his trousers and pulled out a gold band. "You don't have to answer this very minute. I just want you to think about it. And if you're not ready, I'm willing to wait. As long as it takes."

The ring shimmered in the light, like a candle on a cake, the gift of a wish.

Be happy, darling, read Isaak's final letter. *Enjoy a long, splendid life with a man who adores you, children who illuminate your days, and all the happiness you deserve.*

Slowly, she dared to meet Gene's eyes. In

them she saw a genuinely good man, one who was offering all of those things and more. A person she trusted with the whole of her heart. A man who loved her, and, in truth, whom she loved too.

Despite her mistakes, she could give her baby a respectable life, that of an Army officer's child, not the bastard of an executed traitor. She could even save her parents the disappointment and disgrace of having an unwedded pregnant daughter. And through it all, she would never have to hurt the kind man before her.

There was only one decision that made sense.

"Yes," she said, barely audible in her own ears.

"Yes . . . you'll . . . think about it?" The tentativeness in his voice matched his expression.

She pushed out the answer before second thoughts could intervene. "Yes," she said, "I'll marry you."

He appeared to be suppressing a smile until it broke free and overtook his face. After sliding the ring onto her finger, he shot to his feet. He gave her a kiss, brimmed with exuberance, and wrapped her in his arms. "I'm going to take care of you, Vivian. For the rest of my life, I promise you that."

She clung to his pledge, his embrace, and said, "I know you will."

53

Audra now had a convenient excuse. Still without word from Sean, she'd been tempted several times to drive to the farm, wanting to clear up the issue. This morning, a voice mail on her cell phone gave her cause to follow through.

"Hi, Audra," the woman had said, "this is Taylor, Sergeant Shuman's wife. Sean Malloy asked me to do some digging for a genealogy project of yours. I left him a message about it, but haven't heard back. Since he gave me your contact info, I thought I'd try you directly. I did uncover some things about Jakob Hemel that I think you'll find interesting. . . ."

It was both troubling and a relief that Audra's calls weren't the only ones Sean was ignoring. She had honestly lost all interest in hearing about Jakob Hemel, and she would let the woman know there was no need for more investigating. But first Audra would make sure Sean was all right and, if so, assure him Jack's antics had no real connection to his family.

At the front door of Luanne's house, Audra knocked and waited. In the reflective glass panel she noticed strands fallen from her bound hair. She tucked them in and smoothed her fitted cotton shirt over the top of her jeans. She knocked again, but nobody answered.

Late morning on a Wednesday, she figured the chances were good of someone being home. She rang the bell with reluctance, not wanting to disturb Luanne if she was napping.

Again, no one came.

Since yesterday's visit to the cemetery, Audra felt a renewed desire for closure in any area possible. There were only two days left until the start of summer break. Then Jack would be home full-time, limiting her opportunities to tie up loose ends. She had hoped to catch Luanne as much as Sean, still wanting to apologize for pestering the dear woman.

Audra scanned the property. Except for her own car, there were no vehicles around, though they could be parked in the garage. She retained hope based on the unlocked gate and chickens roaming the grounds.

Then a noise caught her ear — a thump — from the direction of the barn.

She treaded past the large apple tree by the weathered fence, where the goat and donkeys were grazing in the sun. They bleated and brayed a few notes of contentment.

Once at the barn's entrance, she found its sliding door partially opened. As she proceeded inside, a square object flew through the air and hit the wall of an animal's stall. It looked to be a chunk of hay, pitched from the loft above.

"Hello?" she called up.

The room was scented with straw and feed and the animals it kept.

"Sean?" she hollered.

All sounds of movement ceased.

It suddenly occurred to her that Luanne could have hired a helper, but then Sean stepped up to the edge. Protected by work gloves, he gripped the long handle of a pitchfork. Patches of sweat darkened his gray T-shirt, untucked from his jeans. He pulled out his right earphone, releasing the wire connected to an MP3 player.

"What are you doing here?" he said.

"I've been . . . trying to reach you."

He shifted his eyes away from her. "Sorry," he said. "Been pretty busy."

She ignored his stock excuse. "Sean, could I talk to you?"

He used a forearm to wipe the dampness from his hairline. Dust and dirt smudged his unshaven face. "I really gotta get some stuff done."

"You can't take a short break?" she said, trying to determine whether his aloofness was specifically directed at her.

"Carl should be here soon. He's a friend of Aunt Lu's. Supposed to help me put in some fence posts. So some other time, okay?"

Audra conceded with a nod, the exchange

486

just as labored as their drive from the gallery. She could push harder, but her energy was running on reserve.

"Is Luanne around by any chance?" A chat with his great-aunt could still make the trip here worthwhile.

"Nah. She went to meet some people. Her knitting group, I think."

So much for that idea.

"All right, then." Audra shrugged. "I'll stop by another day."

"Great."

If his tone alone hadn't make it abundantly clear that her company was unwelcome, his next act did. She didn't so much as say goodbye and already he had returned to his work, no longer in view.

This was her cue to leave, but she couldn't. His shift in personality too closely resembled that of her son.

She wasn't willing to walk out of here without at least trying for an explanation. From what little she knew of him, this wasn't Sean.

Audra made her way up the ladder. Before she stepped off, he glanced toward her, less than thrilled. His earphone still dangled down his chest, confirming he could hear her.

In an attempt to alleviate the tension, she scrunched her nose. "If you haven't noticed, I'm not the kind who gives up very easily."

He let out a sigh, almost a huff. "I noticed." He dropped the pitchfork onto the floor, cushioned by stray leafs of hay. Down on one knee, he snagged a pocketknife from his jeans and cut twine from a bale with a sharp yank.

"Sean, if it's about me talking to Luanne at the gallery —"

"That's not it."

One possibility eliminated.

She slid her hands into the front pockets of her jeans. "To be fair, I should probably mention that I'm *really* good at playing Twenty Questions."

He cut another piece of twine. "It just isn't a good day, all right?"

A shallow laugh slipped from Audra's mouth, not at him but at the mere suggestion. "Well, lately the occurrence of good days in my life is pretty unpredictable. So I've learned not to wait around for them."

He paused for a while, as if he might confide in her. But then he went to work on loosening square blocks of hay. Audra walked over and sat on the bale closest to him, determined to root out the issue. Something had happened on First Thursday; if it didn't involve her, it was somebody else.

She reviewed the event in her mind. After they'd arrived, he had a run-in with a crabby woman over a parking spot. But he'd laughed it off and didn't appear agitated until his mother mentioned a friend keeping an eye out for him.

Audra had assumed the guys didn't cross paths . . . .

"The person who came to see you at the gallery. That's what this is about, isn't it?"

Sean affirmed her guess by the forceful way he threw more hay off the loft.

"Sean, who was he?"

As he flung another handful, the scenario came together.

"He served in the war with you," she realized.

Sean stopped. Without looking at her, he said, "Seeing the guy's face . . . it brought back memories I thought I wanted. But I was wrong."

She waited for more, but he shook his head and sat back against the bale he'd been trying to destroy. He took off his gloves and shuttered his eyes, either viewing the scene or blocking it out.

Audra moved down to the floor and settled beside him. "You can tell me," she said. "If you want."

After a moment, his eyelids lifted, but he wasn't seeing the loft, not the bales or barn wall in front of him. This much was clear in his gaze, same for his tone when he spoke.

"We were on patrol in the Humvee, headed to Bagram from Kabul. I was the A-gunner. I'd hardly slept the night before, filling in for another patrol. So I decided to get some rest during the drive. In the rear, you could lay the seatback down and curl up on the floor. I remember Sarge was cracking jokes when I dozed off. Felt like I just blinked before everything exploded."

His voice gained a slight quiver as he gripped the top of his bent knee. "There was blood and the sounds of screaming, but I was dizzy and couldn't think. I blacked out after that. You realize I only lived because I was taking a damn nap, right?" He released a low, dark laugh. Then his smile dropped off and he raked his fingers through his hair. "Christ, what the hell was I doing over there?"

Audra had no clue what to say. There was no logic to be carved from a tragic fluke.

Aching with a need to comfort him, she reached out and laid a hand on his stubbled jaw. He flinched, startled from his thoughts. She expected him to stand, craving his private space. Instead he angled toward her. The grief and longing in his gaze were mirrored in her own. She had never been remotely close to a war zone, yet still she understood. It was futile, the struggle to comprehend why you survived when others around you didn't.

She opened her mouth to say as much, but he leaned in and smothered the words with his lips. His hands rose to her face. He kissed her with power and wanting, and though she was first taken aback, any resistance quickly dropped away.

On pure instinct she ran her fingers over the broadness of his chest and down the length of his shirt. At his hips, she lifted the pool of fabric and reached beneath, seeking the feel of his skin. His stomach muscles tightened and his breath slightly hitched. As he laid her down, his kisses moved to her neck. She caught a sound, vaguely, and dismissed it when his teeth grazed her ear. The pressure of his body set off a charge inside her. But it wasn't just desire. It was more than that, a sensation she couldn't describe.

Not caring to try, she rolled her head to the side, an urging for his lips to follow the curves of her neck, to which he hastily complied. His hands had just grasped her sides, the vulnerable slope of her waist, when a voice sliced through the haze.

"Sean, you in here?" a man called from below.

They both froze, their breaths rough and heavy.

"Sean?"

"I'm here," he answered, collecting his words. "I'm . . . just finishing up. Meet you outside in a few."

"All righty."

Footsteps shuffled out the barn door.

As reality returned to the loft, Sean's body lingered over hers before he pulled back to sit up, giving her room to do the same.

"Audra . . . I, um . . ."

"Yeah," she said. "I should go."

He nodded, looking as flustered as she felt. Once they stood, he gestured toward her. "Your, uh, shirt," he said.

Audra glanced over her shoulder and brushed hay from the back of her clothes and hair.

"Thanks."

"Sure."

She pasted on a smile, her pulse not yet slowing. "I'll see you around, then."

"Yeah . . . right."

"Good," she said. She went directly to the ladder and climbed down. She didn't look up or reduce her pace until she was in her car, at which point she promptly zoomed toward home.

For half the drive, Audra couldn't stop smiling. She wouldn't be surprised if a blush covered every inch of her skin. She was a teenager after her first make-out session, a game of Two Minutes in the Closet — except a hundred times more exhilarating, aided by experience, and without an ounce of awkwardness. If you subtracted the abrupt ending.

And then she thought of Devon.

Her husband.

Her first love.

Only a day ago, she had knelt at his grave, grieving his absence, cherishing his memories. Yet not once had he come to mind while Sean's lips and hands were on her body. Recognizing this, she waited for a rush of guilt or betrayal, which she expected would always follow her encounters with another man.

But it wasn't there.

The truth was, she felt alive and, in a way, liberated. As though the part of her that she had taken for dead had merely been asleep and was finally awake. Maybe later she would reflect on the day and feel differently, but not now. For now, she would relish the sensation, unconcerned of what it meant or where it would lead.

Once parked at the apartment, most of the lot empty, she took a minute in her car to reset her nerves. Particles from the barn dotted her shirt. Tess's advice flew back to her, about the need for a good old-fashioned roll in the hay, and Audra had to smile. She wiped off her shirt and pants. In the rearview mirror she checked for hay in her hair.

That's when she noticed a man in the reflection. Sunlight made his face difficult to see, but one thing was clear: He was headed straight for her car.

54

Out of the morning quiet came an inquiry from the person Vivian least expected.

"Are you absolutely sure about this?" Luanne said pointedly. "Because if you're not . . ."

At the vanity, seated in her bathrobe, Vivian lowered the cardinal-red lipstick she was about to apply. She turned toward her roommate, who stood at the closet in her freshly buttoned dress.

"Please, don't get me wrong," Luanne continued. "I adore the thought of calling you my sister. And I know it might be unfair of me to say anything, with the ceremony only hours away. It's just that everything's moved so fast. Especially given how much he's been out of town."

Vivian admitted to her: "I do understand why you'd be concerned."

When Gene and Vivian announced the news right after the proposal, Luanne had smiled and bid them good wishes. There had been an uncertainty, however, underlying her manner. Not unlike the doubts that festered in Vivian. Still, the week had rolled on without dissent, until this moment.

"This isn't just about me, Viv." Luanne took a step closer. "You haven't even told your parents. Don't you think they'll be upset to have missed it?"

"They'll be fine — after a while. Besides, it's best this way. I don't want the fanfare of a big wedding and neither does your brother." What's more, an event like that would take months that Vivian could not afford to spare.

"But shouldn't your father at least give his blessing?"

"Gene was going to ask him, but there's no guarantee when my father will actually return. Then there's the business of my parents not even being at the same house. Don't you see? This helps avoid all of those issues."

"Well, yes. I suppose . . . ."

"Luanne, good grief. I thought you were overjoyed we became a couple."

"I was. I am. But still —"

Vivian could not bear any more of this. "Gene and I are going to be happy together." The declaration shot out with such potency, she wondered which of them she was trying more to convince.

After a pause, Luanne gave a look of regret. "I'm sorry, Viv. I didn't mean to imply that you wouldn't be."

Vivian shook her head, bridling her emotions. "It's okay. You were right, it has moved fast." She shrugged and said, "We're just eager to make it official and don't see the point in waiting. The same as a lot of other couples these days."

Given the recent rash of deployment, sprints to the altar had become commonplace, even for people who had scarcely met. The fact that Gene was stationed in the States hadn't stopped Vivian from using this rationale as a source of self-assurance.

"We love each other, Luanne. We really do."

Though truth upheld the words, Vivian withdrew her gaze, fearing it would reveal more than she wished to share. As she busied herself with powder, Luanne slipped into a pair of heels and approached the vanity. She gave Vivian's shoulder a tender squeeze.

"I still need to pick up your bouquet," Luanne said with notable lightness. "I'll see you there?"

Vivian smiled without turning. "See you there."

Some would say it was bad luck, letting Gene view her before the wedding. But Vivian had come to learn that in spite of one's efforts — avoiding cracks, crossing fingers, flinging salt — most in life occurred with little control.

The only element she could count on was the ease she would feel in Gene's presence.

This was the reason she had insisted he escort her to the courthouse. She knew she would need that comfort in order to carry on with the plan.

And for a brief while, it worked.

He stood at her door in his dashing dress uniform, his eyes glimmering beneath the bill of his hat. "Shall we?" he said with a smile, and offered the crook of his arm. He guided her to the waiting cab, carrying her suitcase for their hotel stay downtown. Packed among her clothing was a silken nightgown for what would be their first time together in that way.

What she had not figured into the equation, however, was the intrusion of her conscience. For the better part of a week, it had stalked her from a distance. But here, en route to the courthouse, it was squeezed in like a third passenger. She could not ignore its existence. From her heightened awareness, each kindness from Gene transformed into a punishment. His compliments over her appearance, on her wedding suit and Victory curls, were like lashes to her skin. He held her hand, and the sincerity of his touch burned through her thin ivory gloves.

Were the sensations but a warning of what was to come?

Months down the road, Gene would cradle the baby as Vivian lurked in the background, haunted by a secret. That was assuming, of course, the child's birth would not have already exposed the truth — when gray-blue eyes, light-blond curls, and an early delivery shouted proof of another father.

The faster the thoughts spun in her mind, the thicker the air became. She leaned closer to the open window, but the August humidity blocked any reprieve. She sought an escape, a means to break free.

"Sir, could you pull over?" she said to the driver.

"Sweetheart," Gene said, "we still have several blocks to go."

"I need out. Now. *Please.*"

He looked at her, befuddled, but affirmed her request with the cabbie. The instant they halted at the curb, Vivian jumped out and headed to nowhere in particular. It was as though she had blinked and the golden path of her life had twisted and darkened into a merciless maze.

"Vivian, wait for me!" Gene called out. Travel bags in hand, he caught up to her near the fountain of a city park, where three children waded about, scavenging for pennies. When Gene turned her around, she jerked her eyes away.

"Doll, what is it? Tell me what's going on."

"I can't. I can't do it." She cringed inside, disgusted by what she had almost done.

"It's all right," he said. "We'll just wait. We don't have to rush."

"Gene, you don't understand."

He studied her face, searching for clues, until a splash from the fountain hit his sleeve.

"Come over here with me." He guided her to a corner of the park and onto a shaded bench. He set their luggage down. As he sat beside her, a hot tear leaked down her cheek. She went to wipe it away, but he gently beat her to it.

"Folks get cold feet all the time. Nothing to worry about."

"No," she whispered. "That's not it."

He hesitated, looking afraid to ask. "What, then?"

If only he hadn't surprised her with that proposal. She had been fully prepared to confess it all. After six weeks of his absence, trading only a handful of letters and phone calls, she could not have seen that coming. No girl in her right mind would have seen that coming.

"Why did you ask me?" she said. She was desperate for the road map that had delivered them here, to pinpoint the wrong turns they had taken.

His forehead creased, the pondering of a trick question. "Because I love you."

"We were apart for more than a month, you never even mention marriage, and the minute you come back you get down on one knee. Why?"

He parted his lips to answer. Then he tucked them in, tight as wire. Gazing away from her, he sank into the bench.

Finally, he said, "I'd made a mistake before. Years ago. I loved a girl, and she believed we'd get hitched one day. Have kids. Live happily ever after. Everybody around us did."

It was his old girlfriend, Helen. Vivian knew this without asking. The story of betrayal had never been more painfully significant.

"I wasn't sure, though, that I ever wanted to get married," he said. "When I told her that, after years together, she pulled away for a while. One thing led to another and . . . it didn't work out. I realized too late that I should've explained more to her, so she'd have understood."

He shrugged a shoulder in a manner that was anything but nonchalant. "Thing of it is my old man was a decent guy — until he drank. Usually he'd just throw a fit, start breaking things. But one night my mom accidentally burnt a roast. Money was tight, and he exploded. I was at the table when he slapped her hard enough to knock her down. She caught the edge of the counter with the back of her head and wound up with four stitches. I was twelve. He never did it again, not that I know of anyway. But part of me never forgave myself for just sitting there, scared as hell in my seat, not defending her like I should have."

Vivian had never noticed how rarely Luanne talked about home. All those years, she had always seemed so sweet and carefree, no one in school would have imagined.

Gene cleared his throat and turned to Vivian. "Point is, with me being away from you, and feeling a distance growing, I just . . ." He shook his head and clutched her hand on her lap. "I couldn't risk losing you, Vivi. Not when I know we're supposed to be together. I know it in my heart. And I have no doubt anymore about being a good husband. I'd take such good care of you, if you'd let me."

"Oh, Gene. I know you would . . . ." Her tears were falling now in a stream she couldn't slow, couldn't stop. After what he had shared, her confession would gain another layer of cruelty. "That's why there's something you need to know."

He waited for her to go on, clearly recognizing her conflict as more than cold feet.

Perhaps, to some extent, he would relate to her feeling of deep regret, of being unable to change the past but wanting direly to make things right.

Vivian amassed the remnants of her courage, recalling a time she could now identify as both the beginning and the end. "I was living in London with my parents," she said. "One day, I was at the market alone when the air-raid siren sounded. It was just a routine alarm. We had no idea — or at least I was too ignorant to realize how close we were to war. And how, because of it, my whole life

501

would change."

A rivulet of sweat slid down her back. She shifted her vision to an unseen, distant spot. She could only complete the tale if not faced by Gene's reaction, including the inevitable revelation that the "friend" from Germany she had asked him to help was actually Isaak.

"At a vendor stand," she said, "I knocked over a tomato. It landed on a man's dress shoe, and when I looked up he was standing there. And he smiled at me."

From there, Vivian pressed on, covering the highlights of moments that had shaped her life for the past three years. Meeting Isaak at the London cinemas, the secrecy of their courtship and his family in Munich. His professor at the university, the information gleaned from her father, the letter at Euston Station. She described the reunion at Prospect Park, igniting confusion and fears, the resurrection of interred feelings. She spoke of Agent Daniel Gerard, the dealings of espionage that prohibited her from confiding in anyone, including Gene. And with a tightened throat, she detailed the legal dealings that had led to Isaak's execution.

"Before that, though," she said, fighting the shake in her voice, "I went to his hotel room to deliver a message. I never meant for anything more to happen. I swear to God, I didn't. I was certain it was over for us — whatever it was that he and I'd once had.

After he died, I was going to move on with my life. With you. But then, weeks later, I was at work, and I fainted. And they sent me to the doctor, and . . . and I . . ."

Struggling to finish, she angled toward Gene. She found his eyes lowering to her stomach, where her hands had unconsciously settled. He inhaled a sharp breath, and his neck trembled as though his head had become too heavy. He moved his jaw in several attempts to speak but failed.

"I am so, so sorry. Gene, the last thing I ever meant to do was hurt you."

He rubbed his hand over his mouth. A bead of perspiration trailed from his temple, just below his hat. When his gaze slid toward her, it was clear he could not see her. He had succumbed to a daze she too often made her home.

"I'd understand if you never wanted to see me again," she told him. "But I pray that somehow you'll find a way to forgive me."

An infinite beat passed before he rose woodenly, wordlessly from the bench.

"Please," she said, "don't go yet." She touched his sleeve, and he held there for a moment. If only he would look at her, he would see in her eyes and face how utterly sorry she was, how desperate she was to make it up to him.

But he didn't turn an inch. He merely

503

walked away, abandoning his belongings, leaving her behind.

55

The man strode onward with purpose. Audra detected this even in her rearview mirror. But not until she'd stepped out of her car did she catch sight of his face, and astonishment grabbed hold.

"What do you want, Robert?"

He slowed his steps and came to rest a few yards away. He displayed his palms in a show of harmlessness, a great irony in that. "I came by hoping we could talk."

From the beginning, Russ had advised her that a potential settlement could be reached if both parties were willing to compromise. By now, it seemed an unfathomable option. "That's not a good idea."

"I'm just asking for a few minutes. Then I promise to leave you be."

She suddenly wondered how he could have known when she'd be returning home. The timing struck her as too much of a coincidence. "Have you been following me?"

"No. Of course not."

She had come to doubt any words from his mouth. Did he know where she'd been, what she had just done? The liberation of only moments ago instantly receded.

"I've been sitting in the parking lot waiting for you. I knew you'd be here to meet Jack before long. I would've called first, but didn't think you'd want to see me."

"And you would have been right."

The hurt that flashed in his eyes made her regret the snipe — though not entirely.

She reminded herself what he and Meredith were attempting to steal from her life. "As you said, Jack will be home shortly. I'd rather you not be around then. If you have something to say to either of us, your lawyer can contact mine."

Leaving it at that, she snagged her purse from the car and shut and locked the door.

"Just listen for second. Audra, please . . ."

She charged toward the apartment, pulling out her cell phone. She was prepared to summon the police if needed.

"Audra!" he called to her. "We're dropping the case."

The declaration stopped her cold, spun her around. She had to have misheard him.

He walked over with a gait that now looked weary. Again he settled close by. "Last night, Meredith and I had a long discussion. And we realized we made a big mistake."

Audra shook her head, too stunned to be

relieved. She tried to trace the change of heart and could only imagine one cause. "Is this because of the cemetery? Just because you saw me at Devon's grave, now I'm worthy of being Jack's mother?"

"I'm not gonna lie. Seeing you there, the shock of it, that did get us talking. But that's not why we're withdrawing the petition."

"Oh, really? Why, then?" She worked to keep her voice level.

In silence Robert gazed off toward a passing car. Over the past month, the skin under his eyes had drooped and darkened. "You remember hearing of Meredith's bout with depression? Back when Devon was around six months old."

Sure, Audra remembered. Robert had referred to them as "the baby blues." Although she'd long ago surmised that the postpartum affliction had been worse than the family let on, the mention of it now turned her stomach. After all the turmoil the couple had caused, he was resorting to a sympathy plea.

"I'm sorry," she said, "but if you actually think I'm going to feel bad for Meredith —"

"Now you hold on," he shot back, his eyes like daggers. "I'm gonna say what I came to, then I'll be on my way for good, if that's what you want. But there's something you've got to hear first."

Never had she seen him this stern. She swallowed against the dryness in her throat and nodded begrudgingly.

Robert folded his arms, inhaling a shaky breath. He proceeded in a tight but gentler tone. "For years before Devon was born, Mere taught piano lessons at the house. A few were adults, but most were kids. I used to say we lived in Grand Central, with the way people were always coming and going."

The piano in Meredith's music room, stored beneath a canvas, returned to Audra's thoughts. Not once had she ever heard a single key played.

"There was a little girl in the bunch. Name was Paige. She was a petite thing, cute as a button. Always smiling and laughing and loved giving hugs. But then her mom got remarried, and Mere noticed her attitude started to change. Got real quiet during her lessons, smiled a lot less. Mere assumed the girl was just adjusting to the lifestyle, that maybe her mom was paying her less attention, wrapped up in the excitement of being a newlywed. But then, Mere . . . she saw . . ."

He broke off when his voice wavered, and he cleared his throat. "She saw bruises on the girl's wrists. Her sleeves had ridden up while she was playing a song. When Mere asked about them, Paige said she'd been roughhousing with a neighbor boy. Later, Mere noticed the girl was wearing long sleeves and pants every time. She started missing lessons and her piano skills were getting worse."

"Did Meredith ever bring it up to the girl's

mother?" Audra had to admit, the question was slightly pointed. It was difficult not to feel that such a concern should be reasonably investigated before delivering assumptions to authorities.

"Mere did ask her about the marks," he replied. "Did it in private right after the spring recital. But the woman claimed Paige was just a tomboy. The mom was such a nice lady, Mere didn't want to think the worst. She certainly didn't want to butt her nose in or make accusations that were wrong. Mere was still worried, but days later she went into labor with Devon. She took a break from teaching, being busy with the baby. Then late in the fall, she called around to let her students know she'd be offering lessons again in the new year. And that's when she learned the news."

Audra wished she could reject Robert's appeal, but the nature of the story made that impossible. Despite his ominous tone, she hoped with all her heart the outcome wasn't horrific. "And . . . what happened?"

"That August, on a hot summer day, Paige had snuck a damn Popsicle. Her stepfather gave her a blow to the head that caused her brain to hemorrhage."

"My God," Audra said, her stomach turning again.

"Meredith blamed herself so much for not speaking to the police. She slipped into a pretty bad depression. It took a lot of work, a whole

509

lot of tears and prayers to get out of that slump. So when we noticed some of the same signs with Jack — well, we thought maybe you'd changed after losing Devon. Grief, I know, can do strange things to people . . . ."

He paused and shifted his feet. From the shame in his eyes Audra realized he was referring not just to her but also to him and Meredith. That perhaps the court filing was part of their own grieving process.

"Audra, I hope you can understand. When you talked about being in a rush to move, we got flat-out desperate. The way things were going, we figured there was a good chance we'd never see Jack again. Above all, we knew if anything ever did happen to him because we didn't try to protect him — even from you — we would never forgive ourselves."

No question, when recent events were outlined on paper, Audra was well aware how she'd appear as a parent. Meredith's history aside, the suspicions weren't exactly unfounded. "What makes you certain now that Jack is safe with me?"

"Our lawyer told us about the police report. How they'd given Jack a thorough check and were satisfied. I admit that it helped put our mind at ease. Beyond that, seeing you in person yesterday, I guess you could say it woke us up. It reminded us how much we really do know you. And that you're a good person, Audra. More important, you're a good mom.

Deep down, we've always believed that — even when you seemed to have doubts about it yourself."

A mix of emotions whirled through her. She tried to respond but couldn't assemble the words.

After an exhale, Robert rubbed his jaw and said, "Frankly, I wouldn't blame you if you never forgave us. If I were in your shoes, I'm not sure I'd be capable of that. But I do want you to know how deeply sorry we are. We love you, and we love Jack. No matter where you decide to go from here, I hope you always remember that."

A quiet beat passed before Robert submitted a smile and turned for his car. He climbed in and drove off, around the corner, out of view. But still Audra stood there, her spirits both blooming and wilting in the afternoon light.

56

The day grew quiet as the sun retired from its post. Children at the fountain had come and gone. Mothers and nannies had pushed countless strollers down the path. A welcome breeze fluttered its fingers at the tree above the bench where Vivian remained.

Since Gene's departure from the park, she had lost all concept of time. She had shed the tears that begged to fall, but once again the numbness protected her from ruin. She was gazing at the mosaic of filtered light dancing across the grass when a large shadow appeared on the ground.

"It's time to go."

She raised her head, expecting a park patrolman to usher her along. Instead, it was Gene.

"I said I'd take care of you." His tone was tense but level. He didn't look in her eyes. "I made a promise."

"Gene . . ."

He grabbed the handles of their travel bags

and started toward the street. He was several strides away when he paused, a signal for her to follow.

Alas, he had returned here out of decency, to keep his conscience clear. With nightfall soon arriving, he would ensure she made it home before he walked away forever.

Wearily, she came to her feet. She accompanied him to the sidewalk and on toward the bus depot. They continued in silence over a stretch of city blocks and into Foley Square. When he began to climb a wide set of concrete stairs, she realized where they were.

"This is the courthouse."

He proceeded without speaking.

"What are we doing here?"

Again, no response. Just more steps.

"Gene, stop." She grabbed his arm to cease him. "Tell me what we're doing."

He shifted his body toward her, though still avoided her eyes. "The baby needs a father," he said coarsely. "The way I feel about everything else . . . I don't know what to make of yet. All I know is there's an innocent baby in this mess — a baby that ought to have two parents. There's no reason it should have to suffer."

Vivian withdrew her hand. Pride commanded her to refuse. A strong, independent woman would not allow a man to do this, no matter how charitable his intent.

513

But pride, she realized, would not feed and clothe her child. Nor would it provide a respectable standing on which that child could build a life. Her unborn baby deserved much more than Vivian could supply on her own.

After all the damage she had unwittingly caused, she could do this. If Gene was willing, she would do this.

With a single nod, she acquiesced and the two resumed their ascent. She followed him through the doors, into the corridors of justice, and prepared to say her vows.

Before long, the papers were signed and scripted words recited. The official pronouncement was made. There was even an official kiss, though it passed with all the warmth and length of a pinprick. Gene paid two extra dollars for strangers to stand as witnesses. Luanne and an Army buddy had long since left the courthouse by the time Vivian and Gene arrived.

"I'll call them tomorrow," he had intoned when Vivian asked about updating the others to explain the delay in the ceremony. She imagined he would create a plausible excuse, perhaps cab trouble or temporary cold feet, but he did not confirm this. In fact, he said nothing more.

At the hotel, she soaked in the tub until the water had cooled her to a shiver.

Dressed in her white, silken nightdress — she had packed only this for sleepwear — she left the haven of the bathroom. Gene was lying beneath the covers on the far side of the bed. One hand under his head, he gazed at the ceiling. Lamplight outlined the bare surface of his chest, the muscles she had felt only through a layer of fabric.

"I see there's a bottle of champagne on the bureau," she said. She craved conversation of any kind, the slimmest sense of connection. "Are you thirsty?"

He flicked her a glance. It was the same attention he had extended during the ceremony and every minute since. "No," he said.

Vivian simply nodded.

She clicked off the tasseled lamp on her nightstand and slid beneath the covers. Moonlight slanted between the drapes, drawing a line across the carpet and over the fluffy down bedding. The room was relatively spacious, by Manhattan standards, the décor elegant in soft yellow and cobalt blue. She could understand why Gene had chosen it for their first intimate encounter. Their first night of marital bliss.

She lay there for several minutes, clasping the pressed sheets covering her chest. From the hallway came the laughter of a couple passing by the door, an enviously happy sound. Then it went quiet, save for the city noises below. It was the sort of quiet that could turn a person mad.

At last, Vivian rotated her head toward Gene. Her groom, her husband. The pillow rustled like cellophane in her ear.

"Gene," she said, before considering what would follow. There was so much to say, but with endless doubts of how to phrase it.

"Does anyone else know?" he said.

It took her a second to comprehend the question. "No. Agent Gerard is the only one I've told about Isaak."

"What about the baby?"

How stupid of her. Naturally, that's what he'd meant. "No one but the doctor knows," she assured him. "And now you."

Gene angled his eyes in her direction. She strained to read the emotion beneath them, veiled by the dimness. "For now we keep it that way," he told her. "And the secret of its father, that stays with us for good."

She nodded and whispered, "Of course."

His gaze lingered over her face. It already seemed an eternity since he had truly looked at her. After a notable stillness, she uncurled her stiffened fingers. She edged them over to touch his shoulder, needing even scant reassurance that he did not despise her.

Barely had she brushed his skin when he rolled the other way.

That's how they remained through the long hours of night, together in their solitude, both grieving over a life that would never be theirs.

57

Everything had changed in a day.

The custody case had been officially dropped, releasing Audra from the bindings of a darkly tenuous future. She and Jack could at last continue on a path with promise, the fresh start they would launch together.

Now, if only Tess would share her enthusiasm.

"You do realize you don't absolutely have to move," she said to Audra, emphatically pointing with a potato chip from lunch. It was the umpteenth time she had stated the reminder since the legal development a week ago.

"I'm pretty sure you've mentioned it." Audra put a fifty-cent price sticker on an old purse. She returned it to the spread of garage-sale items covering her bedroom floor, where she and Tess were seated cross-legged.

"Seriously, though. Why would you want to live where people say things like 'shiesty' and 'wicked good'? Those don't even make sense. It's like a bad translation of a foreign film."

Audra smiled, unable to argue. "Well, considering I've given notice on the apartment, and I'd actually be employed in Boston, I'd say it's the best option."

"Oh, please. Hector would hire you back in a millisecond. I'm not kidding when I tell you the new girl's weird. Her name should've been a clue. Cheyenne. What normal person is named after a city in Wyoming?"

Audra started tagging the pile of baseball caps. "I thought you were the one who recommended her."

"Yeah, well. She had a good résumé. There's no way I could've known she'd talk to every patient in a coochie-coo baby voice."

"Maybe it's . . . a phase she's going through."

"Like how she doesn't shave? Legs I get, but armpits? That's plain wrong."

Although the vision did make Audra wince inside, she aimed for a solution: "So, just don't look under her arms."

"I've tried. It's as easy as *not* watching a train wreck." Tess picked up another CD and groaned. "Audra, really? You still own *Cher's Greatest Hits*?"

Tess had taken the day off and was supposed to be pricing the music and books, but between commentary about work, the East Coast, and every eighties album in the stack, she wasn't making much progress. Good thing they still had two days until the PTA's community flea market. Hosted by Grace's school, it was a convenient way to clear out anything Audra didn't want to pack for the big move in three weeks, all while supporting a worthy cause.

"Mom?" Jack asked gently from the open door, his arm now free of a cast.

"Yeah, buddy? What is it?"

"Can I get a hundred coins?"

Grace called out from the living room couch: "It only costs two dollars! Then his penguin can buy a jumbo flat-screen TV for his igloo."

Audra hated spending money on Internet games that trended like pop music hits. But, with her savings mostly intact, there was less need for frugality. Besides, she wasn't about to discourage any of his positive social interactions.

"I suppose that's fine," she said to Jack. "Nothing else though, okay? We don't need a whole penguin village living in my laptop."

" 'Kay," he replied. Before he turned for the couch, he sported half a smile.

His nightmares were still a regular part of their routine, but Audra hoped the depletion of her anxiety would soon rub off on her son.

Tess waved a CD in the air. "Now, *this* one I'm keeping. I love the Go-Go's." She set the case aside and continued through the pile.

Audra laughed and began to organize board games that Jack had long outgrown. She was collecting cards for Candy Land when Tess spoke in a secretive tone.

"Hey, you have to tell me. Have you figured out anything about Sean?"

519

The question pulled Audra's head up. She hadn't told Tess about the hayloft, as she still hadn't processed the encounter, and worried what had given her away. She answered in an equally hushed voice. "What about him?"

"Did you figure out why Jack wanted to find him at the festival?"

Internally Audra sighed, her thoughts redirected. "I'm not sure it happened like that. I think he just . . . recognized Sean from his picture in the paper."

"Or . . . ," Tess drew out, "he could have been looking for him, but in a different way than you originally thought."

"I don't follow."

"It's like in that movie, *Sleepless in Seattle.* How the boy snuck off to New York, in order to meet some stranger, because he wanted his dad to have a new wife."

Audra gasped at the revelation. "Ohhh, so you're saying Jack wants me to have a new wife."

Tess sat back and rolled her eyes. "Just think about it. When you consider what Jack told you about wanting two people together, maybe that's his real message. That he wants you to be with someone — like Sean — because he wants you to be happy."

So finally she can be with him. Granted, it could apply, but Audra doubted that was the case. It was no different from a tarot-card reading: Look hard enough and any prediction could

520

be stretched to fit.

"Tess, if this is another strategy of yours, pushing a romance to keep us from moving, it won't work. But I do appreciate the effort."

With a grin, Audra returned to the board game pieces. She wasn't about to share that Sean had called, asking to see her tomorrow. After all, there would be no chance for a relationship. That's why she had suggested a coffee shop near the apartment. A public meeting place not only clarified expectations as platonic but would also reduce her own temptations for more. Her goal was to simplify. The day would be complicated enough, as it would be her first trip to her in-laws' house since the case began.

After several days of pondering Robert's words, she had been tucking Jack into bed when he asked about his grandparents. *Can we go visit them before we move?* he'd asked, and she was reminded that he knew nothing of what had occurred. *Of course we can,* she'd answered, a verbal reflex. In the late hours of the same night, she had concluded it was time to reach out. Though part of her still harbored resentment, it was impossible to discard compassion in light of the couple's past.

At this point, it was a toss-up as to which meeting tomorrow would clench the prize for tension and awkwardness, but as a means for proper closure they were tied.

The phone rang.

Tess salvaged the cordless from the mound

521

of books and checked the screen. "It says *Shuman.* Do you want it?"

The name didn't sound familiar — at first. Then recognition set in. Audra had forgotten all about the woman's voice mail. Cringing from her blunder, she answered the phone and finally connected with Taylor Shuman.

"I'm so sorry. I completely meant to call you back. With summer break starting, and everything else, it's been pretty hectic."

"I totally understand," Taylor said. "I was just worried you didn't get my message, so thought I'd better try your home number too. I do have some information for you, if now's a good time."

The polite thing to do, obviously, was hear the woman out. Then Audra would thank her profusely and assure her it was the perfect amount of details to finish a family project. Another way of saying there was no need for more.

"Now is a great time. I'd love to hear it."

"Wonderful. I have the file right here." Papers faintly shuffled over the line. "Let me tell you, Sean was right about this guy, Jakob, being a challenge to track down. It became a personal mission of mine. I even recruited a friend to help out. He's an archivist at a military museum and has a knack for uncovering this kind of stuff."

The more Audra learned of people's wasted efforts, the worse she felt.

"Anyway, it took some digging, but we did

locate a file that was recently declassified. Actually, it might have been the one you had trouble viewing online. Turns out, he was, in fact, one of the spies convicted in that saboteurs' case in 1942."

Audra grappled with the statement. She hadn't expected the connection. No article she had read ever included him. "Are you sure about that?"

"I'm looking at a summary of the case right here. It states that Jakob Isaak Hemel was tried by a military —"

"I'm sorry. Did you say *Isaak*? As in, his middle name?"

Tess scrunched her brow at Audra, direly curious from catching a single side of the conversation.

"That's right. Apparently he was tried in a separate case. That's why he wasn't listed with the others. According to this document, he was declared guilty and given — hold on, where'd it go? — oh, yeah. He was sentenced to fifteen years of hard labor in prison."

"So . . . he wasn't sent to the electric chair."

"Looks like he got off for collaborating. Only two others in the group weren't executed. Eventually, at different times, the three were deported to Germany. And that's the most intriguing part."

Audra pressed her hand to her temple, fully aware that she wasn't prepared for the rest. "What is?" she asked.

"There's no record of him after that. Not a shred of evidence he ever made it there."

At the suspenseful pause, Audra sank further into confusion. "What does that mean?"

"Honestly, I don't know if they're linked in any way, but there was a memo in Jakob's file. It mentioned a missing plane over the Atlantic within a few days of his release. An Army transport. From what we can tell, something about it was covered up, though we don't know what."

A shiver ran through Audra's body from scalp to toes. She gripped the phone tighter.

Tess demanded in a whisper, "What's wrong?"

But Audra couldn't answer. Her mind was too consumed by the thought of her son in the next room, a young boy who once again threatened all that she believed.

58

Vivian would have outright rejected the idea just years ago. But much had changed since then, and the task of becoming a dutiful housewife had become her penance.

Her bouts of nausea had fully waned. Though her pregnancy was eleven weeks along, the small swell of her belly was simple to hide. At Gene's insistence, they had yet to announce the news, not even to family. It was only the first trimester, he had pointed out.

If in actuality he was hoping a natural mishap would eliminate the need, she could hardly fault him. In her own darkest moments — prior to the day a fluttering brushed her insides, a discernible whisper of life — she could not deny having had the same thought.

"Are you sure you're okay with all of this?" Luanne once asked, after Vivian resigned from her job. From years of friendship Luanne knew her well enough to question the stark transition. No one else would have batted an eye at a new bride's dedication to the role of a model homemaker.

"Why? Are you doubting my Betty Crocker skills?" Vivian teased, and swiftly changed the topic.

While she already missed Luanne's regular company, their mismatch of schedules did offer a benefit: fewer chances of the truth slipping out. Charging forward would be easier without the weight of added fear.

The first goal was to establish a routine.

Three days a week Vivian washed, starched, and ironed Gene's uniforms. On alternating days, equipped with her ration book, she shopped at the market and tidied their home, a modest two-bedroom apartment a stone's throw from the base. Every morning she sent Gene off with a lunch pail, packed with more nutrition than mess-hall meals, and every evening she greeted him with a supper prepared by six o'clock sharp. Makeup and hair in place, she sat at the table and attempted small talk as he quietly ate her casseroles and dinner molds, the vegetables freshly picked at a Victory garden. On occasion, her meals even achieved the promise of their recipes in *Ladies' Home Journal.*

Afterward, as she washed and dried the dishes, he would read the paper on the davenport or listen to updates on the radio. The current broadcasts covered American bombing raids in Europe, the German march toward Stalingrad, the Japanese stronghold of Guadalcanal. Vivian could not imagine a single headline in the bunch of which Gene wasn't already informed. More likely, they were but fillers for his evenings.

Sometimes he would tune in to a comedic program. A witty punch line from Jack Benny or a one-liner from Bob Hope would induce a smile on Gene's face. But when Vivian entered the room, drying her hands on her apron, the smile would inevitably vanish. And soon they would retire to their respective sides of the bed. In every way, they were parallel rails of a single track, traveling together but never crossing. They had become two halves of a couple she most feared.

They had become her parents.

The other officers' wives welcomed Vivian at their gatherings, though the inclusion had a compulsory air. Most conversations revolved around their children, to which Vivian could not yet relate, and personal jokes placed her further on the perimeter of their circle.

One day, as she sat smiling on cue and sipping flavorless Earl Grey, she recalled how hard her mother had tried to fit in with the British socialites. Vivian had been wrong to criticize. Maybe her mother had always been on the outside, even in DC, making the decision to remain in New Hampshire all the more alluring.

More than once, Vivian was tempted to address the topic with her mother, but other subjects always took precedence — such as her confession to marrying Gene. It took her several weeks following their nuptials to make that particular call.

"Vivian Maureen James," her mother declared. "Tell me you're not serious."

As expected, the woman was less than delighted — more distraught over not being present, it seemed, than the lack of showy display. Faster than a lightning bolt, she jumped on a New York — bound train. Fortunately, already an admirer of Gene, she quickly forgave the offense, assured by the knowledge that, technically, he and Vivian had been acquainted as far back as their early teenage years. The translation was that their marriage would not suffer the consequences of spontaneity.

Days later, Vivian's father, now back in the States, also paid them a visit. He was more accepting, less judging, than his norm. The war appeared to have loosened his views on situations not mortally critical. It didn't hurt that Gene feigned ample pleasantness throughout their supper, just as he had done with Vivian's mother, this time trading educated insight on war and politics. By the time Vivian served the coffee and peach cobbler, her father had ruled favorably.

Gene's performance was so convincing, in

fact, Vivian actually forgot it was a mere reflection of the man she used to know. A man she missed beyond words.

After waving good-bye to her father's taxi, with the dishes put away and lights turned off, she and Gene slid beneath the covers. He murmured, "Good night," a step that would precede his turn toward the window. But before he could complete the act, Vivian inched her way over.

Emboldened by the darkness and her after-supper schnapps, she laid a kiss on his neck, followed by another, and another. She created a path along his collarbone and over the surface of his chest. His skin prickled at the touch of her lips and strands of her hair, and as her fingers traveled downward his stomach muscles cinched. She sensed a firming beneath the covers, heard him gasp in response. His body otherwise refrained from all movement.

When she raised her head, to see if she should continue, his gaze latched on to hers. Before she could think, he shifted her onto her back. He pulled off her nightgown in a single motion and flung it away. He kissed her neck and shoulder with ravaging force, pausing only to maneuver out of his drawers. His hand moved over her breast, down her side, and up again, hungry and searching. A burning sensation rushed through Vivian. Arching her back, she closed her eyes, eager for more. Yet after his knee parted her legs, she felt him hesitate. The first thought in her mind was the baby. He was worried about hurting the baby.

"It's all right," she said, her breaths gone shallow. "The doctor, he said it's perfectly fine."

Somehow she knew, even before she opened her eyes, that her words might as well have been ice water.

Gene held in place, sobering from the short-lived spell, then sat up on his side of the bed. His legs over the edge, he stared at the window, saying nothing. When he stood to replace his boxers, Vivian drew the sheet up over her chest. She wished the mattress would swallow her whole.

"I'm sorry," he said quietly before leaving the room. And those two words, coming from Gene, nearly broke her.

Vivian was still feeling the wound of that night when a phone call arrived days after. It was this weakness, she reasoned, that caused her to concede to a meeting with Agent Gerard. Either that, or on account of the guilt that would always bind them.

And so, on the first Thursday of September, she again ventured to Prospect Park. The spot had been her suggestion; it seemed, in a darkly odd way, appropriate for an ending.

When she arrived at Binnen Bridge, where

birds chirped and water rushed, Agent Gerard was already there. He was fanning himself with the brim of his hat but stopped when she came into view.

"Afternoon, Mrs. Sullivan. It's nice to see you."

It bothered her how he'd known of her married name and new residence without her divulging either one. An occupational advantage.

"What is it you wanted to see me about?"

He nodded, acknowledging her desire to bypass frills. "Now that it's over, I thought you deserved to hear how everything wrapped up with the case."

Part of her preferred not to hear a word. Yet in her mind, a greater part knew that closure would come only through enduring such details. Thus, she gripped her purse upon the railing and waited for him to continue.

"Four weeks ago, a military tribunal did make a ruling on the other spies," he said. "All eight were found guilty."

The announcement brought clarity to a fuzzy memory. "I thought you said one of them helped turn the group in?"

"There were actually two that collaborated. One was George Dasch. He got thirty years in the federal pen. His buddy, Ernest Burger, got hard labor for life."

She shook her head, astonished. "That was

their reward for coming forward?"

"They were originally sentenced to death, like the others. Only reason that changed was because Hoover and the Attorney General made an appeal to FDR. The rest got the chair, just a few days after the trial."

Vivian leaned toward the railing and looked out onto the water. A pair of young boys stood down by the boathouse, skimming stones across the surface.

She caught the vague sounds of Agent Gerard talking. Something about hysteria and paranoia, and the relocation of Japanese Americans. About the possibility of people feeling the same toward citizens with German blood.

"Point of the matter is," he went on, "I need you to keep all this to yourself. It'll be released to the press, but not for a while."

Vivian almost asked why he bothered telling her a thing; he had no obligation to do so. But inside she knew the reason. He wanted her to know that Isaak Hemel hadn't been singled out. That once again the system had run the show.

"I trust you'll keep this confidential," the agent stressed when she didn't answer.

Still gazing at the boathouse, she considered the alternative and laughed to herself. "Who would I possibly tell?" she said. It was hardly a boast-worthy accomplishment. She exhaled her morbid amusement and turned to face him. "Is there anything else?"

He paused a moment. "I suppose not."

"Then, I'll say good-bye, Agent Gerard." She headed off without waiting for a response.

How wrong she had been to come here; the final details were not a source of closure.

"Congratulations," he said, "by the way."

The comment stopped her short. His casual tone clashed with the only reference she could summon: the three-month-old baby growing within her.

This, she realized, could be the true purpose of their meeting. But how could the man have known? Had the FBI tracked her every move, confiscated her medical files?

She pivoted back a quarter of the way, her purse over her middle. "On . . . ?"

"On tying the knot. I meant to tell you that on the phone." He proffered a smile and placed his hat on his head, adjusted the tilt. "I do hope you and your husband will be real happy together."

She studied his features, his voice, for an encoded message. An insinuation, perhaps, about the extent of her relationship with Isaak. But his well wishes appeared genuine.

"Thank you," she said with a nod, and resumed her strides without looking back.

59

Audra had a sudden impulse to drive straight by and never return. But she had made a promise to Jack, giving her no choice but to stop at her in-laws' house. While she appreciated their reasons behind the petition, the fact remained: Even for a short time, they had viewed her as a mother who would abuse her child.

She pulled over to the curb. Although the driveway offered more shade from the morning sun, she chose not to park on their property. It would be too familiar for where the relationship stood.

Then again, she wasn't sure where anything stood.

The phone call from the day before — linking Jakob and Isaak, the saboteurs, and a missing plane — had left her mind rattling like a screen door in a storm. Open, shut, open, shut. Her skeptical defenses had grown weary from the turbulence. Again, the theories could be as easily believed as mocked. Currently she didn't have the brainpower to determine which was more deserved.

She rolled up the thought, snug as the keys in her hand. She smiled at Jack while walking him to the front door. Before she could even knock, Robert flung the door open. He must have been keeping lookout from a window.

"Well, good morning, Beanstalk! How's life treating ya?"

"Good," Jack said softly.

"Gee whiz, I think you grew another two inches. You keep up this pace, your grandma's gonna put a brick on your head to slow you down."

Jack lowered his eyes, but a chuckle sounded from his chest and his face brightened. Any reservations Audra had about bringing him here shrank in that moment.

"So, what are you waitin' for? Get on in here." Robert ruffled Jack's hair. When the boy entered the house and disappeared around the corner, Robert turned to Audra with a thoughtful look. "I appreciate you doing this," he said. "We both do." This was the only time besides the day of Devon's funeral that she ever saw tears mist Robert's eyes.

"It's the right thing for Jack."

Robert nodded. Gesturing behind him, he said, "Could I persuade you to come inside?"

The image of Meredith at the cemetery, her gaze averted and lips pursed, held vividly in Audra's thoughts. To face the woman again was a daunting thing. If not for the desire to hug Jack good-bye, Audra might have delayed the confrontation.

"Just for a minute."

Eagerly Robert moved aside, enabling her to step past him. The rich aroma of chocolate-chip cookies enveloped her, and with it the feeling of returning to a place she once treasured as a second home.

Robert closed the door, sealing her in, just as Meredith appeared in the foyer.

"Hi, Audra," she said with a stiff smile. One of her hands was squeezing the other as if molding a block of clay.

"Meredith."

In the brief pause, a rare meekness from the woman made itself known. "Robert, dear, why don't you see if Jack wants some milk for his cookies?"

"Sure thing, Mama." He proceeded toward the kitchen, patting his wife's shoulder in passing.

Audra had expected to feel a simmering of betrayal once in Meredith's presence, and it was certainly there. What she hadn't anticipated was an urge to cry and hug and declare all was forgiven. But she kept those emotions in check.

"Robert told me that he spoke to you," Meredith said, "about what happened . . . before."

"He did."

Meredith nodded slowly. "Well. Even so, I want you to hear how sorry I am for any hurt we've caused. It was wrong — *I* was wrong. I realize it's not an excuse, but I hope you can see we had only the best intentions for Jack."

"I know that, Meredith. He and I wouldn't be here otherwise."

"Of course."

Hands still clasped, Meredith gazed back at her. After a moment, they both angled their eyes toward the walls, the polished wooden floor. Tension could be wrung from the silence.

Perhaps this was enough for their first exchange. There was no indication they would ever resuscitate even half their former closeness, but nothing to say there was a need for it. Pleasant civility for Jack's sake would be sufficient.

"I'll go tell Jack I'm leaving," Audra said. "Then I'll be back around six if that still works."

Meredith nodded and formed another rigid smile. "Six is perfect."

Audra gripped her keys, a small asset of escape, and headed for the dining room to reach the kitchen. She was steps away from the formal table when Meredith spoke.

"I was afraid you were forgetting him."

More than the words, it was the faltering tone that turned Audra around.

Moisture welled in Meredith's eyes and her lips quivered. "I know how much you loved Devon. In my heart, I've always known it. And I understand you need to move on. I told myself this when you sold the house, and the furniture. But then you made it clear you wanted to be far

537

away from anything to do with him — and us. And when you talked about the soldier you met, a new man in Jack's life . . ."

All at once, Audra saw Meredith's efforts from an altered view. The stories in her lily garden, the visits to the cemetery, the pictures of Devon on shelves and tables, the resistance to Audra and Jack moving.

Both women had been treating the same wound with two vastly different remedies — neither of which had worked.

Meredith shook her head, her face growing mottled. "You have every right to do all of those things, and truly you should. I mean that. Devon was my son, but you're my daughter, Audra, and I want you to be happy."

Audra sucked in a breath. She never would have foreseen the effect of those words.

"I'm just so terrified he'll be forgotten," Meredith said hoarsely. "That little by little, Devon will fade from Jack's life, and that one day Jack will have no idea what a special father he had —" The rest dropped off as she covered her face. She wept quietly into her palms, her shoulders shaking.

Audra couldn't stop her own tears from rising. Right or wrong, her will to hold a grudge drifted away as if pulled by a current.

She moved closer to Meredith and laid a hand on her arm. In a whisper, a single word spilled out: "Mom . . ."

Though nothing followed, Meredith lowered

her hands and reached out for an embrace. Audra accepted without pause, the connection so long overdue she could have cried for that alone.

"I could never forget him," Audra said softly.

How pointless to have ever tried. After all, part of her would always love Devon, and she would forever see him in Jack.

Meredith nodded against Audra's shoulder, as if she had heard her thoughts.

Once the moment had settled and they had both caught their breaths, a question nagged at Audra. She debated on discussing it another day, not wanting to reverse the progress they had made. Given their past, it could come off as a challenge. But now, more than ever, she needed to know.

"Could I ask you something?"

Meredith looked at her, a smile in her eyes. "Anything."

"After everything you've been through, how do you still have faith? I mean, there are so many tragedies that are just so senseless."

Meredith thought on this a moment. She sniffed and wiped the streaks from her face before answering. "I've had plenty of my own doubts," she admitted. "I think that's normal when it comes to believing in anything you can't absolutely prove." She sighed and shrugged lightly. "But one day I realized that faith is a choice. For me, it's a hunch I feel in my heart.

And once I understood that, the decision was easy."

Audra took in the words, an idea to mull over, and nodded.

"Sorry to interrupt, ladies." Robert looked tentative at first, then pleased at the scene.

"What is it, honey?" Meredith asked.

"Just wanted to see if there's any objection to me whipping up some omelets. Jack said he's getting a little hungry."

Meredith regarded Audra. "Would that be all right?"

Memories of the omelets Devon used to cook, his favorite "breakfast-for-dinner" feature, made Audra smile. "Jack would love that," she replied, and added, "It was his dad's specialty."

The corners of Meredith's mouth rose and her eyes glinted.

"Audra, any chance you'd like to join us?" Robert asked.

Before Audra could respond, she remembered her awaiting meeting. "I'm afraid I can't today."

"Ah, well," he said wistfully. "Another time, then."

In lieu of an open-ended delay, she said, "How about next Saturday?"

60

With no plans for the remainder of the afternoon, Vivian ambled through the city. She had left her meeting at the park in what felt a lone procession of mourning. Not until her feet throbbed from the endless clacking of her shoes, however, did she realize which grief surprised her most. For it was Agent Gerard's parting words that seized her still, the wish for her to be happy.

At one time in her life, she'd had a clear picture of what happiness entailed. But no longer. It had become a term in a language she barely recalled. A dream she mistook for truth until waking, and like water through her fingers, it had slipped away.

She was reflecting upon this when her mind registered she had landed at the apartment. She fished the key from her purse, only to find she had left their home unlocked. Inside, she closed the door behind her. She had just set down her handbag when the clock chimed four.

Had she been gone that long? She had intended to swing by the butcher shop. She would have to rush there and back to have any chance of preparing a decent, timely meal.

Again she retrieved her keys. Clutching her purse, she opened the door.

"Going already?"

She spun around, heart racing, before she placed the voice. She calmed herself with pats to the chest and shut the door. Pulling on her six o'clock smile, she proceeded past the kitchen and found Gene tucked away in the living room. He sat on the sofa chair, slouched and cross-legged, a small glass in his hand.

"I didn't know you'd be home so early," she said.

"You don't say." He gulped down the drink, which she presumed to be water until he snatched the bottle from the end table, and he poured a hefty amount. Vivian had no need to read the label to recognize it as gin. It was not a liquor Gene typically owned, but she knew the scent from her mother.

He put the bottle aside uncapped, almost catching a corner of the table. "Well, don't let me keep you, if you got somewhere else you wanna be."

Due to his father's past, Gene never indulged in more than a few beers at a time. A little wine or schnapps when hosting guests.

"I was just going to the store," she said. "Gene, is everything all right?"

"Which store?" he said.

"The butcher's. I'd planned to buy meat on the way home, but I forgot."

"Must've had a lot on your mind. All that running around keeping you busy." He swirled his gin with a loose wrist. His words slightly dragged as if formed by a swollen tongue. "What is it you were out doing anyway? If you don't mind me asking."

She kept her answer simple, her uneasiness growing. "I just went to the park."

"Ah, yeah. The park," he said. "And . . . ?"

"And then . . . I walked around the city."

"That's it, huh? Nothing more to it?" He threw back half a glassful.

"Gene —"

"Who'd you meet at Prospect Park, Vivian?"

The question jarred her, as pointed as his gaze.

"As chance would have it," he said, "I'd accidentally left a file for work here. When I came to grab it at lunchtime, I ran into Mrs. O'Donnell. Told me I'd just missed you. That she tried to say hello, but you were in such a rush you didn't notice. Seems wherever you were going was pretty important."

On the table, beside the bottle, lay a crumpled piece of paper. It bore words Vivian recognized and a jagged edge. He had ripped it from the scheduling book she had

543

stored in her vanity.

Prospect Pk. — 2pm, was all she had written.

Her first instinct was to protest over the invasion of her privacy, and, more than that, his presumption of her guilt. Yet she reconsidered. She had entered an interrogation room, not her home. And this man wasn't her husband, but an Intelligence officer on a mission.

"So?" he pressed.

"I assure you, it was nothing inappropriate. You've got the wrong —"

He slammed his glass down. "Tell me who you saw!"

Liquor splashed and Vivian flinched. She thought of Agent Gerard and envisioned Binnen Bridge, the setting of a past reunion she and Gene would never discuss, from a portion of history they pretended did not exist. These were the reasons she had skipped any mention of today's outing.

Of course, if he wanted to know, she would supply every detail from the FBI — regardless of confidential status. But not now. Not in light of his current state.

"We'll talk about this later," she said evenly, "when you're thinking clearly." She turned for the bedroom to prevent their argument from exploding. Yet she went no farther than the gaping door, stopped by the sight.

Her garments had been scattered over the

bed and floor. Drawers of her nightstand and vanity had been upended in a search. For what? Evidence of an affair?

Her jewelry box since childhood lay on its side. Trinkets and brooches had cascaded into a mound. Vivian's head pounded as she knelt on the carpet and scooped them up. The necklace chains were kinked and snarled, a precise reflection of everything in their lives.

"Viel Feind, viel Ehr," Gene said, now filling the doorway. He was reading the engraved necklace that dangled from his fist. "Let me guess. It means he'll love you for eternity — am I right? That somehow you lovebirds will always be together."

Tears stung her eyes. Stiffly she shook her head. "No."

"What, then?"

"It's just an old German saying. It doesn't mean anything."

"So, why'd you keep it? If it doesn't mean anything." His neck muscles flexed as he answered his own question: "Because you still love that Kraut traitor. That's why!" He pitched the necklace across the room.

Vivian recoiled into herself, her arms and legs quivering. Every second slogged by as if dragged through mud. She doubted she would ever move from this spot.

After a time, she registered only quiet in the room, aside from her choppy breaths.

She edged her head upward and found

Gene still there, yet with an altered demeanor. Hands fisted at his temples, he stood with his back against the doorjamb. Though his eyelids were shut, she knew what lay behind them. It was not fury, but pain and fear. He wasn't battling Vivian, or even his suspicions, as much as himself.

She unfolded her body and rose to her feet. Tears rolled hot down her face. "Gene, please . . . listen to me."

He showed no sign of agreeing, but she walked toward him regardless in slow but determined steps. "I know I hurt you. With all of my heart, I am so sorry for that. If you need to hear it a thousand times, I will gladly say it. Or if you need something else, please tell me. Otherwise, you have to stop punishing me for a past I can't change."

She was a few feet from him when his arms lowered to his sides. His eyes eased open, but his gaze remained on the floor.

"If we're going to be a family," she told him, "if we're going to have any chance at happiness together, you have to find a way to forgive me, for both of our sakes. And the child's." She moved an inch closer, wanting to reach for him, but afraid to scare him away. "I know you still love me. And I love you too, despite what you might think."

She waited for a reaction, anything at all.

Finally, gradually, he raised his eyes but stopped before her face. "I have to go," he said, and turned to leave the room.

"Gene, no. We have to talk." She followed him toward the door. They needed to finish this, to see this through. "Don't run away." She grabbed his arm to keep him there, but he jerked himself free, throwing Vivian off-balance. She stumbled backward into the wall and slid down onto her tailbone.

Gene stared, frozen, but just for an instant. In a panic he collapsed onto his knees. "Oh, Jesus." He reached for her belly but drew back, as if his fingertips were fashioned with blades. As if somehow, the hands of his father had replaced his own.

She saw this in Gene's face as he said, "My God, what have I done?"

"It's all right . . . ." Vivian felt only a throbbing on her backside, the coming of a bruise. She knew with certainty no harm had befallen the baby, and very little to herself. "It was just an accident. The baby's fine."

Gene nodded, though absent of conviction. "I'm getting a doctor." He went to rise, and Vivian grasped his sleeve.

"Everything's okay. Gene, please, sit with me."

In his eyes a flood of emotions mounted. His lips tightened, upholding a crumbling dam.

This time he would not fight her. With great care, he took a seat at her side.

Together they sat in silence. No words

would serve as a treaty. No utterance would magically rebuild the bridge. But Vivian had faith that if both were willing, they could repair the connection one plank at a time.

The thought brought to mind Mrs. Langtree's house, a project not entirely different. In fact, it was during the eve of that day, riding in the truck Gene had borrowed, that he and Vivian had shared their first deliberate and meaningful touch.

Praying it could work again, she placed her hand over his. Just as before, he said nothing; just as before, he did not pull away.

Vivian tipped her head to rest on his shoulder. He smelled of soap and pine and home.

Seconds later, he did withdraw his hand and leaned forward as if readying to leave. Yet to her relief, he was only shifting his body to lay his arm over her shoulder. When his chin settled on her crown, she could have sworn a few tears dampened the top of her hair. She closed her eyes, treasuring his hold, and felt the numbness of her soul start to lift.

Years later, Vivian would look back at that day. She would realize it was in that very hallway, the two of them stripped to little more than bones, that not just healing began, but love. Real love, in the truest and deepest sense. A far contrast to the dizzying, volatile whirlwind she had once taken to define the word.

The most wonderful type of love, she had learned, was the kind built with care and over time, through forgiveness and understanding, compromise and compassion, trust and acceptance. It was hidden in the minutiae of everyday life; it was in the traded smiles during a radio show or the peaceful lulls on an evening stroll.

Pain and fear would not be erased like the marks on a blackboard. Nothing real ever disappears that simply. But over days, weeks, months, the good outweighed all, until the initial impetus of their wedding dissolved into the background.

Never did that hold truer than on the morning when the nurse summoned Gene. "Would you like to meet your daughter?" she asked.

The moisture welling in his eyes supplied the answer. As if handling fine crystal, he cradled the small bundle in his arms, and Vivian knew right then, with certainty beyond measure, that Gene — her beloved husband — would never treat their darling Judith as less than his own, that together they were a family sealed by a bond. A bond that nothing, and no one, could break.

61

It was the start of a family reunified. From the turn of events with Meredith, Audra's mind was still reeling when she arrived at the coffee shop.

At a far table by the window, Sean raised his hand.

The mere sight of him placed all other thoughts on hold. In a flurry of images, their encounter in the barn came rushing back. She fended off the memory. There was no room for complications with just three weeks until the move. She was only here to say good-bye.

She walked steadily past the line of customers that stretched from the entrance. Patrons filled most of the tables in the room, chatting with friends, shuffling through newspapers, typing on laptops. The scents of espresso and warm muffins led a path to Sean's table.

"Morning," he said.

"Hi." She glanced at his mouth, remembered how it had felt on hers, and wondered if he was thinking the same thing.

"Oh, here. This for you." He slid a paper cup

across the table. The string from a tea bag dangled from the lid. "I got here a little early and the line was getting long. If you want something else, I'd be happy to grab it for you."

She recognized the flavor printed on the tag, a decaf favorite named "Calm." After the morning she'd had — make that the entire month — nothing sounded better.

"Thank you," she said, taking a seat. "It's perfect."

He nodded. As she settled in, he drank from the slot of his lidded cup. He looked freshly showered and shaven in a collared, short-sleeved shirt. The bronze fabric complemented his eyes, which had notably relaxed since she'd last seen him.

"You look better," she observed. "Not that you looked bad before. You just — never mind."

A slanted smile crossed his lips. "It's okay. I am doing better."

"Good. Good, I'm glad." She saved herself from tripping over her next words by focusing on her tea. It needed to be stirred and the temperature was just above comfort level, but she drank it regardless. She felt his gaze on her all the while.

"Audra," he said finally, "about last week."

She set down the cup, preparing herself for how he might phrase it.

"I shouldn't have dumped all of that on you. You've got enough to worry about, and . . . I hope you didn't . . . that is, I'm sorry if . . ."

"Sean, please. Don't." Clearly he saw her participation as a merciful act. And he couldn't have been more wrong. "I think it's safe to say, we were both there for each other at a time when we needed it. Simple as that."

He accepted her reasoning with a close-lipped smile. When their eyes connected, she had to prod herself to look away.

"So," he said after a moment. "How's Jack doing?"

It was the question she asked herself daily.

She pictured him building cyber igloos with Grace, zooming around on his scooter, welcoming his grandparents' affection.

"We'll have to see, but I think he'll be all right," Audra said.

True, Jack wasn't the same child from two years ago — the boy with an easy laugh who drummed on Cool Whip tubs and played with potato bugs — but perhaps he wasn't supposed to be. He was growing up and changing. They all were. Maybe it was time to acknowledge this, to stop forcing each other into a mold that didn't fit.

"That reminds me," Sean said, "I got a message from that sergeant's wife I told you about. I haven't called her back yet, but if she has any info —"

"Actually, she got ahold of me."

"Oh, she did? Great," he said. But when Audra didn't expound, he asked, "Did she find anything that might help?"

"Nothing worth repeating."

It was a truthful response. The woman's report only raised more questions, none of which would ever really be answered.

"Turns out," Audra said, "there's a strong chance Jack was getting his ideas from other things. All logical ones. Looking back, it was pretty silly on my part." She underscored the claim with a smile. "From now on, I've decided to focus on the present world — which I already have a hard enough time figuring out."

"You and me both," Sean said lightly.

She laughed, grateful for the elevated mood. They both sipped their drinks as a female barista called out customers' names for drink pickups at the counter.

"So, how about your summer?" Sean asked. "You two have any special plans?" Obviously he intended to perpetuate their casualness, not knowing it was a subject Audra suddenly dreaded.

She shifted in her chair. "We'll be . . . moving to Boston. In the middle of July."

"Boston?" he said. "You never mentioned anything."

"Sorry, I probably should have. It's just that the custody battle left us in limbo for a while. But they've dropped the case, so we're able to stick with our plans now."

Despite the disappointment in his eyes, it was ridiculous of her to feel even a twinge of guilt, or regret. They hadn't known each other for even a month.

"Sounds like it's all great news, then," he said.

"It is. Really great."

They were like two singles who had met at rehab, a transitional place meant for healing, not romantic hookups. Still, she hated the idea of walking away after all he had shared with her.

"What about you?" she asked. "Are you going to be okay?"

"Me? Oh, yeah, I'll be fine."

When he sat back in his chair, she searched his eyes for a genuine answer. "Are you sure?"

He contemplated the question and shrugged. "Each day's getting a little better. I will admit, though, most nights have been pretty restless since the memories came back."

If anyone understood that struggle, it was Audra. "Feel free to call me next time. I'm probably awake."

He grinned and nodded as if he just might. Boston, after all, was only a phone call away.

"Are there other memories you're getting? Good ones, I mean."

"Yeah, more and more so. It's like my mind was blocked by what happened over there. Now that it's open, the rest of it's starting to come through. I'm actually starting to feel like myself again."

"Sean, that's wonderful."

He angled his body forward, hand resting on the table while holding his drink. "You know, I even ran into an old friend from the TV station I used to work at. Looks like a position's opening up. So I was thinking of applying."

"Oh, you definitely should. That's amazing." In her enthusiasm, she barely caught herself from reaching across the table to squeeze his hand. She pulled back and sipped more tea.

After a pause, she made a show of glancing at her watch. "You know, I ought to get going. Lots to do, with packing and all that."

"Yeah, I should go too. I told Aunt Lu I'd run some errands for her after seeing you. So . . ."

"You told her? And she didn't warn you against seeing the crazy woman?"

He smiled. "She doesn't think you're crazy." He almost sounded convincing enough to believe.

"Either way," Audra said, "I've sort of accepted that crazy is the new normal."

"That's a huge relief — for me, that is." The corners of his eyes crinkled before he rose from his chair. "Come on, I'll walk you back on the way to my car."

They tossed their cups into the trash and walked toward the apartment.

With the distance of one block, they rounded her building all too soon. Audra was searching for a non-cliché parting of *If you're ever in Boston* when Sean came to an abrupt stop, his eyes straight ahead.

Perhaps another memory had come crashing back.

"Sean, what is it?"

"Aunt Lu," he said, bewildered.

"What about her? Did you remember something?"

He shook his head, and motioned forward. "She's here."

Audra followed his indication and found Luanne in the parking lot. She had just stepped out of her car when she looked in their direction.

The expression on her face said the day's discussions were far from over.

62

The announcement unleashed a torrent of emotions. In August of 1945, the Japanese Empire submitted its unconditional surrender. Vivian's initial joy was as genuine as that of any serviceman whooping and hollering through Times Square. One by one the Axis powers had fallen — first Italy, then Germany — and now the six-year war had come to an end. *Good had defeated evil,* people proclaimed, a justification for atrocities best left unspoken. They would cling to this oversimplified truth while trading pats on the back and placing flowers on graves.

In the meantime, newspaper headlines would revert to Hollywood scandals, and radio broadcasts to programs of entertainment. Foreign lands and borders worth the fiercest of battles would soon be reduced to a footnote.

But not every facet of war would fade so easily.

Among the survivors, few were left unscathed. Vivian was no exception. Once the whooping and hollering quieted, she felt the tender flare of old wounds. Much had been sacrificed on the road to victory. It was this thought that brought Mrs. Langtree to the forefront of her mind.

Vivian had made a habit of sending baked goods to the lone widow, whenever Gene went over to help with upkeep and repairs. But this time, on a bright September morning, Vivian would present the dish herself.

On the bus ride there, with little Judith at her side, it occurred to her that if the woman was as stringent about etiquette as she had been about rules, an unannounced visit might be unwelcome. Yet it was too late to fret; they were already on their way.

They soon disembarked in Ditmas Park to reach the gray and white Victorian house. With a warm pie pan in hand, Vivian guided her daughter up the steps of the wraparound porch. The planks were the very same that Vivian and Gene had painted together.

"Be on your best behavior, now," she reminded Judith, before ringing the doorbell.

The two-year-old nodded, bouncing her pigtails, then fidgeted with the ruffles on her pink dress, the latest indulgence from Vivian's mother.

Judith was a petite creature since birth. Hence, for those who bothered to calculate, premature delivery made for a natural assumption. For the ones who enjoyed more scandal, it could be theorized that an intimate premarital date had hastened the couple's vows.

Either way, a paternal question was never raised, thanks in no small part to Judith's looks. Aside from a slight curl to her hair, she was the spitting image of Vivian, with thick brown locks and copper eyes.

Only on occasion would Vivian note a flash of Isaak, from a slyness in Judith's smile or the way she crinkled her chin, suggestive of a dimple. And if the situation allowed, Vivian's mind would dip into a well of the past. There she would bathe in her fondest memories, scenes from another lifetime, and emerge at least comforted by a sense of Isaak at peace.

Still waiting at the door, Vivian followed up with a knock.

"Piddy," Judith said, pointing to the lace curtains on the large bay window.

"You're right, lovey bug. Those are very pretty."

Among the greatest aspects of motherhood, Vivian had learned, was experiencing the wonder of things, even the seemingly mundane, as if for the first time. She was reminded of this now while admiring the house, with its charming turret and columns and latticework. The whole neighborhood, in fact, could have been plucked from a storybook. As could Judith, for that matter, a precious pixie of a girl with a heart pure as Gene's.

Finally, the door opened.

Hair in a loose French twist, more silver now than blond, Mrs. Langtree peered through her spectacles. Though her floral housedress was finer than most, the absence of a suit came as a surprise. Vivian realized this must be how the woman began to dress after retiring from the switchboard, when the operators made way for the military staff.

"Mrs. Langtree," she said, "I'm so glad you're here. I hope I haven't disturbed you."

In deciphering the silence, Vivian could not tell if the woman was merely surprised or recognition had yet to settle.

"I . . . apologize for dropping by unexpectedly. We thought you might like a nice autumn dish."

Mrs. Langtree glanced at the gift that wafted with sautéed garlic and onions. "A Victory feast," she guessed. She said this with a fitting hint of dryness. The sweetness of victory had been tamped by the bitterness of personal loss.

"Nothing that fancy, I'm afraid. Just a shepherd's pie fit for supper."

Mrs. Langtree studied Vivian's face, as though in search of her true motives. The woman was once known for her keen detection of lies. Which, come to think of it, might have unconsciously been Vivian's reason for not coming here sooner. Secrets were but a branch on the tree of deceit.

Thankfully, Judith intervened with a squeak, a sun sneeze that flopped her wavy pigtails.

"Bless you," Mrs. Langtree said, beating Vivian to the phrase, then dipped her head toward the girl. "I take it you're the Judith I've heard all about."

Judith tugged at her lip in an almost bashful gesture.

"According to your father, you're a brilliant, enchanting, and very artistic young lady."

In lieu of replying, Judith returned her focus to the ruffles on her dress.

"Gene tends to be a bit biased," Vivian said out of humbleness but also reserve. Such flattery from the woman was uncharacteristic. "Anyhow," Vivian went on, "here you are." She handed over the meat pie. The perfectly browned crust attested to her vastly improved cooking skills. She had accumulated countless tips from fellow Army wives, generous friends she had come to adore.

"That's very kind of you," Mrs. Langtree said.

"It's our pleasure."

Quiet rose between them, and Vivian worried that her presence had stirred up old tragic memories. "Well, I'd say we've taken up enough of your time. Judith, tell Mrs. Langtree good-bye."

Judith stepped forward. But rather than speaking or waving, she wrapped Mrs. Langtree's legs in a hug. The girl overflowed with affection at home — especially for Gene, who doted on her to the brink of spoiling — but typically not to strangers.

Vivian was about to apologize, out of courtesy, and nudge the toddler free when Mrs. Langtree tentatively returned the gesture. The lines on her face visibly softened.

After Judith let go, Mrs. Langtree cleared her throat. "You know," she said, "I was just going to put a pot of tea on. Would you ladies care to join me?"

Vivian blinked at the invitation. "We wouldn't want to impose."

Mrs. Langtree looked down at Judith. "I think I could scrounge up a few shortbread cookies, as well," she said, and with something resembling a smile she guided Judith into the house.

That single afternoon, much to Vivian's amazement, soon graduated into weekly visits. Over tea and cocoa, and a pie or cobbler when they had saved enough sugar — one of the last items still rationed — an unlikely friendship steadily bloomed.

They would talk about canning and gardening and Judith's latest feats. Mrs. Langtree would relay humorous switchboard tales in exchange for descriptions of London. Past these, she and Vivian discussed marriage and their parents and childhood trips to the shore. Sometimes Mrs. Langtree tossed out amusing tales of her late husband — though it was still a rarity for her to speak at length of her beloved son, Neal.

They continued this way for months. Of course, they included Gene, too, in their periodic suppers.

Then on a Friday afternoon in the middle of March, after Judith had devoured her cupcake, leaving chocolaty crumbs and three burnt candles, Mrs. Langtree turned to Vivian with a serious face.

"There's something I've wanted to tell you," she said. "And now is finally the time."

63

Audra hurried to fill a glass of water for Luanne, anticipating what the woman had come to say. Same as their initial meeting at the farm, tension lurked just beneath the surface.

"Thank you, dear." Luanne accepted the glass, seated on Audra's couch. "I hope you don't mind my dropping in like this. When Sean told me that he was coming here, I realized it would be best to talk to you both at the same time."

"I don't mind at all," Audra said, settling beside her.

Sean borrowed a chair from the dinner table to join them in the living room. Squared to the couch, he sent Audra a curious look over the purpose of the gathering.

As Luanne sipped her drink, her attention drifted to the framed photo of Jack on the end table, an old snapshot taken at the zoo. "Is your son around by any chance?" she asked with forced nonchalance.

No doubt, the woman had been thrown off by

Audra's transcendental theories. Rather than dismissing them as she should have, perhaps Luanne sought grounds for validation.

"Not for a while. He's at his grandparents' house until tonight."

"Ah." Luanne nodded.

"Speaking of which," Audra said, utilizing the segue, "I've been wanting to tell you how sorry I am for all my rambling at the gallery, about Jack and those ridiculous ideas. I really hope you haven't wasted time on any of them."

"No reason for apologies," Luanne said, her eyes sullen behind her bifocals. "Not from you anyhow."

Sean leaned forward, listening closer. "What is it you want to tell us, Aunt Lu?"

Luanne placed her glass on the table, the water's surface rippling from the shake of her hand. She curled her fingers, layered them on the lap of her summer dress. "Audra, when your son came into the studio that night," she said with a grave pause, "he called me Miss Moppet."

Fabulous. The poor lady came all this way to decode a name derived from a cartoon character. "I can explain that. It's just a silly game we play. He was actually calling you Miss Muppet — a cute name he made up."

Luanne brushed right by this. "Do you know who Little Lulu is?"

"Um . . . yes. If you mean from the comics."

"As a little girl, my friends often called me

Lulu, short for Luanne. My brother, Gene, gave it a twist of his own. He must have used the name till I was twelve, when I insisted I was too old for it."

"I'm sorry. I don't understand the connection . . . ."

"Little Lulu's last name," she replied, "is Moppet. Gene was the only person who ever called me 'Miss Moppet.' "

Audra flashed back to Jack's journal. Indeed, *Little Lulu* was one of the comic strips pasted inside. But then, so were *Blondie* and *Calvin and Hobbes.* "I'm sure it's just a coincidence."

"The plane Jack was holding when I saw him. Does he carry it around a lot?"

"Yes — I suppose."

"He rubs it like a worry stone." It was less of a guess than a statement.

Reluctantly, Audra nodded.

"A family friend once carved Gene a toy wooden soldier. He took it everywhere as a kid, was always rubbing it with his thumb. The facial features were barely there when he was done with it."

Audra glanced at Sean, who seemed to arrive at the same implication: that Jack's behavior could be traced not to Isaak, but to Gene.

The clues skittered through Audra's head. As an officer in Intelligence, Gene would have had knowledge of submarines and aircrafts and likely the saboteurs' case. It was just as plausible, married to Vivian, he would have been

566

acquainted with the necklace.

Again, though, the links were interpretative and far-reaching, skewed by personal hopes.

"Luanne, I'm sure there are similarities. But really, I was wrong. I shouldn't have given you the impression that —"

"You talked about unfinished business. How some people believe that's why spirits return, in one form or another. And I was thinking, maybe there are even souls who are in charge of carrying another's message."

Audra preferred to discount all of this but no longer felt an authority on absolutes. "I guess . . . it's possible."

Luanne nodded and looked thoughtfully at Sean. "Dear," she said, "the letter and necklace out of your grandmother's things — do you remember much about the day you found them?"

Sean shrugged, pondering. "Just that they were stored away in the basement. To be honest," he said, "I didn't realize you were aware I'd kept them."

Until now, Audra had forgotten she still had the manila envelope he'd let her borrow, containing the referenced letter and article clippings.

"You brought them to me one day," Luanne said to him, "when you happened across the box. You wanted to know about the notes and letters, all of them from Isaak. That's what he went by — his middle name — though his given

567

name was Jakob."

"Jakob?" Sean said. "You're saying it's the same person?"

Luanne answered with a quiet, "Yes."

Sean looked at Audra, who nodded that she already knew. What she didn't know was how much more information awaited. And she couldn't deny being intrigued.

"Please," she said, "keep going."

Lifting her posture, Luanne continued. "Sean, there's a very specific reason you kept that necklace you're still wearing. It belonged to a man who, by blood, was your real grandfather."

Sean narrowed his eyes. He shook his head. "What about Grandpa Gene?"

Luanne sighed and murmured, "I'd hoped this would be easier, telling you the second time."

"Does Mom know about this?"

"Not yet," Luanne said. "Once you found out, I knew it was finally time to tell her. But she was so worried, with you shipping out just a few days later. And you agreed that delaying it would change nothing at this point . . . ."

"Wait . . . I remember now." The recollection was assembling. "You and I were going to talk to her together . . . after I was back from my tour."

Luanne nodded. "We were."

He shoved his fingers through his hair. "Grandpa Gene knew. Didn't he?"

"Apparently so. Of course, he never said a word to me. I only learned this from reading it

568

in Vivian's diaries." She suddenly turned to Audra. "Oh, I know that sounds horrible, invading someone's privacy like that."

Audra was well aware how it sounded, having committed the infraction herself. "It's okay, I understand," she said, but Luanne proceeded to explain.

"Just after they died, there was a night when Judith had been crying up a storm. She still missed her parents tucking her in. I was exhausted and missing them just as much. I pulled out some of Vivian's old diaries, to hear her voice again. What I came across was a story about her first love. How she'd met Isaak in London, but lost track of him. Then one night he showed up in New York, in a German uniform of all things. He asked for her help to turn in a group of spies, just as you talked about. And they managed to succeed — but not before the two of them . . . had . . ."

Wrinkles around Luanne's mouth deepened as she trailed off. The insinuation spoke for itself. "She wrote about feeling confused and regretful. But when I realized Isaak was Judith's father, that my brother had only gotten married for honorable reasons, I shut the book. All I could think about was getting rid of any evidence in order to protect Judith. I lit the fireplace in the middle of the night while she and Fred were asleep. I was about to toss it all in: the letters and notes from Viv's jewelry box, the diaries, even the necklace. But I couldn't go through with it. Rightfully they belonged to Judith."

Luanne closed her eyes briefly, as though viewing the flames and pile of keepsakes. "Someday I was going to tell her the truth. But it was never the appropriate time for a conversation like that. I guess, eventually, I'd pushed it so far out of my mind, it just seemed like a bad dream."

Sean appeared to be remembering all of this and more. "That's why you've always avoided the subject. Especially when Mom wanted to hear about her parents."

Luanne's face, as before, gained a pinkish tint. "Also, because I was angry with Vivian. Or at least I wanted to be. That way I wouldn't feel guilt over their deaths."

At this, Sean sank back into his seat, increasing the distance between them. If Luanne had told him this part before, he clearly didn't recall. "Why would it be your fault?"

Once more, Audra yearned to reach out and comfort him, wary of what was coming.

"Because I was jealous," Luanne replied, and slowly shook her head. "See, what no one knew, except for my parents, was that I came down with an infection when I was seventeen. I couldn't have babies anymore. So from then on, I wouldn't give a fellow more than two dates before I'd casually mention how I had read the most interesting article about orphans, and I'd ask him how he felt about adopting someday.

Back then, adopting was different than it is now. Every fellow would dismiss the idea, insisting he'd have his hands full with his own children. And later, when they phoned looking for another date, I'd simply have lost interest.

"Finally, though," she said, a soft smile forming, "I met Fred. I was so crazy about him that I waited until the fourth date to give him my test. I was terrified to get the usual answer, but he shocked me. He said he had no qualms whatsoever about adopting, even preferred the idea of giving a child a home that otherwise wouldn't have one. As it turned out, he had been adopted as a baby himself. If he'd proposed that very night, I would have said yes."

Her pleasant expression held for a moment. Then, as if Sean's question returned to her, the reminiscent warmth swiftly waned.

"We'd only been married a few months when Gene and Vivian asked us to watch Judith. They wanted to go to Cape Cod for the week, a belated honeymoon of sorts. By then, I'd fallen completely in love with that little girl. So much so, part of me secretly wished she could be mine . . . ." Luanne attempted to say more but failed as her eyes clouded over.

It was then that Audra heard Tess's words, an echo of her tough-love talk at the cemetery. Just like Meredith, even like Sean, they all harbored guilt over a tragedy that couldn't be stopped. In the absence of someone to blame, it was all too easy to point that finger at yourself.

This was Audra's thought, yet Sean was the one who voiced it.

"You know there was nothing you could have done, don't you? Aunt Lu, they didn't die in a boating accident because you wished you could somehow trade places."

"Oh, yes," Luanne said with little hesitation. "I realized that — after a while. All part of the healing process, I suppose."

Whether from this particular story, the collection of admissions, or the emotional drain of the day, Audra was overcome by the ease with which she could lay down her own burden. She just regretted that it had taken the catharsis of other people's turmoil to get here.

Audra offered, "I'm still sorry, Luanne, for bringing up parts of your past that you probably wanted to leave alone."

"Well, I'm not," Luanne said, seeming genuine.

Audra couldn't imagine why anyone would be grateful about all of this, until Luanne continued.

"After we spoke at the gallery, I forced myself to go pull out that box. For the next several nights, I read the rest of the diaries. The last entry was dated about a year before they passed away. The busyness of life, I assume, hadn't left Viv with much time to write. But leading up to that, it was filled with how much she and Gene had truly fallen in love. I'd sensed it from being around them, of course, but reading it in her own personal words helped confirm what I'd always hoped inside."

Sean was leaning forward again, more relaxed now. By rebuilding another section of his history, maybe his nights would become restful sooner — much like Jack's could if only someone knew the answers.

At this stage, Audra figured, what could it hurt to ask?

"In Vivian's diaries, it didn't say anything about what really happened to Isaak, did it?"

Luanne replied solemnly, "It did, dear. She said he was executed."

Oh, boy. Audra would have to find a tactful way to provide the latest update.

"About that," she began, and Sean raised a brow. "There's a woman Sean put me in touch with to help do some research. She claims Isaak was only given prison time. And that years later, he was granted clemency for collaborating and was deported to Germany. But then he disappeared."

Luanne's eyes widened. "I never heard a thing about it."

Audra immediately saw there was no need to speculate over Isaak's true demise. If there was ever an airplane connection, it seemed they would never know.

"Whatever the case," Sean said to Luanne, "I'd say it's time for us to follow through and tell Mom together."

In a heavy manner, Luanne agreed. "I don't expect forgiveness — I've withheld too much

573

for too long. But she does deserve to know."

"I'm sure she'll understand," Audra assured her, "if you explain everything like you did just now."

Luanne extended a grateful look. Then she shook her head and let out a dry laugh. "I was a fool to think I could outrun the past. It has much quicker feet than I do anymore."

When Sean's lips spread into a smile, Audra's did the same.

It went without saying that the past kept a faster pace than them all.

64

Throughout supper, Vivian consciously focused on the present, not the future. Her discussion with Mrs. Langtree from earlier that day made this a difficult yet necessary task. The topic wasn't appropriate for company until Vivian could broach the matter with Gene, even if the guests were both family.

Luanne and Fred, married three months now, had come to celebrate Judith's birthday. The couple had first met at a diner just blocks from the law firm where Luanne worked as a secretary. When they announced their engagement four months later, ending Luanne's long run of passing courtships, Vivian's initial shock fast became delight. Gene was as cautious as any big brother ought to be, particularly one in Intelligence, but Fred gave no grounds for objection. He was a kind, average-looking fellow enrolled as a medical student at NYU. He had discovered his interest in the field while serving as an

Army medic primarily in Burma. Although he didn't say much about his tour — a commonality among combat vets — his political opinions tended to flow a bit more after a glass of wine.

"I know there's some folks out there who question it in hindsight," he said between bites of glazed ham, "but I, for one, am grateful we dropped those A-bombs."

Gene took another gulp of his milk, not one to indulge ever again in anything stronger.

"Those Japs never would've given up otherwise. I'm telling you, we'd be fighting Tojo to this day."

Gene continued to eat his scalloped corn, adding nothing.

His silence was not missed by Vivian.

"How bad is it?" she had recently asked, regarding his analysis reports from Japan.

He had answered with a shake of his head, his eyes moistening before he looked away. And Vivian knew he would never burden her with gruesome details of the explosion's aftermath. Nor would she press for more.

"Last I heard," Fred went on, "Truman's estimating up to a million of our soldiers were saved because of those drops. Is that about right, Gene?"

"So they say," he replied, and took a hefty bite of his roll.

The sacrifice of a few for the good of many was no doubt a noble stance, but not one as readily accepted when those few had a face. Vivian could relate to this much firsthand.

At the sudden lull, she swooped in with a smile. "Who's up for some lemon meringue?" From that point on, she aimed to keep the conversation as light as their dessert.

All the while Luanne stayed blissfully pre-occupied. Making the *vroom* sounds of a plane, she flew spoonfuls of peas into Judith's mouth. The youngster wriggled in her wooden high chair, giggling from giddiness, as she always did with her aunt. Luanne indeed was a natural-born mother.

It was for this reason that her lack of interest in Judith, back in her infant stage, had been an unsettling surprise. Despite Gene's vow of secrecy, Vivian had wondered how much his sister truly knew. But then one evening, during a visit with Luanne, Judith suffered a spike in fever that resulted in a seizure. The episode was short and ultimately harmless but terrified both women regardless.

Therein a fresh bond was born, and once more Vivian witnessed the seeping of light through a moment of darkness.

An hour later, with Luanne and Fred gone, the dishes washed, and Judith bathed, Vivian prepared for her approach.

From the door of Judith's room she watched Gene tuck their daughter into her crib. She looked so cozy in the new pajamas Luanne had made.

"Kiss 'Ippo." Judith held up the floppy giraffe he had given her to mark the special day.

"Good night, Hippo." Gene gave the animal a peck, snuggled it under the blanket, and said to Judith, "Sweet dreams, my little monkey."

"Ooh-ooh, ahh-ahh," she replied on cue. Gene had coined the nickname when, as a newborn, she would squirm, cling, and suck her thumb like a baby chimp.

Then he said, "I love you, Jujube. With all my heart."

"I wuv you too, Daddy."

He leaned over the rail and kissed Judith's forehead. When he stood up, rather than clicking off her lamp, he rubbed her face with his thumb. The soothing motion caused her eyelids to droop, her blinks to lengthen.

While there was beauty in the scene, Vivian also sensed a heaviness. It was the tone of Gene's voice, the intensity of his eyes. Over the past few weeks, she would frequently jar him from spells of thought. His work at the base appeared to be taking a greater toll than usual.

Perhaps he was picturing the images he had seen, the Japanese and European youth caught in the cross fire. Children who would never again hug their stuffed toys or sleep restfully in their beds.

Counting her blessings, Vivian left the sweet pair to their privacy. In the bathroom, then bedroom, she readied for sleep. As Gene did the same, she sat in bed, waiting. Propped against her pillow, she absently perused a magazine. At last, he settled beneath the covers in his boxers and undershirt.

"I saw Mrs. Langtree today," she said, faster than intended.

Gene mumbled his acknowledgment and set the alarm on his two-belled clock. Vivian slowed her pace.

"Her sister, the one who lives in Tampa, she's asked Mrs. Langtree to move in with her. Since Mrs. Langtree needs surgery on her knees, and with the start of her arthritis, she doesn't think it's wise to live alone much longer."

"Yeah?" he said, putting the clock down.

"She's considered listing her house on the market. With the flood of buyers these days, she could surely get a pretty penny. But, well, you see, she was hoping" — and here it went — "that maybe you and I would be interested."

Gene adjusted his head on his pillow.

"Honey? Did you hear me?"

"Sorry. How was that?"

She withheld a groan, knowing better than to take offense. He typically afforded her his full attention. She set the magazine on her night table and cut to the point. "Mrs. Langtree wants to sell her house to us. For a whole thousand dollars under market value."

Surprise shone in his eyes, though only a flicker.

"I know we were going to wait until next year to buy a place, but this is just too marvelous to pass up. Don't you think?"

"I don't know, Vivi. Maybe."

When it came to major decisions — marriage proposal excluded — he was not one to act on impulse. Yet in this case, the window of opportunity was narrow and closing.

"You've practically rebuilt half the place as it is. And Judith loves it there. Plus, it has all the things you and I have always talked about. A nice neighborhood, a large, airy kitchen, a wraparound porch. We could even hang a chair there to swing on."

He sighed, eyes toward the ceiling.

Though at risk of pressuring him, she would have to address a sensitive but vital factor. Without it, he would not agree.

"If it's a matter of the down payment," she added, "you know I can help with that."

"Vivian —"

"Please, just listen." He was looking at her now. "I've thought about it all day. The can of money I've put away since I was a little girl. This should be what we spend it on."

"Doll, that's not what you saved it for."

"No," she conceded, "it's not."

What he didn't know was that using the fund for something other than a cross-country family trip was not a new thought.

During the last year of the war, she had served as a volunteer for the USO. Most often, she would hand out coffee and donuts to soldiers at Grand Central. Occasionally, while Luanne babysat Judith, Vivian would find herself near the ticket booth, daydreaming of buying a pass, jetting off on a whim. But those moments were fleeting, and any notions of regret vanished at the sight of Judith's grin or the milky scent of her head. At night, Gene would wrap Vivian safely in his arms, even in his sleep, and a feeling would overcome her, that everything in her life had led to this place.

"Gene, someday I'd love for us to travel together. But all of that can wait. Besides, you know I want to work again when Judith gets older, so I could just save up again. Until then, the house would be so big, it would be like living on our own island." The thought of the home's spaciousness guided her to the last missing component.

She ran her hand over the fabric of his shirt, the slightly softened muscles. "I should tell you, though, there is one problem with the house." Arching a brow, she said, "We'd have an entire third bedroom to fill."

He didn't respond, even to her playful tack. Few decent men would accept a dime from others, including their wives. At least not without minimal protest. This she had anticipated. But his resistance seemed to stem from something else. Something he wasn't saying.

She flattened her palm over his heart, wishing she could read his pulse. "If there's another issue," she said, "you know you can tell me."

He layered his fingers over hers, snug to his chest, as if to prevent her from floating away.

"Gene?" she said, leaning closer.

For several seconds he gazed at their hands, then into her eyes. Softly he replied, "We'll buy it."

She stared at him, disbelieving. "We'll buy . . ."

"The house."

"But — I thought — you haven't —" She dropped her chin. "You're not teasing me, are you?"

His lips curved into a smile, and he shook his head.

Vivian covered her mouth to keep a squeal from waking Judith. Like their toddler at supper, giddiness poured through her. She planted kisses on Gene's cheeks, then lips, and it didn't take long for those kisses to intensify. When at last she drew her head back, their breaths were equally ragged.

"So, what's that you were saying?" he asked. "About a new bedroom to fill?"

She gave a shrug. "I thought a sewing room

might be nice."

"Sewing, huh?"

"Or a storage room. You know, for Judith's old clothes and toys." She worked to keep a straight face. "Unless you had another suggestion."

She had barely finished her sentence when he rolled her onto her back. Her giggle became a soft moan from the feel of his mouth — on her neck, her shoulder, her chest — and the pressure of his body covering hers. His kisses then slowed, so sensual they made each of her toes curl. "I've got a few ideas," he whispered, and he slid her nightgown upward.

In a daze from their night together, Vivian waded less than efficiently through the morning routine. She dribbled apple juice on Judith's dress, added cream to her own coffee — she always drank it black — and fried Gene's egg to a crisp. Not that he minded much. At the front door, his good-bye kiss made clear he had other things on his mind, like ways to demonstrate more of his ideas.

Returning from the entry, she asked Judith, "Are you ready for some toast, lovey bug?"

"Yep, yep, yep." In the high chair, the girl had covered her tray with applesauce designs.

Vivian knew she should reprimand her for playing with her food, but Judith's toothy grin won out. "Whatever am I going to do with you?" Vivian said with a smile. She grabbed a dishrag from the counter and discovered Gene had forgotten his lunch pail.

Apparently Vivian was not the only one distracted.

"I have to go catch Daddy," she said, snagging the container. "You stay here in your seat."

"I go too!" Judith stretched her arms and leaned over the chair, willing to dive headfirst. Tenacity was clearly a trait Vivian had handed down.

"Okay, okay. We need to hurry, though." No time to fetch a sweater. With Judith on her hip, she sped out the door, through the building, and into the sunlight. Gene was already two blocks down. "Gene, wait!" she yelled.

"Gene, wait!" Judith parroted, loud enough to turn him.

Vivian raised the black lunch pail, summoning him back. Against the morning chill she held Judith close as Gene returned. He bypassed the metal pail to tickle Judith's side. "Who you callin' Gene, missy?"

Judith gleefully wiggled, making Vivian laugh. "Go on, now, Captain. You don't want to be late."

He smiled and kissed them both but stopped short of leaving. "Say, Vivi, why don't we take a trip? Just the two of us. Get away for a while."

"Well, I'd love to . . . but Judith, she's so young."

"Oh, she'd be fine with my sister. They adore each other. Don't you, Jujube?"

Judith was too busy licking applesauce from her fingers to reply.

Suddenly Vivian recalled last night's discussion. "So, yesterday we were watching every dime, and now we're the Rockefellers?"

"I wasn't thinking of Paris, for Pete's sakes. Somewhere like . . . Manchester, or Cape Cod. A cozy inn with candlelit dinners, strolls on the beach."

"In the middle of March," she said. "A little cold, don't you think?"

"It'd be plenty warm in our room."

She pressed down a rising smile. "I'll think about it."

"Good. I'll help pack when I get home," he said, and with pail in hand he resumed his walk toward the streetcar.

"I didn't say —," she started, but finished with a groan. She looked at Judith and laughed to herself. "And here I was thinking you got your stubbornness from me. Good grief. Tell your incorrigible daddy good-bye."

"Bye-bye, Daddy!" Judith waved her sticky fingers.

He turned to wink and disappeared around the corner.

"All right," Vivian said, "let's go finish breakfast." She adjusted the girl's weight to prevent her from sliding down, and headed for the apartment. "How about we bake some muffins today? And we could write letters to Grandma and Grandpa. You remember they're coming to see you in a few weeks." It could have been Vivian's imagination, or just hopeful thinking, but the couple actually seemed more compatible than ever.

"I wanna chocolate!"

"Oh, you do, now? That sounded a lot like a royal order. How about we rephrase that into . . ."

A man at the end of the block stood beside a parked black Ford, staring in her direction. Something about him withered her words. She used her free hand to shade her eyes from the sun, and her heart stalled mid-beat. The embodiment of her past peered back from the eyes of a suited fellow with a head of blond curls. A face she had once known. Features stored deep in the well of her memory. It was a reflection of the impossible.

"Mommy?" Judith tugged the chest of her apron. But Vivian could not move. Her legs were ancient redwoods rooted to the earth.

A minute passed, maybe an hour, a century. There was no sound, no motion, until the driver stepped out of the car. He tapped a shoulder of the blond man and, after a pause, guided him into the backseat. The door closed and engine revved. And as the car started away, what appeared to be slate-gray eyes gazed out from the rear window.

65

Audra could still see the shocked expression in her mind. The way the girl's face had hardened when Audra, in a desperate free fall, had denied Isabella affirmation of heaven. More than a month had passed since then, yet the little girl's reaction neglected to fade from Audra's memory. In fact, it had gained clarity in the last two days, following Luanne's confession.

Maybe it was the woman's talk of "unfinished business" that revived thoughts of Isabella. Maybe the whispers from Audra's conscience were easier to hear, or harder to silence, when surrounded by the quiet of night.

Either way, she heard them now, sitting on the side of Jack's bed. Light from the hall slanted a soft beam into the room as she caressed her son's hair. The air contained a sleepy scent that Audra wished she could bottle.

Jack appeared so serene curled up with his pillow, calm after the fright of his nightmare. His stillness reminded her of a glassy lake at dawn. Its surface offered a different view for each person who stole a peek. She wasn't necessarily convinced about the link between Jack and Gene, but then, there was no reason she had to agree. As promised, regardless, she would bring her son to visit Luanne before the move to Boston.

Boxes around the bedroom, packed with half of Jack's belongings, reminded her how soon that would come. Of course they would be back, to visit friends and family. But in a matter of weeks they would call a new place home.

Tomorrow, then. Sunday was as good as any day to reach out to Isabella — if the family would allow it. Audra had no script planned aside from an apology. She imagined Luanne had approached Judith with similar preparation. There were aspects of life, no matter your efforts, that appeared set on a particular course.

That wasn't to say Audra saw everything as predestined or orchestrated in detail by an almighty power. Upon review of her life, however, neither could she claim that everything happened by chance. That much she knew merely by the sight before her. For as she gazed at Jack's face while listening to the gentle rhythm of his breaths, her love for him went far beyond science. Or logic. Or provable theories in any book.

Overflowing. That's what Devon had called the type of love he felt the minute Jack was born. It was the feeling of your heart expanding, brimming to such fullness that the seams could split in your chest.

"You were right," she whispered, savoring the stretch of that emotion now. "*Overflowing* is exactly the word." She spoke this into the darkness, and though she might never know for sure, she sensed that somewhere, somehow, Devon heard her and smiled.

A sprinkling fell through the morning, but by noon more than half the sky shone blue. It seemed to be a good omen, as Isabella's mother had been warm and forgiving on the phone and agreed to let Audra stop by. Such welcoming acceptance made more sense toward the end of the conversation, when the woman mentioned that Tess had long ago explained the gist of Audra's loss.

At the family's house, the mother ushered Audra and Jack inside. "Come in, come in," she said with the gentle lilt of her accent. She wiped her hands on her apron and yelled up the stairs, "*Mija,* the doctor is here now!"

The pair of matching Shih Tzus pounced around Jack's feet, little pink tongues hanging out. In the living room, Isabella's two younger brothers, maybe six and eight years old, were playing a race-car game on the TV. A waft of hot spices traveled from the kitchen.

When Isabella didn't appear, the mother shook her head. "I'm sorry. She knows you are coming. I will bring her down."

Under the circumstances, Audra hated the

idea of ejecting the girl from her comfort zone. "Would it be better if I went up to see her?"

The woman considered this and smiled. "*Jes.* I think so. It is the room on the left." She turned to Jack. "Would you like to play with the boys?"

Jack's gaze was already locked on the game, which made the activity an easy sell.

"I'll just be a few minutes, buddy," Audra said. "Then we'll grab some lunch."

"Can we get a treat?" he asked her.

"We'll see."

He nodded and followed the mother toward her sons, who were giggling over deliberately crashing their vehicles.

Audra ventured up the carpeted stairs. She stopped at the partially open door, where a handmade poster spelled out *Isabella* in glitter glue.

"Isabella?" She gave a knock before poking her head inside. "May I come in?"

Propped against her ruffled pillows, the girl sat on her bed with a sketch pad. She shrugged her indifference without looking up from the picture she was drawing.

Audra perched on the side of the mattress and glimpsed the artwork. It featured a young girl, with a black bob like Isabella's, on the back of a stallion in a green pasture. "Wow, that's really pretty."

Isabella didn't reply, her eyes on the paper.

"Do you like to ride horses?"

The girl shrugged again, pressing harder with

her brown colored pencil. "I can't till I'm twelve. My mom thinks they're too big."

"Yeah, I can understand that." The same thing had concerned Audra when Tess invited Jack to ride her sister-in-law's thoroughbred.

Audra considered mentioning the animal now, as a means of conversation, but foresaw a dead end. She would get to the point.

"Isabella, I came here today to tell you that, well . . . what I said to you about heaven . . ."

Annoyance rolled over Isabella's face. She had no interest in the stock apology that was surely forthcoming, or a feigned reversal in religious stance.

Audra couldn't blame her.

"The fact is," Audra finished, "I meant it."

Isabella snapped her head up, her attention undivided.

"At least, I did at the time. You see, a few years ago, someone I loved very much died, and it made me doubt a lot of things I used to believe in. I was angry and sad that it happened because it didn't seem fair. But, after a while, I had to look closely at those beliefs again and decide, for me, what had been true all along."

Isabella lowered her sketch pad while gnawing on her lip. "So . . . you really do think there's a heaven?"

Audra debated on how to respond. If referring to a holy place in the sky with pearly gates and cherubs and angels soaring on feathery wings, she couldn't in all honesty say yes. On the other hand, she had learned there was more to our world than what any of us could see or fully comprehend.

That's when it hit her: Maybe heaven was much like a lake at dawn, offering a different view depending on the person. Maybe heaven entailed more than a soul residing in a single place but instead having pieces of yourself spread among the hearts and memories of people you've touched.

With this in mind, Audra reexamined her personal beliefs, and indeed she found her answer.

"To be perfectly honest," she said, looking Isabella in the eye, "I really do."

A slow smile spread across the girl's lips. "Yeah," she said softly. "Me too."

As Audra drove away, an internal radiance filled her from recapturing a sense of certainty. This in itself seemed cause for celebration.

On a whim, skipping a sensible lunch, she steered the car into a parking lot and pulled into an empty spot. The neon sign of the donut shop glowed vibrant red in the window.

"Mom?" Jack said from the backseat. "Are we going here?" The suppression of hope rang clear in his voice. She twisted around to face him.

"You and I," she declared, "are having dessert first."

"Really?"

"Really."

Jack's face beamed, though with a touch of disbelief that kept him in his seat.

"The donuts here don't come to the car, buddy. Better get in there before they run out."

That was all it took to send Jack clambering out of the vehicle.

At the counter inside, they ordered an apple fritter for her, a sprinkled donut for him, and a maple bar to share. To wash it down, they drank from squatty milk bottles, but not before Audra challenged him to a bubble-blowing contest with their straws. When he giggled over his win, Audra could swear she heard an echo of Devon's laugh, and it only broadened her smile.

Once they finished and were wiping their hands with napkins, Audra thought of Judith and how much, as a young girl, she must have craved knowledge about her parents. Audra decided right then; she would never again rob Jack of that gift.

"Baby, I want you to know," she said, "if you ever want to ask about your dad, or hear stories about him, or anything like that . . . I want you to say so. Okay?"

After a pause, he nodded and his eyes regained the faintest trace of an old, sweet glimmer.

Together they disposed of their garbage and exited through the glass doors. Outside, a couple of kids were fawning over a woman's Maltese, its hair trimmed in a puppy cut. Audra caught Jack watching with a smile — though how could he not, with a dog so cute it appeared to require batteries?

A canine companion might be good for Jack one day. Not a rush. Just something to consider.

They had just reached the car when Audra heard a buzzing in her purse. She retrieved her phone and recognized the number.

It belonged to Taylor Shuman.

Though with reservations, Audra answered the call.

"Audra, I'm so glad I reached you," Taylor replied. "I have some news about Jakob Hemel."

"Actually, Taylor, I'm not sure we need any more information."

Due to either the cell connection or the woman's enthusiasm, Taylor continued as if she hadn't heard. "We did some more searching, me and my friend at the museum. We were trying to figure out why Jakob disappeared. Audra," she said, "I know what happened to him."

66

This time around, Vivian didn't bother with trying to reach Agent Gerard on the telephone. She went straight to Foley Square to confront him face-to-face.

"Ah, this must be your little one," he said in greeting after opening his office door. He wore suspenders over his white shirt, his tie loosened and sleeves rolled up. His hair had receded a tad more over the past three years.

This was the first that Vivian had seen him since their meeting on Binnen Bridge, but just like then, she had no interest in pleasantries.

"Judith, honey, go over and sit down for Mommy."

As Agent Gerard closed the door, the girl bypassed the chair to investigate items on the desk. She knocked a cup of paper clips onto the floor, turning him around.

"Was it him?" Vivian asked.

The agent shifted his attention, perplexed.

"I saw a man this morning. A man who

looked like Isaak was outside our apartment." She clenched her purse handle. "I need you to tell me I'm wrong. That he hasn't been alive all this time."

Agent Gerard dropped his shoulders. His skin paled, though surely not to the degree Vivian's had that morning. He muttered to himself, "Those bastards had no business . . ." He shot a glare toward his door, as if meant to reach agents in another office.

The confirmation weakened Vivian's knees, but only slightly. She already knew what she had seen. What she did not know was the reason for the lies. "For heaven's sakes, just tell me the truth."

He hitched his hands on the hips of his pinstriped trousers and glanced at Judith, who was now on her knees, playing with the shiny mound of paper clips. Finally he answered in the begrudging tone of having hoped to never have this conversation.

"When we brought Isaak in, he spilled it all. The details of their plans, the agents' locations, their training and strategies. Everything we needed to shut down the ring."

Vivian narrowed her eyes. "You told me he changed his mind. You said George Dasch was the one —"

"Dasch collaborated too. That's the God's honest truth. And Isaak *was* found guilty by a tribunal, in spite of me doing everything I could to help. His family was taken care of, like I promised. But in the end, they still slapped him with fifteen years in the pen."

Prison time. That's what they had given him, not a death sentence.

Vivian strained to keep listening through her jumbled thoughts.

"Nobody was willing to risk letting Hitler find out that the reason we caught the spies was because they surrendered. And Hoover was more than happy to let the Bureau look top-notch. Not to mention himself. Now that the war's over, though, Isaak is no longer considered a threat. So I helped push for an appeal and finally Truman granted him a pardon. I suspect Dasch and Burger will get the same before long."

The details burned through Vivian like a flame on a wick, quickened by the potential ramifications. In front of Judith, she fought to keep from exploding. "Does Isaak know what you told me? All this time, did he think I just cast him off? Left him alone in a cell to rot? How dare you —"

"The idea," he cut in, "was Isaak's."

With that, the flame was snuffed out.

"He didn't want you waiting around for him, wasting more than a decade of your life. He pleaded for the favor. He was so desperate when he asked me . . ." Agent Gerard broke from her gaze. He paused before continuing in a near murmur. "Doesn't mean I haven't wondered if it was a mistake. I came close to telling you months afterward, but I gave the guy my word."

The motive behind Agent Gerard's last invitation to meet, that day at Prospect Park, suddenly gained clarity. As did his inability to look her in the eye when he'd delivered news of Isaak's death.

"Normally I wouldn't have gotten so involved," he went on. "But I figured it was the decent thing to do."

Decent? Allowing her to believe the father of her child had been sent to the electric chair, that he had been a traitor rather than an unrecognized hero, conjured many a word, none of which included *decent.*

She wanted to lash back, to seek vengeance for the tears and sorrow based on falsehoods. She wanted Agent Gerard — and Isaak even more — to feel the impact of the injustice they had inflicted. But before she could utter a word, metallic rustlings and a sharp giggle diverted her attention.

On the floor Judith was sprinkling paper clips like drops of rain. Her round cheeks glowed with purity and joy. In a flash, like a story told on the silver screen, Vivian saw an averted path — of prison visits with she and Judith in their Sunday best, of reproachful glares at a convict's child, of a life without Gene Sullivan. And through the thicket of this vision, a burst of gratitude filled her chest.

599

"Where is he now?" she asked, still focusing on her daughter.

"Headed back to Germany. To an American-occupied zone. All three of them will be watched there. But kept safe."

Judith, deep in concentration, crumpled her chin. The echo of a dimple, in its timing, shouted a message of a mother's duty.

"In that case," Vivian said, "I need the address."

There was no sense to be made of the discovery. Then again, perhaps it all made perfect sense. Whatever the case, Vivian spent the day vacillating between two types of betrayal, one the product of speaking up, the other of staying silent.

Dear Isaak,

I have not the faintest notion how to properly compose this letter. Nothing about the past we have shared has been simple or clear. The present moment is no different, as I learned only this morning that your life was spared. I assume you must be questioning, from your view today at a distance, whether the child I was carrying in my arms is

Vivian raised her pen from the page. Seated at her vanity, she scoured her brain for an end to the sentence: *the child I was carrying in my arms is* . . .

What, in fact, was Judith's relation to him? A daughter. A blessing. An accident. A mistake?

Once more, Vivian wadded the stationery and flung it toward a scattering of other failed attempts. Every letter bore a variation of the same inept opening, each one blocked by a wall of consequence.

She yearned to purge her bottled screams but managed to refrain, unwilling to disturb Judith's afternoon nap. Security and peace would fade from the child's world soon enough.

Vivian placed the tip of her pen on the next blank sheet and forced herself to start again. What outcome was she hoping for with Isaak an ocean away? Whether she would ever mail the letter she couldn't say. Certainly not without Gene's blessing. Until then, she would set the words to paper, if solely to discern her thoughts.

From behind came the soft crackling of paper.

She glanced in the mirror, expecting to see Judith stepping on a discarded page; the girl had conquered the skill of climbing out of her crib. Instead, it was Gene, home from work early. He stood near the dresser, reading a wrinkled letter.

Vivian shot to her feet, dropping her pen. She pushed down a swallow. "Before you

601

jump to a conclusion," she began, but a look in his eyes eliminated the rest.

More aptly, the absence of a look. There was no anger or accusation. No bewilderment or betrayal. Strikingly, not even mild surprise.

In that instant she realized: "You already knew."

He voiced no reply. But seconds later, he edged out a nod.

The shock of this caused her an intake of breath. She folded her arms over her middle.

Had every man in her life conspired to deceive her? If Gene had kept a secret of this magnitude, what else was he withholding?

Not to say she herself had always been a model of honesty.

"How long?" she asked, a near whisper.

"Just a few weeks," he contended. "All these years I made a point of not seeking out information. I wanted to put it fully behind us."

Her throat loosened a fraction, though not her arms, still snugly wrapped. "How did you hear?"

He sat on the foot of the bed, facing her. "When I was in DC, I was sifting through some documents for the Nuremberg Trials. I came across a file about the case. Did some digging around. That's how I found out he'd been imprisoned all this time. That what you'd told me about him, about giving up the other saboteurs, it was all true."

Now she understood Gene's recent behavior. As she had guessed, the burden he'd been carrying did involve children of the war, but in a more personal way than she had imagined. She thought back to their discussion the night before, about his reluctance regarding the house, an investment in the permanence of their future together.

"So you also know Isaak was released," she ventured.

He nodded. "Yeah."

In the quiet stretch that followed, she imagined how she would feel if the roles were reversed. She could scarcely blame him for being cautious.

"I'm sure it would've been better," he said, "if you'd heard it from me first. But I just . . ." He looked down at the letter in his hand, then to the floor, at the other strewn pages. "I was afraid of losing you. And Judith. She's always thought of me like a father."

"No," Vivian interjected, causing him to look up. "Not like a father. You are her father."

This wasn't a generous placation but an irrefutable truth. Given his care for Judith since the day of her birth — taking shifts on long colicky nights, his solid discipline formed of compassion, his prideful praise for every significant milestone — no child, nor mother, could want for more.

Vivian walked toward him, longing to

reinforce her assertion with physical contact. But just as she reached for his shoulder, he said, "Vivian, I have to ask you something, and I need you to be honest."

She drew back, unclear where this was headed. "All right."

Gene hesitated, as if needing to gear up for the question. "Look, it's clear how much Isaak loved you —"

She shook her head. "Gene, he lied about everything, even his death."

"— and I know this," he finished, "because if I'd been in his shoes, I would've done the exact same thing."

The sincerity and resolve of his words resonated inside her.

Though she had moved on with her life years ago, it would be false to say she didn't wonder at times if Isaak's feelings for her were real, or if the risks she had taken had been for a virtual stranger.

"What I don't know," Gene continued, "is if deep down you still love *him.* And I've got to know that, Vivi. Because I'd rather hear the answer is *yes* than carry around doubt for the rest of my life."

She considered the issue carefully. He deserved a genuine response, no matter how difficult to craft. Consequences aside, she owed it to him, and herself, to examine what lay in her heart.

What she immediately discovered, however,

was it required no more effort than determining if ice was cold or fire was hot. Some things in life bore such certainty, love being among them, they rendered opinions inconsequential.

Vivian took the crumpled paper from Gene. Letting it fall, she knelt before him and looked up into his eyes. "It's true that on some level I'll always care for Isaak. And in a way, he'll always be connected to Judith. But that doesn't mean what I feel for him is love. Love," she said, "is what you and I have built together."

She grasped both of his hands, the very hands that had held her and protected her and supported her in every way possible. "Gene, on the day we exchanged our vows, goodness knows the circumstances weren't ideal. But I can tell you this. I would relive that day a hundred times over to become your wife."

His eyes gained a sheen matching hers, and the relief in his face was unmistakable. He kissed her hand before leaning in to do the same to her lips. The gesture was as tender and warm as their very first kiss, from the night they stood on those brownstone stairs, but now with a fulfillment only history could bring.

When their mouths parted, his gaze slid back to their hands. There was something more he needed to say.

"Gene, what is it?"

After a moment thick with thoughts, he raised his eyes. "Isaak should know about Judith." He said this as though accepting his own conclusion. Not the type to rejoice over, but a statement of fact.

Vivian tilted her head at him. "Honey . . . are you sure?"

"If I were him, I'd want to know. More than that, I don't ever want secrets to hurt our family again."

Isaak's ban from the States, very likely, played a factor in Gene's decision — to feel more threatened by proximity would only be human. Yet his courage and principles were no less worthy.

She just wished she could borrow his bravery. The papers on the floor still loomed from the practicality of the task.

As if reading her mind, he said, "It's not really fit for a letter, is it?"

She shook her head, aware she would have to compose the missive regardless. Beyond that, already she could sense the excruciating weeks of waiting for a reply, imagining Isaak's reaction, wondering if the message was ever received.

"What if we went to Germany?" Gene said, the suggestion startling her.

"Germany?"

"The three of us together."

"But — how?"

"I'll work something out."

The vision of meeting in person was even more daunting. How would that make delivering the announcement any easier?

"I don't know. It's such a long trip. Judith, at her age . . ."

"Yeah. You're probably right."

Vivian nodded. She had just begun to relax when he added, "You and me then. We can start there. Figure out the rest as we go."

She scrounged for reasons to object. But he laid his hand on her cheek, and from the comfort of his touch the jittering of her uncertainties settled. Yet again, he was the solid rock that steadied her, the balm to her worries.

Vivian released a breath, and nodded.

At their trade of gentle smiles, she folded into his embrace. They would do this together, the way it would always be for the two of them. How foolish of her to believe she couldn't possibly love her husband more.

67

So finally she can be with him.

As much as Audra wanted to erase the phrase from her mind, she was overcome by the feeling that at last it completely fit. Her first inclination after hanging up with Taylor had been to call Sean and Luanne. She was about to dial them up when she realized who, more than anyone, deserved to hear the discovery first.

"Excuse me," Audra said to the gallery manager upon entering with Jack. "I'm Audra Hughes. I'm the one who called earlier."

"Oh, yes," said the woman in cat's-eye glasses. "Judith told me to send you on back to the studio."

On the phone, Audra had asked Judith if they could meet in person right away, by now the topic evident. According to Sean, his mother had taken Luanne's admission considerably well but needed time to process it. Audra just hoped the information she was bringing would be helpful, not a hindrance.

"If you'd like," the manager added, "while you

and Judith talk, I'd be happy to show your son the new artwork we just hung." Clearly, she was aware the discussion called for privacy.

"It wouldn't be too much trouble for you?"

"Not at all. So far, it's been a pretty slow day."

Audra turned to Jack. "Are you okay with that?"

"Sure," he said lightly, already scanning the room.

"Thanks," she said to the woman, who nodded and swept Jack off for a grand tour.

Audra treaded toward the back corner and into the studio.

At the worktable, Judith sat on a cushioned stool, lost in thought. Her hands rested on a nest of iridescent gauze. Beside the material were several items identifiable at a glance: a stack of books resembling diaries, letters and notes aged from time, and contents of the manila envelope Audra had returned to Luanne.

"Hi, Judith."

The woman greeted her with a half smile.

"I appreciate you seeing me," Audra said. "I know you've had a lot to think about the last few days."

"It certainly hasn't been dull."

On this point, they were in total agreement.

Audra stepped closer. "I really don't want to make things worse for you or your family. But there's something I just learned. Something I think you should know."

With an audible sigh, Judith said, "I'm not sure

my heart can take many more surprises."

Audra hoped this was said in jest, because she was delivering a rather large one. Regretfully, she could think of no skillful way to ease it in.

"Judith, the man you've heard about, Jakob Hemel . . ."

"Isaak," Judith said, as if trying to reconcile the names.

Audra nodded before finishing: "He's still alive."

Judith sucked in a breath. Clenching her hands, she turned her face to the shelves above her table. "How do you know?" she said.

"The person who helped me with research called today. Taylor — that's her name — she said she tried to locate Daniel Gerard, the FBI agent involved with the trial. She found out he died several years ago. But when he first learned he had Alzheimer's, he'd asked his daughter to transcribe stories from his life. That's how Taylor knew about Jakob's help with the case, and even about his transfer to Europe."

"Back to Germany," Judith said, "wasn't it?" She continued to stare straight ahead.

"Yes," Audra said. "Before he landed, he was given a new identity for his protection. And later he moved to Switzerland to be with his relatives. That's why it was harder to trace him."

After a moment, Judith asked, "How old is he now?" Her guarded tone was understandable.

A man of his generation could very well be incapacitated, or at minimum incoherent.

"He's ninety-four — but from what Taylor gathered, he's one of those George Burns types. Still youthful and lively, like your aunt, Luanne. Apparently he takes walks through town in the evenings, knows just about everyone in Lucerne." When Judith didn't respond, Audra added, "And he loves to paint."

Judith suddenly angled back to her. "He's an artist?"

Audra nodded, watching the woman recognize the potential source of her own traits.

"Does he . . . have a family?"

"His wife passed away some years ago, but he has two daughters and a son."

"You're telling me I have siblings," Judith said, voice tightening.

"Nephews and nieces too." Audra smiled to emphasize the positive nature of the news. "Taylor had sent out some e-mails to track down information, and his oldest daughter, Ursula, is the one who responded."

Judith covered her mouth with her slender fingers, her eyes moistening.

Perhaps this would only magnify her resentment from not knowing all of these years. Audra hoped that wasn't so, but still she felt confident in having come here. It wouldn't have been right to withhold any more secrets.

"I'm sorry to upset you. I just thought you should know."

barn, replied, "I think I'll see how the setup's going."

It had been Sean's suggestion to expand an hour of donkey rides into a holiday barbecue, complete with a private fireworks display — which, in Oregon, meant little more than knee-high sprays of colorful sparks, but fun all the same. Then come nightfall, she and Jack would meet her in-laws to watch a big show at a park.

"In that case," Tess said, "take your time." A smile curled her lips before she headed for the house.

Audra hadn't decided how to deliver her message to Sean, as she'd barely had a chance to digest the idea herself. She made her way over, contemplating her words.

"Do you need any help?" she asked.

He turned to her. On one knee, he was arranging the minipyrotechnics on a large slat of plywood. "I think we're just about set."

Here, away from others' ears and eyes, she sat down on one of the lawn chairs Sean had arranged for the audience. As he finished his task facing away from her, Audra's gaze was drawn to the back of his T-shirt, his neck, the strong lines of his arms.

"So, you're going on a trip this summer," she said.

Twisting around, he smiled. "You heard already?"

"Luanne told me in the kitchen."

He came to his feet, brushing dust from his

When tears slid down Judith's face, meeting the shield of her hand, Audra decided it was best to leave; the woman needed time alone with so much to absorb. Yet before Audra could excuse herself, Judith lowered her fingers to reveal a wisp of a smile.

Audra exhaled in relief.

"For so long," Judith said, "I've been searching for who I am. It seemed like part of me was missing . . ." Her sentence faded away, but Audra didn't need the rest.

"I know the feeling," she replied, and Judith nodded.

Just then, a knock turned them toward the partially open door.

"Pardon me for the intrusion," the manager said meekly, "but a customer needs my help. I wasn't expecting him until later. Would it be all right if I sent Jack in here?"

Audra went to answer, but Judith responded first. "Of course. Bring him in." She brushed away her tears as Jack entered the studio. "Jack," she said with growing brightness. "What a treat to see you again."

"Thanks," he said.

"You know what?" Judith said. "I have an idea. How would you like to help me with a new art piece?"

The offer seemed either an excuse to more closely study Jack, in light of Luanne's theories, or a form of payment for the ways he'd inadvertently changed Judith's life. No matter the case,

Audra wasn't about to intervene. Not after his eyes lit up at the shelves of shiny, colorful supplies.

"Guess you'd better pull up a seat," Audra said to him.

He hopped onto a stool. As he picked out a paintbrush from a jar full of choices, Judith grabbed the paints. She squirted a rainbow of colors on a wooden palette and set up an easel with a small blank canvas. "Why don't you start with painting anything you'd like? Then we can add on other materials from there."

It occurred to Audra right then that Judith could be seeking further insight from Jack's pictures. The boy had already endured so much testing and observing, Audra was tempted to end the activity.

But the truth was she, too, longed to see the images now in his head. And so she watched.

He painted the stick figure of a boy. He painted a girl in the same fashion. Once again, the two were holding hands.

Audra braced herself as Jack rinsed his brush in a cup. He dabbed at the palette to obtain another color. With a smooth stroke of green, he placed the couple on the grass.

No flames. No planes. No darkness or death.

He even put smiles on their faces. Adding to the scenery, he hung a yellow sun in the sky, launched a pair of birds upward, and planted trees on the ground. All symbols of the brightness and beauty of life.

Although relieved at first, Audra worried he was simply following orders, depicting "happier things" to appease those around him.

Then he paused, drawing back to study his progress. That's when his mouth curved up in a look of genuine delight — and Audra's mouth did the same.

She did wonder, though, about the identity of the couple; a lot of options had crossed her mind.

"Hey, Jack," she ventured to ask, "who are those people supposed to be?"

He shrugged a shoulder. "Just two people."

She thought about asking him in another way but then realized there was no need. When it came to viewing art, all that mattered was interpretation.

Later that night, Audra lay down in bed and closed her eyes with a feeling of satisfaction. It seemed only a moment had passed when she opened them again, yet sunlight was streaming through her window. Squinting against the rays, she languidly stretched her arms. She reveled in her restfulness until startled by a sense.

Something was wrong.

Jack.

Panic shot through her, the kind from early motherhood, when crib death was only a breath away.

She tore from her bed, heart in her throat, and in the next room discovered his bed empty.

A thousand horrific scenarios sped through her thoughts, interrupted by the melody of a cheery tune. She hurried out to the living room and found Jack on the couch, the computer open on his lap, a bowl of Froot Loops at his side.

"Hi, buddy," she said, recovering.

"Hi, Mom."

"What are you doing?"

"Just playing a game. I'm trying to find Grace's penguin at the pizza parlor. We're supposed to meet at nine."

Nine o'clock. She glanced toward the kitchen to verify the time on the microwave. When the realization struck, she nearly wept from joy.

Jack had slept through the night.

68

"Should we wake her?" Vivian whispered.

In his brimmed hat and coat, Gene stood beside Vivian in the doorway of Judith's room. "Let's let her sleep," he answered, his reasoning obvious. Their little girl looked too peaceful to disturb at this hour. Outside her window, dusk had barely begun to lift.

"I'll just kiss her good-bye," Vivian said, unable to leave without this small token. They had spent not a single night apart since Judith was born.

Silently Vivian padded over to the crib, where the toddler lay on her back, arms spread wide. Her stuffed giraffe was tucked at her side. Its flimsy, spotted body was half covered by the very blanket that had swathed Judith when she had first come home from the hospital. The beginning of their lives together as a family.

Vivian leaned over the rail, hands covering the large buttons of her overcoat to prevent them from knocking against the crib. She touched her lips to the crown of Judith's head, light as an angel's kiss. "Sleep well, lovey bug," she said in a hush, and had to resist the impulse to scoop her up and take her along.

This trip was not appropriate for Judith yet. But if all went well, someday she, too, would make the trek and meet the man who had gifted Vivian with the greatest treasure in the world: the life of her beautiful daughter.

"Vivi," Gene whispered.

It was time to leave.

She exited the room in the same fashion she had entered, continuing into the hallway. Gene paused to send Judith a final loving look before closing the door without noise.

"I'll get our suitcases," he said, and headed to their bedroom.

In the kitchen, Luanne was brewing a pot of coffee, filling the air with its rich aroma. She had arrived already dressed, but a scarf still covered her curlers.

"Sorry to make you come over so early," Vivian said to her. "I would have preferred a later train, but you know your brother. He insisted we take the first one out."

"It's no trouble. Fred was up most of the night studying for his exams. I couldn't sleep well anyway."

In this moment, face-to-face with Luanne, an urge to tell the truth scaled the walls of Vivian's conscience. Gene had insisted the arrangements he made were on the stipulation of keeping them confidential. He had assured his contact that even their families believed they were escaping to Cape Cod, to a secluded inn on the coast with no phones, no radio.

But what if Judith were to have an emergency?

Gene reappeared with two suitcases. "I'll go flag us a cab."

Vivian nodded.

"Thanks again for watching her, Lu," he said.

"The pleasure's all mine."

He smiled at his sister before turning away and maneuvering the luggage out the door.

As Vivian snapped her handbag shut, she imagined her confession stored inside between her handkerchief and powder compact. The trip was too important to risk a cancellation of plans by saying too much. What's more, to name the destination would require an explanation about Isaak. This would come in time, but not yet.

She pulled on her gloves and travel hat, and Luanne trailed her to the door. The departure now imminent, Vivian's thoughts sprinted with any instructions she might have forgotten. "Now, did I tell you where to find the extra crib sheets?"

"You did. In the top of Judith's closet."

"Precisely. Oh, and for bath time, be sure

to pull her out when the water's cool. She'd let herself freeze to the bone if you let her."

"I promise not to let her freeze to the bone."

Vivian caught the teasing but was too focused to be playful. "Also, if she happens to run a temperature, you can use the thermometer in my bathroom drawer. But if the number doesn't seem right, you can usually tell by putting your lips on her forehead. Either that, or —"

"My dearest sister, you will never make it to the shore at this rate."

Vivian scrunched her nose. "Good grief, I'm being dreadful, aren't I?"

"No. You're being a mother. But don't worry, I've read all eight pages of the notes you wrote down for me. And I promise you, for the next week Fred and I will take care of Judith as if she were our own."

Vivian smiled and grasped Luanne's arm. "I know you will."

"Now, then. With that settled, you'd better get out there. My brother must be chomping at the bit. You two enjoy your belated honeymoon."

"Thank you," Vivian said, and embraced Luanne tightly. "Thank you for everything."

On the tarmac, the propellers whirred into a thunderous spin. The Air Corps captain greeted Vivian and Gene at the door of the transport aircraft. Nervousness belied his firm tone. "We're square after this, Sully," he said to Gene, to which Gene agreed.

Vivian was curious about the favor being repaid, but those details were currently unimportant.

The airman relieved them of their suitcases. After storing the luggage for transit, he went up to the cockpit. Vivian followed Gene in taking a seat on the canvas bench that ran along the wall.

"Put this on," Gene told her over the engines. "It'll get cold."

She wrapped herself with the Army blanket he provided. He helped her cover the gap between her shoes and the hem of her trousers before donning his own blanket.

Behind them a row of oval windows were dotted by Thursday-morning rain.

The captain reappeared after presumably speaking to the small crew, perhaps delivering an enticement for their discreet cooperation. His rank was not high enough for him to have finagled the situation without being resourceful.

"Anybody asks," he said loudly, "you two were never on this plane."

Gene gave a thumbs-up that all was understood.

When the officer shot a glance at Vivian, she made a show of nodding in concurrence. A so-called pleasure trip to Frankfurt would never be permitted by usual Army protocol.

Although it was a harmless cargo transfer, the only civilians likely allowed on such a flight were USO performers and members of the Red Cross. Her status as neither would incur even heftier consequences if anyone was caught.

The airman gave a final reminder. "My buddy, Wes, will meet you on the other side. He'll get you back as scheduled. You miss that flight, you're outta luck."

"We'll be there," Gene told him.

The man shook his head, as though questioning his own sanity, and disembarked without another word.

Minutes later, with all the doors clamped shut, the plane started to move. Vivian shuddered and her body stiffened. Having never flown before, she hadn't expected so much rumbling and creaking as their speed increased.

Gene slipped his hand around hers. "Don't worry," he said close to her ear. "I've got you."

The assertion brought back a memory: It was their first official date. He had spoken those exact words as they hung on the Parachute Jump, side by side on a canvas seat like now, dangling over Steeplechase Park.

The revelation of just how far they had come made her smile despite her fears. "I love you," she said, too quiet for him to hear, but clearly he read her lips, and he reciprocated with a kiss. Her heart brimmed with indescribable adoration for him, for their daughter, and for the blessing of every second they had been given together.

This was the feeling Vivian took with her, long after the plane soared for hours over the Atlantic, long after the burst from engine fires had woken them both from sleep, a malfunction that sent the transport sharply down, into the waves, deep into the ocean, too far for recovery.

In that slice of an instant, before panic faded to calm and resistance gave way to surrender, she gave no thought to how their disappearance would be explained; she had no knowledge that a storm off Cape Cod would help fabricate a tragedy, a convenient covering of military tracks. Her sole concern lay with Judith. The girl would grow up without parents, and yet she would still be nurtured and cared for by family, genuine people with good hearts. Yes, she would be fine, Vivian realized — just as she herself would be, so long as Gene was there.

I've got you, she heard in her mind, her hand still in his, and felt sheer peace from the love that would bind them till the end of time.

69

The once serene atmosphere was now a cauldron of vivacity.

Over the farm, afternoon sunlight poured through a fine dusting of clouds. Sounds of happy children drifted on the summer air. The voices of animals periodically interjected.

It was the perfect setting for the Fourth of July.

Arms resting on the fence, Audra stood beside Tess, enjoying the commotion. Sean had saddled the donkeys, one for Jack, the other for Isabella. When the idea first came to Audra — a mild alternative to riding a standard horse — she had called Sean right away. It had taken a little persuading for the girl's mother to agree, but now the pure smiles on the riders' faces clearly trumped all worries.

"*Mija,* look over here!" the mother hollered. Isabella's father pointed a camera toward the fenced-in area, where Carl was leading the donkeys by ropes attached to halters.

Carl was a kind man with snow-white hair and a short beard to match. Audra had barely spared him a glance during her last visit here, while she madly dashed from the hayloft to the car. A widower from down the road, he had evidently made a habit of lending a hand on the farm when needed.

"I think a certain gentleman might be looking for a date," Audra had teased Luanne earlier, after he shot the elderly woman a wink. Cheeks awash in pink, Luanne tsked at the possibility of being courted by an eighty-two-year-old "youngster."

"Gracie," Tess called out, "don't give him the whole bag!"

Kneeling in the field, Grace was feeding carrots to the goat. Orange bits flew from its voracious chomping. "But Aunt Lu told me I could!"

Tess groaned and turned to Audra. "I'm warning you now. When her teen years roll in, don't be surprised if UPS suddenly delivers her to your house in Boston."

"What, are you afraid she'll grow up to be like her mother?"

"Are you kidding? That's exactly what I'm terrified of."

Just then, Isabella's two brothers and Tess's son, Cooper, broke into fits of laughter. Off by the barn, the boys were chasing the chickens in circles. The squawking birds flapped their wings, sending feathers airborne.

"Should we make them stop?" Tess asked.

Audra shrugged. "I don't think Luanne would mind. Not for a few minutes anyway. It'll wear the kids out."

"Spoken like a true mother."

Smiling, Audra returned her focus to Jack. It had been a week since he'd first slept through the night. In between, he'd suffered two separate nightmares, but they were brief and with only a fraction of his prior intensity.

"I still can't believe you're really leaving," Tess said, her tone more serious now.

"I know," Audra said. "But like I promised, I'll send you lots and lots of beans."

"Yeah, because that's what our house needs." Tess puffed a breath. "Speaking of food, I'm starving. Honey!" she yelled toward the deck, where Russ was cooking on the barbecue. "Are we getting close?"

"Ten more minutes," he said, raising a grill spatula.

Luanne stepped through the sliding glass door and used her hands to create a megaphone. "Who out here wants some fresh-squeezed lemonade?"

The kids erupted with squeals and yells. Carl helped Jack and Isabella off their saddles, so they could join the others in a dash to the house. The group had just reached the deck when Judith appeared, wine bottle in hand. "We have chardonnay for the grown-ups," she added.

"Now we're talkin'," Tess said to Audra. "You coming?"

Audra, glimpsing Sean on the far side of the

hands. "My mom's a little nervous. But I think it'll be good."

Audra was delighted he and Luanne would be accompanying Judith to Lucerne. Evidently Jakob, after his wife's death, had revealed his past to his children, including the possibility of an American daughter. Luanne learned all of this a few days ago, when Judith worked up the nerve to contact them — perhaps encouraged by the necklace Sean had passed along, its inscription promoting great risks. As a result, Judith received an enthusiastic invitation to come meet her relatives across the sea.

The fact she had asked Luanne to join seemed a significant sign of Judith's willingness to rebuild trust. Luanne must have recognized this, because she swiftly bought the plane tickets, paid for in part by a large tin of money that had been stored with Vivian's belongings. *If you ask me,* Luanne had said to Audra, *this trip is exactly what she would've wanted her daughter to spend it on.*

Although Audra had never met Vivian, she would dare to guess that was true.

Sean took a seat in the neighboring chair. "You know, I was thinking," he said, "on the way back from Europe, maybe I could swing through Boston. Come see you and Jack for a couple days."

And there it was: a lead-in to the impending subject.

"Um . . . yeah . . . ," she said, hedging. "That

actually wouldn't work out."

His brow pinched for a second before relaxing, nonchalant. "Sure, okay," he said.

"I only say that because we won't be in Boston."

Now he looked puzzled. "You mean, you're not moving?"

"No, no. We're definitely moving," she said. "Just not as far as I'd planned."

"Oh," he said. "So . . . where are you going?"

"Well, I was thinking it was time to buy a house — once I get a job anyway — around the Portland area."

He studied her face, cautious, then the corners of his mouth rose.

It was during the drive here, with the sun's rays warming her face and Jack in the backseat humming softly to a song on the radio, when Audra realized the most rewarding destination was right where they were. Upon being asked for his opinion, Jack had heartily agreed. There was no guarantee of a job — unless maybe Cheyenne permanently banned shaving. Nor was there a school or neighborhood to target. But they would handle those details as they came.

"Just do me a favor," she said to Sean, "and please don't tell Tess yet."

"Why's that? Won't she happy to hear it?"

"Overjoyed. But the lectures of *I told you so* won't be far behind."

He laughed. "My lips are sealed."

At the reference, her attention moved exactly there, to the curves of his lips, and with little thought she leaned in and sealed them herself. The kiss was slow and tender, yet laced with a thrill of possibilities. When they finally drew apart, he ran his thumb down the slant of her face.

The world wasn't perfect and neither were their lives. They, along with their families, had a great deal of growing and healing ahead. But in that moment, Audra knew that somehow, in the end, everything would be all right. Based not on statistics or provable facts, but a hunch she felt inside.

AUTHOR'S NOTE

People have often commented about our eldest son being an "old soul." Even during his newborn days, they claimed you could see it in his eyes: an aged depth that indicated "he had been here before." Interestingly, I remember how during his toddler years he would, in fact, talk about "the grandma that used to take care of [him]." Whether it was a metaphysical reference or just the creative ramblings of a youngster, I couldn't tell you for certain. What I do know is our son, for one reason or another, continues to possess wisdom and compassion far beyond his years.

It should be of no surprise, then, given my passion for WWII history, that a news story about a boy named James Leininger captured my interest. Evidently, at age two, James began to suffer from recurrent night terrors about dying in a plane crash during WWII. His additional knowledge regarding aspects of the era convinced his initially skeptical parents that in a past life James had been a

631

pilot who perished during the war. (For the entire account, read *Soul Survivor: The Reincarnation of a WWII Fighter Pilot* by Bruce Leininger, Andrea Leininger, and Ken Gross.)

Although our family's experiences bear very little resemblance, our oldest son did for some time also suffer from night terrors. As any parent familiar with the episodes can tell you, the task of soothing a screaming, panicked, wide-eyed child in the throes of such a nightmare is a daunting one. Thus, when I heard about the Leiningers' story, the literary portion of my mind began to wonder how I personally would react if our son suddenly spouted details of historical instances that logic dictated he couldn't yet know. What if those "memories" linked back to secrets various people had attempted to keep buried?

From there, a true account involving WWII Nazi spies provided just the inspiration I needed for the historical thread of my novel. Although Jakob Hemel is an entirely fictitious character, the story of the other eight German saboteurs sadly is not. From George Dasch's surrender and FDR's secret military tribunal to the electric chair executions and selective deportations, I am continually surprised that the occurrence is not more widely known. A thorough recount of the events can be found in a book titled *Betrayal: The True Story of J. Edgar Hoover and the Nazi*

Saboteurs Captured During WWII by David Alan Johnson.

Readers of my previous novels are likely well aware of my penchant for including historical tidbits best described as stranger than fiction. *The Pieces We Keep* is certainly no exception. In this case, among those I found most intriguing were: Nazi contact lists printed on handkerchiefs in invisible ink, saboteurs being instructed to wear their German uniforms during the shore landings in America, riders of the Parachute Jump being deliberately stalled mid-air by its workers for sheer amusement, and transport aircrafts mysteriously disappearing without a trace over both the Pacific and Atlantic Oceans.

I was also fascinated to discover a coincidental connection to Fort Hamilton. It was while stationed there that Sidney Mashbir, as Coast Defense Intelligence Officer, led the investigations that uncovered the first German spy to be apprehended in the United States. As for my inclusion of Fort Hamilton, please note that for story purposes I did take a few liberties in the switchboard scenes, namely with the building layout and number of operators. I have the Harbor Defense Museum at Fort Hamilton to thank for providing me with remarkable photographs and information.

Among the many non-fiction books and articles I turned to for research, the following were particularly helpful: *Old Souls: Compelling Evidence from Children Who Remember Past Lives* by Tom Shroder; *Nella Last's War: The Second World War Diaries of "Housewife, 49"* by Nella Last; and *Unspoken Abandonment: Sometimes the hardest part of going to war is coming home* by Bryan A. Wood.

I hope you enjoyed *The Pieces We Keep* and, perhaps, in the process, even learned a little more about a time in history so very rich in bravery, sacrifice, and honor. Thank you for reading!

Warm wishes,
Kristina

■ ■ ■ ■

A READING GROUP GUIDE: THE PIECES WE KEEP

KRISTINA MCMORRIS

■ ■ ■ ■

ABOUT THIS GUIDE

The suggested questions are included to enhance your group's reading of Kristina McMorris's *The Pieces We Keep*.

DISCUSSION QUESTIONS

1. While reading *The Pieces We Keep,* did your interpretation of the title change over the course of the story? Discuss the symbolism of the cover image in the same regard.
2. What does "faith" mean to you? How did you come to arrive at that conclusion? Has a personal tragedy ever caused you to reexamine and/or alter your core beliefs?
3. When comparing the novel's dual timelines, how do the past- and present-day stories parallel? How do they contrast?
4. Memories — cherished and burdensome, lost and recovered — are major elements of the book. Which memories in your life have played a distinct role in shaping your personality? If given a choice, would you erase any from your mind? How different might you be without them?
5. Of the various parental relationships in the book, which are the most interesting to you? Do you identify with any of them? How has your view of your own parents, or your

relationship with them, developed over time?

6. Connections between the past and present were interpreted by characters in different ways throughout the story. Early on, what did you perceive as the source of Jack's issues? Did that change by the book's end?

7. Do you believe in the possibility of past lives? In your opinion, does such a theory complement or contradict contemporary religious and/or Christian principles? Did the story reaffirm your existing beliefs or expand your thoughts about what might or might not be possible?

8. Vivian's view of love and marriage greatly change by the book's conclusion. Upon reflecting on your life, consider how your perspective on these topics has developed and why. How did Isaak and Gene both contribute to Vivian's growth as a person?

9. Every major character in the book wrestles with grief in some form. Discuss the range of ways in which each person deals with this emotion. Have you or your loved ones ever reacted to loss in a similar manner?

10. At several points in the novel, Audra questions her skeptical and spiritual beliefs. What is your personal view of coincidence versus fate or predestination?

11. How do secrets, whether kept or revealed, affect characters in the story? Do you agree with the reasons they were withheld from

others? If you have ever concealed a major truth from a loved one, do you now regret it or feel it was justified?

12. Army Private Ian Downing, whom Vivian encounters at the café, first appeared in Kristina McMorris's debut novel, *Letters from Home.* If you were previously familiar with his character, how does his personality differ in *The Pieces We Keep*?

13. Audra spends a great deal of time doubting her parental abilities. The petition she reviews with Russ reflects and amplifies what could easily be deemed her shortcomings as a mother. How would you rate your own parenting skills, or that of your parents? What ruling might a stranger make based solely on documented incidents?

14. Who was your favorite character early in the book, and why? Did your opinion change as the story progressed? Who was your favorite character by the end?

ABOUT THE AUTHOR

Kristina McMorris is a *New York Times* and *USA TODAY* bestselling author. Her background includes ten years of directing public relations for an international conglomerate as well as extensive television experience. Inspired by true personal and historical accounts, her novels have garnered over twenty national literary awards and include *Letters from Home, Bridge of Scarlet Leaves, The Pieces We Keep, The Edge of Lost,* and *Sold on a Monday,* in addition to novellas in the anthologies *A Winter Wonderland* and *Grand Central.* A frequent guest speaker and workshop presenter, she holds a BS in international marketing from Pepperdine. She lives with her husband and two sons in Oregon. For more, visit KristinaMcmorris.com.

The employees of Thorndike Press hope you have enjoyed this Large Print book. All our Thorndike, Wheeler, and Kennebec Large Print titles are designed for easy reading, and all our books are made to last. Other Thorndike Press Large Print books are available at your library, through selected bookstores, or directly from us.

For information about titles, please call:
(800) 223-1244

or visit our website at:
gale.com/thorndike

To share your comments, please write:
Publisher
Thorndike Press
10 Water St., Suite 310
Waterville, ME 04901